D1541250

Setting the World
on Fire

By the same author

The Wrong Set
Such Darling Dodos
For Whom the Cloche Tolls
Hemlock and After
Emile Zola: An Introductory Study of his Novels
Anglo-Saxon Attitudes
The Mulberry Bush: A Play
A Bit off the Map
The Middle Age of Mrs Eliot
The Old Men at the Zoo
The Wild Garden, or Speaking of Writing
Late Call
No Laughing Matter
The World of Charles Dickens
As If By Magic
The Strange Ride of Rudyard Kipling: His Life and Works

SETTING the WORLD on FIRE

Angus Wilson

THE VIKING PRESS NEW YORK

Copyright © Angus Wilson, 1980
All rights reserved
First published in 1980 by The Viking Press
625 Madison Avenue, New York, N.Y. 10022

LIBRARY OF CONGRESS CATALOGING IN PUBLICATION DATA
Wilson, Angus.
Setting the world on fire.
I.   Title.
PZ3.W68895Se 1980   823'.914   80-14785
ISBN 0-670-63502-2

Printed in the United States of America
Set in Bembo

FOR
ANNE FLEMING

LIST OF THE PRINCIPAL CHARACTERS

GREAT GRANDFATHER MOSSON (d. 1957)

LADY MOSSON (Jackie) – his widowed daughter-in-law and hostess; an American heiress. Her husband had been Lord Mayor of London.

SIR HUBERT MOSSON BART – heir to Great Grandfather, elder son of Lady Mosson; a middle-aged bachelor and banker.

ROSEMARY MOSSON (Ma) – widow of Jerry Mosson, Lady Mosson's younger son who was killed in the Second World War; she is the mother of

PIERS MOSSON – (called *Van* by his brother Tom, because of his passion for the Vanbrugh architecture at Tothill House) and

TOM MOSSON – (called *Pratt* by his brother Piers, because of his devotion to the Pratt architecture at Tothill House).

(UNCLE) EUSTACE GORDON – brother of Rosemary Mosson (Ma).

(UNCLE) JIM TERRINGTON – a Lt Colonel in the regular army, and close friend of Piers' and Tom's dead father.

MARINA LUZZI – heiress of a very wealthy Turinese financier, engaged to Hubert Mosson.

MAGDA SCZEKERNY – a Hungarian refugee of 1956, who becomes librarian and archivist at Tothill House and subsequently marries

RALPH TUCKER – gardener and later steward at Tothill House. Son of a clergyman.

SIR TIMOTHY PLEYDELL – a famous veteran actor.

Foreword

Note about Tothill House

Following the dissolution of the monasteries in the early six-
teenth century, Henry VIII granted most of the monastic
buildings of Westminster Abbey, and all of the land belonging
to the monks, to Thomas Tothill. Tothill demolished the
buildings and built himself a large mansion upon their site. His
descendant, Sir Thomas Tothill, found the old house inade-
quate and determined to build a very grand house for himself.
For this purpose he employed Sir Roger Pratt, who, although
retired to his estate in the country, welcomed this commission
because his London masterpiece, Clarendon House, was just
about to be pulled down. The new house was nearly complete
when Sir Thomas died in 1688, the year of the 'Glorious
Revolution' and William of Orange's arrival in England to
depose the Catholic King James II. He was succeeded by his
son, Sir Francis Tothill, who immediately decided to add a
great hall for his entertaining. He engaged his acquaintance,
Captain John Vanbrugh, the playwright. This was Vanbrugh's
first architectural commission. Some years later, he built Blenheim Palace. The Pratt house, with Vanbrugh's famous Great
Hall built into the middle of it, is substantially what we see
today. Tothill House, the only great house in London with
large formal gardens and a park remaining in private hands, is
situated just behind Westminster Abbey; its grounds extend as
far as the church of St John's Smith Square.

At the end of the eighteenth century, Tothill and all its estate passed through the female line to the family of Mosson, whose vast fortune was founded upon the West India trade and subsequently upon banking. The house is today in the possession of Piers Mosson, the well-known theatre director. It only remains to say that the house and its history are of course the inventions of the author.

PART I

1948

STANDING IN the middle of the vast Hall, surrounded by the huge, smooth, yet twisting black marble pillars, he thought now I am a beetle, the tiniest of beetles, finding his way through the towering trees of the jungle. In the stories he had read, beetles always 'scuttled'. He liked to act what he thought. But he did not know how to 'scuttle'. In any case, he was afraid to move on this endless sheet of black and white chequered marble floor lest he slide and fall. Uncle Jim had shown him all the chess moves, but none of them was 'scuttling'. He hated floors and being a beetle.

But looking up high, high above, he knew that he need not be one. The light poured down in wide beams from the centre of the great lantern to break in pools upon the chess board; Uncle Hubert had told him that it was a 'lantern'. He had never seen one before. He thought it must be the magic lantern of which he had read in stories of children of Great Grandfather's days who hadn't the pictures to go to, and sat in front of roasting log fires and watched magic lanterns of 'lands and people far away'. Hot and dusty and sweaty it must have been, he thought. If he wished hard, this lantern would magick him up and out into the sky above. He would fly on and on to the wonderful dazzling sun, fly and dive and flit and turn and slide and shoot across the sky as he wished, like the swallows that gathered in the evening over his home, like the bats in the air above the back door, like the young man above him who, smil-

ing with happiness, drove the maddened grey horses with
floating manes across the bright blue ceiling and over the tops
of the soapsud clouds. So happy was the young man that he
left his golden cart and his horses to fly on their own, and,
turning and wheeling, now feet first, now head first, he floated
through the sky, dazzling all with his sudden dives and
plunges and somersaults, dropping all his clothes from him, so
that only a long white cloth twisted and trailed across his
naked body as he flew up and down through the blue.

Piers could imagine such delight a little, for it was the delight that *he* felt now that Uncle Jim had taught him to swim –
'The boy's a super swimmer,' he had said to Ma, and 'super'
must mean the smoothness with which he now floated on the
flattened oily-green wave slopes, and now dived his way
through the surging white foam crests as they were about to
break upon the beach where Ma stood, frightened, calling to
him, 'Darling! Do be careful!' If you were really happy, you
couldn't be careful. If you had a need to fly in circles and twists
and somersaults like the happy young man wheeling above
him, you had no time to think of being careful. You *had* to do
it. As the young man *had to* sprawl down from the ceiling,
down and across the columns that stood each side of the great
green bowl, for the story ran on from the lantern down the
great curving ceiling, and then down the walls of the Hall.

Somewhere in the deep bed of the great bowl, green turned
to fire. But the young man did not fear the fire as he made his
shapes and figures through the air. Only two silly marble girls,
who stood each side of the bowl, wept their tears: they were
trapped there now in their stupid crying fright, for their legs
were turning into stalks of plants – trees, Uncle Hubert had
said, willow trees, but Piers thought them more like silly old
cabbage stalks. They were afraid for the young man who was
their brother, as Ma, at the sea's edge, was afraid for him. But
if you are making your own turns and twists, it's nobody's
business to be afraid. And their fear can't hold you back.

Or anger. As the old man with the long grey hair and beard,
looking out of the sky in the lantern, was angry at the young
man's dance through the clouds – the old man who was God

but who also wasn't God. Grandma had explained that it didn't matter, because God was everywhere, an omelette. That was her religion which was Christian Science which Ma said was silly but we mustn't say so.

Uncle Jim had been very *angry* when he found him dancing naked one evening in the hall at home. But Uncle Jim being angry didn't make the dance which he had invented a less wonderful one. Other people's anger, unlike their fear, *could* stop you, because of what they could do to you. But not inside – inside he had gone on dancing, although Uncle Jim had marched him 'up to bed, my lad'.

It was 'plucky' if you turned and twisted through the waves, but it was 'very worrying' if you danced naked in the hall. Yet it wasn't really 'plucky' in the sea because it was what you wanted to do. It was only plucky if, like his brother Tom, you were afraid of the sea but made yourself swim. He had told Tom not to swim if he was afraid. He didn't like Tom ever, ever to do what frightened or hurt him. He wanted always to have Tom smiling and excited as he was when Piers danced for him, or led the way, crouching and slithering, through the rhododendrons' thick undergrowth – a leopard and its cub stalking the springboks drinking by that African lake which were Ma's geese by the mud pond – or when he imitated Miss Muckelow as she sat that day when she came to see Ma and her knickers slipped down below her knees – she was talking, talking, 'my dear, this', and 'my dear, that' while she managed by wiggling and shifting forward on her seat to make the knickers disappear under her skirt. He could do that bit now so that Tom laughed until he wetted himself. But Tom needed to do what he was afraid of, so that Uncle Jim would cry, 'Bravo, Tortoise! Who said you'd be the last?', and Ma would say, 'Darling heart! That *is* brave.'

There was no point that Piers could see in being plucky and doing things you didn't want to when there were such wonderful games to invent. Tom's pluckiness made him impatient. He tried not to see – as this afternoon when Tom had been so afraid to go into the Great Hall. He felt a bit ashamed about this. But he could always make it up to Tom – to most people, come to that. With wonderful games. None of them so wonderful as flying, as he knew from dreams. In dreams you were there with people you didn't want, like the colonel who came over to see Ma and to talk about Daddy's death which upset her, or Mrs McGuire who came in three times a week and broke wind when she was polishing the floor, or even with people you loved like Ma or Tom. And suddenly you were flying above them, away, turning somersaults in the sky, dive bombing, floating. It was the best dream you could have and you woke up feeling wonderful and strong.

He would make shapes and turns as he wanted when he grew up, but it would not be so that the people he loved became angry or afraid. Everyone he loved, no, perhaps everyone everywhere would be happy at what he did, and, like the Vicar read at church, 'stand amazed'.

And, even if the young man did fall, you could see that he was in a delighted magic trance. He had made his shapes, he had danced through the sky. So the fall was only the last movement of the dance. It was like Daddy, a hero's death, for, although a soldier, he had been shot down over the sea at Italy; but Piers didn't talk about it, because it upset Ma, although Uncle Hubert did, for, as he had told Piers, he had loved Daddy, his own brother, as Piers loved Tom.

He glided round the great room again and again, across the marble floors which he no longer feared, gazing up at the young man caught in the sun streaming down from the lantern.

This was called Tothill House, where his great grandfather lived, and even if his great grandfather with all his watch chains and his smell of cigars was like an old ogre, and even if Grandma was always saying, 'Smile with your eyes, Piers. God wants us to smile,' when her own blue eyes were like hard buttons and she only smiled with her teeth, and even if there were too many rooms and too many staircases, he loved the huge house because of the Great Hall, for that's what the painted ceiling, and the magic lantern, and the chessboard floor, and the black barley sugar pillars, and the flying young man, the horses and all the columns were called. The Great Hall. He wanted to be here always. And he was glad when Ma whispered that, if things went on as they seemed to, the house might well be his one day, but he must never, never mention that to anyone.

It must have been the happy young man's magic flying that had saved the house when Hitler had tried to burn it, along with Westminster Abbey and the Houses of Parliament that were so nearby. Hitler who had shot down Daddy to a hero's death. And now the war was over and the Coal Board had gone and the family were back again, although Grandma could not think how they would get her lovely rooms clean again, which he was not surprised at, considering they were a Coal Board. And they would visit here very often, must do, Grandma had said, and Uncle Hubert had smiled. Piers was so happy that he began to improvise a new dance. He had felt sad that poor Tom was frightened by the Great Hall, even though it had meant his now having this wonderful great room to himself.

But now worry about Tom's fright, shame about his own failure to come forward to help his little brother as he could have, anxiety to please those new, strange, important relations, to show as always his love for Ma, all these faded from his mind as he sought to glide across the Great Hall, his arms floating through the air, his legs parted in great leaps. He was nothing now but his dance. Only once, pausing for breath, did he think of the others, and then it was to know that, when he grew up, he would bring them all in as part of the triumph.

It was true. Poor Tom had been very frightened. He had stood, a little window dummy of grey flannel knickers and a maroon and white school blazer and grey woollen stockings bordered beneath the bare knees with the school's maroon and white colours, and he had screamed and screamed until his pretty little window dummy's face with its cornflower eyes and long black eyelashes had melted into a mass of crimson wrinkles and lumps. He had cried and cried with terror, until his crying turned to hiccoughs. Looking for his brother Piers to save him from these fears, to keep the sky from falling down upon him, to check the smiling young man from cruelly setting fire to the world, he had seen that Piers was not with them, had turned to stone, had frozen into himself like all these painted people on the ceiling, all these marble people by the walls. Through the hot, sweet and oily-feeling tears, he had squinted upwards to see if there was one small breathing live part of Piers that would come to help him in his danger. But Piers was gone away into himself, smiling to himself as he stood oblivious on the great staircase. And when Piers was gone from him like that Tom knew that there was no way that his misery could reach him.

Ma had said, 'Tom! Tom!' in reproach; but she added to her mother-in-law, 'He's only *just* six altho' that absurd school uniform makes him look older.' Lady Mosson bent down, for even her slim little boy's figure towered above her small grandson's: 'What is it, dear?' she asked with her faint American accent. 'We're all with you. God is here to love you. He is everywhere. He is omnipresent. Divine love casts out fear.' Something in her blue eyes failed to communicate this to him for he redoubled his screaming and even stamped his feet in turn on the floor.

Great grandfather Mosson took his large gold watch out of his waistcoat pocket and swung it on the end of its chain in front of the little boy, but this too had disastrous results. So the old man said, 'Temper tantrums. That's not a good sign. This war has been bad for all of us. Anyway, I am no good with children. Never was.' He ambled away, his feet turned in a little, like a bear's, out of the Great Hall and up the magnificent staircase, past the unconscious, wonderstruck Piers, and away into the East Gallery.

'Oh dear!' said Ma, 'this has never happened before. *Piers* has his moods. But Tom is such a brave boy, so self-controlled.' Hubert let out a strange discordant cackle that made his sister-in-law start. He and his mother both looked at her with twitching lips. Neither of them cared for humour, let alone absurdity, but if somebody were really unsuitable, like this unfortunate marriage Jerry had made, they thought it right to smile a little at her antics.

'Darling heart,' Ma cried to Piers, 'Why don't *you* talk to your brother? *You always* know what to say to him.'

But Piers had climbed to the first turn in the great staircase and was staring up at the lantern.

'I don't think he does this time,' Lady Mosson said, still amused at Rosemary's vulgar maternal insufficiency. 'Come along, Tom. Let's see if we can find Gates, shall we? He may have some ginger ale. That would be nice, wouldn't it? And if I know anything, Rosemary, he may have made us a really good martini, straight up. That is one thing I saw to that they taught him when I took him over to New York's Plaza Hotel. People told me that it was the best place now for food and drink. And they were right. And our Ambassador's been most generous in sending me liquor. He agrees with me that your new government's rationing is absurd. After all, we have *won* the war.'

Lady Mosson's eyes twinkled at the thought of her coming martini. It was one of the many things in which she did not conform with her fellow abstaining Christian Scientists. But then, as she often thought, if you've inherited millions, you are bound to find yourself doing different things from other people – even in Science. She led the way to the Blue Drawing Room.

They had hardly left the Great Hall when Tom's cries turned to low sobs, and, after he had sipped, then guzzled, the ginger ale that the butler gave to him, he squared his small shoulders and told them how very sorry he was to have behaved so badly.

'Dear little man!' Lady Mosson said. 'How his grandfather would have loved him! And you'd have loved to have seen *him* dressed up in his robes, Tom. He was Lord Mayor of London.'

Luckily Tom looked, and felt, very impressed; he knew of Dick Whittington.

Hubert said, 'It's all new to you, isn't it, Tom? And it's such a big place.' Tom nodded but said nothing.

'Of course, I've talked to the children about Tothill until we've almost been living here.'

Jackie's eyes sparkled. 'Poor Rosemary! You've hardly known the place yourself, have you? What with Jerry's being posted to India and the war coming.' Then, remembering love, she put her hand on her daughter-in-law's arm. 'Dear Rosemary,' she said, 'you will know its love now.'

'I've read a lot about it.'

Hubert took her up now, but not directly. 'I wish we *could* get something written,' he said. 'Armitage was hopeless before the war. But Grandfather liked him. However, he has agreed to my choosing a new archivist now we've pensioned off the old boy. It's so difficult to know. I'm dining at High Table at the House some night this summer. I thought I'd ask them there. There must be a clever young man, or a woman with her head screwed on the right way, who'd love to do the job well. But we must have something that will be published, and under *our* direction, and who will respect Grandfather's insistence that the whole emphasis must be on the Mossons and not the Tothills. As it stands, there's nothing in print worth reading.'

Rosemary said valiantly, 'There's a rather marvellous description in one of Valma Despard's novels of Charles II being entertained here. I read *that* to the boys.'

Jackie said, 'Historical novels! You *are* so romantic, Rosemary.'

Hubert's sudden cackle again made Rosemary jump. She told herself, he's much more like a silly schoolboy than I remembered. She looked to see if Tom was scared, but he sat placidly drinking his ginger ale. And anyway her brother-in-law's tone was now his usual rather overbearing drone.

'When that scoundrel, Thomas Tothill, paraded all his women before the King . . .'

Rosemary said, 'I imagine the King was delighted.' She added, 'Of course, I didn't read them that. Whatever do you imagine, Hubert.' She stopped because she had in fact read the scene about Tothill's mistresses to the boys. She'd been a bit squiffy that night. Jim had failed her. She meant to say that she had been able to tell them all the stories of their father's boyhood at Tothill which she had heard from Jerry. She knew that would please old Jackie and Hubert. But now she felt so cross with them that she couldn't bring herself to mention anything that Jerry had told her. All the same, she must maintain good relations, if only for the sake of the boys.

'My dear,' she said to her mother-in-law, 'you've been so very good about helping with the capital for my Nursery in Hampshire that you must let me re-stock the garden here. It seems that a lot more varieties have been preserved here and there in country gardens during the war than I thought. So . . .'

But Hubert, banker though he was, could not really think this swift substitution of business for a small boy's troubles was good enough. She was useless as a mother, that was clear – and who would expect it otherwise, coming from a twopenny-halfpenny middle-class family with a ne'er-do-well brother? How a fine man like Jerry could have married such a blowzy woman! Look at her dress with stains on the utility skirt. And Mother had brought her new dresses from New York! She hardly seemed capable of knowing which side her bread was buttered. It was so easy to please Mother.

But, in any case, marriage defeated him. His mind dwelt for a second on woman's power, woman's strength, and lust began to distract him. He put the thoughts angrily aside. It was intolerable that a man's secret, his personal life, should intrude upon his home, his family. And if marriage, how much more children – how could he, a bachelor banker with an interest in the arts, be any good with children? All the same, he could not be happy that his brother Jerry's son should be afraid, a son of a fine officer who died a hero's death.

He filled Tom's glass again with ginger ale, helped himself to another martini and drew the small boy down next to him on a high backed sofa.

'You're not a frightened boy as a rule, I can tell,' he said, and really made, in his wish to help, his normally braying voice quiet and friendly.

'The room's so big,' Tom said, 'and I thought that man would bring the ceiling falling down on us.'

'Ah, so that's it. Phaethon!' Hubert said. 'He was a silly chap, Tom. He thought he could drive the sun's chariot without any practice. Nobody but a fool tries to do things he can't possibly do. And Mr Phaethon learned that lesson. You

saw how he was falling down right into that bowl? That bowl
is the sea. And Jove – that's the old chap at the top – saw that
the silly fool was in danger of scorching the world, driving so
dangerously. So he had to throw a thunderbolt at him. Hence
the blaze at the bottom of the bowl. That's fire.'

It all sounded a little extravagant for so small a boy. Worried
by where he had got to, he gave his loud braying laugh – as
always when discomforted. It startled Tom, and his uncle,
seeing this, took the boy by the hand, and led him back to the
Great Hall.

'Your mother says that you are good at arithmetic. I think
you'll find that it will bring this old Hall down to size if I tell
you that it is one hundred feet high from the floor up to the top
of the lantern there, and it is one hundred feet long and fifty
feet wide!'

Piers, dancing alone, heard them in time, and disappeared
through the South Doorway into the garden.

'Like a squirrel, your brother,' Hubert said. 'Always rushing about somewhere. Now, don't be afraid, Tom. Look up
with me,' but he could see from the trembling hand that the
boy was still terrified. 'That's just a glass lantern up in the roof.
And here you see the silly chap asking his father, the Sun God,
for permission to drive the chariot round the world through
the sky. Of course, the god should never have agreed. Never
let anyone take charge who hasn't worked at the job and learnt
it thoroughly. Your mother tells me that you have learned to
swim. But you wouldn't go rushing into the sea if you hadn't
learned to swim, would you?'

The little boy shook his head; his hand was only faintly
trembling now. Hubert felt more confidence. Like everything
else, dealing with children was a matter of concentration and
practice.

'Now you see if Jove hadn't acted so quickly, this chap and
the chariot and the horses would have crashed down on
the earth and we can't say what damage they might have
done.'

Tom said, finding the words with difficulty, 'That's why *I*
was frightened, Uncle, staring up there, all that big sky seemed

to be falling on us and I thought he'd made it fall. The world *isn't* safe, is it?'

Hubert thought for a minute or two. He knew what his mother would have said – 'All little children are safe. God is love' – or some such stuff. But Christian Science was the one thing they had agreed to differ on.

'No, Tom,' he said, 'the world isn't altogether a safe place. It's a bit like an ice-covered pond – even a skater should never play the giddy ox, in case he falls through the ice. There was a chap like Phaethon only in these last years who thought the world belonged to him. Hitler was *his* name. But at the last the silly chap came to a sticky end. Like Phaethon falling into the sea.'

'Hitler killed my Daddy,' Tom said.

The suddenness of it made Hubert choke. There was only one person who mattered more to him in life than Jerry, and that was Mother.

'Your father was one of the fine chaps who knew what they were doing. Trained men who kept their heads. In the end they were too much for Hitler, as level-headed trained chaps always are too much for the dangerous fools. That's why we don't all fall through the ice or into the sea. It's the young chaps like him,' he pointed to the great Corinthian column down which Phaethon's naked body writhed, 'who learn a nasty lesson.'

'He's smiling,' Tom said doubtfully. 'He *looks* happy.'

'Ah!' Hubert saw what had happened. 'Yes. Well that's a big question you'll understand when you get older. The man who painted this stuff, an Italian called Verrio, wasn't very good at his job. He couldn't even get Phaethon's look right. When he meant him to be terrified, he painted him all cheerful. But that's another question. Some years later an *Englishman* came along called Thornhill who could have done it all beautifully but the work here was already done. As a matter of fact,' he said, for even to this uncomprehending little boy he couldn't help making his favourite point about Vanbrugh, 'the architect who built this room, great artist though he was, was a *bit* wild himself.'

His bray as he said this made Tom think of stampeding horses.

'Pratt had designed the hall with the big central staircase that any household needs. But, of course, Vanbrugh tore it all down for the sake of his dome and his other theatrical effects. Never mind the Tothills – let them find their way upstairs as best they could. He thought he could justify himself by being funny at Pratt's expense – "Sir Roger's design was to take you up to bed before you'd even dined." Always mistrust people who say clever things, Tom, they're always wild chaps.'

It occurred then to Hubert that he really had said enough about ice cracking and wild men. 'Come along. I'll show you something else. Something built by another great man, but a steady one this time.'

Taking the boy's hand, he led him through the vast dining room, where Tom could still smell the delicious chicken they had had for lunch, and out on to the West Terrace. He conducted the small boy through a maze of workmen's ladders and junk left behind by the Coal Board to the edge of the terrace, then he lifted him up in his arms. Pointing towards the house, he said:

'This is the work of the original architect. A very great man called Roger Pratt. You must always remember his name, Tom. He's not enough known. He had filthy luck. Most of his work's been pulled down or burned by accident. Even Vanbrugh pulled down his magnificent saloon and staircase to make that great lantern which scared you so. Of course, Francis Tothill should never have allowed it. But a man who let his life become a public scandal! –'

He pulled himself up. This was not talk for small children. That was the trouble with history.

'Now there's a real building for you. All regular and even. A marvellous sense of proportion. Count those windows on the ground floor.'

The boy counted one, two, three, four, five, six, seven.

'Yes, that's right. Seven bays we call them, but window is good enough. Now count the windows above.'

The result was the same.

'That's it. Regularity in everything. Now look up at the sloping roof. You see those little windows that jut out? Mansards, they're called. They were a speciality of Pratt's. The name's French, but Pratt got the idea from Holland, I think. A nice, brave, practical, cautious country.'

Tom counted and again there were seven mansards.

'There you are,' Hubert said, 'a splendid gentleman's house until Vanbrugh came along and did wild things, great man though he was. Look up to the top of the roof. What do we see? That's the lantern, and there are the tops of the twisted pillars that frightened you in the Great Hall. The gilded tops are supposed to make them flaming torches, but they look like kitchen mops to me. The whole thing was quite inappropriate, but Vanbrugh didn't think of that. He only thought of what was in his own head. But we don't have to worry, the world isn't all Phaethons or Vanbrughs. The men that keep it safe and in order are the Pratts, the men who know how to keep themselves in hand, the blokes who do things well and regularly. If it wasn't for them, the ice *would* break, the flames *would* fly up into the sky.'

He realised that his metaphors were mixed, that he had returned to the grim warning, had passed far beyond a six-year-old's range.

'Well, we had better find your brother. Hunt the squirrel, eh?'

Coming out of the South Door, Hubert's hand took so firm a grip of Tom's arm to guide him down the great flight of steps that any less physically spartan boy would have cried out. Looking at the devastation wrought by the Coal Board upon the formal garden in front of them, it seemed to Hubert for a moment that he had done wrong to tell the boy that only Pratt's fine regularity could preserve the world that he would inherit from the shambles to which brigands and bureaucrats between them were steadily reducing it. Grasping the small arm more firmly, almost lifting the small body down the broad steps as he propelled it forward, he made a vow that, as perhaps he would never find it in himself to provide Tothill with an heir, he would watch over these boys of Jerry's so that they

had every chance in this vile world their father had sacrificed
himself for. And they would need watching, too, with a
mother like that. But then he remembered his father's saying
(he had used it in his inaugural speech as Lord Mayor of
London), a maxim handed down through long generations of
Tothills and Mossons – 'Every man his own master.' He relaxed his grip on Tom's arm so that the small boy stumbled and
almost fell headfirst.

'Steady,' said Hubert, a little sharply – that was going to be
the trouble with these boys, all impulse; no doubt it came from
the mother. Look at the way the elder boy had darted off like
that into the garden. But then he saw that Tom was making the
descent of the last few steps with such determination that the
muscles of his small legs were sturdily quivering. Good Lord!
It must be like descending Everest to him. And he remembered
another favourite maxim of his father's – 'We haven't all been
brought up on the Tothill scale, Hubert. A lot of these chaps
are doing their best and they need encouragement.'

'Jolly good, Tom. Next time you come we'll have the fountain playing again to encourage your efforts.'

And then, as though to approve his new optimism, round
the corner from behind the East Wing came men staggering
under the weight of a stone figure which they carefully laid
upon its back in one of the angles of the square, débris-laden
path that surrounded the empty pool into which the fountain
was to rain its reviving waters for Tom. So, men were at work
and things were being done. And the right men, too, for one of
them, a dark haired, slight-figured chap, now left the group
and came towards them.

'Getting into shape again, Pentreath,' Hubert commented,
with approval. It had always pleased him that their head gardener, so slight in build, had such strength. But then, remembering that carrying very heavy loads must have formed a
large part of Pentreath's ordeal on the Burma Road, he prof-
fered, 'I'm glad to see you're getting things properly
moving.'

'Yes, sir, I thought that her Ladyship would like to see her
favourite statue back, even though it'll take us a month or two

to get the formal garden into its old order.'

Hubert looked towards the long-legged, slender stone figure on the ground. His face softened into a smile of reminiscence.

'Ah! Yes. That will make her feel at home again. It has been a horrible homecoming for her, you know, Pentreath.'

The gardener was not a man to comment, but he looked grave. Perhaps his silence reminded Hubert that some feelings were too deep to share even with those who had been in their service since boyhood. He crouched down to Tom's level and pointed to the statue.

'What do you think *he* is?' he asked.

Tom could only see what seemed to be a noseless boy half dressed up as an animal; the boy was sucking what looked to be a delicious long stick of sugar or white peppermint such as he'd only heard of in stories until Grandmother brought them back their candies from America that must be made to last for months.

'Well?' Uncle Hubert asked again. 'What do you think he is? The opinion of the latest of the Mosson line, Pentreath. Worth having. This is Master Tom, Pentreath. My brother Jerry's youngest. Say how do you do to Mr Pentreath, Tom. He's the man who knows all about gardens.'

Tom felt on his mettle to remember all the important things Ma had said about being especially polite to the Tothill servants. Of course there was Deakin who had been Daddy's batman and who came over to help Ma when the car went wrong and brought petrol that mustn't be talked about. But here at Tothill House it was more than that, as Ma had explained. They lived in the past. He felt happy to be polite, however, for meeting this Mr Pentreath had taken away the oppression of Uncle Hubert's hammering question. Uncle Hubert had made him feel all right in the house – that if it was all ice and fire, you could still stay safe if you took care. But outside, here, he had brought uneasiness back with so many words and questions that it was hard to tell pats from raps. Tom remembered carefully what being polite to servants when you're living in the past meant. Ma hadn't made it clear, but

Piers, as usual, had worked it out and had instructed him. You had to bow as well as to shake hands.

He bowed at the waist as Piers had demonstrated and took the man's hairy-backed outstretched hand. Pentreath seemed surprised but he grasped the small boy's hand firmly and said, 'Welcome to Tothill House, Master Tom,' with a very grave smile on his face. All this seemed to delight Uncle Hubert. He relaxed and laughed, but quietly, not with his sky-rending cackle.

'There you are then, Tom. An official welcome.'

Tom was grateful to the gardener and, when Uncle Hubert walked over to a pile of packing cases and frowningly read their labels, he asked this important, friendly man:

'Is it a bear he's turning into? Bears eat sugar, don't they?'

Pentreath was clearly quite lost.

'The stone boy,' Tom explained. 'It *is* an animal skin, isn't it?' he asked, and, peering more closely, he added, puzzled, 'It's got a knife in it.'

'Ah,' Pentreath said, smiling in recognition of the boy's direct appeal to him, 'That's a dagger. There were wolves in those days, you see. And he had his sheep to protect.'

Uncle Hubert was back. 'So you thought the boy was a shepherd, did you, Tom? Well done.'

Mr Pentreath didn't say anything to contradict this. Tom wasn't quite sure whether this silent acceptance of what was not true, although very comfortable for him, made him feel more safe with the man or less.

'It was the wolves, sir,' Pentreath said. 'He's not likely to have heard of *their* threat to sheep.'

'No, no, of course not. This was centuries ago in ancient Greece, Tom.' Hubert didn't expand this, he'd done enough explaining for one day. 'It's a wonderful statue. Your grandmother's favourite. She'll explain all about it to you if you ask her. She knows all about beauty.' He set all that aside; instead he took on a different historical note. 'All that,' he said and he waved his hand towards the far and thickly wooded end of the huge garden where there seemed to be buildings in the distance and Tom could see the spire of a church, 'all that used to be sheep-grazing meadows until long after the Tothills took over from the monks who, of course, were sheep farmers for the wool. Increasingly it became a nursery garden as London grew bigger and wanted feeding. Then, about 1700 or so, Sir Francis and his son began to build on it. And it's never stopped since. Of course, they were quite right, it was needed. All the same, the way things are going we might be better off with the sheep. Not that they'd let us do it. We can pay rates and taxes on half Westminster because we're wicked landlords, but say we want to turn our land back to sheep pasturage and they'd soon tell us what to do with our property.'

Hubert was stopped in his tracks by the look of incomprehension on Pentreath's face, as great as that on Tom's, but with a look of something hard to define, probably nervous embarrassment, too, in the man's lively dark eyes. Ever since the war ended, Hubert thought to himself, it has been growing on me – this mood of melancholy pessimism that makes me talk as much nonsense as if I were Grandfather's age instead of not quite forty. He turned to jokes as the easiest retreat from absurdity. Involuntarily he began with the loudest of his brays.

'Now, wolves you may *very* likely see back here, Tom, although they haven't been seen in this part of England since long before the monks came here, and that was in the tenth century. But, if this chap in our great new government, Dalton, has his way, all the beautiful houses of England are to be thrown open to the public. Encouragement by taxation rebate is what he promises, but it will be compulsion soon enough. Even those of us who had enough sense to see that we can keep up our houses decently and as private gentlemen will be forced to let anyone in who chooses to produce his ration book or some other wretched government pass. Then we will have circuses and zoos to amuse the crowds. Wolves will be the least of it.'

Again he was faced with incomprehension – the man's still difficult to define, politely embarrassed, the child's on the edge of alarm again.

Hubert felt isolated, betrayed, angry – when old servants

and next of kin can't keep pace with your feelings . . .

He said sharply to Pentreath, 'I don't want to see these packing cases lying around here tomorrow, Pentreath. Is that understood? Everything to do with the Coal Board should have been returned to them weeks ago.'

The man flushed, but he answered in a parade voice, 'Yes, sir.' Then he added more nonchalantly, 'I believe the new estates manager has it in hand.'

'Huddleston? Oh, I'll get on to him. But see to it that they are not outside the house tomorrow, won't you? Lady Mosson has enough to put up with, without those sort of reminders.'

Pentreath gave a nod, then he said, 'I don't think there'll be too much difficulty in re-stocking the greenhouses. And then we can get these beds here looking as her Ladyship likes them. I think we should be able to have a little blue for her. Stoughtons have sent us twenty-five plumbago and I shall bed out a few with the geraniums. But I can't get her favourite blue *salvia patens*. The nursery stocks are badly depleted everywhere.'

'Oh, but still, there'll be *some* blue. That's good. All the flowers will be back here, Tom, when you come again.' This was better all round and, looking over to the pool, Hubert saw that the men had got the shepherd boy into position. 'There he is, Tom, playing his pipe again just as he did before we'd ever heard of Hitler.'

He looked over at the men. One seemed very dark. Of course, Pentreath was dark, Cornish, but this man was . . . might be a Cypriot, there were a lot of them coming over, setting up cafés and so on. Probably a good thing. A reminder that we still had responsibilities abroad.

'How are the new men turning out?'

'I think they'll be very good, sir.'

'Oh, I'm glad to hear it. You're the judge, Pentreath. I'd better go and have a word with them.'

But as he turned in the direction of the under-gardeners, they had lost their look of concentrated labour which had made them such a satisfactory group. One was pointing towards the Woodwork, as the Tothill shrubbery had always been called; the dark one put two fingers into his mouth and let out a shrill whistle, while the third held up an imaginary shot gun and calling 'Bang, Bang!' ran down towards the shrubbery. Hubert gave a mirthless chuckle.

'That's not very good, is it?' he said.

Pentreath explained, 'I think it's the rabbits, sir. The Woodwork is a complete wilderness now, all overgrown with buddleia bushes and a jungle of loosestrife. They've seeded all over London. Even the maze is quite lost in it. It's become a rabbit warren too. I tried to explain it to the other young gentleman when he ran down there. I think he was looking for the maze. But he was too quick to hear what I told him. And, of course, he's scared a lot of the rabbits out into the open, those that couldn't get to their burrows. The men shouldn't have left their job, sir, I know, but rabbits in the heart of London is something we none of us quite expected. It's going to be a problem for the garden. For this year at any rate. With the annuals. But nets and snares should answer it.'

From the thick of the shrubbery came a sudden cry, shout – whatever noise, it was one of a declaimed triumph.

Pentreath said, 'I think that's the other young gentleman in there now.'

From the alert expression in Tom's eyes, he guessed that he was right.

'He'd be after the rabbits, wouldn't he?'

But Tom was listening for his brother.

At that moment, nearby Big Ben's loud boom sounded four o'clock. For Hubert, it emphasised the enormity of this anarchic retrogression, this invasion by the wild, by the untamed. They had the place in Sutherland for shooting and that sort of thing. He felt a massive anger, but it was directionless. His braying came to him but unusually empty and lost. To gain time, he said, 'Rabbits! Good Lord!'

He stood for a minute or two, silent. Then he found a direction. He turned to Tom. 'That brother of yours has got to learn that he can't do what just comes into his head.' He was speaking to empty air. Tom was not there. In the distance his small form could be seen running, all fear lost, into the thick, tangled Woodwork. Pentreath looked away, for a strange sound in Hubert's throat suggested to him that there was danger of one of 'His Lordship's rages'. But Hubert regained his dignity.

'Well,' he said in a friendly, easy voice, 'we've better things to do than chase after rabbits and small boys, Pentreath. I have a mass of papers to attend to and you have all this mess to clear up.'

He was gone into the house with a quick step that suggested thirty rather than forty.

Tom, forcing his way through the hedge-gaps where every so often a straggling, leafless branch would bend before him and then rebound to cut against his forehead or his ears, even to make his eyelid bleed, was high up on horseback, riding with a secret message to his captain. A moment later, loose muscled, soft padded, he was a slinking tiger cub, bringing his share to the evening kill. He could feel the soft furred rabbit, loose-hung in his mouth, the rabbit he would drop before Piers, chief tiger at the cave. Caught for a moment in clawing thorn branches as he tunnelled through a hole in a briar thicket, he was freeing himself from the Jub Jub bird – the teeth that bite, the claws that scratch – which Piers' reading had made so frightening a monster. Seeing the half buried trace of a path among the thick green leaves and onion-smelling white flowers that covered the ground, he imagined stomaching along it, knife held firm between his teeth – ears, skin, hair all tightened against the sudden sight or scent of the enemy – swastika badge, slink-eyed Jap resting beneath a palm tree, Red Indian, an open eye or grinning teeth in the long still tree trunk that would turn to crocodile, the sudden smoke bringing tears to the eyes and the nose-filling smell of the robbers' hidden camp.

He was ready for any or all or none, for it was Piers who had shown him how to be all these things, who would decide, would have decided, where they were to be – in tulgy wood, jungle, or forest or ship or desert island or prison camp or, most recently, the dreadful cellar where the V.C. murderer brought his victims. Wherever it was, it was Piers who made it. Piers, who, vorpal blade in hand, long time the manxome foe he sought. Piers, whose strong arms, coming silently from behind, forced back the smooth yellow throat until the little slink eyes burst from the head and only a hissing told that the Jap was still living. Piers who, when all others cringed by the roadside, flung off the rough hand of the masked man from the delicate bare shoulder of the lady and, drawing his sword, cried, 'I offer you a gentleman's death, Mr Highwayman.' Piers, who now – not one word to Ma, or Uncle Jim, or even to Deakin, mind – stepped from the hidden cupboard and, slipping the handcuffs on the V.C.'s wrists just as he lowered his latest victim's body into the acid bath, said sternly, 'John Edwin Heath, I arrest you in the name of the Law. You were once a brave man, Wing-Commander, but now you have become a foul monster.' Piers, it had always been, who, seizing the crocodile's jaws, forced them apart until at last no trace of fire or smoke belched from the dragon's mouth to speak of life, and the great jaws fell noisily together like an old, discarded rat trap.

All and each ran confusedly in and out of Tom's mind as he sought for his wonderful brother, sought escape from the prod and pat of his uncle's questioning, sought to put behind him the sense of being all buttoned up in a coat on a hot day that he felt with this kind uncle who had rescued him from the young man who would bring them all down in fire. Yet he was an uncle full of puzzles – clucking like a hen, then suddenly pecking and scratching the ground around him, then as suddenly crowing like a cock – but it was a grown-up puzzle and it made Tom feel 'kept in', like Uncle Jim had done to him once when he knocked over a bottle of Ma's 'more precious than life itself'. It's dangerous to be clumsy. You may bring anything down.

Piers could be two or three things or more but he was always Piers; and now, after he had danced away on his own when Tom's panic so greatly needed him, he would surely make up for it by including Tom in whatever it was they were both to be. He would make Tom feel that he, too, could in safety be

anything he wanted. But, of course, that meant that he must be
ready to be anything, ready to merge into Piers' wonderful
world.

Yet Piers, dancing alone, often meant Piers, smiling and
testing. 'Come on, Tom, what shall we be?' – 'Come on, Tom,
can't you ever take a chance?' – 'Come on, Tom, make me
laugh.' Well, at least he knew how to do that. Funny grown-
up voices, funny things the grown-ups said: 'doing' Ma or
Uncle Jim, or Mrs McGuire singing 'Red Sails in the Sunset'
when she was dusting. He must get ready, for he could hear,
from where a white flowered tree spread its wide branches,
Piers making voices. And there, between great spreading
leaves and white cupped flowers all yellow centred, he saw his
brother, one hand on his hip, the other swinging his handkerchief to and fro beneath his nose. Yet, for all Tom could tell,
there were no flies or midges. He thought suddenly and desperately that he might not fit in, that he must please. He
thought to make Piers laugh.

He said, and he knew that at least this time it sounded
almost exact, though he couldn't get deep enough,

'Rabbits! Good Lord!'

Piers frowned; then, not to discourage his loved, enterpris-
ing little brother, he said, 'Rabbits are just a part of God's
smile,' then quickly changed voices.

'Come, come, Sir Thomas. Zooks, sir, you have shown us
better than that. You have dined us on fat capons and wild
boar, as fine as any in my kingdom. I had not known there was
such chase to be found on Tothill Fields. After such a banquet,
prate not to me of rabbits.' He put off the drawling voice and
said in his own, 'You must keep bowing. I am your King.'

Tom bowed and bowed after that until he began to feel quite
dizzy.

'Well, Sir Thomas, we have dined and we have seen your
lady. But come, sir, how goes the rumour? You have *many*
fine ladies here, I think. Remember, Sir Thomas, my daily
walk – no, no, it wasn't walk – can you remember, Tom?'

Tom, not remembering, continued to bow.

'Oh, it's sickening after all the trouble I took to hide the book from Ma and learn the words by heart – anyway, at nearby Saint James's, sir, where the caged birds' song delighted us. I have heard the voices of *your* caged birds from there, Sir Thomas, but I should like to see the birds themselves. Come, Sir Thomas, let me see your mistresses.'

The challenging word brought it back to Tom. Ma had read it to them on one of her funny nights. Afterwards she had said that it was a nonsense word, but Piers said they were ladies nobody spoke about. Remembering the reading, Tom knew what to do. He began shaking all over and spluttering. Piers was clearly delighted. He even stopped being King to say, 'Oh, super, Tom.'

'Well, Sir Thomas, Sir Roger Pratt had told me, when he was designing your great mansion here, that you spoke wetly, a veritable rainstorm he pronounced you. Lord, man, you need not be afraid of your King. It's your women I want to see, not your device of fountains. I've been told they're monstrous fine ladies.' Again, Tom knew what to do. He couldn't remember all the words like Piers, but he could *do* the things the book had said. He clapped his hands, and, after a moment's interval, pointed to where 'the mistresses' had arrived.

'Ah, Sir Thomas, six! Why, sir, I fear you are an overmighty subject. I may be father to a good many of the nation, but you'll be father to the whole of Westminster if you go on in this, this, this – how does it go on? – in this manner. Your King is your servant, ladies.' He began to make a little tittering, giggling laugh. 'Go on, Tom,' he said, 'copy me. That's the mistresses.' Tom, too, began to titter, while Piers walked up and down waving a dead tree branch, which he held like a walking stick, and with his other hand he stroked a great moustache in the air. 'So, so. Very pretty indeed,' and he rolled his eyes to where 'the mistresses' stood.

But, through both their tittering, Tom's alert sense could hear other voices.

'I think in two years, Jackie, the whole thing could be one mass of shrub roses. I'd try to have only the old ones from around the time of the house. Like Victoria Sackville-West is doing at her house, I'm told. Rosa Mundi or Old Cabbage.'

'We're not clever people here, remember, Rosemary dear. And, old or new, roses are all the reflection of God. So long, that is, as the colours are soft and the scent is sweet. We don't want any strident vulgar overgrown cabbage things, dear. But I know I can trust you.'

Tom stopped tittering and made signs to Piers, but it was no good – Piers had turned his back and was talking to an imaginary lady to whom he offered an arm. Soon he had taken her behind an overgrown bush and was kissing her. Tom dared not interrupt him.

'Why, there *are* the dear boys,' Grandma said.

Piers turned at that very moment and pointed to where Tom could just see his mother and grandmother through the leaves. It was clear that Piers neither saw nor heard them, for he announced, 'Well, Sir Thomas. I may only partly praise you. Four of your ladies please me. But for *that* one, sir, and *that* one, they are so damnably ugly that, did I not know you are a loyal Protestant, I would think that, like my poor brother, your priests had given them to you as a penance. Stap me, Sir Thomas, if I do not think it's near treason to present your monarch such a damnably ugly old pair of mistresses as those.' He pointed straight to where his mother and grandmother were approaching.

Tom saw that Ma gave a gasp. Grandma's sweet smile froze on her face; she looked puzzled, and irritated, as though a beautiful butterfly had turned into a bluebottle. There was still time to save Piers and he, Tom, must do it. He crouched down on the ground, waggling his nose and his bottom, and, holding a huge leaf cupped in his hands in front of him, began to nibble it. It tasted very bitter. Perhaps it was poisonous. There was always danger. But like Uncle Hubert said of Daddy, he would have to die to save his brother. He chewed jerkily as he had seen rabbits do and wagged his nose continuously.

He said chirpily, 'I'm a bunny rabbit, Granny.'

He could see that his mother wanted to laugh, for she knew that he never said 'bunny' usually. 'There's hundreds in the garden, Mr Pintreat told me. The bombs and the Coal Board brought them, but Mr Pintreat's going to make traps and snares for them. His men pretended to shoot, but Uncle Hubert didn't like it. He said, "Rabbits! Good Lord!"' He worried immediately if Granny would like him 'doing' Uncle Hubert, but he had to go on until Piers found a part.

But Piers had. He was on all fours now and, like a flash when the light fuses, he shot across from behind one bush to another, so slim and sleek that even Jackie was startled – she who found in all modern plays, with her little laugh, so much that was a pity, so much that was Error.

She cried out, 'Good Heavens! The boy's a fox.'

'Mr Tod looked round the corner and kept a careful watch on Peter Rabbit,' Piers said.

Tom said, 'I'm Peter Rabbit, but you couldn't tell 'cos I've not got my blue coat on.'

'The dear boys,' said Jackie.

And Rosemary felt free to laugh. 'Oh, you don't know the half of it, Jackie. There'll be whales and seals in the Woodwork in no time, or owls and pussycats.'

'Dear boys,' Jackie repeated, but she asked, 'Are *you* not a little old for foxes and bunny rabbits, Piers?'

Piers spoke directly to her as a man of the world explaining. 'But Tom's so frightfully good at animals, Granny. He's especially good at rabbits, but he can be a super leopard, or a lumbering bear. I'm better on two legs. That fox was a bit of a fluke. But Tom has all his feet on the ground. That's how he is. As a matter of fact, before Tom came I was doing the history of Tothill House. If you'd been here, you'd have seen the monks and the abbot with the sheep.'

Jackie, to his surprise, said, 'I guess we can forget those old monks, Piers, they just didn't have good thoughts, dear.'

It was American, Ma said, that way of speaking, but he hadn't been told Americans didn't like monks.

He said quickly, 'There were four royal visits here, Granny – Charles II, Queen Anne, George III, and Queen Victoria. I've been all of them this afternoon.'

She laughed. 'Yes, dear, I know the history of my own house.' Then, fearing that she had hurt his feelings, she added,

'But I am very glad that you know it too, Piers. For it is your house as well.'

To their surprise, and especially hers, Piers put out his hand, 'I must tell you how happy I am to be at Tothill House, Mistress Mosson.'

The slight stammer, the elocuted tone were exact – it was the King himself. Even Jackie, who hated pretence, thought that she must reward him for it. She shook his hand.

'And we are very proud to welcome you here, Sir.' And she curtseyed as low as her rather short skirt and the way her knees were nowadays allowed her.

Piers was, even so, a little disappointed. 'Shouldn't you say "Your Majesty", and kiss my hand, Granny?'

'No, dear, not on informal occasions. Not, that is, for a very long time now. Sir, or, to the Queen, "Ma'am". Of course, when we were presented at Court, that was different. I was the first American débutante to be presented,' she told Rose-mary, for it seemed more suitable to communicate this to her daughter-in-law. 'It was the greatest possible excitement. Two years before I married your father-in-law. The most beautiful gown – and the train and the feathers! I do not think I ever saw a more beautiful woman than Queen Alexandra. Although, of course, it was Queen Mary who loved blue so much. And Queen Mary had a great appreciation of the value of things. She greatly admired the snuff boxes here at Tothill. She was a truly fine woman.' She turned to her grandson. 'And I am *Lady* Mosson, Piers. And even if I weren't, you wouldn't say "mistress". That's in the very old days. Back with Queen Bess.'

She felt so young and happy. She had never felt so pretty as that night at the Palace, and Poppa had been so proud. It had been a real reward for all his years of work. And there had been flirtation in the air as well as royalty that night. Of course, it was so long ago now. So much had gone wrong. First, a dread-ful girl making a suffragette fuss in front of the throne, and then, the mistake of letting divorcees into the Royal En-closure. Innocent parties! As if there could be any innocence where there was Error.

And then she felt so happy, too, because, of course, that was it. She had thought, as they came through the Woodwork, that she heard Piers say something so unsuitable, and who could tell with this foolish mother. But she had been unfair to Rosemary. The boy had got all this speech out of some old historical novel – 'Prithee, Mistress Brown and Hark'ee, Mistress Oliver'. She quite remembered something of the sort from novels she had read as a girl. Miss Braddon was it? Or somebody. What time one had to waste in those days. She hadn't even looked after her own money. Poppa had done all that. And then she had not yet found Science.

Piers was looking up at her, then he returned to Rosemary. 'Isn't it super being here, Ma? The Great Hall!' his voice was hushed as he said it, 'and all this wonderful garden to walk in. And Granny to tell us all these things we would never know otherwise.'

His feeling was clearly sincere, intense; all the same Jackie had always been cautious of flattery, a millionairess had to be.

She said, 'You're quite the courtier, Piers, aren't you?' But then she played in with him. She extended her arm, 'You may kiss my hand.' And Piers, bowing, did so.

Tom said, 'I love it, too, Ma. I'm not frightened of the Great Hall now, or the young man falling. Uncle Hubert made me understand.'

There was true delight in Jackie's forget-me-not eyes at this. 'No one understands the Truth better than Hubert. If only he had come into Science he would have made a wonderful practitioner. But then, of course, he has the property and the Bank to think of.' She put her arms round the shoulders of both her grandsons. 'My two little courtiers,' she said, 'I want you always to feel at home here in Tothill House. And you too, Rosemary,' she added. 'We have sensed what you have been through, dear. And we have known the Truth for you every day.'

She guided the boys back through the undergrowth to where they could see the ravaged formal garden. She detached her arm from Tom for a moment and with the back of her hand patted her daughter-in-law's rouged cheek.

'It will be all right again now,' she said. 'You will see.' Then she restored her arm to Tom's shoulder.

Rosemary was so amazed that she hardly knew what to do, for she remembered Jerry's warning even when he was first after her – that, for his mother, physical contact with the non-family was a horror.

She said rather simply, 'Thank you.'

'You must curtsey,' Piers cried. Everyone must take part in this show. It was just as he'd always wanted it.

Rosemary had even more difficulty in making a low curtsey than her mother-in-law, but she tried.

'Oh good Heavens!' Jackie cried.

Perhaps the whole thing would have been a little too much for her, if they had not been interrupted at that moment by the most unexpected sight. Across the ruined paths and around the emptied fountain pool came the little bent figure of Great Grandfather Mosson, with his usual folds of spotted silk handkerchief tumbling out of his right hand coat pocket. He shuffled a little but he looked hale enough as he rang an old cracked-noted bell with his right hand.

'Oh, my goodness,' Jackie cried, 'Grandpa, where on earth did you get that old bell from? The noise!'

'Tea time! Tea time!' he cried, disregarding her; and he added in a funny flat voice, 'And high-tea, too.'

'High tea at Tothill House! Who in the world ever thought of such a thing?' But she was playing up to him, even Piers could tell.

'Tea with something to it,' he repeated, teeth appearing behind his tobacco-stained bushy white moustache in what must have been a smile, 'as my old Yorkshire nurse used to say.'

Piers then could tell what the funny flat voice he was using was meant to be. He'd been practising Yorkshire himself from a man on the radio. Great Grandfather's imitation wasn't good.

'But where's the new footman?' Jackie asked, a little put out, perhaps. 'He should be serving tea.'

'He *is*,' her father-in-law told her. 'To my instructions. I arranged it all a week ago. Hams and brawns and puddings and pies – all the things Nurse used to tell us of. It wasn't easy to get them all. But now the war's over, my great grandsons must eat like lords.' He held out his arms and flicked his fingers. 'Come, gentlemen, let me conduct you in.'

'Go along, dears,' Jackie whispered, detaching herself from them, 'I haven't seen Father like this in years.'

It was all working just as he'd imagined, thought Piers, he'd known it would, whenever he had imagined their first visit to the long predicted wonderland of Tothill. But before they could run to their great grandfather, something of their other life, of the muddle and the storms and cosiness of their home broke through. Piers could feel the familiar touch of Ma's hand pressing against his waist.

'You won't forget the old rickety shack, boys, will you?' she whispered. It was their shared name for their home. 'And your rickety old Ma? In all this splendour and luxury?' She lightly glanced over Tom's black hair with her hand, caressing and stirring it. Piers could see his own familiar sense of guilt and deep affection and fear of old scenes repeated in his small brother's large dark eyes. He pressed his waist against her hand – the secret signal that ended these appeals. 'That's all right then,' she said softly. 'Run along.'

'The Mosson family reunited,' Great Grandfather said when the two boys joined him. The two women recoiled a little from this. But for Jackie, at any rate, any sense of loss was largely repaired, for there was Hubert at the top of the steps. He walked down towards the little statue.

'Do you see who's with us, Mother?' he asked.

Jackie peered, then ran delightedly forward on her old fashioned heels. 'My little shepherd boy,' she cried, 'so they did not stop you playing, after all!'

'We'll soon be rid of all this rubbish, Mother,' Hubert went on soothingly, as he pointed to the débris. The packing cases were already gone. Good man, Pentreath.

But Jackie brushed it aside. 'Oh, my dear boy, we just do not see it. It is not there. We have woken up from that old Adam dream of war.'

As they reached the top step, old Mr Mosson let go of the boys' hands and turned round to face them. 'And blood puddings,' he said in a voice cavernous but kind.

Piers addressed his mother. He wanted to bring her in. 'It's like the ogre, isn't it, Ma?' It was *she* who had been frightened of ogres in stories, when he was very small; he who had reassured her. He ought to do so now.

'Fee, fi, fo, fum. I smell the blood of an Englishman.' The old man assumed his part in the best children's party manner. He hadn't remembered that he could do that sort of thing. But things came back to the Mossons as they might not to less solid people – even in old age.

'But he's a very nice man, isn't he, Ma?' Tom said and he clearly meant it.

And so Piers, supported by Tom, led the whole company through the South Door into the Great Hall.

PART II
1956–1957

CHAPTER I

The First Performance

'O, villains, vipers damned without redemption!
Dogs easily won to fawn on any man!'

The voice, firm and noble, rang out in all the contempt that
need be mustered to crush those who had dared to darken the
sun with the shadows of their mean forms. Piers, standing by
the prompter, thought, I've done it. Cowley, who's never had
a thought in his handsome head beyond springing, deerlike, in
the air to catch the ball at cover point, has come over as a King,
glorious moulder of his realm and his subjects, man of flair and
imagination and regality.

'Three Judases, each thrice worse than Judas . . .' the
young voice heaped scorn. An absurdity came into Piers' mind
– the Lambkin's copy of the play which he had used at rehearsals, all bordered with inane comments in the old fool's neat
hand. Here, against Richard's magnificent violent denuncia-
tion, the ass had written, 'He believes them to be disloyal'. He
had again, as at rehearsal, to stifle his laughter. Mocking
thoughts and words, the wonderful essence of everyday play,
what kept one afloat in face of the stupidities and frets of
school and home and Tothill; but he had learned in these
intense weeks of production that it could not go with creation, with seeing how the play should be shaped and mould-
ing the actors to make those shapes. There was no time
for anything that distracted – even a giggle could weaken
the tension that was needed.

35

It was Shakespeare's words and the way the actors, following all he had taught them, spoke them, that stood first – not the surface show of bodies and faces and movements and costumes and sets. These came second, were but the outward show. Yet now, against the rule he had set himself, he felt the need to open his eyes and reassure himself. Cowley stood the visual test as well – tall, slim, like an elegant hawk in his gold-embroidered, long-sleeved royal robe, his well-meaning, foolish cricket-captain's face looked visionary, inspired, the dull blue eyes flashing with light too intense for anger. And the audience was held, moved – he could see the headmaster's mouth open, for once not in chatter, but in wonder, and his housemaster's lips set stern, not in their usual lines of self-conscious whimsy. A big old woman's eyes looked out scared as a child woken from a nightmare at the King's terrible majesty. There too, surely, were Ma's eyes, showing amazed behind the mascaraed lashes. What was she thinking? 'Darling heart, say it isn't really like this.' He formed the parodied words as he thought of his mother.

He closed his own eyes; he had sworn that he would take no peep at the audience, would judge all by what it should be judged by – the play's speech as he had instructed them. And all honour and glory to Shakespeare, he mumbled quickly in superstitious fear of the harvest of hubris. But to meet any possible failure he would need all his tense nerve, the tightening of the muscle he could feel in his thighs, the tingling fear that had set his balls aflame since the curtain went up. He willed the cast to be as he had shown them how to be.

Now it was Matlock as Bolingbroke. Oh, the happy choice of that oily, cringing voice to deny any grandeur that the audience might give to the usurper simply because by the play's end he had stolen the crown. It had taken a lot to find an actor whose petty, pimping voice would take all majesty from the usurper's words. He did not need to open his eyes to know the face that voice betrayed – a wizen-cheeked boy, with yellowing skin and fuzzy colourless hair and shifty thick-lidded eyes. He had known at once when he had called the audition and saw him that no one else should play great Richard's odious foe – a boy that years ago, back in Transitus form, he had sat near to, and, with others, had shrunk from, for his smelly breath and constant farting. It had been the fashion to hold one's nose ostentatiously when passing Matlock. But he had proved a worthy actor, ready to respond to his producer's instructions to be meanly menacing in Henry's role. Old Lambkin, in one of his tedious prying visits to rehearsal, had said, 'You don't give us much to hope for from the future King, Matlock.' Very much the judicious senior English master. But good old Stinky had not listened. He had been too anxious to please his producer and mysteriously (for the more Piers thought of all these weeks of creation, the more he sensed something – over and above his instructions – moving among them), mysteriously, the boy had invested his cringing meanness with a sort of pathos that, without diminishing great Richard, gave balance to the play. All honour to the players – but keep them in their place. Yet listening to the envious, mean, sad, snarling tones of Matlock's Bolingbroke, he felt pride,

> 'See, see, King Richard doth himself appear,
> As doth the blushing discontented sun
> From out the fiery portal of the East . . .'

Whine away, and snap as you will, you cheap mongrel, how can you even hope to tell what wonderful meteor flashed through the sky when King Richard II reigned in all his magnificence and artistry? Good old Matlock, he'd done his part to point up the real glory of the Tragedy of King Richard the Second.

But now Piers waited with special anxiety, for that moment was coming which so many seized on to make nonsense of this splendid play. Richard's standing away to view the deaths and murders of Kings, not in any bitterness, less still in fear, not in self pity nor in self anything, but just as a statement of life's attendant facts, passing, external, the shadow world of action through which the artist – whether King or player or producer or great Shakespeare – must pass, the tedious Suezes and

Hungaries, Armadas and Guy Fawkes plots. Cowley's voice came, remote yet sad, as Piers had told him, telling life as it is, but his own majesty untouched . . .

> 'For God's sake let us sit upon the ground
> And tell sad stories of the death of Kings:
> How some have been deposed, some slain in war,
> Some haunted by the ghosts they have deposed,
> Some poisoned by their wives . . .'

There it all was – history, the royal chronicle, politics, getting scholarships, going up to Oxford – but it didn't touch Richard's tragic greatness for a moment. Oh, good old Cowley! He could have held the handsome blockhead in his arms and cuddled him in gratitude. For a moment, a vision of Cowley's shocked blue eyes at such indecency came to him and he wanted to laugh, but once again he thrust irrelevance from him. Soon the great moment of Shakespeare's play, of Richard's life, of his own – since, for tonight, the three were one and the same – would have come and gone. And he could relax. The sun would have gone down.

And the words were said almost before he was ready to weep for them, yet tears came without any preparation, so that he was glad to have his eyes shut.

> 'Down, down I come, like glist'ring Phaethon,
> Wanting the manage of unruly jades . . .'

Until at last,

> 'Down court! Down King!
> For night owls shriek where mounting larks should sing!'

It was tragedy's triumph, Richard's great cry of the beauty of defeated majesty, Phaethon's defiance – and that very great actor Bob Cowley, Captain of the Westminster First Eleven cricket team, had sounded its wonderful agony as he had been instructed by Piers Mosson. Opening his eyes for a moment, Piers saw the prompter, his friend Gordon Cheatle, making the V sign to him and grinning broadly, for all alike – cast, stage staff, property men – knew from him that this was the great climax. Indeed, Shakespeare stressed this by now taking us into the world of the Queen and the Gardener – the Queen important to the man Richard, but irrelevant to his majesty – so that we should move on into the last quarter of the play with sad and stately step, but all passion spent in that one great cry – Down, down I come . . .

Tom, who had lived what seemed hours of misery and leg-shifting discomfort for this culmination of the production, as he well knew his brother thought it to be, felt a wetness in his underpants as a small dribble of piss left his cock to relieve the tension of his whole body. Ordinarily, he would have put his burning embarrassed cheeks into cupped hands in shame, but his pride at his brother's success banished all absurd fears for what others might guess. He looked in turn from side to side along to each end of the row – all were intent, held, even the stupidest, most loutish boys, even the little knot of St Paul's girls who had threatened, with their giggling at the opening of the play, to ruin all. His brother had triumphed, borne all before him, as he had at Oxford – 'the best candidate we have known for scholarship entrance since before the war' some don from Christ Church had written.

And then, into Tom's delight at Van's triumph and well done, Cowley, came a fear that for a moment made cold water run down his spine, between his shoulder blades – all humanity, Kings and sons of Gods alike, walked upon ice, trod tightropes above flaming fires – Down, down I come. But the excitement, the thrill of what Shakespeare, of what Van, yes, what even a nit like Cowley could give to us, made the ice seem gloriously to hold, the balancing rope to stay firm. Even he, who could carve no ice shapes of beauty, kindle no amazing fires, felt happy to be alive in this hall at this first night of this school play, where random people of many ages had felt for a moment the rare thrill, the occasional prize that transcended their necessarily flat life of daily duty. And now for the party and the silly talk and then to the many months ahead of hard work needed to get good A levels, to make sure against failure.

Nothing could have been a more splendid manifestation of Van's absolute triumph, to banish any lurking doubts in Tom's mind, than the gathering of masters around Ma and Grandma at the housemaster's party afterwards. One or two, it is true, may have been paying snobbish tribute to the Mosson family's social position, or to their millions. Leckey, the new young art master, might well, though Tom didn't know him well enough to say, be lured by the legend of Tothill, its seclusion from the public, its extraordinary proximity to the school, above all its renowned architectural union of opposites. Old Lambkin had called the new master 'a disturbing testimony to a resurgence of aestheticism in our midst'. But, for the most part, it was simply – though Grandma no doubt thought it was a natural obeisance to the Mosson presence – a tribute to Van's extraordinary success. You could see it in their eyes, and in the eyes of the mistress who had brought the St Paul's girls along – he'd set them alight, and the more so, no doubt, because they'd been expecting to be lulled into an uneasy drowse of boredom. Ma certainly had, as he'd known when she said to him, 'Shakespeare! Oh dear! Tom, darling heart, will there be clowns? And the actors suddenly killing each other with swords? And all those quotations.' And yet here her eyes were shining as he'd hardly ever seen them before (though there was, too, that unrest, that anxiety that seemed to shiver through the happiest times – he was a true son of his mother!), and the shine was not just pride for Van, it was something the play had done to her. The final proof, of course, was their housemaster, Mr Brownlow. He, who so often had made it clear to them that, much though he liked them, no jot of Mosson wealth or position would count for a second in the house. It was to be merit every time; that was the spirit that must reign if a school like Westminster was to survive. Yet here he was, neglecting all his other guests to pay court to Van's family. His only mark of meritocratic belief, a fixed determination to address untitled Ma rather than titled Grandma. Tom saved up this joke to tell Van – it was just his kind of thing – when he brought the cast into the party from the dressing rooms.

But now Brownlow said it out loud, 'Since he has not yet appeared on the scene, I feel free to tell you that your elder boy is a prodigy, Mrs Mosson. I shan't do so, because our language has become so debased that the word instantly suggests an odious little creature with a smirk, a lace collar and a violin. And I hardly need to tell you that Van, as his brother has taught us to call him, has none of those things.'

Tom watched his mouth twitch in the little smile with which he humorously deprecated his own rather pedantic form of speech – the smile which Van had so perfectly imitated among so many other of the quirks of the masters when, during rehearsal breaks, he had wanted to keep the cast amused. Why was Mr Brownlow so pompous when he was really so nice? Every year, Tom thought, human mystery seemed to increase, when he'd always thought growing older would bring more certainty. Yet the answers were there, he felt sure. And one of them was that Van had found expression for all that had been growing in him since their childhood.

Standing next to his mother, he was moved to squeeze her arm above the elbow. She started and slopped a little of her champagne on her dress. Tom's embarrassment at the unfortunate result of his rare show of physical intimacy was turned to shared amusement, for immediately Grandma signified by a little disapproving click of her tongue her doubts about her daughter-in-law's social proficiency and her fear that this social clumsiness had been passed to her grandson. Tom caught his mother's eye and, under the cover of the Lambkin's pompous talk, she whispered,

'We're in disgrace.'

He whispered back, 'I know. But isn't it wonderful that Van's knocked them all so flat?'

'He knocked me flat too, Tom.'

He could see that it was true, and yet there was something that kept her apart from the occasion. He was about to whisper his anxiety to her, but she said very softly,

'We can't hold a Mosson whispering show, darling heart. I

do know my manners even if your grandmother doesn't think I do.' Aloud she said, 'That boy was every inch a King, wasn't he? And I found the girl who played the Queen very moving. She gave such a sense of feeling the King's greatness even at the worst of his troubles.'

Brownlow wasn't having this. 'No, you can't wriggle out of it, Mrs Mosson, just because he's your son. I *know* school acting, as I am sure does Miss Lantry,' he bowed to the St Paul's School mistress who had brought the girl actresses over, 'and, except for the occasional individual performances of some merit, we are usually busy trying to praise what has not absolutely embarrassed us.'

Miss Lantry gave a little smile, perhaps, Tom thought, to separate herself from the characteristic mordancy of Mr Brownlow's speech, but her smile was in general agreement.

'It's quite extraordinary,' she said, 'to have seen a school play in which everything and everyone worked together to make the same meaning and the same beauty. And only the producer could have done that. I congratulate you, Lady Mosson.'

She's not worried about paying tribute to Grandma's title, Tom thought. He liked such social certainty, even if it was snobbish. Brownlow, nice though he was, perhaps because he was such a nice man, kept forever making exceptions, seeing things afresh. It made the house a pleasant place to live in, but, from the outside, he often thought it must seem a disordered muddle.

Jackie's answer came late and vague. 'Yes? Well, I suppose that Shakespeare . . . all that lovely language. Next to the Bible the most beautiful words in English, we always said. I don't know about *seeing* Shakespeare, however.'

Tom treasured this up for Piers, and also he might pretend that Brownlow had answered, as he would have done in class, 'who are *we*, and *who* always says?' – it would make a more complete funny shape. But in fact that sort of invention was too dangerous. Van might believe it and then be annoyed at being taken in. But certainly he could report what Brownlow actually said, although Van would try to make light of it – he accepted praise so easily, whereas Tom believed in approaching it with caution.

'Van's sense of Shakespeare's *language*, Lady Mosson, was superb. Though not so surprising – I must lower my voice – as conveying that appreciation to dear old Bob Cowley. You're not to repeat me, Pratt, you understand?' He had recently learned of the brothers' nicknames for each other, Pratt and Van.

Tom knew his housemaster's mock sternness; it was real. But since he was right to demand order and obedience, why did he always have to present it in a mocking tone – and using their private nicknames?

'But the most exciting thing about Van's production,' Brownlow went on, 'was his unusual *shaping* of the play. As a rule there is nothing I deprecate more than an original interpretation of a Shakespeare play. It usually means the perversity and second rate "cleverness" we've come sadly to associate with the theatre today. But this evening's demand that we see Richard's fall as the fine edge of his greatness, though not without a touch of Byronic show off – Van is very young – seemed to me thoroughly convincing.'

'I am afraid that I don't agree with you.'

So old Lambkin was to be the devil's advocate, Tom thought. Well, no one would agree with *his* views.

Mr Brownlow said, 'Oh, don't be afraid, Lamb. I did not suppose that you would. It would have been the first time that we'd agreed in our lives.' His smile told the ladies that this Mr Lamb was to be taken with a pinch of salt.

'I don't deny the *brilliance* of Mosson's production,' the older man said, 'but I felt it forced. Henry IV was a far more stable man than Richard. History tells us so.'

The housemaster was now even more amused. 'I know it's unfair of me,' he said, 'but I can't help choosing this moment to tell you all that not only did the Christ Church examiners consider Van's papers to be the most impressive they'd seen since the war, but they particularly commended his grasp of late medieval English political and constitutional history.'

The other masters laughed kindly but firmly at this put-down; Tom's love for his brother won over his sense of order and he, too, smiled.

'Nevertheless,' Lamb said, 'Henry won and Richard lost.'

The housemaster did not conceal his patronage. 'Well, you're the Eng. Lit. authority. But *I* should have thought that we mustn't confuse poetry with political victory. Nor with regicide for that matter.'

All this bickering was not giving a very happy picture of the school. Ma, of course, wouldn't notice – what *was* eating her? But Grandma, Tom could see, had her doubts already – it was almost as though her Christian Science distaste for the Abbey had spilled over on to the school. It didn't matter, of course, except that it led to tensions and to lavish portions of her barbed remarks during weekends at Tothill which meant so much to him and to Van. He was delighted then when Van's form master came over to the group.

'Do have one of these little things, Lady Mosson. It's real caviare. Don't worry, it's not on our usual diet,' he said to Rosemary. 'Once *they've* started arguing, you will never be offered anything. Can I get you another glass of champagne? I am your son's form master. You've heard all about how good his scholarship is. I'd like to say that he's the most *interesting* boy I've ever taught.'

Tom saw that his mother immediately looked less preoccupied, younger. Was it the further praise of Van? Was it being called Lady Mosson? Or the man's good looks? Probably just that the conversation was off Shakespeare at last.

'Thank you. I mean about darling Piers. And, yes, I will have a *canapé*. They look delicious. And yes, I should like some more champagne. I can never have enough. And yes, I *am* his mother. But no, I am not *Lady* Mosson. Did I get the answers in the right order? It would be nice not to be bottom of the class all the time. I'm hopeless on Shakespeare, I'm afraid.'

She fitted a cigarette into her long jade holder, flicked her shagreen lighter and lit the cigarette. Tom was transported back to all the parties at the Nursery with his father's and Uncle Jim's brother officers and their wives. Ma could do all the party tricks. 'It's called poise, darling hearts, in the women's mags,' she had told him and Van, years ago.

'*This* is Lady Mosson, my mother-in-law.'

'Hello,' said Jackie.

Tom knew that address as one she used with him and Van when she was cross. She immediately turned away after her short greeting. She was not pleased at something. She addressed them judicially, particularly Mr Brownlow.

'The play had elegance and taste, but then, you are good enough to let the boys visit us at Tothill; it would be surprising if even a stupid boy absorbed nothing from that. And Piers is clever, and, of course, he was so well served by the other boys and girls.' She was smiling what Van called her Lady Mayoress smile. Tom was apprehensive. And it came.

'I think that you are quite right, however,' she turned to Lambkin, who at once looked unsheepish, like a distinguished stork. 'I am afraid that Piers was being too clever in rooting for a natural loser, as my dear father would have said. It's a thing that we Gleasons never did. Nor the Mossons. The Mossons have always played to win. I hope, as you say,' she told Mr Brownlow, 'that it's just because he's at the clever age. I should not like to think that he believed such nonsense.' She addressed herself to her grandson. 'God wants us to give love to everyone, but that does not mean that He loves a quitter. You can get that over to your clever brother, Tom. You are a real worker.'

Tom saw that Brownlow checked his instinct to reply sharply. He felt so angry himself that he walked away as though to examine the food on the buffet table. It was bad enough when she put down Ma in his presence, but to put down Piers in his absence! Then, having selected an éclair, he ate it very slowly, watching after each bite to see how far the cream was oozing from the tube. Consideration conquered anger. The few minutes' solitude, the active eating rather than the passive listening did the trick, calmed him, made him reflect on what Van and he had been saying of their grandmother during all this term. She had been receding ever since the Luzzi had appeared on the scene on that first termtime Tothill Sunday visit in October,

ever since, in fact, Uncle Hubert had looked happy and had
stopped the cackling fits which had frightened him so in childhood, ever since Grandma herself had spoken in an open bitter
way, so unlike her usual sugary nips, about 'being with that
dreadful woman has made Hubert lose his happy laughter'.

She was on the defensive. But Van insisted that, so tough
and so entrenched, she was bound to win. Yet, as he looked
over at her, sitting there beside Ma, among the masters, withdrawn, hardly even bothering to keep up her famous 'smiling
with her eyes', tired, old, he felt that for once he was right and
Van was wrong. She was losing the battle with the Luzzi, and
whatever Van might find diverting and original in the Luzzi's
breathless cascade of smart talk, whether for itself or because it
had given him a new and very funny object of mimicry, Tom
had to place himself on his grandmother's side. She was, after
all, the matriarch, the family, and that should count. Then
again, however she failed to appreciate the majesty of Pratt's
symmetry, let alone the intricate, reckless-seeming order of
Vanbrugh, she did love and respect Tothill, especially all the
objects and 'little pieces' which so bored Van, but which were,
after all, the outward signs that, in her words, 'Tothill has been
a lived-in house for over three centuries.' Her words for it
were all wrong, of course, but she *did* care for it. Just as all that
sugary pretending that everything was good and happy and
loving was her way of dealing with the fact that she knew that
it was not.

She was like him and Ma, *she* heard the ice cracking too. It
came to him suddenly that this was why she needled them both
publicly so much, because she knew their fears; whereas Van
she only dared criticise when he wasn't there, for her digs left
him untouched. It was the first time that he had thought of her
not as remote and frightening, or, in more recent years, remote
and absurd. He supposed this suddenly seeing people in
new ways was part of adolescence, but it was an additional
strain in an overburdened world. After tonight he would
give himself to A levels and nothing else. Meanwhile he
decided to return and stand by her chair instead of by Ma's.
It was, after all, the same family unity that needed em-

phasising, only a different side of it.

And now they were going on about Van going to France, which he knew Van had no intention of doing. Should he stop them? There was no need. He heard Jackie in her most *grande-dame* manner make this clear.

'There never really was any intention of his going to France,' she declared. 'In my day it was only girls who got finished off in France. Young men, of course, went to Paris for their fling, but Piers is hardly ready for that yet.' She smiled up at the French master, Lacordaire, recalling his suggestion. 'Oh, we had fun in our day,' she went on, 'but it had a lightness, a charm that seems to have gone in these days.' She chose to acknowledge the St Paul's mistress. 'I doubt if the modern girl is taught the real art of flirting. However, I want these boys *here*. I shall take Piers away in the Easter holidays. We shall go to Long Island. The girls will go mad about him. And, of course, all these young people today want to go to the Coast. I have never cared for it. But San Francisco is nice, if provincial. All Europeans feel at home there – that amused us all so in New York. We shall stay with Ida Willard on Nob Hill.'

The housemaster could only find a short comment to make. 'Lucky Van!'

The eagerness of his tone made Tom giggle. It suggested Brownlow's longing to elope with Grandma. He saved it up for Van.

Piers' form master intervened: 'I think it is a wise decision. If he stays on here, he'll have the run of the Library. He can cover a lot of the History School's syllabus in advance. After all, the main thing is that he should both get a First and enjoy himself at Oxford. All the same, I think he must have a say in the decision. He may have other ideas.'

Lady Mosson laughed lightly. 'I cannot think what they would be. We want him here. And he wants to stay in England. Doesn't he, Tom?'

Tom, thinking of Van's decision to get any stage work he could until he went up, felt both that he was helping his brother and telling the truth when he answered, 'He doesn't want to go abroad.'

'I knew it,' his grandmother said. 'He wants to stay here with us.'

Tom could see that all the masters were shocked at her possessiveness.

'What do *you* think, Mrs Mosson?' the housemaster asked, asserting the true priority of parenthood.

But Ma seemed to be absorbed in some anxiety. She said vaguely, 'Oh, I'm sure you're right.'

His form master sought to assert Piers' rights. 'I feel that if we can find him another play to produce this summer he'll be all in favour of staying on.'

'Well,' said his housemaster, 'I don't know that there'll be any harm in that. It will get the theatre out of his blood.'

It was Jackie's turn to look amused. 'I was not aware that either the Mossons or the Tothills had any such taint. They have always been wise enough to marry heiresses not actresses. Do *you* have any theatrical blood, Rosemary?'

'I think Mummy played in one or two amateur musical shows as a girl.'

'Ah. Very likely. Well, it won't take Piers long to free himself of *that*.'

Tom could see that Brownlow had had enough of all this. 'Our only difficulty is that the summer production is operatic. And I am afraid that Van doesn't add music to his many accomplishments. But I'll talk to Howerton. He could do with someone with theatrical sense to assist him. His production of Purcell's *Fairy Queen* last year had about as much life as a meeting of the Dean and Chapter.'

Jackie laughed. 'Oh dear, the poor old Church of England! You're *so* right. It turns to dust everything it touches. Even the Bible's lovely language.'

Tom could see from her smile that she was looking at Brownlow in a new, more favourable light.

'Rosemary, my dear, we mustn't monopolise these busy gentlemen. They have done so much for our boys. And there must be other parents.'

It was Ma's turn to be annoyed now. She assumed her own

regal manner that she used for people who wanted the newest
H.T. rose at her famous shrub rose nursery. She turned her
back on her mother-in-law and addressed the housemaster in a
businesslike, parental manner.

'Thank you for all you've done for them both. And we'll be
in touch about Piers' staying on. In any case I'm sure you're
right about his producing another play if it can be managed.
We all need to express ourselves. All work and no play . . .'
She turned to Jackie. 'Mummy's musicals won't have been
wasted, you see,' she said, and giggled like a pert child.

Tom was delighted at his mother's happiness in a rare score
off Granny, but oh dear, he thought, their bickering has succeeded in turning Brownlow from 'special charm' to 'brush
off', for their housemaster moved away very brusquely and
could be heard loudly greeting other parents.

'Good evening, Mrs Cowley. Well, do you prefer Robert
on the throne or at the wicket?' His voice had a more hearty
ring for the Cowleys. And now the little gathering began to
break up.

'Where *is* Piers?' Jackie asked.

And Rosemary said, 'He had to help with putting away the
costumes and so on, and all that make-up takes time to
remove, especially with children.' She spoke, to Grandma's
evident annoyance, as though to another child unnecessarily
fussing. Then, to Tom's amazement, she said tensely, 'Tom,
there *is* a telephone in this house, isn't there?'

'Of course, Ma, you've rung Mr Brownlow before now.'

'I'm sorry, dear, it's just that I can't understand it.'

'And we cannot understand you,' Jackie said. 'What *is* the
matter with you, Rosemary? Piers is being very discourteous
not only to us but to all these people who came to see his little
play. And all you can talk about is telephones.'

'Piers would have been here now if Marina Luzzi hadn't
insisted on going to meet the cast in their dressing rooms. As
though she was the Queen or something. And Hubert tagging
along like the Prince Consort.'

Tom would have laughed at his Ma's muddled historical picture if it had not been for his alarm at her open criticism of

Uncle Hubert in Grandma's presence. Surely there would be
an earthquake, a volcanic eruption. But no, only a sad, spent
smouldering as Jackie said:

'Everything has been very badly arranged.'

Lacordaire intervened. 'Don't be anxious, Lady Mosson. I
happen to know that Reggie Howerton has decided to do a
Lully opera this summer. He is always determined to be original. I know because I am to supervise the French diction.
Well, I have to ask, what a waste of time! Mosson can easily do
that perfectly. Better than I can – he has patience with these
actors. I shall be so glad to hand over to him. And then we will
tell Reggie that Mosson will *produce* the opera. He will at least
give us some fun. With all those mechanical clouds and flaming
smoke, it should be interesting, though hardly serious. But we
shall see. If Mosson does it, he will make something clever of
it, I know. *Ils ne sont pas des vrais opéras, ces pièces de Lully,
plutôt des masques ou des pièces de théâtre avec musique.*
Quinault, you know, wrote really quite good libretti. Yes, it
will be a real achievement for Mosson to bring all that alive.
And I am too busy for operas. Lully! But that is how it goes
now. Anything not to be the same as other people. But say
nothing, please, until I have negotiated. Good night. I hope
we shall meet again soon. We shall be in touch.'

He bowed. Poor man, thought Tom, he little knows how
rare an invitation to Tothill is. And Grandma always interpret-
ed people who said they would keep in touch as intending to
touch her for money. How the play's success had brightened
him. He must remember that for Piers. And then he remembered Ma's anxiety and the Luzzi business and felt the floor
giving way beneath him.

Then the silly man finally muffed his chances. For he
returned.

'What a world we live in,' he cried. 'Anything to be clever.
Lully! Lully! Lully!' And he shook his finger three times in
Grandma's face. As you might with a baby, Tom thought.
Grandma took it in that way.

'Lully!' she said, when he had gone, 'What does the man
mean? Is he trying to say lullaby, Rosemary?'

But Rosemary looked absent and soon was to be so, for a clearly hired head waiter came up to say that Mrs Mosson was wanted on the telephone and she was gone, white faced and tense, in a second. Could it be, Tom wondered, Nursery money troubles? That was the usual thing, but hardly at this late hour, surely? Or was it Uncle Jim and that woman making trouble? Probably Uncle Eustace wanting a loan – at this hour? and how could he know where to ring? But the old family joke of Uncle Eustace's sponging simply wouldn't work to dispel the awful execution-bound look on his Ma's face. He wanted to go after her, but he thought he could best help by staying to cope with Grandma's tantrums alone. He felt suddenly very adult, for he had never done this sort of coping – Van was the one for that. He hadn't charm like Van, what else could he use? Something was needed, for this dramatic exit of Ma's was the last straw for her ladyship. She can't bear all the world having a role but her, Tom thought, and urged himself not to be spiteful, she was old and frightened, but she had been so bloody in public about Van's triumph. All the same, in some placation and to distract her from Ma, he said:

'It's a composer, I think. Lully, I mean. I'm bad about music,' he added when he saw that his words had no effect on her.

'What nonsense,' she was saying, 'and so very unsuitable. All this drama! Urgent telephone calls in other people's houses! Oh my, it's just like Rosemary. Right back to the days of her mother's theatrical boarding house.' Tom looked fiercely at her, and she changed her tune. 'I am sure it is a mistake. The call can't be for her. It must be some message from the house. Perhaps something to do with Grandfather. Old age seems to have become so very real to him since he turned ninety. And then servants fuss so. They live in a world of doctors and illnesses and death. I remember it with my nurses as a girl. Of course I wasn't in Science then. I believed all their nonsense. It's such a pity. But perhaps that is why they are servants. However, I am surprised at Gates. He should have sent one of the footmen with a message. Urgent telephone calls! It's all so theatrical, and cheap!'

Tom could find no way to stop her working herself up. Suddenly she said to a passing waiter, 'Have Lady Mosson's car brought round immediately, please.'

She seemed to be flinging down a challenge. She would have her proper exit at least. And Tom could not stop himself from taking the challenge up.

'You *must* wait and see Piers, Grandma.' At least he attempted to meet her by using his brother's Christian name; she did not like what she called 'this Pratting and Vanning', or indeed their whole absorbed espousal of the rival claims of the Tothill architects.

'My dear boy, I am not staying here until midnight. You boys have to learn . . .'

But he never did, for at that moment there was a commotion at the door and the cast, restored to twentieth century adolescence, burst into the room. Above their chatter came the voice and accent now so familiar from Van's imitations – so familiar that for the moment or so Tom wondered whether it was his brother talking.

'Oh, my God! 'ow boaring it must be at this school! And worse for these girls. They sent me to a convent once. But I screamed and screamed so they took me away. Then I 'ad governesses. They were frightfully boaring, but I didn't 'ave to notice them. 'Ave you tried screaming? – you, the pretty one, the Queen, wasn't it? You should. It's so amusing. Do you 'ave 'ouses like these poor boys? You could scream the 'ouse down. Oh I know that's not what people say now, 'Ubert. Don't be so boaring and literal. It's what your mother would say. You want me to be like 'er. You said saow.'

It seemed impossible that the Luzzi could go so far, as she must know that Grandma was somewhere around. And it sounded so like Van's idea of how 'the great row' they were all expecting would begin. But it couldn't be Van imitating. Even elated by the play's success, he surely wouldn't be so carried away as to say things like that when Grandma was about. Tom looked at her expecting that she might hurl a thunderbolt but she had shut her eyes. Perhaps she was saying the what-do-

you-call-it – the Divine Statement of Being – or more likely
the Spiritual Interpretation of the Lord's Prayer – 'Our Father
– Grandmother God, all harmonious'. But poor old thing! She
looked with her eyes shut more like an old moulting parrot.

And it *was* the Luzzi – silver lipstick, heavy green eye
shadow, in a pale blue satin dress with a tight embroidered
bodice, and the pale blue hair band (the dress had 'simple lines'
but cost a fortune, so Ma said, but it looked complicated to
Tom – he especially wondered how the big shoulder straps
were fixed to the bodice, as large coloured flowers covered the
actual join). Uncle Hubert was beside her as usual, held by her
every word. For Uncle Hubert to be bowing and bobbing to
something so out of order, so unconcerned with order, even
impatient with it, as the Luzzi, frightened and disgusted Tom.
In any case, *she* frightened and disgusted him too, so that he
made himself, as usual in her presence, as remote as possible.
He went to the buffet table and, poised between the choice of
the silky smoothness of a pink pâté on toast or the sweet-salt
delight of smoked ham, cut himself off in deliberation of pleasure.

'No, please, no introductions to everyone,' Marina said to
Mr Brownlow, to whom Hubert had proudly presented her.
'It's too boaring.'

Piers, who, even through the elation of his triumph, was
increasingly worried about the effect that Marina's late arrival
at the party might have upon his housemaster, was now even
more alarmed. Brownlow merely looked amused in a worldly
way and the rest of the company appeared delighted. Piers
thought, it must be because Marina seemed so immediately to
step out of the glossies, to give hope to even the most staid
that, somewhere in the next few days and to someone, they
could casually boast of having lifted off for a few seconds into
the air with the jet set. If only to add, 'I shouldn't want to
spend my life with them, of course, but this Italian – Marina
Luzzi she's called, you've read about her, darling, I'm sure –
was very amusing for half an hour. For longer it would certainly get on one's nerves.' Or a more masculine voice, Piers constructed, 'Very beautiful, yes, but not my cup of tea. All the

women were raving about her clothes. Looked like a peasant
girl to me. Eileen tells me her dress alone was worth five or six
hundred.' And, thought Piers, I'm bowled over, too, even
when she's said things about the production which show how
little she understands '*l'azione divina della creatività*', as she
tells me it is called. So don't let me pretend. She's so out-
rageous, and then she seems to come straight out of the best
Italian films, and she's so sexy and so rude and so inviting, and
then, if she does hit the wrong note, she hits so many notes
that some of them give out a deliciously right sound. As now –

'But I *know* Piers loves all these children's bodies as much as
I do. We were quite a voyeur pair in the dressing rooms there,
weren't we, darling? Oh, not *children's* bodies! That would be
frightfully sentimental. No. Young bodies, growing bodies!
Oh, tell them not to look shocked, 'Ubert, it's too boaring.
You all think you must play this English part for us because we
are foreigners. It's so crude. You are all lovely people, I can
see it. And so naturally you like young growing bodies. You
must do. You couldn't like 'is play otherwise. And 'e couldn't
'ave made such a spectacle for you, if 'e 'adn't loved them too.
This beautiful girl!' She held Jean Leggatt away from her by
placing a hand on each of the girl's shoulders. 'Look at 'er. She
is so lovely. The little breasts, everything just forming.'

Oh God! Piers thought, Jean'll burst into tears as she had
once in rehearsals when he'd criticised her movements as too
boyish, not enough those of a young Queen born to rule. But
now there were no tears. Only delight. She stood beneath
Marina's gaze with the assumed nonchalance that he imagined
would be shown by a starlet chosen at a Hollywood audition.
And an equally delighted woman's voice – presumably her
mother's – said:

'Well, Jean, there you are. You didn't expect that.'

But Marina had turned to Cowley and now was stroking his
neck – oh crumpets! – his neck. 'And this beautiful young
man! The way the muscles move beneath his smooth skin. I
saw it – 'ow do you say? – rippling when 'e took off 'is shirt.
Our Italian boys of this age are so boaring. They want always
to be – 'ow do the Americans say it? – macho. They don't

realise 'ow beautiful growing limbs are. And these ones are specially good.'

She waved her hand in a gesture to include *all* the boys, and Piers noticed to his amazement that Cowley, modest, virginal Cowley, was frowning because he was no longer the sole object of admiration.

'It must be this cricket, 'owever it is played. And so now you see,' she ended, addressing her host with an offhand smile, 'we've missed all the 'igh Table talk. It's a pity. Because I've 'eard so much of 'igh Table talk, but we were feasting our eyes in the dressing rooms.'

Piers saw that Hubert's delight – so constant nowadays that he seemed to have grown quite elegant with it – had turned to teasing, protective laughter – but not the old bray that used to scare Tom so when they were children.

He said, 'Not High Table, Marina, that's only at Oxford and Cambridge. Not at school.'

She smiled wearily at him. 'No facts, please, 'Ubert. *You* should be a schoolmaster, if you weren't amusing as you are.'

Their host felt it helpful to take up the conversation.

'I am so glad that we were able to provide you with such pleasure. As a matter of fact, you are right about cricket. The King you admire so is the Captain of our First Eleven.'

Marina rubbed the back of her hand against Cowley's cheek. Piers could see that he was as proud as when his team won the inter-house cricket cup. What fun it was when Marina was about, and how silly to get fussed about her like Tom, and Grandma. She had made a wonderful end for him to this wonderful evening.

To Cowley, she said, 'Are you, darling? I am sure you are.'

One or two boys cried, 'Good old Cowley' and a few parents took it up. But Marina was clearly a little bored by now. She put her arm round Piers' waist.

'Here's the maestro. 'E's what matters. Next time, darling, you must produce professionals, not schoolboys and schoolgirls. That's too silly. In the theatre you would set the world on fire.'

'Oh, I shall!' he said. 'It's my intention.'

'Yes. I know. You are going to be England's Fellini,' she said to Piers. 'Don't tell me about it now, darling. We must make love to all these people. Where is that brother of yours? 'E's awfully boaring. So stupid. 'E is not even in the play.'

Suddenly order asserted itself. Mr Brownlow as host and housemaster made the official rebuke.

'Tom's a very hard worker, Signora Luzzi. He's got no time for anything but his A levels. That's our qualifying examination,' he added vaguely, but patronisingly.

Tom enjoyed this public testimony, and from the right man at the right time. But he also felt the delicious ham turn sour on him. For he knew what she was up to, breaking the ice beneath them all, especially under poor Van's feet, now that she was 'boared' with her wonderful evening's dance.

'Oh! I know. Don't tell me. A grade. B grade. C grade. Socialist Britain. No surprise you were beaten down at Suez.' She looked at the faces of consternation before her. ''Ubert, are you ready, darling? We must go. We are boaring them all frightfully.' And she laughed in Brownlow's face.

Someone, oh God, don't let it be Van, would take up her challenge – there would be chaos, shouting.

Piers' form master spoke to him quietly, personally. He was trying, Piers thought, to shield him from the tension of Marina's centre piece. 'Is there anything you *didn't* like in what you did tonight, Mosson?'

His affectionate, friendly look almost winked that he was saving Piers from this awful woman's show-off. He tried to respond, to answer with deliberation.

'Yes,' he said after thought, 'Gaunt's dying speech.'

'You mean the touch of send-up you put into it? Do you think it was a bit cheap? I think I did.'

'Yes. But I don't think that matters so much. A producer has a right every now and then to shake the audience out of a clichéd sense of piety. Especially in those famous speeches where everyone looks as though they were in church. But I think it was too much of an imitation of what I have seen some directors do with Polonius' counsel to Laertes. "This Earth, this Realm, this England" – ha! ha! ha! It's too easy a way of swaying the audience to Richard's side. I didn't do it grossly. But any conscious distortions of the author's intention is a crime against the shape. Am I right, or am I just trying to find a mote in my own eye in order not to seem cocky?'

'Right, I think.'

But it wasn't any good. Marina's was the play. And he, as a principal member of the cast, couldn't opt out, although he couldn't find his words in the present dialogue, where she was asking the assembled company:

'Is this where the beatings take place? They are famous, you know, in my country, everywhere in Europe – the public school beatings! Does it bring back memories, 'Ubert? A frisson perhaps? Do you get beatings, Piers?'

Relief, in fact, came from a quite unexpected quarter. The side door of the long panelled drawing room that led to Brownlow's study opened and from this sanctum, whence usually emerged their housemaster in benevolent and playful or grim and threatening mood, came an apparition of flame and chalk white. To most of the boys it must have seemed for the moment as though Dracula had assumed authority there. For Piers and for Tom, it was a moment of horror, for the tall woman, her chalk white face crowned by dishevelled red hair and slashed by bright lipstick, with chalk white shoulders and cleavage above the flame velvet gown, was Ma, her green eyes staring like two street signals demanding passage. And ahead, indeed, she came, her mouth framed in a vague social, would-be calming smile that to Piers and Tom spoke of terror and coming tears. Piers thought, Oh damn!, and Tom thought, I should have known, it's my fault. For, to them, it seemed certain that this was an old nightmare, hardly recurrent now but unpredictable, and, for three years of their boyhood, a perpetual, frightening, threatened presence. Now, when it happened, a sadness and, to be honest, a bore. Ma, the secret drinker. But how had she found it so soon and so quickly in someone else's house? Piers had a vision of a fellow secret drinker's hoard – Brownlow's – raided. Even in his pulsing alarms, he giggled at the thought. They knew, Uncle Jim knew, the doctor knew, her Nursery gardeners knew (or some of them) this secret thing, an affair of her home, her bedroom, of falling down the stairs, of burning her hand on the cooker's hot plate. It was something so much rarer in these last years, or was it that they were mostly away? But never public, Tom thought. By forgetting what happened at home, we've challenged the horror to visit us here, in the heart of our callous hideaway, at Westminster School, Little Dean's Yard, London.

But it wasn't the nightmare. It was something else – an unknown, frightened but charming Ma.

'Darling hearts!' She spoke to the whole company but especially to Mr Brownlow. 'I have to go. Thank you for a super evening! No, no,' she went on, 'there *is* a train, at an awful hour! But then if one *will* live in the country! Oh God damn that Nasser. Without him I could be running the car.'

She spoke it all to an unprepared, clearly apprehensive yet perfectly mannered Mr Brownlow, spoke it, too, as though he was in on the routine stage movements of whatever drama it was she was playing out; and Brownlow responded as though he knew all the lines and moves. Piers thought how useful the man would be in any future play he might produce at the school. But, immediately, all thought of staying on at school or going anywhere else for that matter seemed contingent on some unknown production of Ma's in which she had, no doubt, blocked out all his future movements.

Yet there was one who was out of line.

'Rosemary, dear,' Jackie's voice seemed to come from a distance, but it was at its most sweetly firm, 'I want to speak to you, dear.'

She's 'knowing the truth', Piers thought mockingly – but if she thinks she can change the action of Ma's play now she is wrong.

He was right. Ma merely turned and smiled at her mother-in-law. 'Jackie, dear love, not to worry. I've called a taxi.' Almost as an aside she added, 'To have missed two lovely nights' stay at darling Tothill. Poor me!'

She's going to kiss her hand to us all and make her exit, Piers thought. But, if so, her audience would not be playing, for everyone at the party was busily engaged in conversation, in not being part of the Mosson show. He longed to take over the production – 'Don't just look as if you're enjoying yourselves. Do it,' he would say. At the same moment he thought, with all the protective love that years of Ma's plucky struggle had made an instantaneous reaction for both her sons – I must go after her and find out what's happened. But, even so, a sarcastic voice in him added, 'Darling heart', for he felt a welling bitterness that whatever it was could not have been kept for another night than this one, so precious to him.

Tom's thought, too, was for his brother's big evening. And he acted on it. He went over to his mother before she could leave them.

'I'm sure you're doing whatever you must, Ma,' he said in a low voice, 'but there's something else you *must* do. You *must* tell Piers what a wonderful evening he gave us.'

She looked at him as she often did, frightened. The mascara on her eyelashes was running here and there with her tears. Her lower lip trembled.

'Of course,' she said. 'Go and keep the taxi for me.' She went up and kissed her elder son on the lips. 'That was wonderful, darling.'

Piers felt a flush of shame in his cheeks at her sincerity which omitted the ritual 'heart'.

'I've never felt like that in the theatre. So frightened and yet so excited. *And* so proud of my son who'd done it all. Give me a bit of the strength now that you gave that King, darling. I think you have actually.' Piers made to hug her, but she warded him off with the brightest of her social voices. 'And there's wonderful news, dear,' she said to all the company's hearing, 'you're to stay on in this lovely, happy house. Not to go to France. And you're to produce a musical. Think of that, darling. It's a lovely piece by Lou Lee, I think. Don't see me off, darling, and I shall send Tom straight back. Goodbye, Mr Brownlow. Thank you so very much. Goodbye, Hubert. Goodbye, Signora Luzzi. I *must* learn to say "Marina". That silly block I seem to have about the name.' She was gone.

'Darling, *now* I can see where you get it all from. Your

theatrical talent!' Marina told Piers. 'Lully! All those machines! Darling, you will do it so ahmewsingly!'

'Lully,' Hubert said judicially. 'You know, I believe there's something about him in the Tothill archives.' After Ma's display, he was clearly glad to find any distraction.

'No, really, darling, you 'ave such a pro*vin*cial mind. Lully was composer for Louis Quatorze. You will find The Man in the Iron Mask in one of your Tothill cupboards next. But really, I 'ope it's nothing to do with the *private* life of Lully. That in a boy's school! My God!' and she burst into a coarse laugh. 'No, but Lully, that is really something quite chic. I congratulate you,' she said to Mr Brownlow.

'I'm afraid too soon. Mrs Mosson spoke a little hastily. Our plans for Van's future are by no means worked out. And as to next summer term's opera, our music master has yet to make known his wishes about the whole thing.' He spoke summarily to Marina, showing open dislike.

She laughed. 'Oh, 'ow boaring for you,' she said. ''Ubert, when are you taking me to Claridges? We can't stay at this little party for ever.' She called across to Jackie, ''Ubert's been trained in perfect old fashioned manners. Quite the *cavaliere serviente*. *You* 'ave done it, Lady Mosson. He not only sees me to my hotel, but must give me supper. I love 'im. 'E's so amusing.'

Tom, coming back into the room, saw his grandmother's cheek flinch. He went over and stood by her.

Hubert said, 'Is that all right, Mother? Goddard's here with the car for *you*, I think.'

Jackie's eyes flashed for a moment, then twinkled in love-in-the-mist blue. 'My dear boy,' she said in a regal voice that neither of her grandsons had heard before, 'Signora Luzzi's your little tootsie-wootsie.'

Her grandsons had not heard that phrase before but there was no mistaking its mockery. When the pair had gone, Jackie looked up at Tom like an erring schoolgirl. 'That was naughty of me, wasn't it? But dear Hubert must wake up soon out of this ridiculous dream. The woman is impossible, whatever her millions.'

Probably she felt worried at having said so much to a boy, for Tom saw her smile fade and the dead parrot's look come back. He did not know what to do.

Piers, however, watching the sad pair, did. He went up to Mr Brownlow. 'Is it all right if my brother and I see my grandmother back to Tothill House, sir?' he asked.

'Of course, you must accompany your grandmother home. I'd no idea, Van, I'd no idea.' But he didn't explain of what.

Perhaps in a last bid to set his ideas right again, Lady Mosson did the farewells perfectly. A quiet thanks to Brownlow for a delightful evening, a sincere thanks to Piers' form master for all he had said in praise of her grandson, a special congratulatory handshake for Richard II and his Queen, and even a little wave to Henry IV (how wise she was, Piers thought, not to shake that sweaty palm); she had a personal smile for the St Paul's mistress and a vaguer one for M. Lacordaire. This was perhaps her only mistake, for he followed them into the entrance hall.

'*Au revoir*, Madame,' he said, 'Do not worry. All will be arranged with Lully. *J'espère vous présenter mes félicitations à Tothill House.*'

Her eyes became misty and vague. 'You must get Mr Brownlow's permission, I believe.'

Piers wondered if perhaps the evening's exhaustion had revealed some senility. In the car he asked her, 'Did you know what you said to Lacordaire?'

'The Frenchman? Oh, my dear boy, yes. He's been fishing for an invitation all evening. The French are all the same. Cadgers. They have to be put in their place. I am glad to say that we Americans have always done so.'

She did not let them stay at Tothill more than a quarter of an hour. She gave Piers a cheque.

'A good workman is worthy of his hire. My father always said that. It's work that makes life worthwhile,' she continued, and hastily added, 'and God's love.' She had clearly almost forgotten that her childhood work ethic had been superseded by Science. 'It's an extra Christmas present,' she explained.

It was £500, more than she usually gave. She only had one further comment to make about the evening.

'Poor Rosemary,' she said, 'Marina Luzzi was too much for her. She's not used to the ways of the world as I am.'

The brothers caught each other's glances. How useful is a religion that conditions its followers to arrange the world to their own convenience. They heaved a sigh of relief that events according to Grandma were so conveniently disposed of.

CHAPTER II
The Planning of an Opera

T HEY WERE too early for Marina Luzzi's arrival so they set
off to walk around the Cloisters until it was time. It took
them back three years to those days when Tom had just joined
Piers at the school. It had not been an easy phase, for they had
both wanted to be together in the term just as they were in the
holidays; yet also they did not want it – Piers had his circle in
which he shone, and circles freeze sadly if they are not kept
warm; Tom feared above all in this new world to defy
hierarchy. So they had established a routine walk each day
around the Cloisters – ('keeping in touch', though physical
touch at that time would have been an infringement of growing personality) usually in the lunch break, where, among
nomadic tourists, circles seemed less clear, hierarchies less
exact – until it was time for cricket or for water, time for afternoon school. It was a year at least since they had needed this
routine get-together, for each had his school life and those
lives were no longer so sacredly separated, so that this late
morning's unexpected perambulation brought unexpected
memories, conjured up by the memorial slabs beneath their
feet or upon the Cloister walls, memories of regular jokes and
routine pieties. Here was Anne Bracegirdle – Died 12 September 1748, aged 85 years – to allow Piers to exult that in those
days an actress could make it to the Abbey; but Tom had
always suggested, as he did now, that it was probably simply
because she was so old – and anyway that they were careful not

63

to mention her profession on the inscription.

They only paused for the merest second today to recall this familiar interchange, for Piers was in full spate about the summer production, and what it was to be, and what Howerton, the music man, had said about it, and what kind of man Howerton was, easy enough probably to work with if one let him chatter on about music, but, on the other hand, what would it be like always looking down on a pink circle of shining flesh surrounded by a ring of thick bristly hair?

'I shouldn't have thought,' Tom said, 'that you *would* be looking down on him, bald patch or no. In fact, from what you've said about stage hierarchies, if he's director and you're producer, you ought to be looking up at him.'

'Pooh! *That's* what any sensible character in Vanbrugh's plays would say to *you*, Pratt. In any case, as Howerton kept on repeating, the Lully operas are all *pièces de théâtre avec musique*. So it's the *overall* theatre that's so important. And as the music's very specialised – I mean seldom played now – it has to be left to an expert anyway. Which Howerton is. It seems that the overture was Lully's idea really. He was a great innovator. Lully, I mean; not Howerton. *He* seems rather timid. Which makes the operas exciting. And up to then they had castrati for the women's parts, only the French laughed and Lully, who was an Italian on the make, introduced actresses, which the French very sensibly preferred.'

'You *do* know a lot. It needs sorting out though.'

'Yes, I do. And it will be. And then there are all the machines they had to bring on – for gods and goddesses and to make earthquakes or to light up Hell. Sometimes the machinery made such a noise that nobody could hear the singers, which shows how much they thought the music mattered. But, of course, *we'll* have to find a way round that, because the text, musical or otherwise, is sacred.'

Then he told Pratt the most important part – important to share with Pratt, for he would help with that. It was how, despite Lully's originality, the opera, of course, had been played before Louis XIV himself, and indeed Lully depended upon the King's favour. Therefore the operas had to be done

with decorum, with a sense of hierarchy, so that Quinault, a
fine librettist, had nevertheless to see that there was no
unseemly defiance of the gods by the mortals and so on. Pratt,
as he had guessed, was delighted by this, although he looked a
little sideways at his brother, arching an eyebrow:

'Oh! I'll manage,' Piers said. 'You see even Howerton,
who's very cautious, is sure that Lully was doing something
bold but in a world where he had to give it the colour of con-
formity. Apparently there was something in his private life
that almost did him in but he survived, although Howerton
was evasive about what it was. Not that it matters. The point is
that I've got exactly the situation I want, as I see it. Something
like Vanbrugh, only perhaps in reverse. Vanbrugh struck out
with forked lightning, but he had an absolutely structured
foundation. This bloke Lully was a maverick but he worked
with perfect success in conventions. But what matters is that
there was conflict. And that makes theatre. I suggested something of the sort to Howerton.'

'Ah,' said Tom dubiously.

'Yes. You're right. He didn't understand. All the better. I'll
produce it above his head.'

'Bald patch and all?'

'Yes. I say, look,' he cried suddenly, 'I've never noticed this
before.'

There on the ground were two slabs, side by side. The first
read: 'Johann Salomon Peter. Musician. b.1745. d.1815. He
brought Haydn to England in 1791 and 1794.'

'Ah well,' Piers said, 'that *was* very important.'

'You would know, of course.'

'Yes, I would.'

He felt very happy – not only at the prospect of producing
the opera, but because Pratt was in a rare relaxed mood that
made him want to put Piers down.

'And this? What about this?' Tom asked.

The other slab read: 'Marzio Clementi, b. Rome 1752. d.
Egham 1832. His fame as a musician and composer acknowledged throughout Europe procured him the honour of a
public interment in this church.'

'As yours will,' Tom said, 'as a producer of Lully.'

'Probably, though I shouldn't think I'd die at Egham. All the same, it is an important step for me, Pratt. It'll be experience, not just with a play, but with total theatre.' Before Tom could answer, Piers said, very seriously, for when he sensed that he was concerning himself too much with his own life and too little with his brother's, he became very grave – 'Have you got the Reform Bills absolutely clear yet?'

He worried about Pratt's A level history, that perhaps he had only decided to take a history paper to be connected with his brother's studies.

'I think so,' Tom answered.

'Well, you hadn't last week. You spouted some embarrassing slush about bourgeois revolutions. You must know exact franchises.' He was the historian now.

'A very serious conclave,' a solemn voice said and a bulky form in a heavy tweed overcoat blocked their way. 'What is the subject at issue?' Hubert asked.

'Reform Bills.'

'Ah! On the whole, a mistake.'

Piers smiled. He delighted in Uncle Hubert as Reaction in Person. But Hubert corrected himself.

'No, that's too easy. Whether we like it or not, our Parliament is one of the few forces restraining anarchy.'

Piers frowned at the boredom of this, but although Tom smiled at the platitude, he looked gently at his uncle – here was the voice of reassurance from his childhood.

'You're keeping a lady waiting, which in itself is shocking anarchy,' Hubert said. And there, indeed, framed in the archway through to Great Dean's Yard, stood Marina Luzzi, in simple, costly black, but ablaze with less simple, even more costly jewellery.

'Well,' said Hubert, after Marina had given Piers a firm kiss and a little unwillingly offered the extremity of her jaw to be reluctantly kissed by Tom, 'I leave her in your competent hands. They'll show you the school and the Abbey.'

'Oh, my God! I 'ave seen the school already. Two times a school! No, this is too much. What! It was only a month before Christmas – that play of 'is. 'Ubert, you think everyone is crazy for punishment.'

Hubert stopped in his tracks for a moment. Then a small private smile, unfamiliar to either of his nephews, drew in his floppy white cheeks, pitted by long forgotten acne.

'Very well, you're let off that,' he said. And Marina returned his private smile.

'My God, she can look young,' Piers thought; and Tom thought, she frightens me *very* much.

'All right, my boy,' she said to Hubert, 'you wait and see. I suppose we must go to this Abbey,' she told Piers, who was a little disconcerted.

'Of course,' Hubert said, 'every Westminster boy knows his Abbey backwards. I did when I was here. And Piers is also a distinguished historian.'

'Is there some good barocco?' she asked.

'No.' Piers was honest. 'It's Gothic. But, in its way, Henry VII Chapel is as good as . . .'

Marina interrupted him. 'In Rome the best things are barocco.' She took Piers' arm. 'I shall take you to Rome. You will see Bernini's Chapel of Saint Teresa. You will like it. It's 'ow you say? Theatre.'

'The best thing in London is baroque, too. The Great Hall at Tothill.'

'Yes,' said Marina decidedly. 'I want it very much.' She let go of Piers' arm. 'Well, we go round this Abbey. Is 'e coming too?'

Tom began to say, 'I only just came to say . . .' But Piers over-ruled him.

'Yes, of course,' he said.

Perhaps Hubert felt he could help matters by asking Tom directly, 'Where are you taking Signora Luzzi . . . Marina to lunch?'

Despite the family cosiness of this suggestion of what looked like an impending aunt, Tom was unable to answer. But Piers said casually, 'I've booked a table at Overton's.'

'Is it ahmewsing?'

'It has its own ambience,' Hubert said.

'Well, I suppose so. Now you go, 'Ubert.'

In general she was dismissive, then, taking each brother by an arm, she seemed suddenly to become their age, or younger, half running them forwards down the side of the Cloister to the scattering and annoyance of the tourists. This discomfiture, especially that of an unexpected photographing Japanese trade delegation, reduced her to paroxysms of giggling. When they arrived at the steps to a small door into the nave, all three collapsed in a huddle with laughter, as Piers seemed to remember jet-set people doing in movies of smart country house parties as they ran towards the camera. But there was no camera awaiting them. However, Marina stopped on the top step and turned to face the boys. She looked at the Japanese crowding behind them. She contorted her face wonderfully until it was all slit eyes and smiling teeth.

'Oh, excuse, please, Japanese,' she said, 'not knowing Clistian habits.' And with a pretended camera, she photographed. Piers had hardly seen Japanese close to before, yet he felt that the imitation was exact. Tom, too, could not keep from laughter . . . The Japanese visitors seemed very angry. Delighted at this, Marina bowed her head and went in at the low door.

All down the great nave, it was the same. Even Tom felt carefree, until, suddenly, before the monument to the eighteenth century Admiral, Sir Cloudesley Shovell, everything seemed to him to go too far. There was a lack of propriety, even a note of hysteria, to the absurdity and fun that Marina communicated that offended and frightened him.

There the stately gentleman reclined before them in full bottomed wig and roman toga draped so as to reveal both his manly chest and his somewhat undulating stomach.

Marina went up and ran her fingers sensuously over the rolling surface of naked marble. 'It must be delicious, I suppose. The feel of dead flesh. Quite barocco.' She looked at Tom. 'You think what I say is shocking.'

Tom surprised himself. 'No. I think it's rather boaring.'

She must have been taken aback for she said nothing. Piers, annoyed with them both, said:

'Well, shall we go to see the Kings' tombs?'

She was solemn now, almost muted. Tom felt contrite.

'Let's show her Richard's portrait,' he said, 'before we go to the tomb itself. Life before death,' he added, aiming to combine wit with reproof.

And they led her to the main altar and pointed out King Richard II, set in a gold background with golden locks and golden skin and golden sceptre and golden orb, and a sheep's face.

'Is that your 'ero? 'E looks like a girl.'

'He wasn't a bit like a girl, though he was very young then. He became King when he was ten. But he had to be tough very soon after. He put down the Peasants' Revolt.' Piers said the cliché in inverted commas, he was the more surprised by her ardent answer.

'Oh! I love 'im. 'E is my king. I 'ate the people. Most specially the peasants. They are so stupid. Was 'e really brutal to them?'

'He was disgusting at that point,' said Tom. 'He betrayed their trust. He rode out to their ranks and said "I will be your leader." And then, when they'd surrendered, he had them hanged, and worse.'

'I adore 'im. To make them believe and then to 'ave them killed like the cattle they are. You must make your own play about it. Theatre of cruelty. And such a young 'ero. Piers, it's all made for you. But not yet, first we 'ave Lully.'

'Yes, it's settled. How did *you* know?' for he could see from her face that she did.

But Tom could not let it go by. Even the recounting of Van's future triumphs could not help him to suppress his shock.

'But if you get people to trust you and then casually betray them, you're undermining everything that keeps society together. You are destroying order. If you're a leader, that is. Chaos is what comes from broken pledges. At least,' he added, blushing at his own unwonted show of anger, 'I should think that it would.'

His voice had jumped from manly bass to falsetto and back again. Marina's version of this was finely absurd.

'At least I should think it would,' she imitated with exact stammering and hesitation. 'Isn't 'e boaring? Chaos is the only exciting thing left. I adore chaos. Throwing all the rules out of the window at the old bores. That's what art is about. Exciting art. Your baroque is a good example.'

Piers was impatient with all this. He could hardly forgive Tom cutting off what she had to say about the Lully project. Yet he found himself speaking quite automatically to correct her, for on this topic, above all, he knew himself informed.

'Baroque is based upon order. It must be. Even Vanbrugh at his most fantastic. That's what gives the Great Hall its powers. What allies it to Pratt's work. No, really, Marina,' he tried to put all his charm into assuring her.

But she burst out crossly, 'Oh, no, my God. What is all this? Van and Pratt. It's incestuous. Such closeness between brothers. Do you do things together? 'Ow pitiful! Schoolboys' nonsense.' When she saw their consternation, she cried, 'Oh, forget what I said. Never mind. But it's too boaring.'

Tom was decided. He couldn't bear the thought of missing the lovely food at luncheon, but there were things more important than food, although at weak moments, or moments of delight, he found it hard to believe so. He said, 'I'm going now. I oughtn't to have come anyway. I mean I've got too much A level work for outings like this.' He ached for the security of his study and of his trigonometric problems. 'Goodbye. Thank you.'

Piers was about to speak, but Marina cut in, 'No, no. Let 'im go. We don't like each other. And 'e knows it. That's sensible. Perhaps we can be friends when I am part of the family. It'll be something to 'ave a sensible one about. 'Oo knows, I may come to like you, Tom, that would be good, don't you think?'

'Would it?' he asked.

She was pleased with this. She laughed. 'I like that answer. You're really quite a pretty boy, you know.'

And she tapped his cheek that blushed with embarrassment and anger. She took Piers' arm and led him away towards the North Transept entrance.

'That's enough of Abbey. I'm 'ungry,' she said, ''Ow far is it? Your restaurant?'

'How did you know that it was agreed for me to produce the opera?' he asked.

'I didn't. But I 'ave some news for you about Lully. News that is very exciting for you. But I don't want to talk about it until I 'ave been eating.'

He knew at once that he must obey her. He secured a taxi and soon found himself facing her across a small silver vase of white and pink carnations at a table in the very far, intimate end of Overton's narrow dining room. As he studied the menu and listened to her favourable comments on the fish that was offered, he was amazed and amused at his own thoughts. All down Victoria Street in the taxi, he had passed buildings as familiar to him as any in life save Ma's Nursery, Tothill or the Westminster School buildings – the Army & Navy Stores, the neo-Byzantine wonder of the Roman Catholic Cathedral, the Victoria Palace with its habitual Crazy Gang signs – and yet it seemed as though for the first time he had ridden past them with a sense of his own elegance, with a sense of importance taken for granted.

And at the table, urging the merits of Sole Dieppoise over Lobster Newburg (but she chose the Lobster Thermidor), although he had brought two or three girls that he knew here to lunch – sisters of friends and daughters of officers in Uncle Jim's and his father's Regiment – with Marina he had a sudden sense of being the right young man in the right place, doing the right thing. He ordered Pouilly Fumé with only the slightest of inquiry addressed towards Marina as his woman guest and she obviously approved, although his basis for the rightness of the choice was some memory of Uncle Eustace in a similar situation, and everything about Uncle Eustace was exceedingly dubious. But that was the kind of woman she was. And, let Tom be forgotten, he felt dizzy to be with her.

Sipping at her wine, pecking at her lobster, puffing at intervals at her cigarette which she poised on the ashtray where its burning made him cough (Uncle Eustace would have stubbed it out with a charming smile), she leaned back, clinking her jewellery.

'Well, tell me about Lully.'

'Tell me *your* news that's exciting.'

'No. I want to tease you by making you wait. It makes you all red. That I like.'

It was no use fighting her. He told her all as he had said it to Tom – about the overtures, the castrati, and the machines, and the excellence of Quinault's libretto. He didn't talk about Louis XIV and Versailles and decorum, because he thought they'd spoken enough about order, but he did mention that there was real conflict, and how that excited him.

'So, you don't know much about it yet. But we'll make something of it. What Lully opera does 'e mean to do, this man 'Owerton?'

'He's not sure. It seems that the famous one's *Armide*. It has the best arias, so he's inclined to choose that, I think. But he probably won't decide until next month. Even then we'll have five months before production, four before we rehearse, I should think, which is beyond dreams. I mean so much time for thinking it all out.'

'No. It will not be *Armide*,' she said mysteriously. She had exchanged her lobster now for a praliné ice, and pecking for gulping. 'Is 'e a snob, this 'Owerton?'

'I don't know. How does one tell? He didn't seem very impressed by my being a Mosson or by the Tothill House connection. I tried them out.'

'But of course. Nobody is. That is the trouble. It's all buried treasure. But with your grandmother, what can you expect? Grandmother mia! What a woman! Divine love casts out all fear! Yes, and everything else. What can be done? Darling 'Ubert's been a good background to 'er. And I will make 'im a better one for *me*. But you can't put 'im on the front of the stage. 'E'd forget all 'is words. Well, *you* can see that. The old man might 'ave been some good. 'E's an ugly old brute but 'e's got – 'ow you say? – pushingness. But 'e must be one 'undred years old. Is 'e a 'undred?'

'Ninety, I think.'

'That's too old. These Mossons! Not you, darling. You're

quite ahmewsing. They've grown moss on Tothill 'Ouse so
that no one can see it anymore.'

Piers didn't laugh because she didn't appear to intend the
English pun she'd made.

'We must take all that moss off that lovely 'ouse which you
love and I love. Why is it there but to be marvellous and to 'ave
some fun in it? The Mosson money, the Gleason money –
what was 'e, that cow's father? a cowboy perhaps? – and even
the Luzzi money, and my dear that is plenty. What is the good
of it if it doesn't make life amusing? The Tothills could do that.
That one Sir Thomas Tothill with 'is twenty mistresses and
that Sir Francis with 'is beautiful wicked wife and 'is pageboys,
they are the ones that built the beautiful 'ouse. And they used
it for life. Your grandmother talks about the 'ouse being lived
in. But all she does is shit in it and say Divine Mind denies
Matter. But the Tothills were ahmewsing! We shall bring the
time of the Tothills back. But there must be a man in the family
to lead the way. You will do it.'

'I will?'

'Yes, you are going to produce a Lully opera in the Great
'All. An opera that Sir Francis Tothill intended to present to 'is
King there. But the King – 'e was Dutch, and they are always
so boaring, the Dutch! Peasants! I wish them all drowned in
their canals – he refused to see it because it was a French opera.
My God! But now *you* will do it. You will, you know, because
it was your great Vanbrugh's idea to celebrate 'is finishing the
Great 'All by staging this Lully opera that 'e 'ad 'eard the gaolers singing when 'e was a prisoner in the Bastille.'

'What?'

'Oh, yes. Verrio 'ad just finished 'is ceiling. The Phaethon.
So they must 'ave Lully's opera *Phaethon* sung there. And
then this Dutchman – an English Dutch King! 'orrible! – said
no. But you will say yes. You will be the King this time. But
you must 'urry up and pay. You 'ave enough money, I suppose. We'll talk to the clever 'Ungarian in the Tothill Library.
She knows it all.'

He'd known it was too good to be true – an opera about
Phaethon in the Great Hall. Either the woman was mad, or,

more likely, he thought, she was purposely torturing him
about the dreams that he had not even dared to imagine. Now
it was clear. Hungarians at Tothill! Perhaps it was her idea of
an elaborate joke. Her version of the Commedia dell'Arte.

He said rather scornfully, for he was very offended, 'Miss
Lynmouth is *not* Hungarian.'

'Oh! that boaring Lesbian . . . "I'm afraid we're very much
tied down with Mosson Vol. II, Mrs Luzzi. It's in the proof
stage, you know. We've no time for operas now. Your query
will have to take its turn with next month's research
requests."' The gruff voice might have come straight from the
fresh faced, square set, mackintoshed woman with horn-
rimmed glasses and the grey short-cut hair who ran the
Library at Tothill.

'Impertinent bitch! I don't 'ave deals with freaks, I told 'er.
It was vulgar, but you 'ave to be. These bourgeois Lesbians are
like coarse skinned – 'ow do you say? – "navvies".'

What with excitement and quickly eaten rich food, and
unresolved curiosity, and surfeit of quick worldly maxims
about life – the nature of bourgeois Lesbians for example – that
he'd never encountered before – he felt rather queasy – an
unfamiliar sensation.

'No. I went straight to this girl – Magda Sczekerny. She is
very dowdy. Well, poor thing, coming from a Communist
country. And then it's not better because she's given 'erself
little bracelets and fuzzy 'air and 'Ungarian dress for England.
But they always do when they manage to get out. They want to
be Western and they want to be 'Ungarian. It's so boaring!
And it can't 'ave 'elped 'aving the 'orrible librarian putting
those coarse 'ands up 'er skirt. She brought 'er out of Budapest
'erself two months ago at the collapse of the revolution. So she
thinks she 'as a right to put 'er great workman arms around the
poor thing. Always the same with you British. 'Ypocrisy –
your famous friendship to political refugees is just a kind of
imperialism. Any'ow, she's a clever girl with good Continen-
tal training. I told 'er to find out what this memory of old
'Ubert's about Lully was and she did.'

'But how?'

'Because I told 'er. Any'ow, you will see when you meet 'er.' And he did, and it was true.

But this confirmation was not immediate. In his eagerness and in her masterfulness, and in their joint unspoken determination to avoid all human contact at Tothill House save with the answering footman, they hurried to the Library while they knew that Jackie would still be at lunch.

But so were the Library staff. Marina's noisy impatience jarred Piers, for the Library had been a sanctuary of quiet to him since boyhood. And here she was, transformed by this momentary frustration of her wishes into a wild sow, snorting and grunting, and rooting among papers on the librarians' desks, pulling open drawers here and pulling out books there, opening cupboards, peering into them and shutting their doors with loud irritation. And yet, of course, he understood her impatience – but she ought to know that if you want the curtain to go up, you must tell the actors when to be on stage. At last she peered into a passageway.

'There's some small rooms down 'ere. Per'aps they're there. God knows what they're doing. I think the woman knew I was coming and kept the girl out on purpose.'

'I think they're still out at their lunch.'

'*Their* lunch! I don't know what that means. They are supposed to be in 'ere.' She disappeared.

Piers thought, fuck her. She really is impossible. As if I wasn't at boiling point of curiosity too. She was so wayward that he thought he must protect himself by preserving some scepticism about the whole thing – that it was a mistake – what did she know of Lully more than he? – that it was a malign joke. As soon as she was gone, he felt anxiety about the whole spell that she cast over him. He let himself hope, however. And how could he not? In this most beloved of rooms – not his Vanbrugh Great Hall, nor the terraces that faced his brother's Pratt Façades, but in their *joint* room where, since boyhood, in winter holidays and on cold Easter days and on summer rainy Sundays, they had, in the most happy separateness, browsed and browsed, extending their knowledge, especially Pratt, who could read no fiction or drama or poetry, and enriching their imaginations, especially he, with a sense of peacefully exciting communion that he could not believe would leave him all his life. They had called it the Van-Pratt room, not only for its intricate, almost paradoxical entwining of their beloved architect heroes, but in its union of themselves.

He looked at it now and thought how little he could have achieved without his brother's cautioning voice, ironic curbing and loyal devotion, and hoped that those looks of excitement, of delight that he evoked in return were sufficient repayment. Whatever this exciting, repellent woman did for him, he would not let her separate them. And that her offering was apparently to be in this room made his brother's absence, his arbitrary dismissal, seem less affronting – for it was impossible for him to breathe the air of the Library without feeling Pratt there, in busy, orderly, methodical reading. And as he looked down the long room, his gaze seemed to give him assurance that what they had contributed to one another all these years, they would do for as long more as he could imagine. The winter light in the great patches of five equal breadths was the embodiment of Sir Roger's great art, as were the shadowed white panels that separated the five windows – miracles of proportion and delicate strength. But what of the objects, the curiosities for which Sir Thomas Tothill had asked Sir Roger to design the original Cabinet Room – the mummified marmoset, the petrified lava from Etna shaped like a negro's thick lips, the caul taken from a Berber baby, 'sent home to me by my deare Brother from among the Moors', a sea-serpent turned to rock as it rose in spirals to strike, a mouse taken from the belly of a Chinaman, an anal fistula bottled in spirits, the skeleton of a great bat ('such as did abound in these parts during the late civil disturbances') found in the hollow of a tree in the Woodwork at Tothill, the webbed, eight-fingered hand of a baby born at Tewkesbury in 1620. They had been a source of terror, delight, laughter, and, above all, wonder in his childhood; and, in their boyhood, he and Pratt had suddenly seen that, focus though they were, indeed purpose of Pratt's ordered Cabinet Room, they were in their

shapes so wild and convoluted that they proclaimed propheti-
cally Sir John's work to come. Whereas the Library, the pleasing, comfortable room of gentlemanly study, that Vanbrugh
had in fact made ten years later out of the Cabinet Room at Sir
Francis Tothill's request, had brought order and regularity to
the room of curious monsters. Up the walls and between the
windows stretched rows upon rows upon rows of books, and
all in uniform bindings – each case headed by an identical
broken pediment, baroque as the symbol of ordered disorder.
If this were to be the place where Phaethon chose to descend
from the great lantern and take him up through the heavens in
creative miracle, then where better? This room where order
cradled aberration, and baroque imposed regularity.

He was startled from his reverie by the voice of a schoolboy
gruffness that seemed far distant from any that the tragic defier
of the gods' narrow dictates would offer.

'Was there something you wanted?' asked Primrose Lynmouth, retreating as always behind her thick-lensed glasses,
shrinking as always into her capacious green mackintosh and
mackintosh hood, which she wore come snow, come heat-
wave – today was bright but very cold. 'We're not really here,
you know,' she added, 'from ten to one until two fifteen.' She
looked at the pendulum clock, which announced five minutes
past two.

Piers thought, oh dear, it's always like this and yet she's so
efficient, finding whatever we want, indeed leaving little piles
of books with notes saying, 'I looked these out. I thought they
might be of interest to you.' And he and Pratt had always
found it the same – he tried to break down her shyness, Pratt to
respect it, but neither had any effect in lessening it.

Now he almost automatically attempted an easy intimacy
that he knew would not succeed, but, after all, he'd been
coming into the Library ever since old Hubert had first engaged her eight or nine years ago, when Pratt was still a small
kid.

He said, 'Do tell me off directly, Miss Lynmouth. After all
these years, don't depute your rebuke to the clock.'

He used all his charm and a little more whimsy than he cared

for. But what followed was the flustered blushing and awk-
ward gesturing that, as usual, ended by her knocking two
books off her desk and an even more wild attack of shyness as
when he bent to retrieve the books his head threatened for a
moment contact with her ample breasts.

Only cold businesslikeness could save things now. He said,
'I believe someone is looking out the facts about a projected
production of Lully's opera *Phaethon* in the Great Hall in
1697.' His voice sounded to himself absurdly offhand about
such a life and death matter. He cursed himself. Now was
when he should have appealed by intimacy . . . 'Miss Lynmouth, do you remember when I was very little? How I used
to read aloud? Even then I wanted to be connected with the
theatre. This is a unique chance for it. What's more, it will
bring alive this great house which you and I both love so much
etc. etc . . .'

As it was she said, 'I believe my assistant has some information for you. She will be back very soon. She's usually most
punctual.'

He sat down in a chair. Where had Marina got to? Damn
them all. If he *had* been more appealing to this strange woman,
she would probably have only been in more of a flap, knocked
the whole desk over. Trying to keep his mind from the Phaethon glory, lest he should be victim of a cruel joke or muddle,
he covertly watched Miss Lynmouth – Primrose, what a name
for such a bulldog! Anyway he had no reason to suppose that
she cared twopence about the house. All her time and Hubert's
concern were taken up with the history of the Mosson family
and its trading interests. Old Hubert had even been over to
Virginia to research that end of the slave trade and the sugar.
They'd apparently made a very competent job of the first
volume, 'Well researched, but exceedingly boring' was the gist
of the *T.L.S.* review Hubert had shown to him. He seemed
most pleased with the second point – 'No fireworks, you see,
just plain scholarship, wasn't it, Miss L.?'

Anything that was outside that stupid limit would just be a
nuisance to her. She had been hopeless with Pevsner when he
came to do the architecture of the house for his London vol-

umes. As if the house wasn't the only thing that mattered – but Hubert and old Jackie were so scared of the Tothill scandals through the centuries that they ran away from anything before the Tothill-Mosson marriage of 1790.

Well, they'd got a right old blushing virgin to do their job for them. Why was she so blushing? Ah! of course, he'd forgotten – she was a bourgeois Lesbian. He must remember to look at her in this more sophisticated light. He could see that Marina's description was going to be one of his regular jokes for months to come. Was she ashamed of her sexual desires or of her class origins? It was a joke to remember for Pratt, although he might be a bit shocked. He began to laugh himself, then was anxious that she was rigid with embarrassment. Old screw head! It was hard for him not to return to the name they'd used when they first knew her, for Pratt, who was a tiny kid then, had walked up to her, and said, 'So Uncle got what he wanted.' Apparently, the first time they visited Tothill after the war, he'd heard Uncle Hubert say he wanted 'a woman with her head screwed on the right way' for a librarian. That had only come out afterwards when they were alone together. At the time everyone was frozen rigid and it had been all Ma talking to distract attention. Old screw head! She'd probably heard them use the name sometime and that's what made her so uptight.

As now, when she asked, 'Are there going to be a lot of requests for information about this opera, Mr Mosson? I ask because Miss Sczekerny is in the middle of checking the references in Volume II of the Mosson Chronicle. The proofs have to be back with the printers by the end of the month and the deadlines are very tight these days.'

'Oh, no, Miss Lynmouth. If the fact that Francis Tothill ever thought of such a thing, let alone that Vanbrugh was the original master mind, can be established, that's quite enough. We can go on from there. I mean I don't even know that the school will do it in the Great Hall or that *they'd* agree here. But anyhow we've got six months before we'd be playing.'

'Oh well, I am sure that everyone will be happy to work

with you, Mr Mosson, when the time comes. I mean, who wouldn't?'

He could hardly believe his ears. He thought he'd better look down, it was the only way that he could show that he was shy too. Perhaps she took the removal of his countenance as a rebuke, for she said:

'I am afraid that I shall have to tell Miss Sczekerny to suspend any work on it for the next few weeks. She's so very conscientious, you know. She'll try to do the two jobs at once. And although she looks strong, she isn't really. And, of course, her experiences during that terrible time in Hungary have left their mark.' She sighed and seemed to him for a moment like a pigeon, its sad, gentle cooing a little ridiculous for so plump a bird.

So this was bourgeois Lesbian love, he guessed, well, good luck to her. He would like to have said how beautiful was her desired (or perhaps by now her love) but he had never seen the girl.

Nevertheless something of the amiability of his thoughts seemed to have reached her.

She said, 'Where can she have got to? She's so proud of what she's found, even though I have been cross with her. She'll be excited to tell you. But there can't be any more of this opera research for the moment, Mr Mosson.'

'That's all right. If she's found what I think, I can follow up where it's needed.'

'I'll go and look for her.'

'That's the passage Signora Luzzi went down. She was looking for her, too.'

'Oh, really!' Primrose was indignant. 'That's the door to our Library staff room. I told the Signora the other day. But she does it on purpose. Sir Hubert has always accepted that only staff should go out that way. Even Lady Mosson respects that. I must go and find out what has happened to them.'

There was no need. Piers could hear Marina's voice boring its way through the corridor, and, chiming in with it, another foreign voice, precise, high-pitched, like a schoolgirl reciting or a Dutch doll speaking. The door opened and Marina came in leading a young woman by the hand – short she was with dark hair, frizzed and permed like someone who'd seen an old movie, but if that's what the West had done, Eastern Europe had left its mark, for her lace blouse with its festoons of ribbons made her look as though she were about to sing a native folksong. She looks a mess, Piers thought, but goodness she's pretty, even through all that folksiness. Through all that silly lace and ribbons he could glimpse the smooth stretched skin of beautifully rounded breasts. If he were to touch them . . . but this was not the moment, nor what he had come for. He must think of nothing but the possible wonderful news she had to give him, perhaps the most important news of his life so far. All the same, if his fingers could stroke those hips. Eyes, cheeks, breasts, hips, buttocks, all were rounded and ready for pressing touch. As he salivated, he knew fury with himself, that desire should interfere with the absolutely exact attention he must give to every word that was said at this moment. But he allowed his eyes to feast a little, for the words that came pouring out hardly needed consideration. They were Marina's.

'Well, 'ere she is. Where do you think I found 'er? In the lavatory, eating a 'orrible sandwich. She 'as been all the way to the British Museum in 'er eating time to find something out for you, darling. And she was frightened because she was late back. I told 'er – you are in the West now – you mustn't let them frighten you. We don't 'ave petty commissars in the West, but there are some people who want to be.'

He smiled and gave a little bow to the girl – damn her, the arty foreignness was communicating itself to his behaviour now. But the blushing red cheeks and the smile were worth getting.

'I knew that Primrose didn't want me to spend time on this . . .'

'Preemrose!' The mimicking little girl's tone in which Marina repeated the name was enough almost without the owner's heavy honest Dobbin face to make adequate mockery of the name.

'You should have asked me, Magda. We'd have found some

way.' Primrose turned to Piers. 'It will be some time before she shakes off the dreadful feeling of spying and suspicion that there is in that beautiful city. It took me many days after just a week there at the Library Conference. You're *free* here, Magda, quite free.'

'I know it, Primrose. I know it. All the same, another immigration form has come to be filled in. And the police have telephoned to my lodging to interview me. Is this England, I have to ask? What does it mean?'

He could have taken her in his arms. It was nice to think of all she had suffered. So that he might comfort her, of course. He blushed at the sort of thoughts she gave to him. In any case, they weren't here for all this. They were here for something vital to his whole future. Unless it was all some ghastly fuck-up of Marina's . . .

'Oh, it's just a hitch. I'm afraid we have all too many of them. But it's muddle not menace. Bring me the form, I'll deal with it. It's routine.'

'Routine I knew already in Budapest. No, I am sorry, Primrose, I don't mean that. And you have been so good to me. But I think we young people from Hungary have impossible expectations of the West. We have been waiting so long . . .' Her great Dutch doll eyes seemed to be rounded with childlike devotion and Primrose's bulldog gaze had the air of a faithful Landseer doggy friend looking up to its mistress. And yet she was *so* pretty. It was intolerable.

It all clearly irked Marina as much as it did himself. She cried, 'Oh, my God! Do you want this poor boy to water 'is trousers waiting 'ere for what you 'ave to tell 'im? Show 'im your notes.'

Well, she's had the satisfaction of making the whole Library blush now, Piers thought. Bless her. Lovely awful woman.

'There is not much, Mr Mosson. First I heard what Signora Luzzi told us. That Sir Hubert Mosson remembered something of a Lully opera here at Tothill House. So . . . in Hungary our training always is – check all your references. I found among the Lully references in the catalogue an article about his operas in England – "French Opera in London: A

Riddle of 1686" by Mr W. J. Lawrence.'

She said the name of the author as though he should have known it all his life, when it must be quite new to her. It aggravated him – this putting him back to class. It was her precise, over-articulated little girl's treble. He wanted to shut her up – by kissing her, frightening her, anything to make her a girl not a doll. But she was a messenger, that was all that mattered. Let her get on with it.

'It was in the *Times Literary Supplement* which we respect much in Budapest. From before the war. The article quotes a letter written from a gentleman, Peregrine Bertie, to the Countess of Rutland, written on February 11th of 1686. It is in the English of that time, but I do not know how it is pronounced, so I speak it in modern English: "Today," he writes, "was the French opera. The King and Queen" – I think it is Charles II, no? . . .'

'I suppose so. And Catherine of Braganza? Please go on.'

'"The King and Queen were there, the music" – it is written with a KE at the end. I think it is pronounced as now . . .'

'Yes, yes, it is.'

'"The musicke was indeed fine, but all the dresses the most wretched I ever saw. 'Twas" – it is written like that – "'Twas acted by none but French." Mr Lawrence goes on to say that the opera was *Cadmus et Hermione* – you speak French, I think – and that was the only Lully opera ever sung in England. But it was not, he tells us, the opera company of Lully that came to the English court, for Lully was rehearsing his singers at Versailles for the performance of *Armide*. I think that is the most famous opera of Lully, isn't it?'

'Yes, yes.' Piers heard his assurance of something that he only knew this week made in the same tones as his assurances of commonplaces. Fuck this questioning . . . Fuck the girl, too. He wished he could. But he felt ashamed of his violence. For she was sweet, too, for all her fake sweetness. He wanted to stroke and comfort her, poor thing. But why didn't she get on with it?

'So. No success there. Not at Tothill House. But I am trained in Budapest. We continue to search. Happily Miss

Lynmouth has given to me the English freedom of the Library for the first three weeks I am arrived. No routine, no fixed labours. I am to make myself a friend of the Library, she says. From that, I remember, I have seen the name of Bertie. I looked in the index to the papers and I found this same gentleman – Peregrine Bertie. He was corresponding with Sir Thomas Tothill and, after, with Sir Francis. There are many letters I read – but none speaks of French opera. But I don't despair. June 1697 he writes to Sir Francis – "I am sorry for your late troubles of which no word to any man, especially of Captain Vanbrugh's the music he did hear during his late captivity in France. It appears that the present breeze of peace is to blow but coldly betwixt here and the French shores."'

Piers burst out excitedly, 'Of course, it was after the Treaty of Ryswyk.'

She smiled gravely and said, 'I think I shall continue the letter. "But, Sir Francis, you will not, I trust, allow your disappointment to prevent your giving us entertainment of the English sort when your Italian has finished his painting of Mr Vanbrugh's Great Hall; we have heard such wondrous tales of the beauties of that Hall that we shall expect equal wondrous entertainment, though of a sort better to flatter His Majesty's Dutch prejudices than your former choice." Nothing of Lully.'

She looked at him so teasingly that he felt impelled to say, 'But *you* found something in the end, *I* know, from your look.' Immediately he thought, I should have told her to tell me what she has to say or get screwed. That's the way they had talked in that American book that his brother had lent him. It had got boring, but all the women had done what they were told.

'It is a clue,' she said, simply and dramatically. 'I think perhaps it is the air of your England that makes me one of your famous private detectives. In Budapest it is so dangerous. But I love clues and mysteries and plots.' She said it with an air of such boyish, romantic bravado, like an emancipated Ibsen girl. He thought, all right, I'll cast you for Hilde Wangel when I produce *The Master Builder*. I'd like to do that and a lot more. But meanwhile get *on* with what you're telling me.

'No word, as I said, in the diaries of Sir Francis or of his lady. So I looked in the private journal of Sir Francis' steward, Heneage Brown, for it is in cipher. But it was not a difficult cipher – a simple transposition based upon the Tothill motto – is that how you say it? I have some practice with ciphers. The entries for 1697 are not many so it was easily found. Entry for July 19th 1697 reads . . .' Piers could stand it no longer. He seized the paper from her hand, knocking against her so that she swayed and almost fell. He saw the fright in her pretty round eyes with a satisfaction that disgusted him as he felt it. But his excitement at the text took over from any thought of her as he began to read aloud – '"Today I did with Mr Copley, the Master Carpenter, perform the sad task of destroying all those great Engines and Machines that we had prepared for the playing of the French Opera *The Phaeton* – viz: the Machine to echo the Ocean's Roar, the Gates of the Altar of Isis that did open themselves and the crackling Fire that did show therein, the changing of Proteus by maskes and lights and shadowes from Lion to Tree from Marine Monster to Fierie Fountaine, and the Engine that we did devise for the transporting of Phaeton to the Throne of the Sun God. It was a mournfull pyre and in his miserie at the burning of his worke Mr Copley did reveal that he knew much of our late troubles: of the King's refusal to attend the playing of a French opera or to suffer a French Companie to come hither, and of Mr Vanbrugh's part therein, namely that he did urge the playing of *The Phaeton*, he having heard the airs whistled and sung by his gaolers when he was imprisoned in the Bastille, that Opera having been received in Paris where it had always been the especial favourite of the people."' Magda interrupted him excitedly. '*Phaeton* was of all Lully's work the people's opera, I think.'

Marina's reaction was instant. 'No, we can't 'ave *that* nonsense. People's Operas. My God!'

'I don't think Miss Sczekerny means that,' Piers explained. 'It was just that it was the hit of the moment. Everyone – the cobblers, the porters, the fish wives, the coachmen – sang or hummed the arias as they worked.'

'Ah! That's quite different. That's delightful! Singing as they go about their work. That's charming. The people should always be occupied. Each at his task – the wife, the husband, the son, the daughter. That is charming. It is genre.'

'You ought to play "Happy Families", Marina,' he said.

She made a nasty face. '"'Appy Families"! What is it? It sounds 'orrible.'

He explained the card game to her. 'Mr Bung, the Brewer. Mrs Bung. Master Bung. Miss Bung.'

'Oh, my dear, that is quite charming. You must find me those Bungs. Are the cards pretty? But go on with this steward. 'E is rather a bore.'

'"This discoverie of his knowing that which should not be known alarmed mee greatly which made mee swear him to secrecie upon the Holy Scriptures; which othe hee being a Godlie man I think hee will keepe it. And so ended much labour to little end. Such are our masters."'

'Oh, it's wonderful,' Piers cried, as he took in what he had read.

'That is all,' Magda said.

'We don't *need* any more. With copies of that evidence surely we can persuade Uncle Hubert, or maybe Grandma, or I suppose really Great Grandpa to agree to its being done here. And Howerton ought to jump at the opportunity. But in any case, I don't know how to thank you enough.'

He wondered should he give her a kiss on the lips as he wanted, but, thinking of Screw Head, he decided a warm handshake would be better and was about to rise from his chair. But it was too late, Marina had thrown her arms round the astonished (or was she astonished?) little bundle of national folk costume and was kissing her – crumpets! – but kissing her as he had wanted – on the mouth! And then he saw why. Marina had one eye fixed on poor old fatty Primrose's misery.

'So,' she said as she disengaged herself, 'we shall all be very busy now, our thanks to this girl.' She stood away and looked at Magda. 'You're certainly not *amusing*,' she said, turning up her nose, 'but you will be very useful. So, now you go on with these researches and lookings. But not so important now about the Tothill performance. You can't learn much from what never 'appened. Find out about the way it was produced in Versailles, in Paris, wherever it was. The more you can give this boy of all this fact, the more 'e can use 'is imagination. Can't you, darling?'

'Good heavens! Marina. That's *my* work,' Piers cried.

'No, no. You are the artist. Archives, research, that's not for artists. You are to make it beautiful for us. Extraordinary. Fun. To shock us with your ideas. 'Ow can you do that working in libraries? Look at it 'ere. This room's not beautiful or fun.'

He felt some outrage at her blindness, surely her wilful blindness, about the Van-Pratt room. He was ready to protest, but Primrose did so before him.

'Mrs Luzzi, I am not going to quarrel with you about the beauty of our Library, although I think you would like it if I did. We have already discussed all this and I have told you that Miss Sczekerny *cannot* give any attention to this Lully business until at least the end of January when the Mosson proofs have been fully corrected, and even then we have a backlog of important queries to answer. This is not a Library of musical history, nor is Miss Sczekerny paid to work on the history of opera. In any case I am sure that, as Mr Mosson says, *he* will want to do that work. I must ask you not to come interfering here unless there is some book you wish to consult, and not to give orders to my staff. And particularly, if you please, you are not to wander about in our staff quarters. I am sure I don't know what Sir Hubert would say if he knew.'

'Staff quarters? Ah! You mean your lavatories. Don't worry, I am not going to report any thing to 'Ubert. What 'as been going on there anyway? There was no bad smells. Was there, my dear?' she asked Magda and went straight on, 'In any case soon you won't be reporting to 'Ubert. You will report to me after the marriage. And it won't be Mosson work we shall be doing 'ere, it will be the Tothills. Can you do that seventeenth century language? Soon you must be learning it. Oh, I know, darling,' she turned to Piers, 'the nineteenth century is very amusing, those Victorians, but not sugar and cotton. And look at Thomas Tothill choosing all those mistresses for their ugly looks. I read about it. That's amusing. And Sir Francis getting Vanbrugh 'ere and wanting Lully. And Verrio! That's not 'igh art, thank God. Michelangelo, Raffaele, that's boaring. No. People *talk* about Verrio these days. That's what matters. And all Sir Francis and 'is little page boys called by numbers. They say 'e was very cruel to them. That's amusing. Who knows? Perhaps 'is wife 'ad some little girls, you'd like that, wouldn't you?' she turned to Primrose. 'And why not?'

Piers could not bear to look at Primrose. 'I say, look here, Marina. That's enough.'

She stroked his cheek. 'I know. We've got to think about this Lully. That *is* important. Come along and talk with me about it. I go to see 'Ubert. 'E'll be pleased if 'e thinks it was all 'is doing. But you 'ave to talk to your grandmother, if that's necessary. And to the old man. Now what about . . .'

Miss Lynmouth's voice cut through this discourse. 'Mrs Luzzi, I'd better tell you that I shall see Sir Hubert about all this as soon as possible.'

'You do so. I think you will be seeing 'im anyway. Now, about this 'Owerton, I still want to know, is 'e a snob, darling?'

Once again Primrose's voice interrupted. 'It occurs to me, Mr Mosson, that you'll want a copy of the libretto of *Phaethon*. I looked it up the other day. It's by Quinault. I see that there is a copy of his *oeuvres* in the London Library. I'll get it out for you on our Library subscription. I can send it round to you at the school. 7 Dean's Yard, isn't it?'

'Thank you very much,' he said, trying to give her all his sympathy in his voice. 'That's most helpful.'

He gave a smile. He added a wink, urging her to say no more to Marina, implying perhaps that he would put it all right. But could he?

'Oh, for God's sake. Do you want to produce this opera or not?' Marina asked. 'Then tell me about this 'Owerton. You can tell me on the way to my car.'

As they turned to leave the Library, Magda came close to him and whispered, 'I think you are the important man, Mr Mosson. They all so much wish to please you.'

Perhaps he had made more impression on her than he thought. If he could work *her* in as well . . . But she had moved away before he could answer. She seemed to have a natural taste for conspiratorial behaviour, perhaps it was always like that in Communist countries.

'You see, darling, what I think is I can do so much for this opera. Oh, don't worry! It's not just for your beautiful eyes. I want to launch this place into life and a Lully opera – even performed by amateurs when those amateurs are boys and girls from famous schools – would be so amusing. And even if the Lully is bad, frankly, darling, so is the other Phaethon, the Verrio. But it doesn't matter. It's what they're wanting. It's the ambience that is dramatic. Well, you know.'

He thought that he did know rather better than she did. But he nodded, for he was impatient. As they were walking along the panelled corridor, she stopped and faced him. Her dark eyes had an extraordinary blend of excitement and of contentment in them. As she talked, he wondered how to resolve this new contradictory Marina, and he thought, I am seeing her for the first time, serious.

'Look, darling, this has got to work. This is about making something that could bring this beautiful, boaring 'ouse alive. Oh, I know, for you there's some child's dream. That's not for me to know about. And also it could be the beginning of a real dream – to become a fine theatre man, but I know we are not to talk about that also. All that is your business. But for me also, it matters. If I can do this, I know that I can do more 'ere. And then life will be fun. I shall be quite good to old 'Ubert. Don't ask me – will that last? It never does. You will know that soon. But I want some rest from all this fighting. Oh, my God, why should I tell you all this and why should you listen? Can I get this opera 'appening 'ere, that is all you want to know. And why not? Well, I *can* get it done for you. But you must leave it to me. Come, follow me, I will tell you outside. My car will be at the Lodge. We don't want your old grandmother putting 'er nose into this, or is it God's nose? God knows.'

So, she did understand English puns. Walking down the lime avenue, she continued:

'I can get important people interested. I don't mean the jetset people. I can get them anyway. But musical names. Ben Britten and Pears will come, I think, and Glyndebourne – old John. Then there's a brilliant young man at Cambridge 'oo knows all this French opera, I'm sure. 'E's at all the interesting parties. And then my darling Katherine White, the most beautiful singer of our time. And she's amusing, too. Most singers are so boaring. She'll bring the names from Covent Garden – darling David Webster adores me. And critics will come for me too – Desmond, darling Desmond Shawe-Taylor. You will love them. And I will get some from Milano. Now, I think if your man 'Owerton's a snob – 'e will be, all schoolmasters are – to talk these names to 'im will be enough. It will make 'im take risks, because to produce in that Great Vanbrugh 'All *will be* a risk, darling. But you are not the person to tell 'im all this. For a beginning, you don't know these people, and 'e won't believe you. Because, beside everything, although you are a most beautiful amusing man, you *are* a schoolboy. So let *me* talk to 'im. Write the address down.'

They had reached the Lodge of Tothill House and, while he wrote down in her address book, he steeled himself to say:

'Marina, you did behave very badly to that poor woman.'

'Oh, the poor woman! You don't understand much yet, Piers. She and the old woman "want out" for me. 'Ave you 'eard that? "Want out"? It's American. But Lisa Grote and Ronnie 'Arris are all saying it. Isn't it amusing? No, all that is just women's nonsense. Not for you. Did you see 'ow angry she was when I kissed that little girl? I like to upset these boaring old bourgeois Lesbians. Why not, darling, I don't like it when people can't understand what 'as to be done after I 'ave told them.' She gave him a quick kiss, told her chauffeur to take her to the Goupil Gallery and was gone in her great Rolls.

Piers walked back to the school. Already he could not wait for a sight of the libretto, better still, the first hearing of the score, above all, the first rehearsal in the Great Hall. He would so enter the very being of the actor who played Phaethon that the whole cast, the lantern itself, the great Solomonic columns would be shaped and ordered to his design, and Phaethon would fall at last in all his tragic wayward beauty to the terror and sadness and satisfaction of a fine tuned audience that would stagger from their seats amazed.

CHAPTER III
At Home at the Nursery

'**D**ARLING HEART! *Béarnaise!*'

She had guessed rightly and, to avoid spoiling the sauce, he had to move the double saucepan off the ring until she had gone. How wonderful it must be to cook without people coming into the kitchen at the wrong moment. He promised himself that, after he'd left school, and before University, he'd take a room with a cooker and make delicious meals without any fear of interruption. Something told him that such licence would be punished by the electric stove blowing up in his face. Something else said idiotic puritanism. But he didn't find the second voice very convincing.

Meanwhile she had put her little finger gingerly into the pan and sucked the green-flecked, yoke-coloured liquid.

'Mm!' she said, 'Delicious, darling.'

'It will be when it's cooked.'

She put her arm round his waist. 'Aren't I awful, interrupting you?'

'No, Ma. But I did agree to do the luncheon so that you could be with Uncle Jim as he has to leave so early.'

'I know, darling heart, that bloody petrol shortage.' Her voice had that hysteric shrillness as soon as she mentioned the subject that he'd noticed again and again this weekend. Now was his chance to find out what it was all about, but intrusion was difficult.

'It was angelic of you,' she went on, 'but he and Piers are

92

deep in some thing about the stage sets for *Phaethon* – I supposed it ought to be pronounced as though it was French, but I'm not really sure what that would sound like – and they so seldom seem to find anything to talk about these days, and it makes me so happy when they do, that I thought I must come and interrupt you. I know it's naughty of me. Piers would be furious, he's so keen about your mugging up for A levels.'

'I'm cooking at the moment. Anyway, I don't think anyone mugs up now, Ma. It has quite a different connotation. To do with robbery and beating up in New York. At any rate, it's a new American expression.'

'Oh! I know. Isn't it awful? Jim despairs of everything. He says law and order's a finished thing. And, of course, as he says, everyone feels so let down after Suez that it's not surprising.'

Tom saw no way of discussing something so serious as symptoms of chaos on such a fugitive foundation, so he contented himself with chopping up the chives he liked to add to the salad. He steeled himself to ask about her 'scene' after the play – it hadn't seemed right to spoil Christmas by mentioning it during the holidays, and this was their first termtime weekend at the Nursery.

'Ma, what was all that about . . . ?' But her voice, high, and excessively lively, overrode him.

'I know it's awful of me to keep harping on your being such a good cook.'

'Well, if I *am* any good, it's simply because I learned from you.'

'Darling heart! You're very sweet.'

'Well, it's true.'

'Yes. I think it is. It's the only thing I *have* been able to teach you. Neither of you have ever understood anything about gardening. All the same, I sometimes wonder what your father would have said about you cooking. But Uncle Jim says things have changed about all that and that men do all sorts of things now they wouldn't have done before the war. Not that he can tell an omelette from a macaroon, poor love. I mean, of course, he'll adore his lunch today.'

Tom laughed loudly. 'I'm not giving him either omelettes or macaroons, but he still won't know what he's eating. But what does it matter?'

'Of course not, darling. It's just that I'm so happy when he approves what either of you do. And he always does. Anyway, Useless will love the food. He adores food and knows what he's eating. Half the money he never makes has gone in expensive restaurant meals. Bless him. But I wish he wasn't quite so good at getting round me. I'd put that £300 away towards a holiday. But anyway it would only have been to go to see him and the Pyramids. And now he's not there. One wonders if the Pyramids are. Poor England. What *did* Jerry and the others die for?'

Tom made no comment. He had not yet been able to absorb the reappearance of his improvident Uncle Eustace into any scheme of family life that promised responsible order. It seemed only yesterday – although, of course, they'd been very small – when the errant uncle came back from India to sponge, when *that* closed down. Now it was Egypt. The Albatross of the British Empire, he thought to tell Van. All the same, he *did* usually herald bad weather.

'Anyway, I only really wanted to say, darling heart, that your being such a good cook has a special significance for *me*. It somehow seems to say that out of the worst things in life something good does come. I can remember now, when I got back from hospital with that burned arm, you said, "Ma, I want you to show me how to cook, then I can take it on when you're not up to it." You were only twelve. And yet you perfectly knew that I'd burned myself when I was tight. But you did it so tactfully. And then for all that awful period, or as much as you could be here – three years of it – you took over and cooked for me as soon as you saw a sign that I'd had one too many. And never so much as once did you make it embarrassing for me. The tact of it, at that age.'

He said, trying not to mumble with embarrassment:

'When somebody's as fond of someone, it's hardly to be called tact.'

'No, of course not. To have two such sons! All the same, if

your mother hadn't been a near alcoholic for all those years, you wouldn't be an Escoffier.'

'Well, we don't need a repeat.'

'Honour bright! Cross my heart. It won't happen again.' She turned away and looked out of the window. 'If I said I'm delighted at how beautiful the *daphne mezereum* looks this year, I might as well be talking Greek to *you*. Better really. All the same, I'm rather proud that with a purely shrub rose nursery, we do have something to show at almost any time of the year, at any rate just round the house, if customers turn up to order. And, thank God, they do nowadays. They expect a shrub nursery to be a sort of Chelsea Flower Show whenever they choose to come here. And they come at the oddest times. Of course, half of them know nothing about shrub roses, let alone old roses which I still insist on. "It only flowers once a year! Oh dear!" Then if I say I'll find them a repeat, they think it's something to do with belching.'

Tom always felt hot cheeked when Ma got to the class of customers she called 'them'.

'All the same, we're getting somewhere now. Vita Sackville-West wrote recently, "If we're not careful soon old roses will be the in thing in the suburban garden." And what will poor Harry Wheatcroft do then, poor thing, say I? Aren't I a snob, darling heart? Do you know, this year I had two customers who corrected me on dates – one on Fantin Latour and another on Nuits de Young. And when I looked it up, they were both of them right. So the gospel's spreading. But the *work* now! We're really making some sort of a profit. Even with an extra gardener to pay and all the insurances. Thanks to Labour. At least we're rid of *them*. And although the two pupils from the Horticultural College – sweet girls – bring me a small grant from the Ministry, they eat their heads off at my expense. So they should – I mean eat their heads off. They're very young.'

This seemed to be a record for her, he thought, both in speed and ramblingness, especially as she usually kept off Nursery affairs with her 'garden blind' sons. And why did she look out of the window all the time, away from him?

'I think that's why I get so tired. Did it embarrass you all terribly, Tom, when I got so lit up after Shakespeare? I felt so ashamed. I haven't dared to say a word to Piers about it. I think I was so exhausted with all the work here, and then so excited by the play. And then darling Jackie's a bit of a bind, especially being in such a state about that awful Marina's dead set at Hubert. What about *that*, darling? No, I mustn't say anything against *her*. After all she's doing for Piers. And then Eustace, bless him, reappearing on the scene. And that damned American lecturing us on what we should do when British men and women who'd made their lives in Cairo faced lynching in the streets. That's what Eustace said it came to. I honestly thought I should fall flat on my face at the party. So I decided the best thing was to make my exit as mousily as possible.' She turned and stared at him in challenge.

He must, he thought, take it up, for she *hadn't* been drunk, or anywhere near it, he was sure.

He said, 'It was rather a noisy mouse, Ma. What *was* it that upset you so much on the telephone?'

She said, 'On the telephone? Oh, I was just ringing Victoria Station to make sure of the last train and getting a taxi. It was a bit of a business with my head swimming. I should have asked you, darling, but you looked so absorbed as you always do when it's anything to do with Piers. It's wonderful about this opera, isn't it? I must say your Mr Brownlow was absolutely charming when he rang up about Piers staying on at school and so on after that evening. So I couldn't have been quite as bad as I thought.'

She stopped for confirmation, he supposed, but he felt that he must get more out of her. Piers couldn't do anything outside *Phaethon* at the moment, but something *was* wrong, so it devolved on him. Yet he couldn't see how to approach her. There was a noticeable pause, he realised, before he said rather flatly:

'You're sure there's nothing wrong? That isn't what you said when you came back to the party.'

She said rather crossly, 'I told you I was tight.'

'Is it anything to do with Uncle Jim?' he plunged on. But her voice came to him icily:

'Really, Tom darling, I do not think I need a cross-questioning from my schoolboy son.'

For a moment he thought, in his easy vulnerability, that he would sink in the freezing waters, but he surfaced and said, 'We're awfully fond of Uncle Jim, Piers and I. That's all.'

She came over and patted his cheek with the back of her hand. 'Thank you. I didn't mean to sound forbidding and parental. It's really *you* that's worried, isn't it? You didn't answer when I said it was good about this *Phaethon* thing. After all, Piers isn't really musical and Eustace whispered to me last night that the opera's probably a terrible bore.'

It was too much for Tom. 'It will be wonderful. Van's got all sorts of ideas about it, as you already heard. If Uncle Eustace gets a good filet and *Béarnaise*, he'll sing a different tune. But he won't if I can't have the kitchen to myself for a bit.'

He had shouted. He felt immediately horrified, and he could see that Ma was appalled – Tom, he could see her thinking, for Tom to lose his temper!

He said, 'If I may lose my temper for a moment.' It would allow them both to laugh.

But they had no time for laughter. Piers came in. He said, 'Lovey, what can you have been saying to make Tom shout?'

Tom answered, 'She was going on and on about your old opera, can you pull it off and so on, when I want to make a sauce.'

'*Tremblez, tremblez pour votre fils, ambitieuse mère.* That's what old Proteus says in the opera to Climène, Phaethon's mother, when she asks him about her son's fate. He's a sort of raven's voice foretelling the doom. The Mother's a terrific part. She bore him as heir to the Sun God. True, she doubts, just as his Sun God father does, the rightness of his driving the chariot through the sky. Phaethon's pretty quick to tell her off for it, when she hesitates to support him – "*Quoi, ma grandeur n'est pas votre plus chère envie?*" You'd never let anything be more precious to you than your son's greatness, would you, Ma?' He put his arm round her.

She said rather vaguely, 'No, of course not, I'm

tremendously ambitious for you.'

'Would you mind if he set the world on fire?' Tom asked.

'No, of course not. It's just what I know he *will* do.' Piers
made the up sign to his brother. And they both laughed. Ma
joined them, but she said:

'That's a bit vulgar, isn't it, darling heart? Or did you mean
that Victory sign that Churchill used to cheer us up with
during the raids?'

This set her sons laughing more uproariously.

Then Piers, seeing her puzzlement, said, 'I love you for
your ambition, Ma. I wish you could play Climène for us.
And I promise you this – that I cherish your good name as
much as Phaéthon did Climène's. His anger is terrific when
his rival Epaphos – he's an awful shit, though I'll have to suggest that subtly because I suspect he's given some of the most
heroic arias – casts doubt upon her statement that Phaethon is
her child by the Sun God – "*Votre mère l'a dit, est-ce assez
pour le croire?*" And Phaethon comes right back – "*Osez-vous
attaquer ma gloire?*" I'm pretty sure that for him, like me, his
glory and his mother's good name are indivisible. You see how
I know my text, and I've only had the libretto two days. It's
frightfully important if I am to defend my view of it to
Howerton, since it's so unorthodox.'

Tom said, 'You'll have to use a lot of tact.' He saw his brother's forehead wrinkling in a scowl. 'Oh, I know you will.'

And he suddenly thought, here's a chance to enrol Van in an
attempt to reach Ma.

He said, 'Well, you couldn't be less tactful than me. I
wanted to get it across to Ma that we're at her disposal if she
has any worries and all I did was to seem an impertinent Nosey
Parker.'

'No, darling heart, it's just that everything's very complicated in life as I am afraid you'll find out when you're older.
And you were absolutely sweet to say you were fond of Jim.'

'Was there any question of otherwise?' Piers asked. 'Oh, do
you mean because we aren't so much on his wavelength as we
were when we were kids? That's only surface. It's always
better when he's here. You're better. And look at just this

weekend, how he's helped me over the machines for *Phaethon*. He's doing sketches for them now. He thinks the door of the Temple of Isis that opens itself to reveal flames and phantoms presents no difficulty. But he's more doubtful about Triton's changing shapes.'

A sharp rap of a ladle on the aluminium sink made him look towards a frowning Tom.

He went on, 'Anyway, it's lovely when he's here, Ma. And I think he ought to live here. Oh! I know the problem, but now Marius is about to go to the Seminary, I don't see why you should play up to that woman's caprices any longer.'

Tom thought, he's trodden and the ice has not cracked. It *is* possible. Why does it always crack with me? But now caution was needed. Ma must feel her own confidence if she was to trust them. He tried to signal to Van to give her time to speak. And indeed she began.

'I don't think I should say anything, really . . . at least not yet, but . . .'

Then they all heard his footsteps. She said brightly, 'Come along in, Jim. One more intruder won't break the poor cook's back.'

He looked to where Tom was measuring the olive oil into the salad dressing and made his usual remark at such times.

'Ah! Veronica's soul.'

It dated from his only recognition of Tom's culinary prowess when the appearance of grapes with the fish had startled him out of indifference at what he ate. They also, as usual, didn't take up his joke.

Ma said, 'The boys love us both. They've been saying so.'

He gave a start, jerking the papers that he held in his hand. She put her hand on his arm.

'I don't break promises,' she said.

'Oh, that's nice. That they love us, I mean. Good people.' He took his pipe and his box of matches out of the sagging left hand pocket of his old olive green woollen cardigan and began to light up. 'Well,' he said, between draws, 'I think perhaps I *have* earned Piers' good opinion this morning. I've sketched out all your machines. They can be made to work all right.

R.E.M.E. never fails, you know. But to be honest, I am very doubtful about the noise. Even with the best modern technique, a lot of these eruptions and clouds, and gods appearing in the heavens are going to make an infernal row. What I suspect is that three-quarters of this could be better done with lights. Come into the sitting room and I'll show you what I have in mind.'

When they had gone, Tom said to his mother, 'And you go and rouse Uncle Eustace. I don't want this meal spoilt for anybody's laziness. Anyway, *he* might make an entrance next. This is a kitchen not a stage.'

He was almost ready to serve when Ma returned with his thin, elegant and seedy uncle.

'We can promise you Ritz quality, Useless, with Tom at the stove,' she said.

'Oh, good! That's what I like and what I have mostly been used to. It's one of the absolute hells of London at the moment, any restaurant faintly within one's means spells poison. After Shepheard's it does rather make one hate life. It simply means that one has to live on credit.'

'Darling Useless, you haven't *got* any credit.'

'Oh, you'd be surprised.'

To Tom's embarrassment he began to do a little tap dance and to sing. He knew his uncle's legendary little turns and faintly remembered them from boyhood as menacing. Clearly Ma found them rapturous, for she gazed at her brother with worshipping amusement.

'Altho' my bankers call it treason, I buy you orchids out of season, and tho' my landlord has ten fits, I have a table at the Ritz . . . pom, pom, pom . . . I'm a little bit fonder of you than of myself.' He brought his song and dance to an end.

Ma said, 'Oh, Useless, it's so lovely. You haven't changed the tiniest bit. You're just the same absurd monster. It makes me feel young again.'

Tom, feeling sure that this awful man was here to batten on Ma's hard earned savings, looked away.

His uncle said, 'Mm. Well, I don't usually visit the kitchens before I lunch. Certainly not for long. Shall we find ourselves a completely delicious martini straight-up, as the awful Americans in Cairo used to say? It's not the least of this shit Eden's balls-up that the *Americans*, whom all the Egyptians who count, all my pupils for example, *loathe*, are sitting there today as though nothing had happened and we've been kicked out.'

'Oh, darling heart,' Ma cried as she led him off to his martini.

But it was true that after he'd consumed his filet and *Béarnaise* and his aubergine and his salad and his Stilton and his syllabub, as well as four glasses of the Côtes de Beaune Uncle Jim had provided, Eustace gleamed all his rather shark-like teeth at his younger nephew in approval.

'Mm,' he said, 'you'd better come and cook for me, Tom. I couldn't *pay* you, but I'm sure I could coach you for this whatever it's called exam far better than any of these awful English public schools of today.'

Uncle Jim came to the rescue with one of his parade ground dismissal noises. 'Oh, no, that wouldn't do at all. Is that all clear about the possibilities of lighting?' he asked Piers.

'Yes, indeed. I can't say how grateful I am. I'm sure you're right. And I'll work at it this week.'

'Good. Well, I think that I'll have to be off. I have to sit on a court martial tomorrow. I don't look forward to it. Desertion. Always a very unpleasant occasion. It's hardly surprising that the buggers desert when we scuppered out of Suez like that. Sorry for the language, Tuppence,' he said to Ma. 'All the same, you can't afford to show any leniency in such cases, eh, Tom?'

'I shouldn't have thought so,' Tom said. It was the kind of dilemma that he dreaded to face, yet felt wholeheartedly that it was his future duty to address himself to.

Ma was upstairs for some time helping Uncle Jim to pack his weekend suitcase, and, when they came downstairs, the sparkling of a plucky smile fought the glistening of gathering tear-drops for possession of her eyes. It was a combination that had been one of the great warning signs of the 'bad years', and Tom reacted now as he had then by drawing into his shell. He opened his Moneypenny and Buckle's *Life of Disraeli* and began to make notes.

Piers' reaction was different. Poor thing, he thought, I must atone for my selfish absorption in *Phaethon* before I go back to it as I inevitably will. He said, 'I hope we'll see you again soon, Uncle Jim.'

'I doubt it. This petrol rationing makes visiting a luxury.'

'But surely the Army . . . I mean a little scrounging,' Eustace suggested.

Uncle Jim replied, 'The R.E.M.E. doesn't scrounge. In any case, I happen to be one of Her Majesty's Officers.' He put a touch of chuckle into the last sentence, but Tom could see that he was offended.

Uncle Eustace made a little face at his nephews to show that he knew he'd been reproved.

'Bloody, bloody Nasser,' Ma said hysterically and she stamped her foot.

Uncle Jim, embarrassed, looked away from them all. He took her arm. 'Yes . . . well . . . come out to the car with me, Tuppence.' And, to the company, he said the farewell so familiar to Piers and Tom: 'Well, goodbye all.' He said it in cockney. It was his one concession to playfulness.

'Let me like a soldier fall and die,' sang Uncle Eustace. 'Such uprightness is exhausting after luncheon.'

'Oh, Uncle Jim's marvellous. Make no mistake about that,' Piers told him. 'Just on this business of the machines for *Phaethon* he's been of enormous help. And it's frightfully important.'

But now Ma was back and Tom could see by the trembling of her lower lip and of her hands that she was near to loss of control.

'I'm going into the garden,' she said abruptly.

He thought, I'd better go with her.

He said, 'Can I come too?'

'Certainly not. Piers has explained to me a hundred times about the importance of your putting in some hours' reading each weekend you're down here.'

Piers felt from the way that she had introduced his name that she was calling for *his* help.

'Let *me* come,' he said, 'I can help with the pruning. I like all things that are against the conventions.' He felt proud of remembering about modern ideas on pruning in any month.

'We are not pruning now, dear, it's February.'

'But you said all that about pruning in November or March only was out of date. That's what I *meant*.'

'You *can* prune in February. You can prune any time you like unless it's a disastrous frost. But you wouldn't *choose* February – unless you'd been on a delicious cruise to the West Indies all over Christmas and January. Which is hardly likely with all the calls on my purse.'

They all felt guilty.

Eustace said, 'Well, Rosemary, you know I can't face your wonderful wild garden at the best of times. Let alone with snow about. It's all too Rousseau and noble savage for me. I see its beauty, but it's a miraculous muddle and if I hate anything more than muddles, it's miracles. Now if it were a perfect formal garden. There are some absolutely heavenly sketches of Le Nôtre's shaped peacocks and chariots with a light covering of snow. I reproduce one in my book.'

Ma was clearly conscience-stricken by what she had said. 'Oh, Useless, darling, why don't you do another book of that kind? The wonderful reviews you had! You boys just don't know what a brilliant uncle you have.' To Piers, she said, 'Darling, Uncle Jim was so impressed with all your ideas. He's left this address for electrical equipment. He says they were most helpful when the regiment had a crisis over searchlights.'

'I should think they'd be terribly expensive.'

'Well, the school will pay. In any case, with old Jackie's generosity after the Shakespeare, you can afford a little yourself. She gave the boy five hundred pounds, Useless.'

'Mm.' It was almost a purr.

To Tom, she showed her contrition by stroking his hair. 'Saturday's child works hard for his living,' she murmured and then left.

'Jim never seems to bring me pretty flowers, Jim never seems to cheer my weary hours, how can I go on carrying a torch for him?' Uncle Eustace sang. 'But she can, bless her,' he said. 'There used to be a thing when I was young about woman's mystery. But, of course, there's no mystery about it. It's just that they like being pushed around and thank God for it.'

Tom thought, he's perfectly repulsive, when Ma's obviously unhappy. He must bury himself in the Berlin Terms, otherwise he'd say something rude to the old boy. As it was, Piers would do it for him pretty soon and much more effectively.

But when a pressing urge to pee began to break through his concentration on the book, he came back to quite another atmosphere – one of immense cordiality.

'Well, I could help there. I do know my *grand siècle* pretty well,' Eustace was saying. 'What was the chorus of the Golden Age Prologue which opens the opera?'

'"*Dans ces lieux, tout rit sans cesse.*" Can't you imagine the boredom of such an Utopia? Inane laughter incessantly. I expect the Garden of Eden was like that too. "*Tout l'univers admire l'auteur d'un si doux repos.*" It's like an old people's home with a visit from the board of governors. And yet the music's some of his best.'

'Well, in some ways the boredom, the general gossipy tedium of *Le Roi Soleil*'s court *was* like an old people's home. You can see it in Saint Simon's memoirs. But then, on the other hand, it was the height of civilisation and he was always bringing France victories or claiming to.'

'Goodness,' said Piers, 'all this *is* a help. That's there too – "*ce héros terrible dans la guerre; Il fait, par sa vertu, le bonheur de terre.*"'

'Exactly. Jove, that's Louis, had to be the real hero of any work if it was to be presented at Court.'

'I see. That explains why Phaethon seems so much the motive force of the libretto and yet, as I'm told, so much of the best music is given to all the others. Lully had to present on two levels.'

'Oh, very much so. Everyone did at that Court if they hoped to survive. But especially Lully. After all, he started as the Grande Mademoiselle's Italian scullion and he owed everything to Louis personally. Well, I mean, he was the *Roi Soleil*. And, of course, the old boy knew that Lully was a bloody good musician. Yes, mm, I think you're on to something with this idea of yours to have a conflict in the opera – with Phaethon the ambitious damned as the conventional picture and, underneath, Phaethon as the hero, the innovating artist who dares – Lully himself, in fact. Fascinating.'

Piers' eyes were glowing. 'This is wonderful,' he said. 'In fact, I want to try to play it as both. For both are true, aren't they? The classical and the romantic. Well, Pratt and Vanbrugh, to come nearer home.'

'Exactly,' Eustace drawled. 'You'll make tremendous theatre with it.'

Something in his tone made Tom think, he doesn't believe a word of what he's saying, he's utterly contemptuous. He looked at Piers, but his brother's eyes were aglow.

Eustace went on, 'And now, tell me about these dances you have, *cher maître*.'

His uncle's sneer this time so disgusted Tom, he felt sick – or was it the richness of all the cream he'd put into the syllabub? He made for the downstairs lavatory again.

When he came back, he saw his uncle folding a piece of paper and putting it into his wallet.

'That's very good of you, dear boy. I didn't want to worry your mother, she's got enough on her plate.'

Tom immersed himself in his book, but it seemed to him that all the solid Victorian order rested on the hypocrisies and dotty ambitions of individualism – Palmerston, Disraeli, Gladstone. Only one statesman had real principle – Sir Robert Peel, and he'd split his party into two. He came out of his thoughts to find Uncle Eustace doing a little tap dance in front of him; he was singing, "I don't want to set the world on fire, I just want to be sitting alone." That's it, isn't it, Tom? The *solid* brother.'

Tom shut his book, got up, walked towards the door. Turning back, he said, 'You borrowed money from Ma. And then you borrowed money from Piers on the plea that you didn't want to worry Ma. And I don't suppose you've any intention of paying either of them back.'

'You're quite the little solid shit of the family, aren't you?' his uncle said and, brushing past him, left the room.

With anxiety, Tom realised that he had lost all chance to question his uncle about what he knew of Ma's moods.

CHAPTER IV
The Auditions for Phaethon

'SHE'S DONE it,' Piers told his brother excitedly, bursting against all his own orders to the family and staff into the Blue Drawing Room. For he had insisted that, on their weekends at Tothill, Tom should have a sanctum for his study – to the high approval of Hubert and Jackie. Tom dragged his attention away from sines and cosines and showed interest which he feared was a little forced, for he guessed what she had done and who she was. And his distaste for both strained his concern for his brother's success more tensely each day.

'Apparently she had Howerton to Claridges for lunch. I was terrified when he said it, because I thought she might have patronised him or, at least, that he might have thought so. But no. Actually, he told it all quite amusingly. I like him, Pratt. By the way, we're Reggie now and Piers. "It was a Royal Command," is what he said, "but I think I emerged with good or, at any rate, adequate marks for wit and manners." He thinks she's a bit absurd and very formidable, but that she knows what she's doing. Apparently she's taken the trouble to look up his articles on Rameau and Purcell, which I haven't.'

'But you will,' interjected Tom.

'Yes, yes. All right. I will. More important, she knew, which I didn't, that he'd organised some concerts at Edinburgh that included a Lully overture and some arias from *Armide*. And what's more she was able to tell him that some conductor whom he thinks hugely of had admired what he did

there. He takes what she says with a pinch of salt. He doesn't
think for a moment that Benjamin Britten will come, even less
Sir David Webster. And, if some critics do come, they probably won't write about it. I don't think he would really want
them to. And as to the brilliant young man from Cambridge
"who's at all the interesting parties, darling", he's already a
close personal friend of Reggie's. But there was enough obviously to make him feel that it would all help to put him on the
map. He simply loathes teaching, it seems. But the crowning
thing, strangely, is her bringing this Sylvia Armitage. Even I
have heard of her as a singer. I think she's a sort of Edith Evans
and Sybil Thorndike in one, only of course decades younger
or she couldn't still sing, although I think she's half retired. It
seems that she wouldn't know a work of Lully if she heard it,
or any of the music Reggie's interested in, but apparently that
doesn't matter. She's a great singer and that's that. It's something I'll have to get used to on the stage, I mean about stupid
people who are great actors and actresses. So it'll be good practice listening to her criticisms and comments and trying to turn
them into my own terms. Because obviously experience does
matter, but these people don't have the intellect to convey
what they've felt except by acting it. All this knowing how to
deal with people, Pratt, is going to be a super lesson. And it's
going to be very exciting.'

Tom, who had been watching the elegant loops and coils of
the green monkeys as they sported and postured up and down
the walls, was ashamed to find himself thinking, I'd rather be
one of *them* than all this Piers is describing, there wouldn't be
so much noise. Anyway, the monkeys' capers were bounded
by Pratt's exact proportions.

'There's just listening, too, I should think.'

'Yes. I'll have to imagine that I am you for that. Look, I
won't disturb you any more, but isn't it wonderful? We're to
have a meeting here in the Great Hall tomorrow when Reggie
and the music woman from St Paul's Girls will come with
some of the potential singers from the two schools. It will be
Reggie's first sight of the Hall. And Marina's going to bring
one or two musical celebrities who've been dying for

years to see the inside of this place.'

'What will Uncle Hubert say?'

'Ah, that's exactly where Marina *has* been clever. Hubert's to be there to tell them all about the Hall and the whole house and show them round and everything. And all without his committing himself until afterwards. Reggie saw exactly what she meant and fell in with it. Officially, of course, Hubert can't decide it. It has to be Great Grandfather's decision. But if Hubert *is* impressed, and they flatter him enough, it *is* really his decision, or rather, the old boy will do what he tells him. Apparently he's going through a gaga period.'

'And Grandma?'

'That's your job. What's the point of the afternoon sessions in the State Bedroom otherwise? Marina's made pretty dirty cracks about them. According to her, Grandma's just moved a generation on in her voracious sex appetite. Our Grandmother God all incestuous, she said. It's amazing, she's learned all our Jackie's Christian Science language, which must be difficult for an Italian. But she hates her so.'

'Yes. I know. I don't want to hear about it again. You know very well that I agreed to the furniture history sessions with Grandma because she's lonely and unhappy. And I am not surprised. I know what it's like to have the Luzzi on one's trail. And also because I wanted to do all I could to keep her favourable to the opera's being done here. But I can tell you now, Van, that I've come to enjoy the afternoons with her for themselves. She really knows the furniture in this house.'

'Oh, all that "lived in" stuff. You haven't fallen for that, I hope?'

'No. The best part of the State Bedroom is that it's a Pratt masterpiece. But all the same I *am* beginning to realise that a great house is a shape and it is also the way people have lived in it over centuries and what they filled it with. That's what makes it a strong fortress instead of a weak shell.'

'Yes, yes. I dare say. I don't know about all that. I think you'll become a slave to history that way. One must break the mould of what *actually* happened by what might have been. That's why this avenging of Sir Francis Tothill by staging

Phaethon is so satisfactory. We're not just gradually changing the inside of the house with different artifacts as all our ancestors have done, we're going to make a new work of art out of an old one – or rather I am. Anyhow you *will* bring Grandma round to agreeing, won't you? Though actually I don't know that her agreement is necessary.'

'No. That's why the Luzzi hopes to force the decision through without consulting her. To insult her and to show her power over Hubert. But Grandma's not a fool. Van, of course I'll do what I can for you. But you must consider Grandma yourself. You ought to anyway. She's a very unhappy, lonely old woman, especially now after this fall which she won't even admit she's had.'

'Yes, Pratt, I see that. If only Christian Science didn't make her so bright. And I do know that Marina, for all that she's helping me so much, is a bitch. But Grandma can't have thought that she could keep Hubert to herself for the rest of his life. And she has no right to think such a thing either. As for all this knowing the truth about a badly bruised leg, it won't be so easy when she comes to break a hip.'

'I don't believe that Hubert will be better off with the Luzzi.'

'She's quite good looking, Pratt, and she's given him a new life. Anyone can see that. Besides, the general prejudice is in favour of going to bed with women who aren't your mothers.'

Tom only smiled at this; he was considering. 'I can't imagine Uncle Hubert having sex with anyone. Perhaps that's just because when one grows up with someone, an uncle or so on, you take them for granted before you know about sex and all that. But I've always thought of him like a doctored Tom cat . . .'

'I know what you mean. That's partly because sex is one of the errors that Grandma has known the truth about, and so it's vanished from the very air of Tothill.'

'That's not really true. Oh, I know what *you* mean. But look at how flirtatious she is. And she's always throwing out little hints about old Hubert and "the ladies", as she calls them. She implies that Hubert has had a wild life somewhere away from home. The only time Ma spoke about it, she said he was "a great woman chaser". But apparently not even Daddy had been able to tell her of one woman he'd chased.'

'I expect he has a mistress somewhere. Or some Victorian thing like that. Great Grandfather had one, you know. But Grandma told Ma that it isn't to be talked about. Poor old man! I bet he'd like to remember it. Do you think he's too gaga to be able to tell *us*, if we drew him out?'

'I don't know. I shouldn't think it would be a very happy thing for an old man of ninety to start telling about his past sex life anyway. It would be like all that stuff in the popular Sunday newspapers that so undermines people's ordered way of living – "Revealing all". Brownlow was talking about it last week. He quite impressed me. He's good on the corrosion of values by sensationalism. Anyway Uncle Hubert isn't Victorian, I don't believe he's fifty yet. I must say he doesn't look at all old these days.'

'There you are. That's Marina's doing. She's dragging him screaming into the twentieth century, out of some terrible Victorian world. Prostitutes, I expect. It always was in Victorian times. They age a man, you know.' Piers was pleased to find that such worldly generalities came to him quite easily nowadays. 'Look at the way she's brought him into contact with whole worlds of people outside the Bank and the City and the Estate administration. And, bless her, she's doing the same for me.'

'You were never in any of those places. But I hope she does produce people who will be useful to you. Not just jet set and weirdies.'

'Oh, I think she'll do both. I hope so, anyway. There's no point in meeting producers and actors and designers and all the mass of people I can learn craft from, if I don't spend this next year or two, before I'm launched, getting involved with life of all kinds – and the weirder the better. No, a crazy lady with a power urge is just what I need so long as I keep an eye on her antics. And the Luzzi's no sawdust pierrette. Her kicks are real.'

Tom wanted to say that to him she was like a marionette

controlled by an electric machine that was out of control. He stared at the elegant *chinoiserie* monkeys making their eternal patterns on the wall. If there must be a monkey world, he thought, let it be patterned and confined to wallpapers. The chattering, cavorting, gibbering, imitative monkey world of Marina, so far as he could guess at it, both worried and upset him so much that, recognising the sincerity of Van's statements, he felt completely cut off from the future of his wondrous brother. He saw a lifetime of complimentary stalls for 'glittering' first nights and a lifetime of standing in a corner with a glass of champagne fighting off the threatening din of the meaningless chatter of celebrities in dressing rooms. He *must* do his own thing. He turned back to his book, to the subtle certainties of mathematics and the wondrous flights of pure intellect.

Piers, feeling guilty, tiptoed from the room.

He went as always now to the Great Hall. Each time he looked at it from a fresh angle, to impose upon it, or rather to bring to life out of it, all the fictional life that was bursting inside him, to arrange and then to see in turn each ballet, each character (for characters in fictional art, he felt sure, were small ballets), grouped around the central glorious, tragic flight of Phaethon across the lantern in glory and down in glorious death into the burning malachite bowl. As he squatted at the audience seat-level, he saw in turn again the great scenes of Phaethon's world: Climène, his mother, exulting in her son's triumph; the Sun King, his father, hailing him as hero; Mérops, the Egyptian King, bestowing succession and his daughter's hand upon him; then, at last, Phaethon's glorious flight across the sky – '*C'est un nouveau soleil qui donne un jour si beau.*' And then, for the work was tragedy, Théone, Phaethon's forsaken girl, the inevitable but piteous wreckage that any great bid for glory leaves behind it; Proteus, that croaking raven voice, warning of the cost of the venture; the Earth invoking Jove to save her from the revolution, the newness that Phaethon's daring threatened; and, at last, Jove's thunderbolt thrown in the righteous cause of order and dull peace, bringing death to Phaethon's bid for greatness in the flames of that great bowl which stood between Vanbrugh's marble pilasters – '*O chute affreuse!*'

Could someone from this rather obscure seat to the west of the North Doorway see far enough up to take in Jove, whom he proposed to place high upon a suspended platform beneath the lantern's light, and, above that lesser God, the Sun King, whom he would seat in lesser majesty to receive his son in the South Gallery below? Yes, one could see, but only, he thought, by squinting. How he longed to talk to the designer. Who would it be? Brierly, who carried out his orders so well for *Richard II*, was leaving school before the summer. Anyway it seemed highly unlikely that the high peruke with which he proposed, recalling Louis XIV himself, to adorn the Almighty God, Jove the thunderer, would be seen from here. Did it mean that these allusions that he wished to make to the dimension of contemporary Louis XIV's earthly monarchy in this legend of Greek celestial deity would drive him to clothe the cast entirely in seventeenth century costume? No, he wasn't going to have that. Just suggestions here and there, like Jove's peruke. Otherwise, it would all look conventionally 'clever', like Shakespeare in modern dress. That way he would sacrifice the essential visual reality of the play to its contemporary Court undertones that were, after all, only one dimension.

The play must speak – as he had to take on trust that the music would – of the world of Greece's Sun God, and also of France's Sun King implicitly, and it must speak of both of them to an audience viewing it now, in 1957. And also, of course, and this was his personal essence, the reason for his being the chosen producer, to an audience most of them seeing for the first time that famed, almost legendary Vanbrugh room.

Strange the whole production must be, but with a strangeness all the time that stirred echoes of familiarity.

Oh, of course he couldn't achieve it. He could only hope at best with amateur singers and no experience to avoid a laughable failure.

He must not tell Pratt, but there and then, looking at the

daring, skyward-reaching, twisted pillars that supported the lantern, and the lantern itself piercing the heaven's vault, he begged whatever deities there were (or defied them) that the baroque, the elegant, the eccentric and the thrill-worshipping should outnumber the safe and sawdust-stuffed in the Hall on that first-night performance of *Phaethon*, if the school authorities and his great grandfather (curious associated company) gave licence for its performance.

And then, from behind the very black marble twisted pillar at whose astonishing spiral climb he was gazing, there appeared Magda Sczekerny – a demure yet luscious doll. All those folksy ribbons and smocks, and he'd never played with dolls as a boy, was no practised hand at dressing and undressing them.

'Mr Mosson, I am breaking into your artistic reverie. Do I have the right, please?' And the doll's eyes rounded at him like a little maid presenting a bouquet to Grandma when she was Lady Mayoress. He expected a curtsey. 'Forgive me, please. But I wish so much to introduce a friend of mine who can help you with your production.'

He knew quite suddenly that he had no hopes. And it wasn't anything to do with Lesbianism, bourgeois or otherwise. Her eyes glowed with loving devotion and she held out her hand towards the black shining Solomonic twists and pulled to his feet from a crouching position – not a strange, unkempt, bearded, open-shirted, hirsute-chested, wild, brilliant Bohemian, nor yet a breath-taking apparition of elegance, suavity, worldliness and flair – but a short chunky young man. He had large dull eyes that stared emptily through his spectacles like a toy owl's, and his long arms hung down beside his short body, like the wings of that cute wise old bird; his front upper teeth protruded a human version of an owl's beak. But his cheeks, to match Magda's, were blobs of Dutch-doll red. His sweater and trousers were old and stained but precise and neat. Of the two dolls, he had been dragged across floors and through hedges more than Magda. But dolls they were and as dolls they presented themselves.

'Your researcher,' Magda said coyly, 'begs to present **another assistant.**'

'Your handyman, general cook and bottle washer,' said the young man. His voice was precise, over-articulated yet modest, like one of the more pathetic clergymen that came to read the lessons at the school services in the Abbey on Saints' Days. He had, too, their slight touch of genteel cockney. 'You'll need one for this production.'

'Ralph Tucker,' Magda said. 'He knows Tothill House and grounds very well. He has been chief assistant to the head gardener now for a year, since he came from Horticultural College. Isn't that correct, Ralph?'

'Yes. That's right. In another place I suppose I'd have been in charge of the conservatories or the shrubberies or the formal bed maintenance. But Mr Pentreath likes to run it all himself – with his working gardeners to keep things as they always have been. So as I was chief assistant, he's appointed me general ideas man. The two years at College seem a bit remote, but it gives me a wide range to be odd jobs man on the Estate.'

'Ah, yes, of course – I've heard of you from my grandmother. She's always singing your praises.' Piers heard in his own voice some of the patronising note that, in their different ways, Grandma and Ma had both brought him up to use to 'those who work for us'. It's not fair, he thought, once I get to know anyone individually, these stereotypes vanish. But his grandmother's constant praise of her blue-eyed boy among the staff had made him subconsciously unwilling even to distinguish the identity of the young man. He tried hard to recall one meaningful phrase from the mass of gush that old Jackie always poured out about her rare protégés – 'only a boy but so starved of God's love' – 'a broken home, but he has no bitterness' – 'a rectory, yet these genteel people feel the little privileges they lose so much more than any of us who were born to authority' – 'Pentreath's decided to return to his native Cornwall next year. And better so. We should all be in the place we love best and Cornwall is his. This boy is born to take over here. He loves every inch of Tothill. And he has such a simple but true love of beauty. "The bluebell's got them all beat, Milady" – he said to me.'

Piers had, in desperation, almost complimented the young man on the simplicity of this reported pronouncement. Then he remembered something a little more appropriate.

'You're the one who mended the rococo jewelled singing birds. I can just remember them singing when I first visited here after the war when I was eight. And now suddenly a month ago they were singing again.'

'After Suez,' the young man said sedately. 'Those birds love wars.' But he didn't smile. 'The general maintenance has been bad here, sir, for a very long time. But Magda here told me that there were many machines in this opera you're doing. I'd quite like to have a hand in constructing them. If my help is needed that is, of course.'

'I certainly should be glad of your help, and please don't call me sir.'

'As you like, of course. It's Phaethon's fall, isn't it? Like on the ceiling.'

'Yes. But *I* see it as a tragic fall. I'd better explain that now, as it is an unorthodox view.'

To his surprise this genteel young man said, 'Orthodoxy's about finished in the theatre, isn't it? Exit the dear old well-made play. We all look back in anger now.'

It wasn't quite what Piers had in mind, but he smiled. 'I see Phaethon as more constructive, more daring than Jimmy Porter. His chariot ride is a brave gesture of defiance of the dismal routine life. But, of course, it *is* a tragedy and it turns out to be destructive. The Earth is in danger of a ravage by fire as his horses get out of control. In the opera, the Earth, that is, appeals to Jove to save her people from burning. But I don't think this makes Phaethon's gesture any less dramatic, less exciting.'

'Oh, no, you're right there. There's always someone to moan. And I suppose the old Thunderer throws his thunder-bolt. What else can he do? That's always the excuse anyway. Like Kings – they're regnant so they *have* to reign. Or popes, they're fathers, so we have to obey them. Authority's all in the name really, isn't it? That's not going to be an easy machine to construct, the chariot, you know.'

His voice made no change from its flat but chirpy level as he changed the subject.

Piers thought, he has a lot of comments, but never mind, if he can really do what he says he can.

He said, 'I had the idea to show that by lights playing upon the Verrio fresco on the ceiling.'

'Ah! Interesting. Lights interest me very much. I'd like to have been an electrical engineer.'

'I tell you what,' said Piers, 'I've got the notes here that a friend of mine made for me about possible machines and the use of lights.' He took Uncle Jim's notes and drawings from his pocket and handed them to Ralph. 'Keep them. It's a copy of the original.'

'This friend of yours, is he a professional?'

'Yes. He's an officer in R.E.M.E.'

'Oh, I see. He'll have his work cut out if Phaethon ever gets going. If Jove, that is, tells your friend to jump to it in time.'

Magda, who had been standing a demure, adoring maiden (she was obviously nuts about this Ralph), said impatiently – she managed to make even impatience seem shy – 'Give Mr Mosson your play, Ralph. We must go.'

'Okay, Magda, don't get excited. It's just a play I've written. I know you're very busy at the moment, but it might interest you. At any rate, it doesn't take too much notice of the rules.'

'We must go now. I am supposed to be checking a reference at the Westminster Public Library. Poor me! If I am found.'

Oh dear, Piers thought, this fuzzy conspiratorial business again.

'You don't have to hide *your* movements, I hope,' he said to Ralph.

'No. I am everywhere at once. That's the great beauty of my job here. Not that I want you to think that gardening is not my real interest.'

'Oh, I can believe that, but I am incurably ignorant about horticulture. You must talk to my mother. She runs a shrub rose nursery garden in Sussex. You probably know of it.'

'Indeed I do. The most famous in the country. I was able to get Pentreath to send me down there to collect some plants. I'd looked forward to learning a lot. But Mrs Mosson wasn't talking much that day. I don't think she was too well.'

Oh God, Piers thought, but there was nothing in the stuffed owl's face to suggest sarcasm. He said, 'We're having a general meeting and survey here on Tuesday. I'd like you both to come, but perhaps you can't get away. And then my Uncle Hubert will be here and perhaps you wouldn't want him to see you.'

Somehow their manner seemed to demand that he enter some conspiracy. Then, somewhat to his annoyance, they brushed such plotting aside.

'I think I can usually manage to get away,' Magda said coyly. 'I managed to get away from Budapest.'

'Yes, we'll be here,' Ralph said. 'There's nothing like a roving commission to give you the power to move about without being noticed.'

Strange people, Piers thought, yet both of them could well be useful, and they were clearly talented; but they seemed finally to be as they looked – dull, nebulous, talented, impalpable. It wasn't what he was looking for, life seemed to have been pressed out of them both – hey presto, here, hey presto, gone: visitations more than presences. The life he looked for in the next few years, at any rate, must be a great deal larger than that, moving, frightening, absurd, or all three in one, but large, larger than life. And he would find it for himself out of a wide selection; it would not be planted on him from behind columns. There was something disagreeable in the sense that one's 'artistic reverie' (how awful to be an exile in a foreign land – probably the girl could find the right words in her native Hungarian) had been observed – like Hamlet in that spy-filled court. But he reminded himself that Hamlet's preoccupation with soliloquy was half his and half the play's trouble. He would leave to Tom intuitive doubts, omens and half-fears; if he was to do what he wanted with his life, he must learn to see clearly what was before him, select from it and use it. These people were only two among many, he hoped, who would come into his life in the next months and help him to show to a wider, more talented, more influential world what he could offer to it in display and shape and wonder.

But now to practical matters. He went to the great heavy keystoned North Door and gazed with love and excitement at the Hall. Here must be the entrance for the audience – so that they should have before them this view of the vast lantern and of the great twisted pillars and, above all, of the half-lit mysterious story of Phaethon high above. Such a first vision was an essential of the whole dramatic force of his presentation. Only a fraction of the audiences of the three nights would have seen the wonderful Great Hall before. How it must knock them over!

Everything, then – seating, orchestra, stage, machinery, lighting – must, as far as he could fight for it, be subordinated to the securing of this entrance. For this, above all, he must manoeuvre and please, and sacrifice and insist. For this and for his interpretation of the opera as the glory of Phaethon's flight and the tragedy of his fall. Indeed, to secure those aims, he must be ready to fight for the subordination of stage effects, of costumes and lighting, of dancers, even positioning of the orchestra. Many of these would be his own sacrifices and he must surrender dramatically and splendidly at exactly the right moment and so make it hard for the St Paul's ballet mistress and the St Paul's art mistress, and even for Reggie, not to respond with equal sacrifice. The beginning of this war-world he had sensed with *Richard*, and now he could feel it more keenly. He would now serve a more intense training for the wonderful theatre strategy that he longed for as his life to come.

Every battle needed its own strategy – and this one must be fought on the splendours of Vanbrugh and Verrio, so that what was a mere amateur production of adolescent amateur singing and acting and playing could soar at least a little like Phaethon in his borrowed divine chariot. He could do much to point his shape by giving life, fatal, tragic life, to his rash hero, to the ambitious mother, to his father, the glorious Sun King who acknowledged him for his heir. *They* should move with majesty, but freely, fiercely, giving emotional rein to their acting and singing. Yet the dutiful, sad, rejected girl and the defeated rival of Phaethon; Earth, howling to Jove to save her from burning; Jove, hurling his thunderbolt of security and justice, all these forces of order and of domestic love and of sweet content should be given the moral majesty they deserved, but frozen into statue-like postures as they sang their arias of life's lesser, simpler modes. Yes, that was it, two sorts of acting – dramatic-expressive and plain stand-and-deliver should mark his reversal of Jove's order, his celebration of Vanbrugh's glorious bid to encompass the sky.

Perhaps it was a sudden clanking of his heel upon the marble as he arrived at the centre of the Hall, beneath the lantern, midway between the four great columns; but when he turned and faced the imaginary audience, Phaethon's words – '*Il est beau qu'un mortel jusques aux cieux s'élève*' – died on his lips. All the power and determination for which he had prepared his muscles, in anticipation of what he would teach to his hero-actor, froze, until he stood stiffly in statue guise, just as he proposed to instruct the actors cast in the anti-Phaethon roles to stand. It was a frightening reversal of his intention.

Then, suddenly, he knew why. The high discordant noise that came from the jarring of leather upon stone was not music, but it *was* noise without words. He had no music, hardly any noise, only words. And the opera finally rested upon music. Yet he felt sure, as he stood there, that the room, his vision, his will to succeed *could* find accommodation with whatever Reggie Howerton might think was needed to declare the *music*'s power and beauty. But the discordant noise of his shoe against the marble did not only speak of his deafness to music, to all but words, it suggested something more terrible, an insoluble danger. Supposing this very room, the central glory of all he had designed, distorted or blunted or effaced the very sound of voice and instrument which made the opera, then the whole idea would prove an absurdity, a non-starter. Beside this terrible verdict which Tuesday would pronounce, all other judgments to come – family permission, school agreement, the interference of music or dance with his theatrical design – were nothing. On that single test of acoustics, over which he had no power, on which he could make no guess, depended everything.

The realisation that he had lived far ahead of reality, that all his dreams and hopes depended upon a basic, hardly changeable factor, outside any of his powers, caused a strange near-nervous explosion. It seemed to come from a click in his spine, it sent its little tensing pulsations out over all his body, down to the soles of his feet and into his balls, along his arms to every finger of his hands, up into his brain, so that he felt himself neither to see nor to hear as he normally could. This was stage nerves far beyond anything that he had known. And it came upon him unawares again and again in the three following days. He guessed that such feelings would be a central, though spasmodic, part of his life, as he designed it from now on. And yet the dreams and hopes and changing shapes and designs did not come to him less frequently or less excitingly because they rested on ice that might melt at the first, or, to be fair to Reggie, the fifth horrific distorted note which might echo that Tuesday from Vanbrugh's wondrous lantern. Indeed, these recurrent and horrible physical panics somehow formed part of his hopes and dreams, for surely they only came to true artists.

Reggie Howerton had arranged for the auditions to begin very early – half past eight. He wanted them over, he told Piers, before Uncle Hubert and Marina Luzzi and her brilliant friends arrived at eleven.

'It's not fair on the kids,' he said, 'to ask them to face people who scare even me. At least until they've rehearsed a bit and got used to such grand surroundings. And, in any case, we must make our decisions unaided. It will be *our* production. Although let me tell you that Signora Luzzi knows a great deal more about music than I had supposed. Perhaps one misjudges the first-night smart set. But I don't think so. She's an exception.'

So there they had arrived, even in advance of the appointed early hour. Yet, despite the chill of such an hour, with insufficient breakfast, and a beating, anxious heart and pulse, Piers felt the glory of the room as they entered. At least if *everything* went wrong, if the singers were no good, if Uncle Hubert seemed unwilling, if Marina went too far, if the acoustics were poor, Reggie would surely be so overwhelmed by the room's greatness that he would seek with Piers to find a way round all the difficulties.

But horribly, incalculably, it wasn't so. Reggie hardly looked at the room. He seemed obsessed with the fact that the St Paul's Girls' contingent hadn't arrived. Again and again he said, 'This is impossible. Rehearsals must be on time.' Piers felt both too anxious and too affronted to draw attention to their surroundings. He tried to help a little by, at first, pointing out that *they* were early, and, when eight thirty had passed, by murmuring about the unreliability of the Underground. All to no avail. 'This is impossible. Rehearsals must be on time.' The only variation to this reiteration that Reggie made was again and again to fuss the boys, nervous before their auditions, making them move his harpsichord a few paces here and a few paces there, although he had not yet struck a chord.

Nigel Mordaunt, Reggie's brilliant friend from Cambridge – 'at every party, my dear' – stood, it was true, looking up intently at the lantern and across at the mourning virgins in the niches. But, though his tall, slender figure in its elegant bottle green velvet suit seemed to accord beautifully with Vanbrugh's demands, he only said, offhandedly, 'So *this* is the famous room.' Perhaps he sensed Piers' frustration, but if so he misunderstood its cause, for he added, 'Don't worry about Reggie's fussing with the instrument. He's doing it to distract himself from this waiting about. He's quite right, of course – failure to be punctual is the worst canker of any production. It must be cut out from the very start.'

This initial failure of the room to have the overpowering effect on which he had so relied set Piers in a tense condition such as he had never before experienced. And so it lasted through the two hours of listening to aspirants that followed. He simply could not tell whether the singing was good or bad, up to Reggie's expectation or well below it, a matter of surprised pleasure to Mordaunt or of expected scorn. Indeed, in his tension he could often hardly distinguish one sound from another – except where it was a blatant mispronunciation of a French word.

A plain, spectacled girl who, auditioning for Théone, sought to reproach Phaethon for deserting her, made noises which sounded to him so miraculously beautiful that he could not but believe that acoustics were on their side. But Grayson, the American Consul's son, 'up Wren's', who, he had been told, was a splendid bass singer, shot up into such strange shrieks and plunged down into such grim growls as he pronounced Proteus' dreadful prophecy of Phaethon's doom that it seemed to him that this could be no human vagary but the hideous product of a beautiful room's distortion. Was the Hall an acoustic disaster, as after all had been Vanbrugh's London theatre, into which he had sunk so much of his early hopes? Or would it carry sound through its vault with the same magic grace and loveliness that it carried light? The faces of the experts, Reggie and Mordaunt, gave him only the judges' proper neutral answers that they gave to their candidates. Miss Tankerton, the St Paul's music mistress, appeared to be asleep; perhaps, he tried to joke himself out of his anxiety, she was a Christian Scientist like Grandma and had shut her eyes to 'declare the truth' – 'There is no Error in opera.' But he didn't want jokes. He looked to others; all those seeking parts – tenors, sopranos, basses – looked bemused with their own anxieties; the ballet mistress with the rush of teeth to the front smiled as much as her teeth allowed, but it could have been a grimace of ecstasy or despair; the art mistress, who was under his direction to design the sets and costumes, looked only amazed, expecting Mozart perhaps or even Puccini – could the silly bitch at least not have read a little about Lully before she came? Suddenly he saw near the South Door, half hidden by a column, the two dolls – so, they *had* made it, but with such a need to efface themselves that their nullity defied all interpretation. Once he believed that, at last, he would hear a judgment. The ginger-haired, freckled boy with glasses, who

improbably sought to play Mérops, all-powerful King of
Egypt, overlord of the tributary Kings of India and Ethiopia,
suddenly broke off singing, saying, 'Can I begin again, sir?
The room is so vast.' But Reggie's answer gave no clue. He
said, 'Yes, it is, isn't it? Of course. Begin again.'

Yet all through this agony of doubt, this despair that the
whole wonderful flight might never leave the ground, Piers
observed and, with surprise, observed himself observing. The
music seemed a blur, sometimes expressive and pleasing,
sometimes distorted and hideous, mostly dull shapeless voice-
continuity that reflected Reggie's basso continuo on the harpsichord. (He felt that he knew now what was meant by the
statement that Lully had invented musical recitative – was
there no end to the harpsichord?) But the words, the facial
expressions, the movements of heads and of bodies, the very
rare flashes of characterisation, the even rarer flashes of the
singers' personalities that broke through the thick hedge built
up of the clustering, choking anxieties and efforts and desires
to please – all these he registered immediately, as though his
whole life had been spent in verbal and visual appraisal.

Soon five pages of his notebook had been filled, his own selection of the principal roles had been made,*and* with alterna-
tives to meet purely musical objections that might be made to
his first choices. For Phaethon, Strangley, with subtle, supple-
moving body, eyes excited and proud, sure of success, but also
sure of himself if these failed him, his words incisive, clear,
arrogantly certain of his French. He was a most detestable
creature who'd been in O level class with him, but tremendously ambitious. It would be fun, but hard fun, breaking
down his distrust of anyone but himself. But perhaps his voice
– it seemed what he thought 'shouty' – was disastrous; if so he
would take Purrett, hoping to find intelligence and a slightly
wobbly conceit and mould them into noble arrogance, to firm
up pronunciation by strengthening slurred final ts and ds. But
on no account John Martin, such fun and so intelligent. But
there was no place in Phaethon for wit and irony and argument, no easy intimacy to cause one to forget those drooping
shoulders, the sloppily held belly, or the little twitch of the

eyes that seemed in everyday talk a pleasing quirk. No, not John Martin, though Reggie might say he sang like an archangel. And for Climène – *ambitieuse mère* – he knew at once that it must be Linetta Forbes-Brown – God what a name! – who had ambled on to the stage, spectacled, mousy-looking, prematurely stooped, and had transformed herself as she sang, glasses removed, into a proud, passionate, straight-backed matron, demanding recognition for her son, clearly not only out of maternal love but in pride at her own union with the Sun God. It must be her. He could teach her to pronounce French. But he couldn't, he felt sure, teach Stella Sykes, so handsome and stately, to look other than null and sad. No, she, if Reggie approved, could be offered Théone, whose piteous plaint of Phaethon's desertion of her would be amply expressed by such waxwork posture and great empty dark eyes, such accurate dead French speech. And as to age, they were both only girls; but the one had power to project herself, while the other was a shapely column. As he filled the pages and saw the whole cast being formed, he observed himself as the observer and felt more sure than he had ever been that he must give his life to staging plays, whatever checks and barriers might arise.

As, for example, here, the potential deadly judgment – impossible acoustics. But now he felt a little relieved. They had auditioned the Prologue last. Reggie had just dismissed the chorus of four girls who sought to be Astrée's followers. The sickening eulogy of Louis XIV's reign of peace had come to an end – 'The whole universe stands awed before the author of such sweet repose.' Sweet repose! What a gift to offer civilisation! And now Reggie was signalling that the audition was at an end. He called to Miss Tankerton, over by the South Portico, to two boys who had stood by the North Door, to a group of boys and girls up in the gallery.

'Audibility?'

'Perfect.'

'Wonderful.'

'Couldn't be better.'

'Well, of tone and distortions, I think *we'll* be the judges, don't you?' he said, and his question, addressed to Mordaunt, seemed to take in Piers with an ironic glint of the eye that admitted their joint knowledge of Piers' ignorance of the subject.

The young Cypriot footman approached Piers, who relayed, 'Shall they serve coffee now, sir?' 'Reggie', they had tacitly agreed, was not for public use unless and until the rehearsals grew red hot.

'Oh, I think so, Van. Could you arrange it so that *we* have it here and the applicants are served elsewhere?'

His question hovered between Piers and the footman. Piers noted this social uncertainty with satisfaction. It was snobbish nonsense, of course, but it could give him an upper hand over Reggie when they came to work at Tothill. Immediately he thought superstitiously, I mustn't say 'when' but 'if'.

The footman led the way for the Westminster boys and the St Paul's girls with the ballet mistress and the art mistress towards the East Wing. Miss Tankerton was following them, but Reggie called her back.

'*You're* one of the judges. You can't get out of it,' and, when she demurred, he said, 'No, no. You stay and see fair play. We're not having any women's rights complaints afterwards. Anyway, Nigel's agreed to be referee.'

'I didn't. Oh my God! You'll both hate me for ever after.'

But, looking at him, Piers could see that the elegant Mordaunt was quite prepared to put any music teachers down if it was needed in the cause of art, and with full expectation that they would accept his verdict.

'I don't know when I have been so frightened,' Miss Tankerton said jollily. 'Nigel Mordaunt! Aren't you scared?' she asked Piers, in a jolly way again.

He nodded but he felt that his terror was on a different, higher level than hers. Snobbery again, though not social this time. What a help it was in time of need! So, laughing, the four of them moved to the sofa and chairs around the table by the flaming malachite bowl, where coffee and fudge cake (a standby of Jackie's) were served – only Piers wasn't really laughing, his bowels were churning too much.

'One thing, I am sure you'll all agree. The acoustics are superb!' Reggie said – and as Mordaunt and Miss Tankerton nodded, he added, 'So we needn't worry about that.'

He glanced at Piers. Even through the wonderful joy of Piers' relief at this declaration there wove a thread of annoyance that clearly his agitation had been an object of Reggie's affectionate amusement. There seemed no end to the penalties of being young.

All the same, he felt his stomach wholly settled, he breathed freely, he bit into a slice of sugary, buttery fudge cake. There was no natural objection to overcome. Nature, or rather Vanbrugh's art, had not stood in his way. Every obstacle from now on would be some human objection or disagreement that he could surmount or dislodge by his greater vision or his sharp wits or, at a pinch, and most ignobly, by youth's charm. *Phaethon would* be performed in the Great Hall. He would see to it.

At first he sat in a daze as they talked – 'quite a surprising gift for joining phrase to phrase', 'no sense of the melodic line in that very happy little aria – Lully at his best, I think', 'I would have liked more rhythmic precision', 'Yes, there is a great sense of strain. Rehearsals could be a help, but I'm afraid of the performances. There could be some very nasty noises', 'a very nice gentle pianissimo there', 'it would be a simple enough transposition. I'll think about it', 'I was playing pianissimo as it was. Honestly with the bassoons and trumpets I don't think he'll be heard'; and, like a basso continuo, Miss Tankerton repeating, 'I should have liked a little more *expression*. It's so important if we are to bring an opera of this sort alive.' Piers sat silent, waiting for something that seemed even faintly an intelligible cue.

And then it came. Reggie said, 'And now for Climène. Handsome mother of a handsome son. I think Stella Sykes, don't you? She's a bit of a stick, but her voice is splendid. And that's all really that's required. The spectacled girl with the absurd name sang well but she tries to make the line too expressive. She projects herself too much. I suppose to compensate for the glasses.'

Miss Tankerton said, 'Poor Linetta! But you're quite right. I am always telling her not to try so hard. And Stella is so dignified.'

Piers forced himself to speak. 'I'm afraid I think that's all she is. If her voice is as good as you all say, then I think she should play the poor rejected Théone. She has just the right kind of empty statuesque look. But if Linetta Forbes-Brown,' he pronounced the name casually, hoping to make them a little ashamed of their mockery of it, 'whose glasses have nothing to do with it because she wisely removed them before singing, also has a voice as good as you say, then I am sure that she has all the acting power to make us feel her indignation and her pride and her ambition. It's so essential to the building up of the tragedy of her son Phaethon.'

'Stella for Théone,' Miss Tankerton cried. 'But surely we want a pretty, appealing little thing for the deserted girl.'

'Her appeal is in being deserted, that's all. She must be sad and we must be sorry for her. But we don't have to love her for it. She's not one of the burning, active spirits of life. She's not on Phaethon's side.'

'Golly,' cried Nigel.

'Oh, Van has a theory,' Reggie explained, 'it's not at all bad, though perverse. But I doubt if we can work it into the production.'

'It isn't a question of working it *in*, Reggie.' There seemed no possibility of 'sir' at this junction, though he saw a slightly jarred smile on Miss Tankerton's lips. 'It's a question of the basis *on* which the whole thing works.'

'Explain,' Nigel said. 'This opera could do with a bit of perversity.' Looking down, he added to himself, 'I think the composer would have liked it.'

So Piers explained about Phaethon and his supporters, their tragic, wayward, ambitious, living humanity, and about Jove and his son and their supporters, who included the rejected girl, and their noble, ordered, smug, dead statuary; he described the parallel of Lully's brilliant art and Louis' solemn regality. He felt it wiser not to say anything of Vanbrugh, lest he seemed to be making too personal a plea.

'Gracious!' cried Miss Tankerton. 'I *have* misunderstood the play.'

'You see,' Reggie said, 'it's fascinating but off-key, I think.'

Nigel Mordaunt allowed a little smile to play upon his elegant, olive skinned camel's face. 'I suspect that it is a whole lot of delectable nonsense, but I think you'd both be very wise to let Mosson produce it the way he wants. It has got some surprisingly good music, this opera, but it is, let's face it, a tiny bit empty. And if you do it here, Reggie, you will get some quite lively people arriving just because of the place. They won't be expecting too much musically. And, if I may say so, I think that among both the boys and the girls we've heard this morning there's more than enough well-taught talent to satisfy. But this room will stun the whole audience, I think. It's a stunning place, I'm only just beginning to recover from my excitement when I first came in. But they'll recover too, and you don't want them to be bored by contrast. Now, if we play it Mosson's way, they may, frankly I think they *will* disagree, but they'll be interested. It's been thought out and felt and that will come over. But if we *do* accept your ideas for production, Mosson, they can't, you know, be allowed to permit any choice that subordinates the music.'

'I should have thought,' Piers said very tentatively, 'but, of course, I don't know, that if opera meant anything, the acting, the characters, what I want will come naturally out of the music, if the singers listen carefully enough and feel music more than I probably can.'

'Yes,' said Nigel, 'but not what *you* want finally, what *we* all believe the composer wants.'

'But what about Quinault?' Piers asked. 'What about the librettist?'

'Ah,' Nigel answered, 'I refer that to you, Reggie,' as though a dangerous strike had broken out in his presence.

Reggie said, 'I think it interesting enough to give Van his head.'

'So do I,' Miss Tankerton agreed and gave a smile to Piers such as he had received from his grandmother as a small boy when she gave him a present.

'But,' Nigel added, '*Phaethon is* an opera, it hasn't been played for two and a half centuries and we owe it to Lully that his many very original contributions and his often delightful airs are given the best musical performance that an amateur cast can provide.'

So Linetta Forbes-Brown was cast for Phaethon's *mère ambitieuse* and Stella Sykes was to sing Théone's plaintive cry of '*Ah, qu'il est difficile que l'amour soit tranquille.*' Piers, mocking himself, took Nigel Mordaunt for his hero immediately. And sought imitative hero worship. He tried to look with inflated nostrils as though, camel-like, something disagreeable was within reach of his powers of smell. He decided – a velvet suit, yes, but Prussian blue would be more suitable for his fair complexion and blond hair than the bottle green which truly suited Mordaunt's Levantine colouring.

But he soon learned that Mordaunt was one who meant what he said. He proposed Strangley for Phaethon, and his new hero was down upon him at once.

'The movie star! Oh, no, no. It would be all right if he was a boy Callas – not easy to imagine, is it?'

Reggie and Miss Tankerton laughed delightedly. 'But he isn't. Those ghastly strident noises above the stave. Anyway, all those faces and throwing about of the arms! One would think you'd trained him for silent films, Reggie.'

'Except,' said Miss Tankerton teasingly, 'that Mr Howerton is far too young to have seen one.'

'*He*'s one of those old movie snobs who see nothing else,' said Reggie and they all laughed.

Piers wondered why, when such an important battle was being waged, they wasted their energy on so much flirtatious teasing. He put it down to their being unhappy to leave their youth behind them.

So Purrett was chosen for Phaethon, although Piers protested that, intelligent though he was, and quick, he was not very sure of himself, hardly knew Phaethon's rash daring.

'Then you must give confidence to him,' Mordaunt said. 'That's the producer's job.'

'I'm surprised you didn't choose your friend, John Martin,'

Reggie remarked, 'he's such an amusing, intelligent person.'

'Is his voice good?' Piers asked.

'I'm afraid not very.'

'I am surprised *you* suggested him.'

'We *are* learning,' Miss Tankerton commented.

Piers thought it unwise to make her an enemy, although he couldn't see, once rehearsals began, that they would meet. But she might be difficult about the girls' rehearsal attendances, or influence them against him. He must take no chances. He tried unaffected sincerity as a charm.

'*I'm* learning a great deal,' and he looked at her very simply and – he hoped – boyishly. After all, it was true.

She wasn't quite mollified. 'Are you? I don't trust you. I don't quite know where I am with you yet.' But she gave him a smile to show that she meant less than she had said.

All the same, Piers was cheered to hear the interruption of voices – he could discern Hubert's even above Marina's excited screams.

'I think that's my uncle.'

'It's certainly Signora Luzzi,' Reggie said. 'Well, we've made very good progress. I think we can safely leave the rest of the casting until the end of the week. Could you manage a meeting at my house? Friday drink time, six o'clock?'

From the West Saloon appeared a small party led by Marina. The four at the table stopped their consultation.

'If you will all excuse me,' Miss Tankerton said, 'where will I find my children? No, don't come with me, just tell me.'

'I think you want the East Saloon,' Piers said. 'You can't miss it. There's a large Zoffany on the wall immediately opposite you, showing the Royal Society meeting in their Hall. They look rather like we must do now,' he added, watching a little group of visitors forming between the great columns. Miss Tankerton smiled and was gone.

Reggie said with a touch of chiding, 'A lot of schoolboys and girls eating and drinking would have been a much better guide than Zoffany.'

Nigel laughed. 'He can't help taking Zoffanys and Vanbrughs for granted. Don't be so narrow, Reggie.'

Although all three laughed, Piers thought, there doesn't seem to be a single advantage that isn't a disadvantage as well.

Reggie said, 'I think *I'll* go and see how the boys are getting on. Make my excuses to the smart set, Van. We'll all come back in five minutes.'

Nigel Mordaunt, turning immediately to Piers, asked, 'Why do you dismiss the world and its simple joys so early in life? I hope it isn't that too much Vanbrugh and Zoffany have filled you with youth's ennui.'

'Oh no, I'm only a visitor here. Anyway the Zoffany's one of the least of the pictures, unless it be a portrait of my grandmother by someone called Laszlo. It's just that surely there's more to it than quiet delight. Something a bit beyond everyday pleasantness that's worth taking risks for. Some shape you can make out of life. I suppose Phaethon has always obsessed me since I wondered at the beauty of the Verrio ceiling as a small kid. It's not very good, I know now, but it seemed a miracle to me then.' He suddenly felt that he could say no more to anyone about this. And he stopped speaking abruptly.

'Well, steady on with the Peter Pan stuff. "I want always to be a little boy and have fun" and all that.'

'But I *don't*. And taking risks isn't just having fun.'

'All right. All right. But I warn you – you will surely have problems. Your vision isn't going always to harmonise with Reggie's musical feeling, at any rate with his chronometric order. And, by and large, *you'll* have to give way and you *should* do so. But don't let me discourage you. Out of such battles are born enlargements – celestial visions and echoes, if you like. Anyway, the opera isn't so good that it forbids sacrilege.'

Piers, thank God, was saved from attempting to express his overwhelming gratitude by more than a smile and a nod, for Marina had descended upon them.

''Ullo, Nigel. 'Ow's it gone? Were the kids awful? Where's 'Owerton? 'Ow do you like Piers? 'E's amusing, isn't 'e?' She bent her head towards Nigel Mordaunt and received his kiss on her cheek, indeed he enfolded her mink-clad form in his arms.

'Darling!' he said. 'Your voice! The echoes in this wondrous Hall. But it *is* enchantment. You were quite right. Before you made your grand Brunhilde, we'd just said the acoustics were perfect. Now, I really don't know.'

Marina kissed Piers. 'Isn't Nigel a beast?' she asked. 'But a clever one. Don't forget that, my dear. Oh, it's wonderful. 'Ubert's woken up. 'E was superb telling us all about this 'ouse. Of course, 'e prefers the Pratt. But that's sense too. I think Pratt's the English Palladio. 'Ubert really knows this 'ouse. And to think it 'as all become so dead. These corridors should be alive with people. Life never stopping. Music. Laughing and fun. It should be amusing. That great Gallery! What feasts we could 'ave there. These awful Mossons! They're like – what do you call the people that bury you? And all the servants are dead. No Figaros! No Susannas! Oh, not you, darling Piers. And not my darling 'Ubert after today. I 'ave woken the Mossons up. *She* won't like it, but we shall see who will win. You will 'elp us, Nigel? This schools nonsense is just a start. After that, it's the 'ouse and me – us,' she said, putting her arm round Piers' neck.

Nigel laughed. 'I've never heard you say "us" before, Marina, darling. But, yes, I'd love to help "us".'

'Oh, you'll really hear about "us", you rude beast, this morning. But now we go over to listen to 'Ubert.'

CHAPTER V

A Marriage Has Been Arranged

IT WAS his uncle's peroration, but Piers could hardly believe his ears – his uncle sounded so simple, so direct, of course pompous a bit, loving making his speech, but unboring, even a bit inspired.

'I don't apologise,' he said, 'for showing you Pratt's greatness first. It's so easy to take for granted, even to belittle, after the stunning effect that Vanbrugh has provided here. I'm very proud of my two ancestors who gave the opportunities to these two architects. It would have been very easy for them not to have done so. The old Tothill House must have been a beautiful building, if rather a muddle, as you can see from the stable blocks, though they have been made to look older than their Tudor origin by Vanbrugh. For all his astonishing verve and almost ruthless flair for originality, he had a very special reverence for the medieval that was almost unknown in his time. Yet these two very different men, Thomas Tothill, essentially a slow-moving, hard-headed man of affairs, and Francis Tothill, essentially a quick-witted, graceful courtier, in turn, took the risk of choosing architects who were not easy, safe bets and were rewarded by the wonderful results you have seen. We Mossons couldn't have done it. I know I couldn't. We could take commercial risks – the slave trade, however reprehensible, was no certain investment, nor were the sugar plantations, nor has banking been, as my friend John Wallis will agree.'

134

The distinguished grey-haired man referred to, whom Piers had taken for a music critic, gave a nod that must surely be a signal of assent used at board meetings.

'But for the Mossons, there was always the heavy weight of joylessness. The Evangelical creed of my ancestors that led my great great great grandfather to free his slaves, though very honourable, was not a joyous Calvinism. And you need, I suspect, a sheer joy in letting your imagination go, if you are to invest in a Pratt or a Vanbrugh. The Mossons haven't had it, although, thanks to my dear mother's love of beauty that she brought to us from across the Atlantic, Tothill House, I hope you all feel, still has what my mother calls the beauty of mature repose. You were saying, Lady Beale, how you loved the flower decorations. I only wish that Mother had been here to hear you.'

A fat, jolly woman smiled in response and waved a cheery hand. Piers heard a snuffling beside him, like a wild boar, or a sow with young. Oh, damn, he thought, Marina. But it seemed that Jackie's absence was sufficient to appease her, for there was no outburst.

'But the Mossons have been worthy. Worthiness has kept the building in decent repair. And I am afraid I shall always be worthy. I was brought up that way. But worthiness doesn't encourage the imagination that led so improbably to Thomas and Francis Tothill commissioning this house and what is more, as I've told you, having a good deal of say in what was built. To have employed Pratt, an architect who was thought to be finished, who had come to London a broken man, to see his wonderful Piccadilly mansion, Clarendon House, being pulled down by property speculators, for we've always had those in plenty, that was courageous.'

A heavily built man with a guards' officer moustache, next to Lady Beale, perhaps Lord Beale, said, 'Hear, hear!'

'To employ a man of the past like that to build a great new mansion was a wonderful act of imagination. And marvellous to think of that delightful man, Sir Roger Pratt, the very type of English country gentleman with genius – and more English country gentlemen have genius than is commonly thought –

building here his last and, I shall say, his greatest house, certainly the only one to survive intact today. Of course, it was
not completed, and a streak of worthiness in me tells me it
should have been finished after Pratt's death in the style he had
chosen. But it's probably unimaginative worthiness, for look
at what a miracle we have here. This Great Hall of Vanbrugh's
built into, even extending Pratt's splendid house, has always
seemed to me to explain that otherwise mysterious saying "In
my end was my beginning".'

Piers, turning involuntarily towards the fiery bowl, saw
that Reggie had returned with the St Paul's mistress and all the
aspirants, and that all were standing huddled below the staircase, held silent by the authority and personal emotion of his
uncle's speaking.

'I would almost say, indeed, with my grandfather and my
dear mother absent, I *shall* say thank God that the Tothills,
father and son, were *not* worthy Mossons, otherwise we
shouldn't have this miracle. Although the more lurid aspects
of their lives, so loved by the historical novelists, are what
unfortunately have been handed down to us, those over-
advertised debauches don't explain what they gave us here.
Frivolous debauchees don't have that amount of imagination.
But the historical novelists – I don't of course mean fine writers like Elvira Stuart, whose book on Queen Anne is so much
more than a novel and set me on the track of my ancestor
Francis . . .'

A tall handsome blonde-grey woman made a moue which
suggested that no statement of her difference from the race of
Georgette Heyer was needed.

'. . . but the run of the mill historical novelists who are like
the popular newspapers, they have very little imagination, and
what they have is that of a dirty-minded schoolboy.'

'Shame! Shame!' came from Nigel Mordaunt, and was taken
up laughingly by Reggie and some of the others.

Hubert said, 'There are no dirty-minded schoolboys at
Westminster. I know because I was there. Some, it was true,
had sophisticatedly decorative minds, but I am not going to
complain of them. My own emancipation, such as it was, came
from them.'

Marina said, 'Oh, my God,' but not very loudly.

'Anyway, Francis Tothill had the courage to commission a young man, fresh from the army, not too long out of the Bastille as a matter of fact, soon to be one of our wittiest play-wrights, a young man with no technical knowledge of archi-tecture, so far as was known, whatever. And so we have the first Vanbrugh building. I won't say the best. I must tread carefully here. We do not have the wonderful dome of Van-brugh's next work at Castle Howard, but this magnificent painted ceiling and our lovely lantern, Vanbrugh's tribute to Pratt, have a special beauty, I think. We do not have the glorious landscapes of Yorkshire. But you must remember that in 1697 we looked from the topmost storey here far across the river and straight upon the Abbey. No, it's needed the horse sense of the Mossons to keep Tothill alive, but it needed the imagination and daring of the Tothills to build it. I think there is a Mosson who *has* something in him akin to the Tothills – I mean my nephew. I have enough of my Mother's American blood in me to say, "Everyone, meet my nephew, Piers".'

And now it was like the cinema, Piers felt, as he smiled and responded to bows (mock bows!) and little friendly waves and conforming smiles.

'He, through the lucky and exciting inspiration of Marina – for whom I claim the credit – has the chance to produce a French opera which my ancestor, Sir Francis, on the urging of Vanbrugh himself, intended to produce here in 1697, but which, being French, met with William III's disapproval. He'll tell you all about it. Whether it is to be produced or not depends on what they've discovered about the acoustics and the suitability of the room during their auditions which were being held here this morning while we were looking at the house. When I say "they" I mean, of course, my friend Reggie Howerton, director of musical studies at Westminster School. Well?' he asked Reggie.

Nigel Mordaunt, standing next to Piers, whispered, 'God! *He*'s a gambler, supposing the answer were to be no.'

But already the answer 'yes' was given. Piers whispered back, 'He never gambles, I'm absolutely sure. His life is free from all taint of risk. He must have *known*.'

'We shall be honoured,' Reggie was saying. 'I think it could be a rather special occasion, although I would beg you all to remember that we are school amateurs. There may be some problems about siting the orchestra. For we can hardly dig a pit.'

Hubert cried, 'No, you can't.'

'And I don't want to build up a stage which would spoil the proportions of the Hall as the audience will see it, although, of course, we shall need to build raked seats for the audience on each side of the North Door.'

My God, Piers thought, he's seen it as I have.

And Reggie added, 'Lastly I must confirm the arrangement with the headmaster. But from all he has said to me, I think that's a formality.'

'And I,' Hubert replied, 'will have to talk to my grand-father, which means, since he is now over ninety and not always quite himself, seeking the right moment. But I think I can safely say that that, too, is a formality. Which being so, we can issue an invitation now for next summer. Invite them all to come, Piers.'

It suddenly seemed a bit stuffy and comic, but nevertheless it was a wonderful victory.

'Ladies and Gentlemen,' Piers began, 'We invite you all here to a performance of Lully's opera *Phaethon*, to be held in this Great Hall some evening next June, the date to be announced later, and to be performed by singers from St Paul's Girls' School and St Peter's College, Westminster, Westminster School to all of you. Musical Director and Conductor – Reginald Howerton, Theatrical Producer, me.' He could not prevent himself from giving Marina a big kiss on the mouth. 'Thank you, darling,' he said.

'Oh no!' Uncle Hubert cried. 'You're not instructing *me* in *my* part, Piers. Before that goes any further, I'd better say that this reign of imagination here at Tothill is to be inaugurated by the engagement of Marina Luzzi to be my wife.' And he added, 'More important to you, your hostess at a banquet which I propose to give in the Long Gallery, which many of you greatly admired this morning.'

As though by magic, Gates with the two footmen appeared, bearing trays with glasses of champagne and smoked salmon rolled in brown bread.

Piers found that he had made those around him laugh, for he said spontaneously, 'I wish Pratt were here, he can eat smoked salmon till he's sick.'

And now it was all meeting people. It seemed that Lady Norah, who looked older than mountains, *was* in fact very old indeed, but that nothing was ever done in connection with opera that she didn't know about. She appeared to be much worried about the date of the performance of *Phaethon* and got out a small diary and blinked at Piers a great deal and got immensely muddled about the dates of Salzburg and La Scala and Verona and Glyndebourne and Edinburgh and Aldeburgh, but she kept on reiterating to Piers:

'We don't have to worry about the Spoleto dates. I never go to Spoleto. Although I am told most happy things of Charleston.'

She'd lost the habit of America, she told Piers, because all her old friends at the Met had died off. In the end she almost bullied him into giving a very unlikely date for *Phaethon* which accorded happily with a blank in her diary.

'Will dear Sylvia be singing?' she asked. 'That's what we shall all want to know. But I am sure you're not going to tell us yet.'

Piers realised that she had no idea that the Tothill venture would be an amateur school performance. But Marina rescued him.

'So you 'ave got 'old of Piers, Lady Norah. You always get 'old of the amusing people. Isn't 'e amusing?' She took Piers across to his uncle's group. 'Oh, my darling! Lady Norah 'as 'er 'and on you now. She's terribly important, very old, and 'orribly boring.'

Then Hubert introduced him to this man Wallis, who it seemed was on a number of the boards of directors on which Hubert also sat and was himself a banker and, like Hubert, descendant of an old banking family.

The conversation now, however, seemed a little more relevant. Moreover, it transpired that, despite all those meetings
on boards, Wallis had never connected Hubert with opera
until now (in which, thought Piers, he was quite right), yet he
himself was a tremendous opera buff – he was a Friend of
Glyndebourne and a Friend of Aldeburgh, and a Friend of
King's Lynn and had been a great Friend of Sadler's Wells in
the old days and attended Covent Garden on all first nights
now. And Uncle Hubert had known none of this until today
(as why on earth should he, Piers thought). But he seemed
very happy now that he did know it. Suddenly Piers knew
why, clearly Sir John Wallis (that was his full name) was the
only one of Hubert's business associates who was also in
Marina's circle. He watched his uncle's sense of alienation,
schizophrenia almost, which, for all his new gaiety and liveliness, had seemed somehow to dog the post-Marina Hubert,
fading away.

He said to Piers, 'Are they all happy, your friends? This is
nice, isn't it? Do you realise that Sir John recognised the Louis
XV ormolu commode in the Saloon as the twin of one at the
Victoria and Albert Museum? He thinks they must have been
commissioned as a pair.'

Piers hadn't realised, but he was most interested in the idea.
He said, 'Grandmother will be fascinated by that.'

But he wished he hadn't because Hubert pouted and looked
at the ground.

'I wonder how they got separated,' Sir John said. 'I'll talk to
Griffin in the furniture department at the V. & A. He's
a knowledgeable creature, though hardly amusing. But
there must be something about the purchase in the Tothill
papers.'

And then Hubert had to say that most of the work had been
done on the Mossons and not on the Tothills and Sir John
found it hard to believe, for really, if it came to bankers, the
Wallises were rather more interesting, weren't they? Their
East India connection, and their involvement with the cor-
ruption charges against Warren Hastings.

'And we haven't neglected them,' Sir John said. 'I've had a

young chap, an economic historian from London University, working on the Bank archives and the family papers for some time. But that's a business affair with some domestic history thrown in. The Tothills are a cultural and social history of England in themselves. It was one of them, surely, later, who went with Athenian Stuart to Paestum?'

Obviously the pretty, dark woman, with cascading earrings, who turned out to be Lady Wallis, thought all this was a little too deprecating of the Mossons. She said:

'Darling, really, you and lack of tact! Here are the two principal living Mosson males and you talk about the Mosson family as though they weren't there.'

They all laughed, including, Piers noticed, Hubert, who laughed much more when Marina did her cheek-rubbing act with the back of her hand on his face and said,

'Oh, I can tell you 'e is *very* much there, aren't you, 'Ubert, darling?'

Sir John turned to Piers.

'You're just going up to Oxford, I hear, to read History. So you're the man for the job. You must write the history of the Tothills.'

Piers could think of no more irrelevant suggestion, but he was saved from replying by Marina.

'Oh, Piers 'as got wonderful artistic things to do.'

And Hubert said, 'He's got to get a First. That's what he's got to do.' But he smiled at his nephew almost as admiringly as Marina did.

'No,' said Marina, 'We 'ave a brilliant girl, a 'Ungarian, who will write the 'istory of the Tothills. She was responsible for finding this information about Lully's opera.'

Piers was not surprised when, as it seemed from the floor, appeared Magda. She had a small bouquet of anemones de Caen which she presented to Marina with a curtsey.

'We are so happy at your happy news,' she said.

Lady Wallis laughed. 'The presentation to the Count and Countess to the life.'

Her husband commented, 'Susanna', and she said reprovingly, 'Darling'.

But clearly Hubert did not know the allusions, and Marina was too intent. ''Ere's the girl, 'Ubert, to make the research for the 'istory of the Tothills. And then *you* will write it. And everyone will be so surprised and fascinated. And we will 'ave a lot of parties for amusing people. Do you like that, John, does that fit with your idea?'

Sir John said, 'It sounds perfect. It could be a best seller.'

'Oh, 'Ubert darling, wouldn't that be lovely? And then I will come with you to sign books at 'Arrods. Say yes. Make it my engagement present. Don't be an old bore, darling.'

'It's a good programme,' Hubert said, but Piers thought he was a little cross at being nailed down in public. 'The only thing is the work on the Mosson second volume. And then there's the general Library correspondence to keep up.'

'The Mosson 'istory could be done at the Bank, as John says. Or old Miss Mackintosh could do it by 'erself. My dear,' she said to Lady Wallis, 'the Librarian 'ere is quite extraordinary. Like Elsa Maxwell. Only always in a man's mackintosh. What this poor child 'as to put up with.'

Piers thought a little levity might help at this point, to divert the topic, so he said to Magda, 'Are you allergic to mackintoshes?'

'I shall be so happy to work on the Tothill archives also with my other work,' was her simple reply.

'Of course you shall not,' Marina cried. 'We didn't bring you from Budapest, from those communist beasts, to make you work like a slave.'

Piers thought that if Ma were here, she would think all this business talk before visitors in very bad form. But perhaps that's just middle-class gentility. All this conflict between Tothill and the Nursery standards that he and Pratt had known since childhood was impenetrable. Surely it no longer mattered. But he did look at the Wallises with embarrassment and he thought Sir John had mockery in his brown spaniel's eyes.

Perhaps it was this that urged Hubert to say in a commanding voice, 'We'll make a start on the history of the Tothills next week. And *you* will be in charge of it, Miss Sczekerny. I will speak to Miss Lynmouth. If she needs more help, we can

employ a young library assistant. Does that satisfy you, darling?' he asked Marina.

'You are a darling, 'Ubert.'

'Ah! Hubert's famous in the City for his decisions.'

'Darling,' said Lady Wallis, 'I think we ought to go over and
speak to old Norah. I am always so worried these days that she
may start undressing and trying to get into bed. She has the
vaguest notion of where she is. It's too disappointing that
Sylvia hasn't come, Marina. But we'll wait a little longer.'

'All right, Janey,' her husband said.

'Aiee! Aiee!' Marina said, 'they're *so* boaring. Piers, you
must meet Elvira. She wants to know what you are going to do
about costumes. All those biographies and novels of 'ers are
full of costumes. Darling Giles said 'er life of Queen Anne was
a royal laundry list. Isn't that amusing?'

Elvira Stuart was a formidably handsome, bulldog-faced
woman. She was talking to a slight young man, whom she
introduced as Laurence Frayne, a Covent Garden costume
man, but he said nothing, except 'Lovely, I'm sure' in a cockney accent, when Piers was presented to him.

'Well, how are you going to dress it?' she asked. 'You'll have
to think about Verrio's blues and greens if you're going to
make the most of this wonderful room.'

Piers told her about his ideas for giving Jove and his followers Louis XIV perukes to crown their classical costumes.

'Hm,' she said. 'Don't be too clever. It's always embarrassing. Have you got a goddess as well as Jove and the gods?'

'Yes, there's Astrée. She's the Queen of the Prologue,
which is all about the graceful beauties of Louis Quatorze's
court.'

'Oh, well, you could give her a high head-dress with comb
and lace. It would have the same effect as a high peruke. And
it's quite authentic for Mary the Second's or Anne's reign.'

'Oh, super. It isn't just going to be the girls in classical ballet
gowns. I am so pleased. We have so much of that at school. All
these Greek tunics and sandals. It's so commonplace.' The St
Paul's art mistress had joined them. 'I am so excited to hear
you have *ideas*, Mr Mosson. I was wondering whether Phae-

thon and his rival couldn't wear Roman armour like that statue
of Charles II in Soho Square, or all those monuments in the
Abbey, you must know them. After all, they're young men
and in a sense they *are* warriors.'

'May I think about that?' Piers said. He had already thought
and knew at once that, turning Phaethon into a statue, it
would go directly against his scheme. He saw battles ahead.

But he was cheered by Elvira Stuart's reaction. 'Jolly sound
answer,' she said. 'Stall. Always remember these grand scale
amateur shows can so easily turn into dressing-up-box
charades. There's nothing more embarrassing. Isn't that the
case?' she asked the Covent Garden man.

'I don't know, love, I'm sure,' he said. 'I only do foundations.'

The art mistress smiled quizzically at Piers. 'We'll talk about
it later in a more congenial atmosphere. Why don't you come
over and meet Miss Livingstone, who's going to do the cho-
reography? I wonder what you'll make of *her*.'

It seemed to Piers that, for him, it was more important to
make some link with the people he was going to work with
than with people with important names like Elvira Stuart, so
he risked her displeasure by following the art mistress. However, he was gratified that the popular writer gave him a wink.

'I'll send you some drawings of those head-dresses,' she
said. He returned her wink as he thanked her. So it *was* possible to keep in with two opposing camps. That was useful to
know.

He was disconcerted, however, to hear the Covent Garden
young man say, 'Mm. He's quite the little Lord of the Manor,
isn't he?' as they moved away.

Miss Livingstone was altogether easier to deal with. When
the art mistress introduced Piers, she said, 'He's full of ideas,
Laura. I had to rescue him from that disapproving woman like
a bulldog.'

A stream of words rushed from between Miss Livingstone's
protruding teeth. 'My dear Alma, do you know who you're
talking about? That's Elvira Stuart, the writer. She's very important. Isn't Alma awful, Mr Mosson? But she's always like

that. I am afraid you won't find me full of ideas. I see it quite
simply. I think the dances of the Prologue with Astrée the
goddess and her followers and the return of the Golden Age,
when everything is happy and peaceful, should be as nice as we
can make them, you know, some charming country dance,
with the girls scattering flowers. And that kind of thing, too,
later, for the dances of the Hours and the Seasons. But with the
chorus of Egyptians and all those gipsies and Indians at the
Temple, when they hail Phaethon as the new Sun, I thought
something a little exotic and off-putting. I mean almost not
very nice.' To emphasise this concept, perhaps, she landed a
large gobbet of spit on Piers' coat, but she was obviously used
to such communication. 'I mean both stately and cruel. I suppose you might say a ritual dance. So that we don't feel a part
of them. Beautiful but frightening, if you know what I mean,
like Phaethon himself.'

Piers did know what she meant, and he saw that she meant
exactly what he did but from the opposite side.

So he said, 'That sounds excellent,' and wondered how long
it would be before someone told her of his view.

However, to have dealt with so much in so short a time was
exhilarating, and when Purrett came up to him and said: 'I
expect you know that I have been chosen for Phaethon,
Mosson,' he was ready to lie, and said, 'Yes. After all, I did a
lot of the choosing.'

He noted with satisfaction that the boy's cheeks flushed
with pleasure. He would play on that, and he spoke of the
splendid ambition and daring of Phaethon, the hero. Purrett
was clearly surprised.

'Oh, I thought he was a bit of a twit, falling in the river like
that. But what you say goes.'

'Look, we'll go through the text together on Thursday and
I'll show you how the whole tragedy centres round you.
Don't you want to be the centre of the audience's admiration,
even of their terror?' He was apprehensive of the answer, but
there was no doubt when it came.

'Oh, that's more than fine by me, if you say so.'

Flattery could do no harm, especially if it were honest, Piers thought. So he said, 'Your French diction is first rate.'

'Well, it ought to be. You see, my mother's French. But my German's better.'

'But not so relevant.'

'No, I suppose not.' Purrett did not smile. There was no danger here, Piers considered, of the actor undercutting his heroism by misplaced moments of humour. He felt that it wasn't going to be too hard with all these people, if he remembered the basic urge of all human beings to shine.

He was, however, a bit perplexed when the guards-sergeant-major-looking man who'd said 'Hear! Hear!' about property development came up to him and said:

'The Musical Director tells me you're going to have problems in this Hall in constructing machines for this opera. What sort of effects do they have to produce?'

'Well, the Temple doors open of their own accord to reveal flames and spectres, Phaethon's chariot must fall from the Heavens, and . . .'

'That's enough for the moment. You're likely to have difficult constructional problems on your hands. I am fascinated by everything to do with opera. Here's my card. Let me know if I can help. I must go now.'

The card read 'Lord Beale' and an address in Grosvenor Square.

But *everyone* was going now. The school parties had left and Piers joined Marina and his uncle to say goodbye to the other guests.

Lady Norah blinked at Marina as she said goodbye. 'What a tragedy for you, Sylvia Armitage not appearing for her part. Never mind, you'll have to find some sort of substitute. We can't all get the moon by reaching for it.'

Sir John laughed at the old woman's confusion. 'All the same,' he said, 'it *is* a real disappointment not meeting *la divine Sylvie.*'

'Yes. I am so sorry for you, Marina. I know what store you set upon her coming. And it's not like her to stand anyone up,' his wife added. 'I wonder what can have happened?'

Piers flinched at the flash of anger that was in Marina's eyes, like the spark from a grindstone, he thought.

'Most likely the old bitch is drunk,' she said.

Whether the famous opera star *did* drink, or whether it was a gross slander, he did not know, but he could tell from the expressions of all the dozen departing guests that *lèse-majesté* of a terrible order had been committed. Marina had gone too far. They left with the smallest possible murmur of thanks for the hospitality.

So Pratt had been quite right. Marina walked all the time on the thinnest of ice. He knew now that he must never depend upon her because she clearly had no final self-control.

To help relieve the atmosphere, he asked who Lord Beale was.

''E's very rich and 'e adores opera,' Marina replied shortly.

'Yes, but what does he do?'

''E's a dreadful man – 'e's a property speculator. Pulling down most of the beautiful buildings in London.'

Piers realised that he must have shown his momentary alarm, for Hubert said, 'Don't worry, Piers. He isn't going to pull any of Tothill down. But he's a useful chap to know. And he worships opera.'

At least there were jokes, he thought, to keep one laughing as one crossed the ice. Pratt was right. And he reminded himself to tell his brother the one about the Hear! Hear! man with the destructive urge.

CHAPTER VI
Preparations

Piers looked up from the script of Ralph's play. As he surveyed the Saloon he thought, well, we're back in the Golden Age of the gods with a vengeance here. *'Dans ces lieux, tout rit sans cesse.'*

Well not actually *laughing*, it was true, except Marina who now and again gave one of her great hoots as she came on something in the documents concerning Sir Gervase Tothill in the summary that Magda had prepared which was especially 'amusing'. As for Hubert, his head was bent close to hers – poring over the papers that were their new joint hobby, the public, partial sign of their coming private total union, and he wore now a happy smile far removed from the terrible cackles of laughter that he had once given forth.

Grandma's smile was omnipresent, of course, like God's, but constant and, therefore, improbable, Piers always thought. Yet however unreal it might be, it was surely quite something that it was worn now in the presence of the happy pair and in the room selected by *Marina* for family daily use – the Saloon, with its intricate rococo plasterwork ceiling, an addition to Pratt's work made in the seventeen-seventies by Marina's present concern, Sir Gervase Tothill. Even now, Grandma couldn't forbear to look up at its arabesques occasionally with a contemptuous smile and to murmur something about its childish artificiality, but for the most part she concentrated on her embroidery – a firescreen of a crinolined girl with a poke bonnet standing in a garden ablaze with holly-hocks. And then, despite rococo absurdity, the cabinets in the Saloon walls contained much of her beloved jade collection – the hobby she had shared with Queen Mary. Indeed one mutton-fat jade toad encrusted with sapphires had been that rare thing – a present from the late Queen. Grandma had also brought in a few comfortable sofas and armchairs in pretty flowered cretonne covers to lend a little humanity, a little 'lived-in'-ness to the Louis XV and Louis XVI furniture that Marina found so 'right'. As she said once or twice to her future daughter-in-law with a tiny laugh, 'Men *do* like comfort, my dear. They're selfish brutes but we have to love them.' She usually cast a look of worldly complicity at her grandson at such moments of battle with her future daughter-in-law.

Not, Piers reflected, that he knew in the least what to do with them; they must be meant as a compliment to his man-hood. But he tried his best, for his being there at all was a gesture of gratitude to his uncle. Hubert had asked him espe-cially to sit with them in the Saloon during his Tothill week-ends. 'It's not easy for Mother to accept the situation,' he had said, 'but she's trying to and I think it will help, as well as make it easier for Marina and me, if there are other members of the family there.'

It had not only been gratitude that Piers felt he must show, but an easy response to this unexpectedly intimate, man-to-man approach of his uncle's, a flattering recognition of his own maturity. Actually, Hubert had wanted both him and his brother, but it was enough that Pratt spent so many hours now with Grandma in his mission to relieve her unhappiness, it was up to him to make sure that no more time was eaten out of the hours his brother so badly needed to work for his A levels in calm seclusion. As to himself, it was a mark of the curious sense of harmony that now reigned in this elegant room, that he felt relaxed enough to lay aside both plans for *Phaethon* and his history studies for Oxford and to read Ralph's very strange play.

He was on the side of risk and sensation, of course, against sleepy ease; all the same these places where *tout rit sans cesse*

were a very nice *occasional* relaxation. What with the blazing
fire and the surprisingly strong March sunshine pouring in at
the long windows, he almost dropped off. Then, a knock at
the door heralded the housekeeper, Mrs Tillotson, followed
by two footmen bearing pots of all manner of flowers – there
were hydrangeas and cinerarias and some blue lily Piers didn't
know and scillas and *anemone blanda* – it was a mass of blue.

'Shall I place these, Milady?'

'Yes, do, Mrs Tillotson. Put that deep blue hydrangea on
the ormolu table there where I can look at it. We're beginning
to get spring skies and there's no reason why we shouldn't
have a little of their blue around us indoors to tell us what we
all of us really know, that winter is a false Adam dream that we
can all wake up out of if we try. Aren't they lovely? And soon
we shall be getting them all straight from the garden.'

'I think the scillas and the anemones *do* come from the
Spring Bank down by the Woodwork, Milady. The others are
from the greenhouses.'

'My first blue out-of-doors flowers! I think you can put
some daffodils in with them now. The whole place is already
looking less false, more loved. I am afraid the eighteenth century was a *very* artificial age. That kind of false richness always
breeds its own horrors, like the guillotine. Did Pentreath
select all these? He is getting quite artistic as he prepares for
retirement back in his beloved Cornwall.'

'Oh no, Milady. Tucker always chooses the flowers for
you. He knows just the blues you like.'

'That is very nice of him. Thank him from me. Or rather,
give him a large piece of shortbread. He will know why. I
expect that he will laugh. He was telling me that when his
father, the Rector, was thought to be so ill and they were so
very poor, the one thing that little Ralph longed for was shortbread. Apparently it had been a treat when he was very small
and they were better off and had a cook and so forth. Oh dear!
All that false claim of poverty and illness – it has robbed that
poor boy of so much of his youth. Now if they had been in
Science instead of that muddle-headed Church of England.
Coming down in the world! It seems so real to that class. But I

think that I have been able to help him. There isn't any coming up or going down, I told him. We are in God, secure in his Love. But we've done a lot of good for him here, Mrs Tillotson. There's a smile coming back into his blue eyes. I noticed it the other day. And if that old opera of yours has done *some* good, Piers, it is giving that boy a chance to show his inventive powers. Not too many of the white cinerarias, Mrs Tillotson. White flowers seem so cold, like wreaths. And not that magenta one. It's so strident.'

'Oh, Mama, please.' Marina's girlish manner that she wore nowadays with her future mother-in-law was assumed almost with a wink to the others, Piers noticed. 'The magenta is glorious. It makes all the gilding and the Sèvres and the beautiful little squares of marquetry glow. It's such a rich colour.'

Jackie smiled resignedly. 'My dear, if you like it. Put it where Signora Luzzi can gaze at it. Luckily Pratt's rooms have such order and dignity that they can absorb so much of the exotic. One hardly notices the horrid subjects those old painters chose. The Tintoretto from here is only a mass of warm pinks and browns.'

'My lovely Tintoretto! Don't be blasphemous, Mama! I look at it all the time. The wonderful triumphant look in Salome's eyes as she 'olds the plate in front of 'er, and that greenish colour of the Baptist's 'ead and the teeth just showing white between 'is dead lips. Aiee! It's so exciting! And the Caracci, too. The old man passes 'is knife over the boy's neck most lovingly.'

It was unfortunate, Piers thought, that the two principal pictures in the Saloon should show John the Baptist's head on a charger and the sacrifice of Isaac – they were not calculated to bring Jackie and Marina together. Jackie had closed her eyes and her faintly reddened lips trembled a little. Marina's eyes were glowing with expectancy. *Dans ces lieux tout ne rit pas.* It was his uncle's look of helplessness that urged him to try to make the place laugh again.

'The sensational side of Scripture,' he said.

Hubert laughed relievedly and Marina returned to their transcribed documents.

'Oh, no! But really, this is wonderful. This 'Ell Fire Club.'

But Jackie was not to be deterred. 'Oh dear. It is so easy to make the Bible ugly and sad. I remember it like that when I was a girl. That is one thing Science has done for me. That old language – "Charity is not puffed up." We always say "Love is not proud." Charity is so unfortunate, so Victorian and smug. And then even the Lord's Prayer. "Our Father" – Mrs Eddy makes it so clear in her spiritual interpretation – "Our Father *Mother* God".'

'They met in caves, 'Ubert. And they said the Lord's Prayer backwards. Now I ask, did Sir Gervase ever 'old the wicked meetings 'ere at Tothill? Because you know, those old monks 'ad been 'ere. Wasn't there an underground passage to Westminster Abbey? They could 'ave 'eld their 'Ell Fire meetings there.'

Hubert laughed indulgently. 'I'm sorry to disappoint you, my dear. That old story just isn't true. Anyway, it would have been St Stephen's Hall. Nearer to Parliament. Miss Sczekerny was telling me that she has looked at two old plans – one from the monks' days and one from shortly after, Edward VI's reign, I think, and there's absolutely no trace of the famous passage. The monks obviously went across the fields in all weathers.'

'The stupid things people can do. Backwards! As if God minded in what order we said his prayers. In any case, prayers are loving thoughts, not words.'

'And all the girls were naked, 'Ubert. *And* the serving boys. Sir Gervase tells it all in a letter to 'is brother 'ere. And all of them dressed as monks. The Prior was their 'ost, Sir Francis Dashwood. Were they Catholics, the Tothills, then?'

'No, no, this was just a sort of masquerade. Rather coarse fun. We don't want to make too much of it, darling. It rather falls into that category of sensational stuff about the Tothills that I was talking of. No, the only Roman Catholic in the Tothill family was Sir Rayner's wife at the time of the Gunpowder Plot. We ought to look into that, by the way.'

'There was so much Error about in those days, Hubert. It does seem a pity to rake it all up again. But there you are, wherever the Roman Catholics are, they are working against God's real purpose. Miss Spooner was saying the same only the other day.'

'The Church working against God!' Marina burst into contemptuous laughter. 'It's so lucky I 'ave lapsed, Mama. Do you say lapsed? But you're right, 'Ubert. Fun it was! All kinds of fun. This Sir Francis 'ad whips and God knows what. What do you think of that, darling?'

Hubert seemed desperate. 'It's Sir Francis Dashwood, Mother, Marina's talking of. Not Francis Tothill.'

Grandma wasn't looking appeased, so Piers thought he must try to help.

'You're quite right, Grandma. Ralph's very useful. He's so inventive. And he doesn't waste time. He saw at once that any mechanism for actually flying Phaethon's chariot at the end would be quite beyond our means and possibly dangerous to the fabric of the Hall. So he's followed up Uncle Jim's idea and he's already got some wonderful effects by playing lights on Verrio's ceiling painting.'

Jackie said vaguely, 'Uncle Jim?'

'Oh, you know him, Grandma. You've met him at the Nursery. I can remember one summer, when you came down to see Ma's new white garden, he was there.'

'Probably, dear. I have met many people in a very full life, I am glad to say.'

So that was that. He'd try again. 'I want to say now that Tothill has supplied so much to the making of *Phaethon*. I don't mean only all that I have to thank the family for,' Piers took in Marina with a smile, 'but Ralph Tucker and Magda Sczekerny, too. She started it all.'

'She's a useful little creature,' Marina said. 'I must try to get 'er not to wear those terrible clothes. All those bows. Really it's quite 'orrible. So childish.'

'Oh, Marina,' Jackie cried, 'don't stop her making her life a little prettier after all the evil that she's had to live with in that country of hers. Anyway, she's like a little Dutch doll. It makes me happy to see her and Ralph together. Tothill has brought them great happiness, I think. Not that there is anything silly between them. They are like two Dutch dolls.'

Piers thought, so in some strange way Grandma and I *are* on the same wave-length. He stored this up as part of human behaviour that he must puzzle out. Then he thought, really it's like me and the dancing mistress – the same wave-length from opposite ends.

A knock on the door this time brought the girl Dutch doll into the room.

'Mr Mosson,' she said, 'I thought you would like to see these pages. I remember in what they are saying in the Great Hall'at the big reception that Sir Gervase has been to Paestum in Italy. These are some extracts from the journal he writes there.'

Piers thought, how had she heard that? He remembered Sir John Wallis saying it, but he didn't remember her presence. She seemed, like God, to be omnipresent.

'Paestum! Oh, 'ow wonderful, I am so fond of Paestum,' Marina cried. 'All the best Greek architecture is there and in Sicily. All that in Athens and in your British Museum is awful 'and sweet and sentimental. What do you call it – the Parthenon – it's bad like the Victorian imitations, like that 'orrible shepherd boy in the garden.' She clapped her hand to her mouth, with a look of a naughty girl at Jackie. She's getting very coy with all this land of laughter stuff, Piers thought. 'But Paestum and Agrigento and Erice, that is different. That was what Italy did for the Greeks, made them strong and bold not sweet and weak and sentimental like these Athens Apollos. Give me those papers, Magda. My dear! Paestum! It's the place that made Goethe and Wincklemann 'appy! We must send you there to follow where this man went. Isn't that right, 'Ubert? Would you like to go to Paestum, Magda?'

'I shall be very happy. I have never been to Italy.'

But further exploration of the idea was cut short when the door flew open and the room was filled with green mackintosh and tweed.

Piers could see that Magda was scared, or was she? There was something else in her look as she cried, 'Oh, Primrose! Just think, I am to go to Italy. Mr Mosson is sending me to Italy!'

As the storm broke around him, Piers determined to get out
of the rain. He buried himself in Ralph's play – 'You're fucking right, you won't. You keep out or we'll put the muckers on
you.' The language of the play continually surprised him, but
its action and violence kept him going. Thank God, he'd not
told Grandma he was reading her dear Ralph's play or she
might have asked to see it. And then there'd have been another
storm.

The noise of this one was growing too much for his concentration on the violent obscenities, though he realised, tearing
himself away, that he was flattered to be offered so avant-
garde a manuscript for his opinion.

'Sir Hubert, this *must* be decided. Either we are employed
by you or by this lady.' Primrose indicated Marina with a
sweep of her hand, but 'lady' was not what the force of her
voice implied. Piers was conscious of a shuddering noise
like poplar leaves and he realised that it was her heavy frame
trembling in its waterproof cover. He liked her; she had
been good to him; he longed to say something to help or
comfort her; but he felt absolutely sure that he must not be
involved. He could not tell what women's strange storm
was brewing.

'This lady, Miss Lynmouth, is to be my wife. She will
always show you full consideration, I know, for the loyal service you've given to us at Tothill, but, of course, she will
decide what work is needed on the archives as much as I or my
mother have always done.'

'Lady Mosson has never . . .' Primrose began, but there
was a knock on the door and Mrs Tillotson brought in a mass
of daffodils. In silence, Jackie rose and took them from her.

'I will arrange them, Mrs Tillotson, thank you.'

As soon as the door had closed after the housekeeper, Primrose burst out, 'You've never given orders to my assistants
without asking me, Lady Mosson, have you? Ever, ever.'

'My mother has not concerned herself greatly with the
Library, although she appreciates as much as I do all that you
do for us.'

Piers could see that Jackie was busy underlining this statement, breaking up the sky blue anemones and blue scillas with shots of sunlit yellow. She had, Piers felt sure, the same resolution as he had not to be involved.

'How can you talk of appreciation when, after all the work we have done on the Mosson chronicle, you take Miss Sczekerny off it? And with the splendid second volume to be checked?'

'That's all been settled, Miss Lynmouth. We've been through it two or three times. We can't go over it again. Miss Sczekerny's working on the Tothills. You have Mr Arrowsmith at the Bank giving you his very expert assistance when you need it.'

'But I have trained this girl for the work. I have brought her over here. We worked so well. And now I can't even leave the Library to go down to the Bank to take documents to this man, but it's left unattended. We've always kept the Library with someone in attendance except at lunchtimes. Even when we had only a half-time assistant.'

'You take it all too seriously.' Piers felt Hubert really was trying his best. 'It's not a public library.'

'Any place of work has to have some discipline, Sir Hubert. I told you to stay there, Magda. You know my rules.'

'I think, in England, you have to obey those who pay the money,' Magda said.

Marina was delighted. 'That is very good. Your little doll, Mama, is quite a realist, you see. Well done, my dear.'

To Piers' surprise there sounded a tiny laugh of materialist appreciation from among the blues and yellows, but his grandmother said nothing.

'How can you talk so cynically, Magda, after all I've done for you, all we seemed to mean to each other when you first came to England.'

Marina gave a small coarse laugh. Damn, Piers thought, there's going to be more trouble. 'Bourgeois Lesbian' had seemed so worldly the other day, but now it was an annoying embarrassment.

The mackintosh swished round towards Marina like a whiplash. 'Oh, you can laugh. But I've seen what you've been trying to do with this girl. I saw you kissing her on the mouth the other day. I appeal to you, Mr Piers, it was disgusting, wasn't it?'

'I really think she wasn't . . .'Piers began,but Magda shouted him down.

'No, really, Primrose, this is too stupid. To ask the boy such questions. Signora Luzzi was just having fun. She was teasing you. You have been so good to bring me out from Budapest. You are a good woman. But you are foolish. You let yourself get too fond of me. Ralph has said so.'

'Ralph!' The name was the last straw. Bursting into tears, Primrose sobbed at them. 'After all I have done. Not one of you can . . . I give my notice, Sir Hubert. I am clearly not wanted.' And with a whirr of crackling material, she had run from the room.

'I am so very sorry,' Magda said.

'My dear Miss Sczekerny, it is not your fault. She's let herself overwork. A holiday is needed. We'll leave her alone and she'll come to her senses.'

Piers wondered if he was hearing his uncle's City voice; it seemed more like a scene at school than in the boardroom of a great bank.

'She must go,' Marina said. ''Ubert, you must get rid of 'er for this girl's sake. It's not fair on 'er – all that old maid's repressed sex.'

'Oh dear!' Jackie cried, 'how unpleasant all this is. And to involve a boy of Piers' age. One has to put up with nonsense like this in a badly run girls' boarding school, but at Tothill! Piers, come and tell me, dear, do you advise a cream hyacinth or a pink one here next to the mauve? I want a soft shading.'

Hubert had sat silent. Now he said, 'Mother, you know how loyal she's been. Can't you talk to her?'

'My dear boy, it is all quite outside my experience, I am glad to say. You must manage your own affairs.'

Piers was watching Marina's anger. He thought, she's going to make a scene.

But she said, 'Poor old 'Ubert. You mustn't be worried with all this women's nonsense. Come, darling, we shall be late for

Annabelle Gilroy's luncheon. She will never forgive me. You
are 'er new catch. She says it's so wonderful to find unspoiled
people these days. You make 'er laugh so much.' Hubert
looked like a pleased child as they left.

'Poor Hubert,' his mother said. 'Another of these smart
luncheon parties with all their false talk. And then he will complain about all manner of imaginary indigestion pains. Now
you, Tom and I are going to have a good, wholesome Tothill
luncheon. I believe that Gates murmured something about
spring duckling for the greedy Tom.'

Here they were in the great State Bedroom, its elegant Pratt
proportions and its Gibbons carved chimney piece beaming at
them. Grandma walked across the room and stood beside the
console table. She still hobbled from the fall of a week earlier,
and Tom felt the concern for her that had come with his growing affection. But it would upset the whole afternoon if he
mentioned the error of bruised thigh and, in any case, her
bravery, he thought, deserved consideration.

'Well?' she asked.

He answered at once, 'Gilt. Ebony. Marble top.'

'Oh, we want more than that – what country?'

'England.'

'English marble! You can do better than that.'

'I meant the wood and the carving.'

'Where's the *marble* from? Carrara?'

'No,' he said, 'I know it isn't *that*. I don't quite remember.
Wait a minute. You *did* tell me. Could it be Siena?'

'Correct.'

'And it's designed by John Vandy who was an architect.
And its date would be . . . 1760.'

He couldn't get the words out fast enough when he remembered something. Partly, he felt so pleased to remember all
that she had taught him, it augured well for his success in all
the years ahead of exams if he was to become a lawyer – a secret
ambition told not even to Van, for fear it might seem like
empty boasting and provoke disaster. But, partly, he spoke so

quickly because he was anxious lest the Saturday afternoons he spent with her were time he had no right to take from his exercise or studies, as he knew Van thought. Mostly now however, he spoke quickly to keep sealed the happiness he knew he had brought to her and the understanding she gave him of the certainty of Tothill, that it was something real – objects, values, rooms, purposes – not just the abstract shapes or the dreams that it seemed to mean to Van.

He heard her voice now suddenly, with a teasing note that she'd only recently begun to show to him.

'Woolgathering? Or just shamming deaf because you don't know the answer?'

He blushed as he always did when convicted of inattention.

'I am asking you about this,' she said, patting the green satin seat cover of an armchair.

'Gilt. I should think the wood's probably walnut veneer on oak. It's by Mathias Locke,' he added proudly, but, as it turned out, unwisely.

'By?'

'Oh, well, in the style of. I don't see why that matters so much.'

'A false smile, in the style of a true one. But God knows the difference.'

If only she wouldn't. It all seemed so false and she wasn't really false. He frowned.

'All right, Tom,' she laughed. 'All you men are the same. Hubert's embarrassed when I speak of God's love for us all. I was talking to Miss Hovendon, our first reader, about it last Sunday and she said her son is just the same. "We simply have to know the truth for them, Lady Mosson," she told me.'

Holding on to the arm of the Locke armchair with her left hand, she leant across and placed her right hand over the name of the watchmaker of the Grandfather – he corrected his thought – pendulum clock, some feet away. He thought, she'll fall, but I can't upset her by offering to help her. But then he remembered his fears a week ago, soon after her accident, and how she had laughed, not her usual sweet ripple, as Van called it, but a hard barking laugh. 'My dear boy,' she'd said, 'I won't go falling about the place, don't worry. Half the world now wants to bring down the rich and the secure. Imagine how they'd laugh to see an old woman like me come by a fall. But I have no intention of giving them that pleasure. It's pride that keeps old women like me going. And we have to be particularly careful not to relax or get sloppy just because we have someone we love with us as I have when I am with you or Hubert. *I* shall not fall, however rickety I look. Don't worry.' And really, he told himself, he shouldn't; she wouldn't fall.

But now she had taken her hand from the clock face. 'Time's up,' she said, 'You didn't know, did you?' The silvered letters read 'John Ellicott, London.'

'Oh, I remember about him.' Tom realised the words were rushing out now to make up for his earlier lack of concentration, so he deliberately slowed down. 'He was a Fellow of the Royal Society and he did a great deal to improve the technical efficiency and regularity of clocks. The book you lent to me said his cases were the most elegant in all eighteenth century England.'

'Yes.' He noticed as she spoke now that her voice was neither sweet nor bitter, but solemn, for her, almost passionate. 'Regularity and elegance. They are the important things. Especially when chaos is trying to take over. Keeping beautiful things going. And really knowing *about* them, caring for them. Do you know who has brought all these splendid pieces here?'

He felt carried away by her – that she voiced in her own way so fully what he felt about the way things must be. He said, hoping greatly that he'd got it right. 'Was it Celia Tothill, the heiress who married Sir Gervase?'

'Yes, it was. She was an alderman's daughter. The last one to grease the Tothill wheel before Amelia Tothill married Samuel Mosson forty years later. And then the Mossons took over with all their wealth. And then I came along with my vulgar dollars just in time to grease the Mosson wheel when *that* was getting rusty. And now it's Marina's turn, with her Turin fortune. Or so it seems. Part of the regular pattern. Or we must try to think so.'

She sounded so sad now that, in his admiration for her support of order, he risked, as rarely, the ice.

He said, 'I expect you and Marina will become fond of each other in time.'

He tried to say it casually. But she sat down in the armchair, her back very straight, and looked at him very directly.

'Tom, dear. Do not try to talk above your age. There is no call for Marina and me to become fond of each other, as you call it. We are not blood relations. She is engaged to be married to my son and I hope she'll make him a good wife if and when she marries him. He will have to settle down and be less of a stage door Johnnie,' she gave Tom a little arch smile. 'She's not a classic beauty. I should call her a *jolie laide*. But she has poise and elegance. She is very *soignée*. What your great grandfather calls a good dresser. She is sociable in her way, although her set seems rather shallow to me. She has money. Not the sort that my father would have respected. I cannot imagine him needing to smuggle money into Switzerland. But then Italy is not the United States. And times have changed. She is intelligent. Far too intelligent, I hope, to try to pretend to sentimental feelings for her future mother-in-law. Sit down, Tom. I want to talk to you.'

It was turning into an interview with Brownlow, he thought, but he was held by her force, so lacking in either her usual sweetness or her occasional bitterness.

'I think you are trying to be kind to me. You think I may be lonely. And so I may be. But that is not why I get you along here on Saturday afternoons to learn all about the things that make up Tothill. It is much more serious than that. You see, the Tothills in the past and the Mossons in the old days took it all for granted. Tothill House was them. They were Tothill House. That's really how your great grandfather is. Of course, he's getting old now and he has foolish fancies – his ideas about owning St John's Smith Square and so on – but on his good days he can tell you most of what is here without a lot of fuss about art or culture or explaining it to the people. He knows the house because it belongs to him, and the things in it belong to him. And if he doesn't know some of them, that doesn't matter either, because they are part of Tothill, which is his. Of course, that's the old days.'

She got up and walked across to the window. He felt annoyed that she was breaking her own spell, would stare out into the garden or something. But she turned to face him and continued her speech.

'Even your grandfather couldn't see it quite like that. He liked to have special visitors – royalty or ambassadors. He needed just that touch of outside attention to feel sure that Tothill stood firm. Even when he was Lord Mayor, he always found time to conduct special visitors round the house. I believe that he was never so proud of me as when Queen Mary said that I knew my possessions better than anyone in England. And Queen Mary was *the* expert. Of course, I had to learn it all, but that was half the meaning of marrying the heir to Tothill. Things have changed again since then. Hubert, I am glad to say, has no wish to open to the public. And we have no need to. But he thinks it more important than I do to open the house at the request of every charity that writes to us, although I have been responsible for seeing that we are more selective. And now it looks as though it's changing again. This opera of Piers' and all the parties Marina plans to give. There seems to be less and less confidence in *ourselves*. Tothill doesn't need showing off any more than we do. It's there and we're there. It is because I believe, Tom, that you are a boy who cares about things for themselves, a solid boy, that I have encouraged you to learn about the place and the objects in it. You have such a lot of influence with Piers and he is to inherit. Although now, of course . . .'

'Thank you, Grandma. I'll do my best.'

Having said that, he felt he could ask a question. 'What happened to Marina's husband?' he asked.

'He was killed, dear, in the war, towards the end of it, I think.'

'Like Daddy?'

'Oh no, not at all. It was all to do with Italy. Politics play such a large part in those places. I do not know the ins and outs of it. And we shouldn't understand if we did.' She rose. 'We

will go and have tea now. I can see the greedy look in your eye.
I cannot think why you don't put on weight, Tom, eating so
much, bless you.'

'Oh, I take a lot of exercise. P.T. And I play squash regularly. If you get too fat you may fall through the floor, I always
think.'

She laughed. 'No one falls through the floor, Tom. God
holds you up, however fat you are. There now, that has given
you a nice imitation of Grandma doing her Christian Science
stuff to tell to Piers. Come along to tea.'

As they walked along the corridor to the Blue Drawing
Room, he said, 'Don't be against Van, Grandma. This opera
means a lot to him that we can't understand. But he cares about
Tothill House as much as any of us. You can rely on him.'

'I hope so, Tom. He did not do much to stand up for that
poor silly Primrose Lynmouth the other week, although it was
clear that she'd always helped him when he needed books.'

Tom had sensed this when he had heard Van's account and
he felt more defensive.

'Well, what did *you* do, Grandma?'

'Me! Oh, my dear boy, I can't mix myself up with all that
nonsense. Besides, I never *use* the Library. I sent her a nice
letter, of course, and a cheque.'

The answer sickened Tom a little. Now the ground seemed
firm, now it seemed treacherous and marshy. He felt no security anywhere.

He said, 'Anyway I think this opera's going to be quite
something.'

She stopped and turned to him. 'I hope Piers is not counting
on it *too* much. It needs your great grandfather's approval.
And although he's not himself, he can be very obstinate.'
When she saw how horrified he looked, she said, 'Don't
worry. I'll do what I can to persuade him. I have quite a lot of
influence with him.'

To the footman in the Blue Drawing Room she asked, 'What
are you offering us for tea, Lucas?'

'Chef's made buttered scones and quince jelly, chocolate
cake with rum butter filling, *petit fours* and éclairs.'

'Ah!' she said to Tom as she picked up the silver teapot, 'you will like those. Tuck in, Tom. And I think we must make these sessions with the furniture once a month now, not a fortnight. I am much too fond of you to let you neglect your real work. But we shall have tea together every fortnight, won't we, dear?'

Made confident by food and love, Tom felt able to tuck in.

They stood at the South end of the Great Hall. Ralph flashed two torches, one against the other, across the ceiling – miraculously the horses tossed their white manes, the chariot lurched, Phaethon stood upright, serene and proud, now the whole chariot and its steeds heaved and shook, a wild bloodshot horse's eye showed madly and then a hoof kicking fiercely from a knotted, slender white furred leg, then one horse had tumbled, its neck writhing, its legs kicking fiercely upward; then, in two terrible twisting turns, Phaethon was falling – and now the torches shone on to the burning malachite bowl. It almost worked, Piers thought, there was a real sense of movement, although he was aware that his own imagination was magnifying it, speeding it up to bring alive the terrible drama he wanted to see.

'And Bob's your uncle. Anyone want a nice piece of roast Phaethon? Can't you hear all the old dears, "Oh, well, he only got what he asked for." Poor bugger!'

The more that Ralph became accustomed to his company, the more Piers noticed that he spoke the same brutal language as the characters in his play, yet all in his over-articulated comic curate's voice. It was off-putting, but what didn't he owe to him?

'It's not quite convincing yet, tho' it is marvellous.'

'Can't be. Stands to reason. But come the night, you'll have your proper arc lamps working from the back there and your noises, tho' I suppose most of that will be in the music. You'll need amplifiers there. You're going to have to make room behind the audience for the lights. I should think five or six properly distanced should do it. I can teach your blokes how

to work them, if you like. And then the twit that's playing
Phaethon must drape himself as dead as he can in the bowl.
Arms hanging over the edge. Lights on him. Christ! he's dead.
Curtain. That's how I see it anyway. We might be able to work
it out with silhouettes, magnified slides. But you'd lose
colour, I think. And to try to fly it, as I've said before, would
mean goodbye to the fabric of the Hall. Or near. Anyway,
there it is.'

'Thank you very much. If you could give me a costing for
the lamps, I'll discuss it with the Musical Director.' Then he
added, 'No, I won't. It's my decision. It's taking me some
time to learn what's my sphere and what isn't.'

'Action's where the muscle is. That's the system, isn't it? By
the way, I hear they've given old Primrose the boot.'

Piers, thinking of Magda, stopped before replying to this.
But he felt he must do justice to Primrose. 'It's a bit sickening.
She's always been such a loyal, hard worker.'

Ralph chuckled. 'This'll learn her then. It's like the old lady
in my play when the kids beat her up in the alley. What do you
think of it, by the way?'

'It's very funny. Some of it. I liked the vicarage dinner party
when the bishop gets locked in the loo. I'm sure you must play
against the farce, though, to get the best effect there.'

Ralph seemed pleased at this. 'Genteel middle-class comedy
with farts to it. Yes, I like that. Any other suggestions?'

'Well, a general tightening. And then I don't think an
audience could bear the last scene if it was well played. Those
children laughing and jeering round the Guy Fawkes pile
where the old aunt is being burnt as a guy. It would be too
horrible, even if it were not played realistically.'

'Oh, it's got to be played for laughs. After all, she's very old
and she's bossed them around all the first two acts and now
they're feeling their muscle. Of course, if you want "silver
threads among the gold" and all that, then it's not your play.
But it shows the logic of the system.'

'What system?'

But Ralph wasn't to be drawn – or was it sidetracked? He
went on – Piers had never heard him so animated, and as he

talked he swung one of the torches, picking out now the gallery, now the lantern, now the mourning girls.

'And then, below that, there's something about the very old, that makes you want to have a bash . . . I mean, look, if you were to find yourself stopped in your tracks by some old buzzard . . .' His torch swept to the staircase on to an old, old face.

'Am I on stage then? What are my words?' The voice chuckled with delight.

It was some months since Piers had either seen or heard his great grandfather and the old, mummified face, the eyes blinking, coming at this moment, almost made him lose his command.

'Well, right you are then, I'll be off.' Ralph's very mundane reaction to the weird coincidence restored Piers to control of the situation.

'You're welcome to a part, sir, if you're willing to sing with youths and maidens.'

'You haven't heard my singing voice, or you wouldn't say that. Anyway, you've taken the spotlight off me and I feel dazzled. You had better light me downstairs, or I'll tumble and that can be very unwise at my time of life. Is this a rehearsal?'

It's here, Piers thought, let it be good news. Great Grandfather's amiability had seemed to him from childhood the smile on the face of the tiger; and now that he lived mainly as a rumour of senility, he seemed to be the very symbol of the Unsure. Remembering what Pratt had said of Grandma's doubts of the old man's agreement, his uncle's bland assurances to everyone that he would arrange things seemed hollow indeed.

He could only trust to his instinct. 'No, sir, there's no question of rehearsal until we have your agreement.'

'*My* agreement? Then why didn't you come and ask me? Your uncle talked about it all, but it isn't his business, it's yours. Or so it seemed. But then there was all that about this Italian girl of his and some of her friends. And we can't spend money on staging operas for foreigners at Tothill. And then your grandmother seemed worried that I hadn't agreed to it.

She started on old age being an illusion and I must get about
more. And *that* upset Nurse Harper. So I couldn't have it.
She's a damned nuisance, the nurse, but *I* have to live with her.
Anyway I wanted to hear it from you. That's why I came
down here. I heard your voice upstairs. Nurse'll be in a tizzy.
I am not supposed to move about on my own yet. Now, what
is it you want to do?'

Piers explained it as shortly and simply as he could.

'Yes, yes. I understood it was a seventeenth century French
opera that Francis Tothill would have presented if the King
hadn't objected. I'm not a child. I can understand what I'm
told. I can't say it sounds very interesting. I mean if it wasn't
done, it wasn't done. And if Dutch Bill was against it, that's a
pity. He was a nasty asthmatic little runt, but he was one of the
best Kings we ever had. It took a Dutchman to know what
England needed and to get it for her. One of the best operas I
ever saw was by a Frenchman – Offenbach. Frenchman with a
German name. *La Belle Hélène*. I saw it three times. And
then there was Balfe's *Bohemian Girl*. That was my favourite.
Oh yes, music hall was my standby, but I went to opera quite a
lot. I heard Patti when I was very young. That'll make you
think. When are you putting it on?'

'In June, sir, if you really agree.'

'Of course I do. I've just been telling you. I might come
myself. On the first night, of course. If that damned nurse will
let me. But I can't dress up, you know. Too old. Is it tiaras?
Your grandmother loves wearing her tiara. Thinks she's the
fairy queen. Have you got any pretty girls in it and dancing?'

'The heroine is very pretty, yes. And there are a lot of ballets.'

'Good. A chance to see their legs. Not that that's much
excitement to your generation.'

'Not really. Anyway their dresses will be very long. They're
based on Verrio's ceiling and the mourning statues round the
great green bowl. A sort of fantasy of ancient Greek costume.'

'Never mind how long the dresses are. They can always kick
their legs up. That way, with luck, one of them will drop her
knickers.'

He laughed so much that he began to cough violently. Piers banged him on the back. He saw to his relief that the old man was soon recovering his breath. Then suddenly a middle-aged woman appeared in the gallery at the top of the stairway.

'Oh, there you are, Mr Mosson. Are you all right? I don't know how I'm going to look after you now that you're better. One never knows where you are.'

'Well, if I really get better, I won't need you, will I? Don't worry, Nurse Harper, my great grandson here has been entertaining me. Haven't laughed so much for years. Told me a story about girls' legs. Can't tell you, though. It would make you blush like a young girl. That would take some doing, wouldn't it, Piers?'

Luckily Nurse Harper interrupted any reply he might have made. 'Come and have your tea, Mr Mosson. There are meringues.'

The old man's eagerness recalled Pratt's greed. Piers felt very warm to him, especially when he called over the banister, 'Come and tell me some more of your choice stories. And keep a seat for me on the first night. That boy's done me good, Nurse. Young blood, that's what I need.'

'You certainly seem to have livened him up,' Nurse Harper called to Piers, but he couldn't tell whether her tone was approving or acid.

So he'd done it himself. Uncle Hubert and Grandma had done their best. But it was he who had done it. And, thank God, he had the assurance himself. For, tending to treat the old man like a child, the others might have easily given the green light and then at the last minute the old boy might have forbidden it.

He felt so happy and excited and personally in charge that he at once ran down the corridor to the Saloon to tell of his Victory.

He could hear Marina's voice, as he approached the room. She was obviously in high spirits. Shouting and laughing. Well, he could match her for that this afternoon. He opened the door and had it on his lips to announce his news, thanking them all, Marina included, but reserving final credit for himself – why not? He was producing the show.

But, as he peered in, Marina turned from addressing her future husband and mother-in-law, and waved her hand towards him in a grandiose operatic gesture, almost as though she was exorcising his presence.

'And there's this boring boy now,' she cried. 'All right, go and sit down. Go away. You and your boring opera! I am nearly losing the friendship from Sylvia Armitage because of the stupid play. She wrote me, "You invite *me* to see a rehearsal of a school production of a Lully opera. You must be mad." I 'ad to go on my knees in 'er dressing room last night. She 'ad been Anna Bolena. She was superb. Not this stupid Lully rubbish. Go and sit down!'

Her scream was so powerful that he shrank to the wall. He stood there for some minutes as her tirade continued, then he sought to run away, out of the room, but in her dramatic mood she strode across the room and was guardian of the door. He felt quite cut off from safety. The only thing to do was to efface himself as much as he could. He crept along the Saloon until he found shelter behind a large Chinese vase. The brutal misery of these three people unfolded itself before him.

'Oh, my God, it's so boaring here,' she cried, 'Do I want dinner parties every night?' The little primping voice must, Piers thought, be an imitation of one of them, but it sounded like a small boy 'baiting' another at his prep school. 'Yes. I do want dinner parties every night. It will tire dear Mother. I 'ope it will, if she is going to be there, the more tired she is the better, then we won't have all this boaring talk about blue. My blue flowers! My blue nose! And God is love. Oh, my God.'

'Marina, I cannot let you talk . . .'

'No, no, Hubert dear. She's overwrought. I do not take any notice. Remember, you are giving the garden party, Marina. Surely that is enough to begin with. It's only that we cannot have too much entertaining even in this big house while Father is upstairs. Old age needs quiet and peace.'

'So 'e will die! So all right! Isn't that what you want? 'Ow long do you want 'Ubert to be a small boy waiting to be the heir?'

'My dear,' Hubert said, 'let's not say more about that. As I told you, it will work itself out. Now, what are your ideas for the garden party? About how many guests do you think?'

'Garden party! What 'orrible words! It's a *fête champêtre!*'

Jackie gave a very small laugh; so far as Piers could tell it came from her quite naturally. 'How ridiculous!'

'It's your garden parties that are ridiculous. And your gardens. It should be a baroque garden. All the beds should be amusing shapes. But they are all square with geraniums. It's a little provincial park. And Rosemary's famous wild garden, well, perhaps they're all right, those old rose bushes. The Nicolsons 'ave them. It's amusing. It's English. But what about those terrible trees? I must 'ave them cut down, 'Ubert.'

'Cut down the elms?' Jackie laughed. 'My dear woman, they are eternal.'

'Marina,' Hubert said, speaking very patiently, 'you don't seem to realise that we're in the heart of London. If we cut down the trees, we'll be open to everyone. And we should be seen from all the ugly buildings going up in Westminster . . .'

'Ugly buildings! Aiee! That is the 'ole point. This wonderful 'ouse is in *London*! There are buildings all over and people and life – some ugly, so, some beautiful, and the most beautiful *this* 'ouse. That's it. You want it to be *pretty*, I suppose. My God, you 'ave the minds and taste of provincials. We might be living in Foggia!'

Jackie said as though to a child, 'It's a secret garden, Marina, that's the secret of it.' She gave a tiny chuckle.

'Ah! *Giardino segreto* – very well. Let's 'ave some orgies there. Oh no, we must 'ave a garden party.' Piers failed to see why Marina treated these two words with such scorn. 'Very well, let us 'ave a garden party. A *burlesca. Belle Epoque.* Or 'ow do you say, Edwardian? With a vulgar rich American lady trying to be an English lady. To love pretty things, and art and beauty! Little garden statues of shepherd boys! Stupid imitations of Donatello! Well, now you won't 'ave your shepherd boy. I sent 'im away.'

'What do you mean, you've sent it away? How dare you? Where has he gone?'

'Oh, I don't know. I told the gardener – Pintit, what's 'is name? – to get rid of it. Some people came and took it away. It will sell well in some 'ouse in the suburbs. Don't worry, your little shepherd boy will 'ave a nice little bourgeois 'ome.'

Piers watched his grandmother peering at Marina's face and suddenly, to his shock, tears came pouring from her forget-me-not eyes down her carefully powdered old pink cheeks. And she didn't even produce one of those small lace edged handkerchiefs that played so large a part in her life as he knew it. She cried and cried like a frightened child.

'Oh, Mother, darling, for God's sake, really! The two of you. We'll get it *back*.' Hubert seemed to Piers miraculously to be able to be merely cross when the two women were over-wrought.

'He meant so much to me, Hubert. I used to stand by him and listen to his pipes in my fancy. And all the Error, all your father's sillinesses with other women went away. You were only tiny children playing round it – but Jerry noticed. "Mummy's listening," he said, "is de music nice, Mummy?" And then they shot him down.'

'Mother, darling, the last thing Jerry would have wanted is for you to upset yourself about a garden statue. I really think you're being a little sentimental about it all. You've let your-self get carried away.'

Marina laughed scornfully. 'She's not carried away. She is, what do you call it? A calculator. She knows what she is doing. There is no trick that old bitch won't get up to with you. So you wanted a little shepherd boy's doodle to play with, Mama, eh? 'Cos I am takin your 'Ubert away from you. Rub my doodly, Marina, 'e says, – is that 'ow you told 'im to say it?'

Hubert rose from his chair; his floppy cheeked face was scarlet. Piers thought he was going to hit Marina and she must have thought so too, for she dodged away. Then Hubert drew back and in a tight controlled voice said:

'Marina, I will not have you . . .'

'No, you won't 'ave me and I won't 'ave you. Do you think I want to see your white bottom any more – "Make it red, Marina." Get 'er to do it. Go back to your prostitutes. I 'ave done enough for you.'

Hubert gave one of his old frightening cackles but this time
it turned not into laughter, but into hysterical crying. Jackie
with difficulty got down on her knees beside him and began to
stroke his hair and his cheeks. As his crying died away into
sobbing, Marina broke out again, but differently.

'Oh, 'Ubert, *please*, I wanted to bring you 'appiness and
laughter 'ere and fun. You know 'ow lonely I 'ave been. I was
only a girl when they married me to 'im. But *'e* thought me
fun, 'e and Ciano. And then they shot 'im. And the family is
never fun, only money. And so I've gone on my own – she's so
rich, Marina Luzzi, and so crazy, she's always on the move.
But I wanted to 'ave this lovely 'ouse and not to be on the
move. And look 'ow I 'ave made you laugh in these days. I
would 'ave done anything for you.' She, too, was crying now.
But he only buried himself in Jackie's arms.

Jackie looked up. '*Prego di non parlare come questo qui*,'
she said, '*Andate, andate*.'

This sudden speech in her own tongue must have alarmed
Marina, for she cried:

'Oh my God! It's no 'ope. I can't live with it,' and, opening
the door, she ran from the room.

Jackie remained kneeling on the floor, Hubert's large head
cradled in her lean bosom – she kissed him on the forehead,
and, yes, the lace edged handkerchief did appear, she wiped his
tears from his cheeks.

'My dear boy, she was the wrong one for you. Someone fine
will come along to make my boy happy. You mark my words.'

As quietly as he could, Piers sidled along the wall, as though
he were trying to escape from a marksman's shot. He said,
almost in a whisper, 'Great grandfather agrees to the opera
being performed here.' He was going noiselessly out of the
open door when Jackie, not looking up, said in a very formal
voice:

'We are delighted that Grandfather has approved your little
adventure. Although, of course, your uncle had it all in hand.
Shut the door please, dear. Always remember to shut the door
when you leave a room, my dear boy.'

He went slowly down the corridor, wondering how long it would be before he could purge himself of all this pity and disgust, and how he would do it.

CHAPTER VII
The Family Lunch

'OH, MY God, it's so boarring! Your secret garden, 'Ubert. With its old white bottom and its pretty little Donatello imitation doodle. I am so boarred with it.'

'Marina, dear, God is blue. *Fête champêtre* indeed. We do not have silly ideas like that in this house. You will not get my dear boy a little heir in that way. *Non parlate come questo qui.*'

Piers had reduced the whole scene now to surrealism mainly in the form of a dialogue between the two women. There had seemed to be no other way of banishing its horror. Although, when he had first told his brother on that very evening, he had found himself repeating it with emotional difficulty and yet, in the end, reproducing every word that had been said. But he had had to be rid of it.

And it appeared not to have affected the future of the production. Reggie was in full excitement about the opera. He and Nigel Mordaunt, who was still closely involved, were to meet with him before luncheon this very Sunday. And at Tothill, when he had talked again of Great Grandfather's friendliness towards the scheme, both Grandma and Uncle Hubert had seemed delighted. They showed no recollection of his having been present at the terrible scene; there was no mention of Marina; Grandma was perhaps a little sweeter, Hubert's cackle sounded occasionally, but it was hard to think that it had all gone very deep. At any rate, it was clearly not to be lived with, was a soon-to-be-forgotten past.

174

Marina, so Nigel said, had gone to New York; it was known in her set that some sort of quarrel with the Mossons had put an end to the episode, but it had not hit any gossip column. As to the important people she had interested in the opera, Nigel thought that those who had intended would still come. He had met Sir John Wallis, who was full of Tothill's beauties. Elvira Stuart had written to Reggie asking if she could help about period details. Everything was all right. For a moment, it was true, as in the opera, the temple gate had opened to reveal not the gods but fiery flames and awful spectres. But it had closed again. And, as Marina would have said, the memory must be made into 'fun'.

So he kept up the surrealistic rehash for Pratt's benefit as they were talking together in Dean's Yard this Sunday morning with a full family luncheon in prospect at Tothill House.

'Oh, 'Ubert, it's such fun 'ere at Tothill with the boys' throats being cut and dead saints on the plates. Thank you for it all, Mama.'

'My dear Marina, at Tothill we can give you Our Father Mother God all harmonious.'

Tom was laughing with his brother because the absurdity was just very funny, but, as laughter came, he wished to reject it. Van had made it absurd, and they were both agreed that it was hard not to be amazed and fascinated by the suggestion of their uncle's secret vice. But from the very first moment that he had heard of the scene, he felt that an earthquake was making the ground tremble under them. He felt desperately unhappy for his grandmother and his uncle, although he was relieved that Marina should be gone. But more than compassion, he felt a dread. He was sure that such violence could not end there. He sensed bad luck in the air. Above all, he wished that Van had not been present at the scene. Not just his emotions but his reason – yes, he felt sure it was his reason – told him that they would find it hard to forgive his brother for having heard such things. But Van seemed to feel that, by giving them all comic voices in retrospect, he had defused their explosive potential. Trust was broken. He must, little though he wanted to, check his brother's happy eagerness.

He said, 'I think today may be rather a strain. Ma at Tothill is never the easiest thing. And she's still in a state, *I* think. Oh, I know I exaggerate. But there *is* something wrong. And then bringing Eustace! I know you like him and I don't. But what *will* Grandma make of him? And how will he behave with Uncle Hubert? And can you imagine him with Great Grandfather? After all, the whole of this family luncheon is to celebrate the old man's being out and about again. At ninety it's pretty good! And Eustace isn't even Tothill family. Why ever did Ma want to bring him? And then you're going to be late for lunch . . . Do you *have* to go to this meeting with Howerton and Mordaunt?'

'Yes, I do, Pratt. It's very important. Anyway, I shan't be more than a quarter of an hour late. And we've agreed that you'll hold the fort. You're supreme at holding forts.'

'All right. But I do wish you hadn't heard all those awful things. I am sure they must have hated you being there so much. I know you say they've been nice about the opera since, but I suspect they connect it all with Marina, they're bound to. And then this tremendous family occasion and then your being late because of the opera. Look, I hate lying and I'm frightfully bad at it, but do let's find another reason why you're late.'

'I say – lies! Grandma won't like that in Truthful Tom.'

'No, I am serious, Van.'

'Well, okay. Let's think. It's Sunday. Say I had to go to a special service in the Abbey.'

'But why should you go, if I don't?'

'Oh, say it's all the people who've won scholarships to the universities. That the Dean is giving us a special talk.'

'But why should he?'

'Well, why shouldn't he? Anyway, *they* won't know.'

'Uncle Hubert will. You know what he is about his old school.'

'Things have changed since his day. It'll give Grandma a bit of a grumble to keep her quiet. "The stuffy old Church of England" and all that. But they'll have to accept it. And they'll never know.'

Tom was not happy at it, but he said, 'All right. I'll try. But you must promise me something in return. Don't talk about *Phaethon* at all with them today. After all, it *is* a family day. Great Grandfather's really. And I'm sure it will be safer. Please.'

'All right. I'll do my best. Although how we'll get through the day. What on earth will Grandma say to Eustace? . . .'

But further conjecture was cut short, when a tall, sharp-voiced boy came up to them.

'I say, Mosson, I've been looking everywhere for you. Brownlow told me to find you and tell you that your mother's been on to him on the telephone. She's coming to Waterloo not Victoria. She's been staying with friends.'

'What friends?'

'How on earth should I know? That's what she told Brownlow or at any rate that's what he told me. But the chief thing is you're to meet her at Waterloo. Twelve o'clock. The train from Andover. You're both to be there.'

'Good Lord! She's been at Uncle Jim's.'

'I have no idea – I don't know your Uncle Jim. Anyway, is the message clear?'

'Yes, yes. And very rudely delivered.' But the boy was gone.

'I can't go,' Piers said. 'It's nonsense anyway, I'm sure.'

'I'd better start now,' Tom said. 'If I go now, I can't get any more confusing messages making it more of a beastly muddle. I'll walk. I'd like that.'

And so he had. All along the Embankment, the sight of the river flowing past and of the clear, spring sky above gave alleviation to his anxious speculations and foreboding. 'Against their bridal day, which is not long, Sweet Thames run gently till I end my song.' There was no wedding expected. He had only attended one wedding and remembered nothing but the disappointment of the wedding cake, on which the icing had been hard yet powdery. Nor, he reminded himself, further to banish gloom, was he giving vent to song. How terrible it must be to become one of those half-mad people who walk the streets talking to themselves or singing, how frightening to be out of touch with the normal, the rest of humanity around one. But, with the river flowing as it had done for centuries, and the protective sky overhead, such fears, all danger of unrule or chaos, seemed remote. As indeed did the people down below on the Embankment that he had just left. He began to cross the bridge.

Then suddenly there was no road nor traffic nor people but water whose depths he could not see. And then, looking up, high, high above him the sky, across which some clouds were moving. At once the bridge's pavement beneath him was insecure, trembling. The clouds above looming closer, threatening – the skies would fall in. He pulled his back straight and threw off the strange thought. He noted other passers-by – an old woman telling her daughter of something 'green and ever so large it was'. A double-chinned man whose head thrust forward showed what 'sunk in thought' meant. But they were nothing – he felt only himself, his own body totally alone, himself, Tom, and, high above, the sky, nothing, nothing between to save him from its fall, and below, the trembling bridge, the bottomless water. The sense of the aloneness of his body terrified him, and all the passers-by were only a dream – none of them were there, no one was there but him, he felt, and nothing, nothing, would save him from finding safety in the depths of the river below, nothing could save him from throwing himself down where he would be cradled from all this frightening void above and around him. He began to walk more quickly. If he could get to the other side he would be safe . . . He tried, hurrying, to look again at the passing faces, but then as each person passed he thought, that's the last one I can appeal to . . . he wanted to stop these laughing girls, this tall young businessman, this smart lady, and ask them to take his arm, to carry him, to save him. In his haste he pushed against a woman who said, 'Do you mind?' and he nearly knocked over a small boy so that the father called, 'You'd better watch what you're doing, see!' But he couldn't, he mustn't watch anything until he had set foot on dry land, had escaped the closing in of the emptiness, the suffocation that surrounded him, the desperate certainty that, to avoid it, he would throw himself over the parapet into the enfolding water.

He set his eye on the Festival Hall. Mr Lawton, the new young history master, said it was the best clean simple piece of recent London architecture, but Uncle Hubert said it was an eyesore that should never have been allowed. The Festival had been in the year he came to the school but he'd never gone to it. To him it was simply like a large box. It had nothing he could dwell on to forget his absurd, immediate terror. He began to run . . . he fixed his eyes on the shot tower . . . for a moment he found relief, wondering what such a vast chimney did that it had that name – were people fired from it as from circus cannons? It was a fascinating idea but nonsense. Was it an arsenal? But why then like a chimney? He followed it up to where its brick ended in the void and then his eye must go on and on until it came to the looming sky above . . . there was nothing, nothing to save him from this fright . . . only to get to the other side . . . he could see that as he ran faster people were staring at him . . . he was one of the odd ones that had lost contact with order and rule . . . a young man shouted, 'It's no good, mate, your train's left.' And now, suddenly, he looked down and it was warehouses beneath, not water, and soon he was no longer lost under the sky, but under the safety of the shadow of a building. He had crossed the bridge. His heart began to beat less fiercely. He was there.

By the time, seven minutes or so later, that he had found Ma's arrival platform, he had almost forgotten his panic, was filled only with anxious speculation about Ma's request for them to meet her at Waterloo. There were so many things connected with Andover, with Uncle Jim, that it could be anything, but perhaps, at last, they would find out what had been worrying her so all these last months. Perhaps Uncle Jim had let her down. If it had been that he was getting a divorce and could marry Ma, she would have been so happy, so eager to tell them. But if he had decided to cease seeing her, if that beastly wife had forbidden him to come to the Nursery, Ma wouldn't want to discuss it at Tothill, yet she would want him and Van to know so that they could help her to get through the

day. That must be it. It wasn't going to be a very happy luncheon – not least, because it meant no more Uncle Jim the reliable, and, even worse, that Uncle Jim wasn't reliable, had let
Ma down. He felt himself straightening his back ready to act as
Ma's cheerer and protector, and then, recognising his physical
movement as that which he used when he acted as Grandma's
stout arm, he laughed at himself – who was he who had just
panicked on a bridge to be the mainstay of women in their
unhappiness?

Now the train was coming in, and a moment later he could
see her among the alighting passengers – he wished she didn't
use all that funny make-up and hair dye – women didn't get
themselves up like that now, it seemed specially wrong for
mothers, it made her look so old. But he waved to her and
almost at the same moment found his Uncle Eustace beside
him doing the same. He could see that his uncle was annoyed
at his presence. He probably had hoped to have Ma on his own
to borrow some more money from her. Thinking this, and
remembering 'little solid shit of the family', Tom glowered at
his uncle. But luckily nothing had to be said before Ma was
upon them.

'Darling heart,' she cried. 'Oh what rapture to see you!'
Tom managed not to cower before her overwhelming
embrace. 'Useless, darling, what bliss.' And then she looked in
disconcerted amaze for Piers. Tom began to explain, but, 'No,
let me guess,' she cried, 'the darling boy's gone off to the
public loo to see if his tie's straight or something like that. I
know the angel's vanity.'

'I'm afraid it isn't that,' Tom said, 'he's had to go to a service
in the Abbey. There's an address by the Dean particularly for
those who are going on to university with scholarships like
Van.'

It sounded so silly that he felt that he must add, 'I should
have been there but they let me slip away when they knew you
wanted me here.'

That made nonsense of what he'd said, because of course he
hadn't got a scholarship. Oh, dear. How difficult lying was.
For a moment he could see Mama's face literally fall. Oh God!

he thought, she's been relying on Piers. Something is *very* wrong.

'Oh dear, what a bore! If he's late at Tothill, Jackie will be livid. And it's not very complimentary to the old man. But what bliss to have this little meeting first. And the delicious weather. The *tulipa clusiana* at the moment! I've never seen them better. I've decided to have Black Parrots in the formal bed and some Bizarres. It's this awful business that, though we don't really flower until July, people expect a spectacle at any time.'

She was on to her hobby horse, but to Tom's ear, so familiar with the complaint, it sounded as though she were speaking by rote. Uncle Eustace obviously felt so, for he rushed away to buy cigarettes.

'There's something wrong, Ma, isn't there? You had something special to tell us.'

She gave him a look he couldn't decipher, but then she seemed to have made up her mind.

'Well, not really, darling. It was just that I was talking with Uncle Jim. He sends his love by the way. He's so fond of you.' Tom tensed himself in readiness. She plunged in, 'It's just that I couldn't decide what we should or should not say about the Luzzi woman. Jim said play it by ear . . .'

'Is that really all, Ma? But why ever did you want Uncle Eustace to decide that? And it isn't a problem.'

'Of course it is, darling. And Eustace is such a man of the world. I was saying you'd know what we should say or not say about this Luzzi woman, Useless. You know her, don't you? She's a tremendously smart rich woman that Hubert was going to marry. I thought she was simply hell, but then she thought me madly dowdy and poor. And she was right, of course. Anyway I can't say she's missed much, having Jackie for a mother-in-law. Oh, I mustn't say that to you, Tom, you and Grandma are such friends. But she isn't the easiest mother-in-law. And really I shouldn't have thought poor darling Hubert would have been the most exciting of husbands. Like a doctored Tom really.'

Uncle Eustace began to sing, 'Hold your hand out, naughty

boy. Hold your hand out, naughty boy.'

Tom thought, how on earth can he know? It made him dislike his Uncle Eustace even more, as though he had some secret powers.

Ma said, 'Useless, darling, the songs you dig up. That was old Uncle Edgar's favourite tune. And not very polite when I am talking. Now, what should we say about the "broken engagement"?'

'Nothing,' Tom said, 'unless they do.'

'Nothing,' Uncle Eustace agreed, 'very wise.'

'Oh there you are. I knew you'd be a help,' Ma cried.

'Is that *all* you brought me to Waterloo to discuss?' Uncle Eustace sounded cross and, Tom thought, a shade disbelieving.

But she didn't really look more relaxed, he soon decided, not even when, as they emerged, she drew a deep breath and said, 'What an absolutely heavenly day. Let's walk across the bridge.'

Oh no, Tom thought. But then he decided that it would be all right with companions – he took his mother's arm and she smiled and patted his hand.

But Uncle Eustace was horrified. 'Are you out of your mind, Rosemary? Walking is absolute hell.' And he at once hailed a taxi, disregarding the waiting taxi queue.

It hadn't been all that easy on their arrival, Tom reflected, as a new young footman presented him with the cold snapper soup which Grandma loved to serve as a gesture of her Transatlantic loyalties. Everyone had been very Mosson, greeting him lovingly as the youngest of the family, deploring Piers' absence as the direct heir, making Ma feel at home as a daughter-in-law, so that there had really seemed to be no place for Uncle Eustace. Tom had even found himself for a few moments feeling sorry for his stinking uncle. It wasn't as if he'd never been to Tothill so that he could be 'shown round', and yet there was no inclusion of him in the family ring.

Great Grandfather had merely stared at this intruder, and

repeated the name 'Gordon' quizzically once or twice, so that
Ma had been forced to say coyly, 'It's your granddaughter-in-
law's maiden name, you know.' But this sort of relationship
conundrum had not been the most suitable for his ninety years
plus comprehension. Nurse Harper had said at once jollily and
sharply, 'It's the greatest pity Mr Piers Mosson should be late.
He does Mr Mosson so much good.' It was clear that Uncle
Eustace didn't, for Great Grandfather sat like a cross idol in
his chair, resolutely uncomprehending.

Tom's unhappiness was that, in this uneasy atmosphere, the
absence of Van, who could have set it all right, kept on presenting itself as a topic to fill in silences. He felt so untrue to his
promise, for he could find no way of intervening. It was a sign
of the unsuitability of the whole occasion that he, the
youngest, who should have been the silent, polite follower of
adult conversation, should be called upon like this, and he
comforted himself that that was why he couldn't help as he'd
promised he would. It was contrary to all proper protocol.

Uncle Hubert, it was true, had taken over Eustace and there
had been some exchange about Britain's disgracefully tame
acceptance of Nasser's treatment of British subjects in Cairo.
But Grandma had been quick to scotch this by saying sweetly,
'There wasn't much the British could do, was there really? But
I don't think politics, do you, Hubert dear? They will not help
to welcome Father downstairs.'

Tom had wondered for a moment whether Uncle Eustace
would attack her as he whispered to his nephew, 'The Americans weren't exactly helpful, I assure you.' Then he added,
'But still, we mustn't sing for our supper. I hope it's coming
soon. We all depend too much on their largesse to wish to
offend.'

Tom thought back with horror to this whispering, both its
content and its manner. He had felt sure that his uncle would
whisper too loudly and then the ice would break.

There had, indeed, been some near disasters. When Uncle
Hubert had said, 'But you used to be a member of the Travel-
lers', surely,' and then had stopped short in embarrassment.
Obviously something awful had happened with Uncle Eustace

at the Club, probably dud cheques. Well, at any rate, Tom
thought, it made something quite clear to him: people who live
on their wits are a perpetual menace to order and cohesion.
And he reflected now, as Eustace next to him toyed with the
snapper soup which he obviously disliked, at least if I do
achieve my ambition of becoming a lawyer, I shall have the job
of keeping people like him, parasites and frauds, out of circula-
tion. Why had Mother brought him? Man of the world indeed!
He wasn't of their world, as Grandma had made quite clear.
He couldn't help loving her for it. For when Eustace explained
that he'd resigned from the Club because of living abroad,
she'd asked him why he did so and he'd murmured, 'Oh, taxation.' As if he had any money to tax! The lying and pretence
was so awful. But Grandma, out of her great wealth, had rumbled him, without realising that his claim was a pretence. 'Oh
yes?' she said brightly. 'People seem so often to speak about
taxation. I am glad we have never had to worry about it. It
seems such a pity when money, that can bring so much happiness and joy, is allowed to become a burden.' Eustace's face
had been worth seeing – the longing for a little more burden!
Tom chid himself for being so spiteful.

But really this cultured man of the world had done nothing
to help the situation. He'd only made one attempt, and that
had been a disaster. He'd peered at some picture when they
first came into the dining room and said, 'What a delightful
little Lancret. There's something about his work that tells you
at once that it's his.' Grandma had given a silvery laugh. 'Is
there? We have always been told that it is a Watteau. But if
something is as beautiful as that little thing, the name doesn't
matter, does it?'

How certain she seemed in her movements, as now, when
she squeezed her silver lime clip on to the snapper soup and
took the least particle of jelly into her tiny lip-sticked mouth.
All with brisk little gestures and small quizzical flashes of her
bright blue eyes from one side of the table to another. Like a
thrush breaking the life out of a snail in two quick turns of its
beak, Van said. But if that was her way, so efficient and
uncomplaining, of crossing bridges that he knew frightened

her so terribly, he admired her and hoped that he could one day be as orderly and safe.

'You're all getting English Sunday roast beef,' she said. 'I do apologise, Mr Gordon. I know that you are a gourmet. But this luncheon is for Father. And that is his choice.'

Eustace murmured, 'Delightful', in his particular drawl – perhaps that was what was 'man of the world' about him. And then, 'Oh really!' he began whispering, 'Those Grinling Gibbons snipe and woodcock round the fireplace would be rather more delicious than beef, wouldn't they?' But this time Grandma *had* heard. She produced a tiny amused laugh.

'Oh, I can promise you that the beef will be more tender than wood. Even than Gibbons carving.'

Eustace tried to laugh too. 'An enchanting room,' he said.

Something – could it have been Grandma? he wondered – inspired Tom to give his uncle a peck. 'It doesn't happen to be the season for game.'

Eustace was clearly offended. 'And *I* happened to know that.'

Tom could have kicked himself. Instead of helping, he'd made things worse, for Ma, perhaps in defence of her brother, perhaps in desperation, began one of her longest things. And, as soon as she began, he knew that there would be no stopping her.

'I'm sure poor Piers is feeling awfully miserable about this Abbey service. Poor pet! Not that that's any real excuse for lateness, I know. You were quite right to have lunch served, Jackie. I mean if there's not some discipline, as Jim was saying to me only the other day, we're quite finished. Of course, *he* felt that so much after the war, with all those national service men being drafted into the regiment. Thank goodness, *that's* soon to be over. I thought the poor darling would have had an apoplectic fit sometimes. And all the other officers I know agreed. When I go over there I find that there are so many of Jerry's friends still left in the Regiment, Jackie. I always think you'll be pleased about that. And they remember Tothill. Those that came here. Arthur Caplet – he's a colonel now – was recalling it last time I saw him. He married a frightful creature. He spent a night here with Jerry on their way down to Tidworth in 1940. Like a great tomb, he described it. But that was in war-time, of course. And the bombs. Anyway it was like a palace to them all. And it is! Here one feels one can expand. It seems all wrong that poor Grandpa should be so confined. But then, better confinement in a vast palace than prison. Except that prison cells probably don't seem better . . .'

Thank God, Tom thought, she's stopping. He began, 'Grandma, what . . .' but Ma's loudest contralto note drowned him.

'How beautiful it all is! The rooms, of course. I haven't dared to wander into the Great Hall. It seems somehow so sacred to Piers. I wonder if you're all looking forward to his opera as much as I am, Grandma. I don't know when I saw an opera last.'

Grandma, with a hint of a smile, said, 'Perhaps you never *have* seen one, Rosemary.' And Hubert chuckled.

Thank goodness they were taking it all so easily – even the forbidden subject.

Uncle Eustace commented, 'Mm. Well, I hardly think Lully, do you?'

Old sarkey boots! But he'd have to get them off the subject before Van arrived, because he knew his brother wouldn't be able to resist if it was in full steam. But, ah, thank God for Ma. She was off again.

'And the wilderness that's grown up at the end of the garden. Such wonderful shapes the bushes have made, like those creatures that jump out at one in dreams. It's the sort of effect that I've tried to create with the shrub rose end of the Nursery. But customers only think of flowers. Never of shapes. All the same, our propaganda for the old roses is bearing fruit. I had a letter asking for Cuisse de Nymph. Imagine that!'

Tom translated the name of the rose and thought that Ma could hardly have chosen a worse thing for them all to imagine. What could Uncle Hubert's thoughts be? And in Grandma's company! Oh dear! Nymph's thigh!

'I do believe I really saw a rabbit when I walked down there before lunch. And within yards of the Thames! I used to hate them for eating everything in the Nursery. But now they just sit in the roadways, all blind and deaf, and get killed by the cars, I can't think how I could have been so greedy and unkind. But most people are until it's too late, aren't they? No, Gates, no wine. Do forgive me, Hubert, I'm sure it's very special. Burgundy, is it? Could I, do you think, Jackie, have another large gin and tonic? It's either being upset by Piers' lateness or being so hungry, but I long for another gin. My wretched tum keeps rumbling. I think it's hunger tho', because I heard Grandad's tum rumbling, too. He doesn't hear me, does he?' She plunged on. 'I believe Piers has got a wonderful smart new suit. Hasn't he, Tom? We must remember to praise it. Or perhaps we shouldn't now he's late. Shag suits, you call out-of-school suits, don't you? They have a word for everything, it seems. But, of course, you'd know that, Hubert. You and Jerry must have been major and minor. Like the boys, only always shorter, of course. They have the Gordon height. Do forgive Piers, Jackie.'

'The boys and I,' their grandmother said, 'share a love that is more powerful than lateness for lunch, Rosemary. The wilderness, my dear, as you call it, is as old as Pratt's house, perhaps even older. Charles II certainly. It isn't called the wilderness. They called it the Woodwork and the name has been kept through the centuries by Tothills and by Mossons alike. Of course it has its shapes and paths for those who know it. But perhaps it is rather overgrown. Will you give me a memorandum pad, Gates? I will just make a note to speak to Ralph Tucker about cutting back the bushes if they need it. Your visits are always so good for us, Rosemary. You always have some little oversight or muddle to bring to our attention.'

Eustace whispered to Tom, 'Oh, God! Rosemary's put her foot right in it. I'd better help out. I'm doing this knight errant ride for you and Piers – so remember that when he comes into millions.'

He looked at the arrangements of tulips and winked at his nephew.

'What an enchantment of flowers, Lady Mosson! And how suitable tulips are for this seventeenth century setting. Too bad you don't have the Bizarres and the wilder Parrots.'

Grandma gave the sharpest birdlike look. 'That's so nice of you, Mr Gordon. May is a bad time for flowers, I think. Tulips never appear to me to be true flowers. They are too stiff. You must see my lilac arrangements in the Saloon.'

'I long for it. But tulips stiff! Oh come! The colours! The *enchanting* pinks!' he cried, 'Lady Mosson. The *delicate* mauves, the rich *purples*.' He drawled and stressed the adjectives in his most dandy manner, indicating each elaborate Constance Spry-like confection with a languid wave of his long-fingered hands. 'Flowers do *make* a room, don't they?'

Grandma gave a tiny coarse chuckle. 'I hardly think a Pratt and Gibbons dining room needs much making. And I think you know that, Mr Gordon. I am an Edwardian, you know, and I like flower decorations. Flowers and sunny rooms,' she added vaguely.

Then Tom saw to his amazement that she had stretched out her delicate little hand, a little knobbed with arthritis, and laid it on his uncle's arm as he crumbled his bread on the table.

'Dear Eustace – I am now going to call you that – we welcome you here as Rosemary's brother. You do not have to sing for your supper with us.'

Tom could feel his uncle's body tremble. He saw a flash of anger in his mother's eye, but she did her best while he was doing nothing. He felt ashamed. All he could do was to sit back and let her prattle on, hoping she would clear the fences.

'Have you been getting out on to the terrace in this lovely May weather, Grandad?' she shouted to the mummified figure.

Tom waited for the old man's answer as they all did. His rheumy bloodhound eyes were sorrowful as always, but they fixed upon Nurse Harper's hands as she cut up his beef for him into little digestible fragments. Tom turned away from this culmination of disintegration. But Ma was only stimulated into nervous talk again.

'Darling hearts! I'm afraid he doesn't hear me.'

'Oh, I think he does, Rosemary, but I doubt if he will answer while Nurse Harper is cutting his beef. Feeding time is very important to him nowadays, you know. It's a manifestation of living, I think. And living has become his principal occupation. But I can answer your question about the terrace. No, he does not go out now at all. When it is not feeding time, he prefers to sit upstairs conserving his strength.'

There was an icy note in his uncle's voice that made Tom wonder whether he was rebuking Ma or just longing for his grandfather's death. Probably both.

Ma smiled vaguely at Hubert. Tom made a vow to say something before she could speak again. But, surprisingly, Great Grandfather suddenly waved a hand more like a fin in its scaliness and its blue-patterned veins. The hand bade the nurse leave off mashing his roast potatoes. Taking a fork in his trembling fingers he proceeded to risk a little of his own energy in feeding himself – and in addressing Ma in a high but small voice. As he spoke, Tom saw his napkin shift a little, showing a huge Adam's apple bobbing about in his wasted chicken neck.

'No, Rosemary, I don't sit on the terrace. There's always some dangerous little breeze or other even in the conservatory, let alone on the terrace, in these sunny days. We're in England remember, not Madeira. I've got to live to ninety six, you know. If not a hundred. Hubert expects it of me. And Jackie believes that there's no age in God's love, or something like that. So you see it means a lot of care.' He stopped and his chin fell on his napkin as though he had died, but Tom could see that he was staring at the beef and potato with greed. He understood that, as he tucked into his own delicious, toffee-ish pieces of outside that Gates had specially served to him. However, before the old man started to eat, he addressed Ma again.

'We're pleased to see you, you know, Rosemary. But I'm afraid you must be spoiling Piers. He's with us every Sunday fortnight, is it? Yes, fortnight. And he's never been late before. It doesn't help to spoil boys, you know. We lunch at one, as he well knows.'

'I do indeed, sir.' Piers had made a sudden entrance. 'And I'm greatly ashamed and very apologetic. And very hungry.' He held out his hand to the old man.

Oh, thank God, Tom thought. I can hand over now.

The old man had laid down his knife and fork and was shaking Piers' hand. 'We're very glad to see you, my boy, though you *are* late, and might well be kicked out for breaking the rules. But your mother's here and her brother and they're not hitting it off very well with your grandmother. So your presence will help.'

Piers gave a wide smile to the whole company at the old man's embarrassing frankness. Tom felt he could follow this up and he laughed and said, 'You *are* needed, Van. I've been hopeless.' And in a minute everyone was joining in the laughter.

Piers shook hands with his Uncle Hubert and exchanged with him a smile at Grandma's so immediately blaming the whole mischance upon the Church of England.

'I can just imagine the stuffy old sermon you have had to sit through in that beautiful Abbey. It's a mercy that old Church of England doesn't scare every child away from God's love. Do you know,' she asked Eustace, 'what is the worst thing I can remember from my childhood? Father was an Episcopalian. And, can you imagine, every Good Friday as they called it, they had a *three hour service*. My gracious! As if God's love could want anything so morbid for his little children.'

'Mm,' Eustace drawled, 'but that's the length of the service. Always has been.'

Grandma wasn't bothering with this. She kissed Piers and asked, 'Well, haven't you got eyes in your head? There's your mother. Go and say you're glad to see her.'

Piers rubbed the back of his hand against his mother's cheek. Tom could see tears welling in her eyes. Something was wrong.

'I don't think Ma needs to be told that, Grandma.'

Even Uncle Eustace, who was not given to sweet emotions, said, 'That's a noble suit, Piers.'

'To be honest,' Piers, who was seated beside him, spoke

quietly as though to an habitual confidant, although he hadn't seen the old thing for months and months, 'it was my vanity in changing into it after Abbey that's made me so late, Eustace. I'm glad it's all passed over so easily. Although I am afraid poor Tom has had to hold the fort longer that he need when the fault's mine.'

'Oh, but one always does that with people. One can usually make it up to them later.'

'I really think,' Grandma said, 'that we ought to write and say that you are not to attend these long Abbey services. Would you like me or your mother to do that, Piers?'

Tom exchanged anxious glances with Van. Now they were in for it. Ma had seen their glances, however, and she rushed to their aid.

'I rather wonder,' she began, but there was no need, Hubert was more horrified than they.

'My dear Mother, the Abbey is the equivalent of the School Chapel.'

And Eustace came to Hubert's assistance, 'Oh, I really think, Lady Mosson . . . I mean you see, if they were at Eton . . .' The two men exchanged public schoolboy glances of embarrassed amusement at her feminine and American ignorance and insensitivity.

'Oh, men's fiddlesticks!' Grandma intervened.

But she was overruled by patriarchal authority. The old man was by now ladling waves of cream-spumed juicy stewed rhubarb into his toothless grinning fish's mouth. He paused in his gurgling greed, and said, with a little stream of white flecked red juice running down to the left of his chin, 'They have to go to the Abbey, Jackie. It's the school place of worship. As well as the national one. They don't teach you these things at ninety ninth church. But then *we* don't have women readers – or not yet. Nurse Harper or one of those nurses read me something about women clergy the other day. If we ever *do* restore the family chapel, as I hope we shall, we shan't have any of *them*. That's where the whole family will worship once it's restored. And no nonsense about it. But I was overruled. That was *our* family chapel and we let Hitler's bombs turn it into a concert hall or some such nonsense. The family's never been right since. That damned scoundrel! He did for the Mossons.'

Suddenly the old, grey pouched lizard's face was shot red with anger and the rheumy sagging-lidded reptile's eyes flashed. Piers looked at his great grandfather and wondered at his ancient anger and grief. The truth was that his father's death did not affect him as it seemed to do the old man and, looking at Pratt, he saw that his brother, too, felt only embarrassment, no special sadness for his hero father whom he didn't even remember. Perhaps, Piers thought, grief and anger are special properties of old age, like Lear's.

The reference to the bombed nearby St John's Smith Square as the family chapel was more fierce in its effect on everyone, he could see. It announced untimely that old age had its fires but also that those fires smouldered away in delusion. Lunacy in the old is embarrassing, but, like all lunacy, it is also private. Piers could see that Tom shared his anxiety at being confronted by what had previously been known to them only by whisper – Great Grandfather's belief that he owned St John's Smith Square. But the anxiety was in the older faces too, of course. Eustace, after all, was not family to Grandma and their uncle. Piers could see that the stranger registered the general emotion but had no clue to its meaning.

'The family chapel?' he asked in his most charming, urbane manner. 'I'm culpably at a loss. I knew nothing of one.'

Grandma took on the office of explaining. Her low chuckling-sweet voice was well adapted for undertones. But she was not risking too much, for she said, 'Father always sees St John's Smith Square as a fitting family chapel to Vanbrugh's Tothill House. And for him it is so. Well, Mrs Eddy quotes Shakespeare, "There's nothing either good or bad but thinking makes it so." ' And she gave a little chuckle to help Eustace digest the meaning.

Alas, thought Piers, he was the wrong recipient. He hadn't written his famous scholarly article for nothing. He would tolerate no inaccuracy. What Tom has been going through, Piers thought.

'But Thomas Archer was the architect of St John's.'

'There was,' said Hubert, 'a long standing attribution to Vanbrugh, you know. St John's was thought by many authorities to be his church and not Archer's right down to 1800 or so.'

But the old man caught on to it. 'You're one of the chaps then who thinks that we owe our great buildings to the signs of the Zodiac, are you?' He levelled his knife tremblingly towards where he vaguely thought Eustace to be. 'Or perhaps you think *this* great house was built by Fred Archer the jockey.'

'I've heard talk of him, of course,' said Eustace stiffly, 'but he was long before my time. And I am not a racing man.' He laughed in assumption that the old man was joking, but the shaking knife shook more fiercely. Eustace smiled in turn at Jackie and Hubert, and then, in desperation, at Rosemary. 'I really don't understand what all this to-do is about,' he drawled.

What an ass he is, thought Tom, why can't he leave the subject alone? And how indecorous for a man who boasts of being 'civilised' to dwell on an old man's madness. Piers thought, they've been savaging Eustace before I arrived, and he wants to get back at them. But he hasn't a chance, I'm sure. Whatever did Ma land him in a lion's den for?

'Archer won the Derby five times and the Oaks four. And now no one remembers his name,' the old man said.

'Oh, *I* do, Grandfather,' Hubert answered, calling on them all with his eye to see him do wonders with the old. 'He was the Steve Donoghue of his day.'

But to Piers' satisfaction his song had no magic power – tiresome old nanny. Great Grandfather was drama, not a child in the nursery. Through the old man's sobbing came another nostalgic groan, but his voice, high and cracked, had unmistakable spite in it.

'Steve fiddlesticks! A man in his prime like you shouldn't live in the past, Hubert. Lester Piggott should be your man. We old people *have* to cling to the little rock of memory that's left to us until the mighty stream bears us away. But you don't need to blast that rock away bit by bit from under us. Club us on the head, it's cleaner and quicker.'

The unexpected fierce note in his great grandfather's voice touched Piers. That was how he would play it, that was how *he* would play Lear – pathetic, a nearly dead oak tree, from which oftentimes the thunder would sound and the lightning flash to make all quail. But, to his consternation, Ma rushed in where silence was the correct tribute.

'You don't know how tactless you've been, Grandfather, with all your talk of jockeys. I'd almost forgotten my fatal fling last year. Wasn't it shocking, Hubert, but I lost fifty pounds on the Oaks. That Captain Lister who writes about rock gardens came down to the Nursery and told me one of his "sure things", as he calls them – I ought to have known better, but you know silly me!' Piers hoped that she would not see the stormy look on all faces, but she did. Nervously, she added, '"said she coyly"; I can't resist a flutter. And so I lost my money.' Silence greeted this flat ending. Even Eustace looked depressed.

Then Great Grandfather Mosson said, '*My* money. Not yours.' But he was not deflected from his lament. 'When he was very old, my father used to say that old people should be quietly put away. I used to think he meant Euthanasia as the Shavians called it – God, what a hypocritical crowd! And to be honest I often thought he was right. But I don't think he meant that now at all. He meant he wanted to be put away from all of us and our noise and our kicking.'

Piers looked with contempt at the embarrassed faces around him. Here it was. A tomb had opened and the skeleton had spoken its mind. And all they could hear were senile ramblings. And they were red in the face as though a parrot cage had been uncovered and the parrot had said 'Fuck!'

Tom thought, when our seniors opt out of life, we should respect them, but surely, if that was how he felt, Great Grandfather could not be arbiter at Tothill. He could see his brother's worshipping face, and he understood, for at least the old man was serious. But his seriousness was that of a mystic, someone who'd withdrawn, not of a man whose word ruled family life. He hoped that Van would not let his imagination lead him to offend the others, for, in the end, surely it was the active – Grandma, Hubert – who would decide now in Tothill affairs. Perhaps Grandma's competence would intervene. Her lips had been moving silently – she too was seeking her God. He wished he didn't find religion so incredible, for it was one of the rocks on which safety was built.

Suddenly Grandmother spoke. 'They're still alive, your memories, Pater.'

Pater! She must have dredged the funny name up from her memories of her early wedded days in England. Perhaps she was on the old man's side, Piers thought. But her next words soon made it clear – it was just her usual Christian Science.

'God is omnipresent, Pater. "Behold I am with you always." All the beautiful things always are.' She smiled and signalled to Gates to serve the old man first with the cheese soufflé and to the others to say no more for the moment.

Tom felt a shiver of horror going through Uncle Eustace's thin frame at his side. And, though he didn't wish to, he could not but share the beastly man's embarrassment. He felt angry that the Mossons should let themselves down before such a cheap sponger.

But the old man mumbled, 'Always bending things! We aren't all bits of wire to be bent by you, Jackie, you know. They're my thoughts, not yours. Leave them alone. I wasn't talking about *beautiful* things. Public hangings is what I said. Those aren't beautiful.' His seriousness gave way to tears again.

Smiling towards Nurse Harper, Grandma said, 'Yes, I wonder perhaps, Nurse? Whether he wouldn't be more comfortable? Certainly not the cheese soufflé, do you? His digestion, you know. Perhaps his little tray on his own in future. What do you think?'

To Piers' disgust, Uncle Hubert followed her lead like a stupid sheep. 'Yes, I think, Nurse, you know, Mr Mosson would be altogether more comfortable . . .'

Piers could hardly put up with it. It was George III all over again – that fine mind, that large if obstinate nature tortured and brutalised by stupid doctors and an uncaring royal offspring. At Kew they had put the old King into an iron chair, and he met iron with irony, he'd called it his coronation chair. It was like the old man's answer to Jackie. What a part! Why had no one written it? But, to produce it, he must feel with the old men, fight for them against a heartless world unaware of the tragic grandeur of old age. Even his brother Pratt sat red and embarrassed. The grandeur of old age recalled Vanbrugh's work – massive, eccentric, even brutal, but splendidly tragic. An ironic voice questioned this relation between his Victorian merchant great grandfather and his soldier-architect and man of the theatre, but he suppressed all such ridicule fiercely. And to his delight the ironic voice was silenced. Scepticism and irony *must* be silenced if creative powers were to live.

He broke into Hubert's dialogue with Nurse Harper about the old man's future regimen in his upstairs banishment. He addressed the old man directly.

'I don't think, sir, that was what your father meant by "being put away" or, at any rate, what he wanted.'

Coming so suddenly his voice sounded abrupt, even severe. He saw Uncle Eustace flinch at the prospect of more such talk and fuss. Uncle Hubert frowned. Grandma began, 'Piers, darling, Nurse Harper was talking . . .'

But Piers went straight ahead.

He had found a gentler note, now that his first horrible nervousness at coming on stage was over. 'Nor you, sir, I believe. Or if you do, then it's very selfish. For there's nothing that young people, my generation, that is, well, people like me, need more than to understand about your memories, to hear about them, to feel them, if you can help us. I mean what's the good of most of the humanities that we make so much of at school – I mean those of us that aren't on the science side – if we can't connect with people who've lived in the past, been involved with it all? It seems to me nonsense to try to feel literature or history – I mean as more than language puzzles or facts on the page – if you can't be told by old people, people like you, sir, what remains with you of all you've known.'

Nurse Harper said sharply, 'Mr Mosson's very tired.' And indeed the old man, who had ceased crying, sat like a limp puppet, eyes very wide open but dead, mouth a little gaping.

Piers swept on, 'Oh, I know there are many wonderful things that happen to one, and dreadful ones – public hangings – that are for oneself only. I've had some already, even at seventeen. I'm not being insensitive and impertinent, I hope. I mean when I say, "I hope", I'm using it to mean "I know". Although Pratt's nearly falling off his chair for fear I may be. But if you would tell us how it seems to you, how you recall it . . . the things that you feel are for telling, naturally . . . I should think everyone would be grateful. Certainly I should. I mean, what, for example, were *your* public hangings?'

The old man's wooden incomprehension turned to an equally wooden patronage. But he did break his apparently senile silence.

'There weren't any public hangings in my day, my boy. I'm not as old as all that. The last public hanging was in the eighteen fifties, I think. Ten years or so before I was born. But you can look all that up in a book.'

Piers could see how the others looked delighted that his question should have been answered so matter-of-factly. He felt anger with himself for having bungled. Sadness for his great grandfather at being lost to response. Shame, too, for the old man's conventionality, his dead emotional shyness. Shame for his own failure to feel enough with the poor, lost, angry old man, shame that his self-conscious play-acting, his awareness of 'drawing the old man out' had perhaps stifled the real bond of feeling that had come to life in him. Yet he was conscious with fury, too, that the audience was growing restive, that they were relieved because the old man's down-to-earth answer had broken the spell. He could hear his grandmother's little laugh patronising the disillusionment of youth. He sensed that Nurse Harper had wiped her nose, placed her hankie in her handbag and was snapping its metal clasp shut, preparatory to good sense and action. Uncle Eustace, he saw, was eagerly spooning deep into the second cheese soufflé that the footman was now serving.

He *would* hold them; yes, and above all he would *not* let that strange moment of life be swallowed up again in the tomb of his family's daily life. What came to him seemed to him banal, but it was the only connection he could make.

'Perhaps there weren't any public horrors when you were young, sir, I mean, they'd all become private.'

'I don't know about that. If you walked about in the East End at night when I was a young man – Limehouse or Wapping – there were plenty of horrors. You couldn't go there unless you went with the police or Scotland Yard, of course. A friend of mine arranged it once or twice when I was in my twenties. A jungle world. And Seven Dials was worse. Only you had to go *there*, of course. Desperate sights. But plenty of laughter, too. Not the miserable world the welfare people have built. Animals, too. A chap took me over to see a dog fight on an island in the Seine. They weren't allowed in this country. Horrible thing to see, Piers. Dogs tearing each other to bits, lumps of their bowels all over the sawdust. Enormous crowd. Mostly Englishmen, of course, the dogs were trained to it. It was a sport.'

'Of course, of course.' It was all a bit mad, an endless surge of waves of dead prejudices and unresolved feelings. Piers felt desperate – there must be more to it than this. Perhaps the paradoxes themselves offered some key to that strange outburst, that marriage of public hangings and deep affections. But the audience was beginning to mould the play to their own comfortable assumptions.

Hubert said, 'You're quite in form today, Grandfather.'

And Grandma with a little laugh said, 'No *beauty* in those old days, Father? I think there *was*.'

The old man continued to address himself to Piers. '*Public* horrors? Oh, yes, there were public horrors all right. But that big horror, the Great War, put an end to *them*. That was one thing in its favour. The *only* thing. Those of us who were too old to serve and the women knew nothing about it, of course – except through telegrams and newspapers. And that sort of grief, though it's bad, my boy, can be exaggerated. At least as a memory. Is that what you meant when you asked if there were no public horrors when I was young – that I was too old for the trenches? If so, you're a cleverer lad than I thought.' He spoke in short rushes of words interspersed with silences which Piers dreaded, lest one of the family should be able to break the spell. But by now everyone seemed held. 'Yes,' the old man went on, 'those of us who were too old for the trenches had to thank our lucky stars. But we missed history and all the big public memories and private ones too, I suppose. The worst horrors of our times and some of the finest a man could imagine.'

Piers said, 'My public memories and my private ones are often mixed. Such as I've got at my age. Nothing's happened since I can remember. After all, even D Day is a kind of blur to me.'

The old man laughed. 'I don't remember that either,' and he was clearly puzzled. 'When was it?'

But Piers didn't have to answer.

'All the same, you're perfectly right,' the old man went on, 'about the mixture, and very mixed up they can be.' He was talking now as he must have done at seventy, twenty years before. Like an easy, garrulous old club man, Piers thought, and he remembered a visit to the Junior Carlton with Uncle Hubert.

'When your Great Uncle Jasper was wounded in '17, I was working with McKenna at the Treasury over War Bonds. I was able to sort out a lot of the muddle they were in. They had no head for Finance, the Coalition Government. It was their legacy from Asquith and the Liberals. And as the Bonds were the great thing of Lloyd George's, I was quite a pet of his. So when the telegram about Jasper came, I pulled a lot of strings and they let me go out and see him at the Field Hospital. Civilians weren't allowed there, of course. Base hospitals, yes. Field hospitals, no.' He glowered at Uncle Eustace as though he might be about to challenge this and then went on, 'It was my first experience of the noise of the guns and of shell fire. You felt such a fool because it was the daily life of three quarters of men. Most of the men out there at Popperinghe could hardly remember anything else. So you had to try not to show how scared you were, and excited, too. And the ghastly objects on the stretchers. Yes, well, that's not luncheon talk.

Anyway, they took me to Jasper's bedside.'

He paused as if to draw breath, then went on, 'He was alive when I got there, but he never regained consciousness. I was only by his side for half an hour. It was going down into hell though. I could have got him some office job at home easily. He wasn't strong. I kept thinking, in that nightmare place, there with the screams you could hardly hear for the guns and the stench of vomit, that he was only there because I'd kept my mouth shut. But of course he would never have spoken to me again. Nor his mother. She thought he must go. I don't know. Anyway, I felt in hell and then he was dead and there was nothing for it but to go back. But as we walked through the wards, one of these unrecognisable forms, more like landed fish than men – you know, white and gaping and every now and again threshing out to show there was still life in them – called my name. Three times before I realised it, because he was spewing his lungs up at the same time. It took me some time to recognise him, though he said "Mr Mosson" and some other words. At last I got it. Sweetings! He'd been a young waiter from Sweetings Chophouse in the City where I ate my lunch most days before the war broke out. I didn't know what to say. But he seized my hand and wouldn't let it go and as they told me he hadn't a chance, I got them to give me a packing case and I sat down beside him. The retching and the blood and the bits of guts were awful.' He stopped speaking and looked round the table. 'I shouldn't be telling you all this,' he said.

Grandma said, 'If it's tiring you, Pater . . .' and Nurse Harper nodded vigorously. But Piers leaned across the table and looked very directly at his great grandfather.

'I shan't easily forgive you if you don't go on now. You can't just leave us in hell, you know.'

The old man smiled and Piers could see that, though he had probably always been ugly, he had known moments of ease and charm.

'No. I suppose not. But I'll cut it short. It turned out that the boy's mother had been a little girl I kept up at St John's Wood before I married. Back in the late eighties. No, no, the

boy wasn't my son or any of that sort of Ouida rubbish. Sorry
to disappoint your romantic heart, Rosemary. In any case, he
was far too young. She was a pretty little girl and very sensible.
As soon as she knew I was going to get married to your great
grandmother she accepted some young chap who'd been after
her. A commercial traveller, I think he was. I told my guvnor
about it before the marriage and he insisted on my giving them
a house as a breaking-off present.' He was silent for a moment,
searching for his memory. 'In Half Moon Street. They ran it as
lodgings for single gentlemen. Very well, I believe. At least, I
heard it well spoken of. But of course I never went near it. I
fell in love with my wife after we'd been married a year or two
and never wanted to look at anyone else again. But what this
boy managed to tell me was that his mother had never been out
of love with me. I could just get the gist of it between all the
heavings and spewings. And soon after I'd got the hang of it,
he sat up and spewed a flood of blood that covered my suit.
And he was dead. Yes, it was a public hell all right as well as a
private one. And as to the girl having loved me all her life, that
was a waste. And yet right at the heart of it all, it saved me.
There was something wonderful about it. After all, she'd been
the first love in my life. Of course, I told your mother-in-law
about it, Jackie, when I got home. I never kept anything from
her. And we agreed to say no more. But I knew the girl's birth-
day and her size in gloves and I had a dozen pairs sent to her
every year. Until in 1932, I think it was, Harrods told me that
the owner at that address had died.'

He seemed pleased with his generosity as though remembering giving a large Christmas tip to a goddaughter. This self-
satisfaction was the only flaw in a perfect and moving work of
art as far as Piers was concerned. But, in a way, it was a very
satisfactory final note, too. Here was this old man, who, to all
appearances, for all Piers could ever remember of him – ten or
so years – lived on the most mundane, materialistic, unimaginative level possible. And, out of the depths of old age, had
come this revelation. He, too, old Mr Worldly Wiseman, had
gone down into hell and had found illumination, a moment's
grace there. Sucks to old Bunyan! Of course, it wasn't a grand

firework illumination, a real baroque, *Phaethon* affair. A bit of
a Victorian magazine story really. He could see Uncle Eustace
had found the sentimentalism of it all far too much for him.
His uncle was singing under his breath, 'Goodbyee. Don't
sighee. Wipe the tear, baby dear, from your eyee.' But for all
that, the old man had had his moment of flight and, more important, he'd allowed himself to remember flying and to
crown that memory by making a shape out of it. For that's
what the story was – Great Grandfather's only work of art.

And absurdly, but touchingly, Piers noticed that the release
of this memory had made the old man alive to them all in mind
as well as in body, and benevolent.

'Tell the Chef, Gates,' he was saying, 'that the cheese soufflé was excellent. A very good luncheon, Jackie my dear.
Hubert, you take a rest this afternoon, you work too much.
And we must have a talk, my boy, 'bout these ideas you have
for the house. I don't say I'll agree, but I'll be interested. I
shall go upstairs now. I shall sit in the Blue Drawing Room, if
Nurse Harper will help me up there. It will make a change to
snooze there with those blue monkeys capering up the wall
around me. Perhaps we've ordered the rooms a bit too closely.
Oh, I know that's how Pratt intended it. This room here is
clearly the dining room and nothing else. Gibbons' succulent
carvings tell us that. And very fine it is. Each room has its own
function. A gentleman's house. But that wasn't what Vanbrugh intended when he changed things. He made a palace
where the King's will is law. Or the Queen's. That's you,
Jackie. But principally the King, that's me. If we wanted to
dance in the Library, that's where we'd dance. Or if I wanted
to dine in the State Bedroom, that's where we'd dine, even if
Jackie was in bed. All the more so, for the King or Queen often
held court or dined in bed. I wonder if Tom there would enjoy
his food as much in a bedroom? I loved to see the way you
licked your lips when you ate that soufflé, my boy. It was
good, wasn't it? Of course all that changing rooms wouldn't
do for my grandfather's day, even less for my father's. No, the
Victorians had to go back to Pratt and a gentleman's house.
And quite right too. But still we could probably do with more

flexibility. And will do, I dare say, in these boys' time.'

The excitement with which they had both listened to this exposition of their constant argument must have communicated itself to him. He added, 'You've got a very nice pair of sons, you know, Rosemary. By the way, my dear, before you go, come up and talk to me in the Blue Room. You're looking tired. That nursery garden's too much for you. You probably need to employ more labour. We can talk about that. Well, Nurse Harper, take my arm, and you boys, you can tell your Headmaster and the Dean that they won't be able to make you late for luncheon much longer. We shall soon have the family chapel in Smith Square in order again, and then the family will worship there.' He looked fiercely at Piers. 'Remember to tell them that. But you've not got time for Headmasters and Deans. You've got your opera to produce. I'm looking forward to the first night. A French opera, Harper, what about that? That's more important to youth than any family chapel, isn't it, Piers?' As he got to the door that led to the Great Hall staircase, he turned and bowed to Uncle Eustace. 'Good day to you, sir,' he said, 'and if you come to England again, we may be able to receive you.'

It was obvious that no benevolence could let in the stranger without the Mosson gates. Eustace looked so glum that Tom whispered:

'Thank you for helping us through,' and then felt ashamed at his falsity. Piers, too, winked at his uncle to help him on – but he did so feeling that the production was over, so he could afford compassion.

In general, however, the family mood after the old man's departure was a happy one. Ma came and put her arm round Piers' waist and squeezed it. She said, 'I knew it would be all right once you arrived.'

'We will have coffee on the West Terrace, Gates,' Grandma instructed. She, too, seemed in a generous mood. 'The dear boy helped you, Rosemary.' She touched Piers' elbow. 'I have not seen anyone bring Father out like that in years. Poor Father! So much error mixed with so much that is true. St John's Wood!' Her small laugh tinkled somewhere between

flirtation and disgust. 'But we are all reflections of the Divine
Mind. You must reject the false claim of tiredness, Rosemary.
When I think of all those beautiful roses you grow. They deny
tiredness, don't they? All the same, *I* should have been glad to
help the Nursery myself, if you had asked me. Money worries
are only in the mind, dear, and they make you restless and
edgy for these dear boys. So we shall have no more of them. I
shall see to that. Eustace, I want you to see my lovely blue aga-
panthus. There are pots of them on the terrace. Such a lovely
blue. Young Tucker brings them on early for me.' To Piers'
delight she even included the new young footman, who was
gaping vacantly. '*You* love flowers, don't you? That's good. I
expect they remind him of home,' she added vaguely as she led
the family past Gates and through the open doorway and
down the steps on to the terrace where white doves tumbled
and pouted among the great lead urns full of swaying aga-
panthus lilies.

Piers nudged his brother at Grandma's absurd remark to the
footman; but the response was a very half-hearted laugh. They
were the last to come out on to the terrace.

Tom said, 'Well, you've saved the situation. I could do
nothing with them before you came. All the same, I know you
won't agree but I wish you hadn't had to do it by letting the
old man make a show of himself. The head of the house!'

It was clear from Piers' silence that he did not agree. Yet
Tom could not reconcile his image of Van who could turn grey
into gold with being pleased to show off an old man's ramblings.

He walked out on to the terrace and looked back at the
exactly proportioned, seven-bayed, two-storeyed, red brick
West Wing, its sloping grey slate roof clear cut by the mansards.

'Isn't it smashing?' he asked. 'So exactly right, Grandma, in
every way. Good old Pratt.'

Jackie smiled. You could see that she found this architectural enthusiasm of her grandsons tedious. But the worst was
that Piers took no notice.

Since no one else answered, Uncle Eustace said, 'It's certainly a most elegant building, if a little lacking in verve.'

To have only this rotten ally made Tom suddenly very cross with his brother, with them all. He said, loudly, 'It's the quoins, of course, that are Pratt's master stroke. Quite as emphatic as Vanbrugh's giant keystones, yet strictly in proportion.'

Surely Piers would know that he was quoting from that book they had both read, and would know that he was upset, wanted some notice. But no reply came from anyone. He said more loudly, 'From here, no one could tell that a beautiful house had been gutted and vandalised.'

So loudly that Grandma said, 'Yes, dear. But don't wake your great grandfather. Do all the boys speak as loudly at Westminster?'

And even Ma said reprovingly, 'Tom!'

He had to accept defeat and recompensed himself by eating two delicious large truffle chocolates and dwelling on their rich creaminess.

'Help yourself to a spot of brandy, Piers,' Hubert told him. 'I can recommend the Courvoisier.'

Jackie said, 'Brandy, Hubert? Don't you think a *crème de menthe*, dear? Have a *crème de menthe*, Piers. I often pour out one for myself, if only for the glorious colour. Like spring-time in the meadows.'

'Syrupy stuff like *crème de menthe* for someone who has talked to his great grandfather man to man! No, you take a brandy, Piers. Your great grandfather was very fond of your father, you know. His death was a terrible shock to him. Uncle Jasper in the First War, your father in the Second. Perhaps you could get him to talk about that, too. I think it would be good for him.'

Piers felt happy that his uncle should shed his well-known reserve so far with him, but he knew that he was even more pleased to be treated on this man-to-man basis. Perhaps he could break his uncle's reserve down a little, too, get him to meet life on the basis of real intelligence that surely was hidden under all his pomposity.

He said, 'Great Grandfather's uniting of the evil in life with the joy seemed to me so absolutely true. I don't believe in these sort of Manichaean divisions. That's why I don't accept so much of Conrad. The heart of darkness – yes, all right, but even in the heart of darkness there must have been joy.'

But it was Grandma who answered. 'It's all joy in reality, Piers, dear. There is no darkness in light.'

He wouldn't be put off. He said as lovingly as he could, 'Yes, I am sure you're right, Grandma, but I'll have to come to that for myself, won't I?' He addressed his uncle (or perhaps his uncles) again, 'You see, Conrad says, "The horror, the horror", but even in that strange primitive rite there must have been joy. At least, that's how I should produce it.'

None of his family appeared to have read Conrad, for there was a blank silence. Tom, to break it, and to deflect Piers, for he sensed danger, said, '*Lord Jim*'s been set for A levels. What's it like?'

But Piers was not to be separated from holding his audience. 'I suppose you and Grandma have heard Great Grandfather's romance and its terrible setting many times, Uncle.'

'I don't think grandfathers usually say much about their mistresses to their grandsons, Piers, less still to their daughters-in-law. In any case, Mosson men have never be-lieved in a lot of breast baring. Too busy, I suppose,' Hubert told his nephew.

Piers tried hard to suppress any sting he might possess, but he *had* to bite. Something had to pierce his uncle's layers of self-protective convention.

'I'm jolly glad we were idle today, then, or we might not have had time to see childish tears turn to a moment of joy.'

Grandma bit too, then. 'My dear boy, we are grateful to you for putting Father in a good mood, but it was all very childish. The tears *and* the talk. Not that it is for us to dwell on it. Poor Father! Ninety years old! But it won't be long now before he wakes up from his years of Adam dream.'

Rosemary took Piers' arm with her left hand and patted it with her right. 'Well, *I* was very proud of you, darling heart.'

Tom had been watching Eustace trying to make sleepiness look like admiration for the blue lilies. The sight distracted from his anxiety for his brother. But suddenly his uncle stirred like a great lizard.

'I fancy the little moment of revealed humanity owed everything to clever production, my dear Piers,' he said.

'Oh, no, Eustace, you are a pure aesthete, aren't you? Great Grandfather's *experience* was all that mattered.' He felt his mother's hand pressing his arm, he could see her tiny loving moue denying his modesty. Eustace's flirtatious smile warmed him. He risked registering their dangerous applause. He had to. Or else it would *all* die away. He said, 'Of course, I admit it needed shaping.'

'Well, to be able to *shape* one's great grandfather,' Eustace said, 'I congratulate you. That's quite something.' He bowed to Piers and Piers bowed back again.

Tom said quickly, 'Grandma, hasn't mooching time arrived? It's getting late. I want to spend the rest of my Sunday wandering round the treasure house. You won't mind, will you, Ma?'

But Grandma had had enough. 'Piers, my dear boy, the idea of your *shaping* your great grandfather's life! Really! It is too good.' Her tiny laugh was hard and pecking. '*I* never was able to do it.'

Hubert laughed. 'And what your grandmother can't do in the human management line, I shouldn't advise you to try, Piers.'

Despite the thunder in the air, Piers said, 'I think if you have a creative instinct . . .'

But Tom rushed in, 'Oh, it's Piers' great historical sense, don't you recognise that, Uncle? He's famous for it at school. Nobody over thirty can say anything without Piers putting it into its historical context, as he calls it. I think it's a bore. But *that's* why he got the history schol. To the House. You can't have one without the other.'

'I see. Well, that is kind of good to know. You have to be grateful to Tom, Piers, for interpreting to us. Tom has a very wise head,' said Grandma. 'Your great grandfather, of course, *is* a real piece of history. You know how proud we are about the scholarship, dear boy.'

'Indeed,' Hubert added. 'When do you go up? October? We must have a ways and means talk very soon. If you take my advice, you'll try for rooms in Peck. The proportions are far and away the finest in the whole of Oxford.'

Ma said, 'I think Piers brought Grandfather out from affection as much as from any historical interest. He's a very loving boy.'

Tom said angrily, 'Of course he is. Everyone here knows that, Ma.'

His mother smiled at his brotherly defence. But he need not have rushed forward. He had saved his brother already. Piers' audience was still intact.

Grandma flipped her neat little feet from off the garden chaise longue. 'Well, shall we all go about our business? The boys have done us all good today. They deserve to be free of us for a little. Rosemary, will you look after your brother? You can both tell us so many of the mistakes we have made in the garden.' Tom noted, happily, that her smile was teasing. 'Hubert and I have Tothill business to discuss. There will be some tea in the East Parlour at about four for anyone who wants it.'

So the Saloon and all its biblical horrors had gone, Piers noted; well, he would be pleased not to have to face his grandmother and his uncle with the memories of the recent past around them. John the Baptist's head came back to him, its white teeth grinning out of the green dead skin, and strangely from between the lips came the long hooting note, mockingly it said, 'My God! How boaring it is!' And the visit had indeed been boaring and difficult – but Great Grandfather was looking forward to the first night of *Phaethon* and that was all that mattered.

Tom and he were last to leave the terrace to the doves, to tumble and pout at will. But as they turned the corner towards the South Façade and the formal gardens, Tom said, 'Well done. Not a word about the opera from you, and I know what it cost you. But I was right. You got Great Grandfather's express wish to attend the first night. And no one said otherwise. Not even the nurse. She's not very friendly, is she?'

'Oh, I don't know. I think perhaps one shouldn't be always doing psychological interpretations of rather dull people. Look at all the auguries you drew from my being at that Marina scene. But they've clearly come to terms with it.'

Suddenly Tom felt angry. Really, Van had no sense of reality. 'Well, I saved your bacon this time,' he cried. 'A nice display you'd have given. The Mosson show you produced. They were starting to ask for their money back. All the same, I apologise for Ma explaining the decent part of your motives. Well, I mean, anyone who knows you . . .'

Piers said, 'The decent part, as you call it, and the display are all one. But you wouldn't understand. You won't ever need to. I expect you're lucky, really. Go and feed on Pratt's sense of order and civility.'

'Sorry,' Tom said. 'I tell you what, Van. I have a feeling that Ma's going to break out sometime before the day's over. And I shall need all my order and civility then. We must get old Eustace into the act. He's sulking and he could help.'

'I propose to talk with your uncle. But thanks for the advice.' Piers put on his elder brother voice.

'It's ripping of you to listen to a squit like me.' Tom had found the phrase in an Edwardian story and it had become one of their favourites in a mock quarrel.

Their partnership affirmed without any capitulation on either side, the brothers parted, each to his own delights.

But Piers, as usual, deferred his supreme pleasure of the Great Hall until he had tasted every aspect of the house and its gardens. All his growing up that he could remember had consisted in learning that no play can be simply a curtain, however compelling. It must be a thing of scenes and acts, each building up towards its inevitable climax. This afternoon, a sense of having made something unusual and done so at risk deserved indulgence of lengthy savouring. Also the momentary guidance of his brother's hand as he had skated elegantly over the family ice rankled a little. A longer walk than usual would give time both to savour success and to expel doubt. He would go down to the extremities of the Woodwork, to that bosky wilderness

which cut off the great house from the common gaze of
Labour's Transport House and Conservative Central Office
alike, a promenade of a full quarter mile in this *hortus mirabilis*
that still survived in Central London. And the walk would
have the additional advantage, he felt sure, of allowing him a
talk with Ma and Eustace, for she was sure to take whatever
problems had brought her to London, to Tothill House, down
to the wild garden which alone in the great estate made any
sense to her imagination. Probably Pratt was right. His
instinct for pessimistic interpretation of people was much too
strong, but it was often built on some justification. Ma *did*
look at times very preoccupied. He must explore. He couldn't
let any neglected problem break through and ruin the fair
prospect before him. And, too, he mustn't let the fair prospect
cut him off from understanding and helping her if she needed
him.

He made his way down the long avenue of limes and
through the strangely complicated plantation of walnuts to
where the mazy paths wound and turned and turned sharply
back again between hedges of holly and cypress and box and
yew, to which, as Ma always lamented, the Victorians – 'the
Mossons', she called them – had added, like some displeasing
skin disease, golden privets and Portuguese laurels. The
splotchy, yellow skin disease seemed less in evidence now in
this compact, complex green labyrinth – perhaps the winter
had killed them off. He must tell Ma – the thought of a Mosson
death always cheered her. If only he could get her alone . . .
And he was in luck's way. For there she was, or rather her large
bottom stretched her tired, old, worn blue skirt towards him
as he approached the high brick South Wall which shut them
off from modern London. She was bent almost double, cutting away among the roots of one of the rose bushes that
formed the last of the garden's mazes. When she turned up her
face towards him, her creased forehead was flushed almost to
the colour of the smudgy rouge on her cheeks, but her large
grey eyes were more smiling and happy than he had seen for
many months.

'Darling heart,' she said, 'the Mossons take notice of me! Of me, unpresentable Rosemary! They really do. First of all they've got rid of all those disgusting yellow privets. And second, they've actually made their awful gardeners do *some* pruning of the shrub roses I gave them.'

He felt sure that was part of Ralph's excellent influence. What a difference that peculiar little man had made to his life.

'At least there are only a few suckers to every bush,' she went on. 'Last time I was here I thought the suckers were sure to have taken over. I expected a wilderness of dog roses by now. Not that it wouldn't have been authentic or whatever it's called. But rather dull. I *did* try so hard, you know, to see that the roses I planted here were all of the right period and yet to give variety. After all, in 1680, or even 1700, the choice *was* limited. I *did* cheat a little because, of course, *rosa foetida bicolor* was one of *the* roses then. But I really couldn't risk the black spot it would bring – even in London. It's *the* carrier, you know. And I think anyway that flame colour's rather a mistake in roses. Oh, as if you would know all that. But I do think it's a good sign that they've followed my advice, even if they'd never admit it. She snubbed me over this being called the Woodwork. As if I hadn't read every description of this garden from that eighteenth century Miller's dictionary onwards. But I was wrong, they *have* taken notice.'

Her delight so delighted him that he could only say, 'Good, darling.'

'It almost tempts me to try to introduce some later roses. I'd love, for example, to have a great tangle of Malmaisons up and over the wall. Do you think one or two varieties from later times would matter? I know Eustace would disapprove terribly, but luckily it's nothing to do with him. But *she* might rather like the idea of cascades of roses. God's smile and all that. Isn't it embarrassing, darling heart?'

Piers said, 'Of course it doesn't matter. History's there for us to create the shapes we want out of it.'

'Oh, darling, you *are* bad for me. You encourage me so much. Bless you! I knew I could rely on you. Jim said I could.'

He saw that this was his moment to explore what might be

looming, but he couldn't spoil the happiness he'd brought her.
No, *he* hadn't brought it. It was Tothill, wonderful Tothill.
But the spell mustn't be broken.

He said, 'Wouldn't it be marvellous if Uncle Jim could be
with us here? I'm sure he'd charm them all in no time.' Perhaps
by saying this he'd cleared the air.

She seemed to blush, but it was hard with Ma's rouge to tell
a blush. She frowned slightly. She said, 'Don't try to make me
too happy. Anyway, I must get on with this pruning, if these
bushes are to be done before tea.' She flashed the pruning knife
at him and bent down once more to her task.

If he had not dared to disturb *her* unaccustomed joyous-
ness, he could at least try to pierce Eustace's tricky defences, to
make sure that the day wouldn't end in his uncle borrowing off
poor Ma, or, worse still, trying to borrow from Uncle
Hubert. Here was an adult task before him and probably a bad
tempered Eustace to wake from after-luncheon snoozing.
Truth to tell, he couldn't really find any place for Eustace in
his cast. But if the old man's speech had not brought a deeper
harmony to *all* the players, his shaping would have failed.

But as he approached the parterre he saw Eustace, stork-
like, standing on one leg, while on the raised knee of the other
he balanced a small notebook in which he was writing intently.
That his uncle should accept discomfort was strange enough,
that he should accept inelegance was extraordinary. Most
strange of all, Piers came right up to this foxlike, wary, intent
man without being heard.

'Is it an erotic drawing?' he asked. They had developed the
steps of their dance together over the years, but in no other as-
sociation of his life was Piers so uncertain that his partner
might not change the whole measure abruptly to suit his own
ends.

Eustace stared at him for a minute with what Piers saw was
genuine incomprehension. Then he closed his eyes.

'My dear boy, I am neither still a virgin nor yet impotent. It
is hard to see why anyone should *write* about sex unless he
were one or the other. Or, of course, a cad – like Byron or
Rousseau or those bores, de Sade and D. H. Lawrence. No, I

was doing a pleasant exercise.' He showed Piers the notebook's page – it read:

'Species and varieties wrongly planted by the owners of
Tothill House in very bad taste and total incompatibility
with the parterre gardening either of Pratt's foundation of
the House in 1683, or with Vanbrugh's completion of it in
1697.'

There followed a list of all the blooms that Piers recognised as
growing here in the summer months, and many other names
he did not know. Then followed another heading:

'Species and varieties of flowers suitable for planting in
parterre beds of the late seventeenth century; all to be
found in Thomas Hanmer's notebook of 1659; largely
supported by Evelyn.'

Here were very many more names of which Piers could recognise only – *Spring beds*: Five kinds of tulips, fritillaries including Crown Imperials, anemones, iris, polyanthus, hyacinths.
Summer flowers: mallows, scabious, amaranth, cornflowers,
lupins, peonies, tomato or love-apple, mimosa raised on a
hotbed.
   'Tulips, above all, of course, were the glory of the time. As
we saw at lunch from those hideous mauve and purple tulips,
the municipal park gardener or whoever else your grandmother has instructed to produce such monstrosities does
plant tulip bulbs somewhere. But what is wanted here in the
formal beds are the wonderful freak tulips of seventeenth century taste – the Parrots, the Agated and the Bizarre which the
lively fancy of those days provided. As to the rest, what
subtlety or delight one could have here for six months in the
year by keeping to my authentic list. And I've made that from
memory, without reference to any book. There must be
dozens of plants I could add to replace these coming horrors.'
And he pointed to the flowerless bedded-out plants. 'Of
course we can plant out exotics, too. After all, the Mosson

futures were built on delicious trading in spices and slaves. But
in their full horror these beds must be more like a terrible blazing Kipling ballad of the late Victorian Empire than any reminder of the old East India Trade. And then the awful regularity
of these squares! I've sketched here some typical patterns of
seventeenth century parterre knots.' They looked to Piers like
a sketch of the fragmentation caused by a broken tumbler or an
atomic explosion. 'I thought perhaps I might put some of my
ideas before your Uncle Hubert. He's rather an old woman
and he's got his funny little habits of which the less said the
better. But he's a gent. Well, you saw how sensible he was
about your attendance at the Abbey. As to your grandmother,
if she must have her beastly blues, she'll get more of them than
she does now with this public park nonsense – I'll give her hyacinths, cornflowers, lupins, but tempered with other more
subtle colours. We don't want Woman to be without her
Whims, if only for the delicious fun of tempering them for
her.'

His look seemed to be calling Piers to some special partnership, but Piers had no idea to what he was being invited. So he
let his uncle's look of complicity fade away unacknowledged.

'Of course, I should want a small fee for the designs. Partly
because I think such things should be on a business footing
and partly because frankly, dear boy, financially, May's never
a good month for me.'

Piers tried not to smile. He heard so much of his uncle's
'bad' months.

'How do you think they'd respond?'

In his excitement, all Eustace's slyness seemed to vanish,
even his shabby, neglected clothes took on the elegant look his
posture and manner intended them to have. Piers had not realised what a handsome, charming and boyish man he could be.
He swallowed his own scepticism rather than dispel his uncle's
new elegance or restore his old tarnish.

'I don't see why not,' he said. 'You make it all sound so
attractive. And these colours clash horribly here in summer,
you're quite right. Certainly with my idea of what I'd hope to
see after coming out of the Great Hall.'

Eustace was clearly delighted. He said, 'Your youthful passion for Vanbrugh, my dear Piers, is a constant refreshment in
the painfully vulgar age in which we live. Of course,' he went
on – Piers had never seen him absorbed in something outside
of himself – 'to be authentic, all the borders of the knots and
beds would have to be upheld with low, coloured boards or
tiles. How do you feel about that?'

It was a delighted child's question and Piers felt free to give a
loving adult's reply. 'I think I should leave that out,' he said,
consideringly.

Eustace was equally impressed by his nephew's sagacity. 'I
am sure you are right,' he said, swallowing his usual high
drawl in a manner that was his nearest vocal approach to
respectful regard. Piers left him adding names to the list of
desirables.

Passing along the West Terrace once again, he found the
tumblers and pouters still tumbling and pouting, but as a
décor for Tom, totally absorbed in reading. Piers had no wish
to disturb him, but the doves gave up their antics at his
approach and with whirring wings flew feebly and clumsily on
to the sills of Pratt's ground floor windows.

Tom raised his head. 'What's your book?' asked Piers.

'It's a new way of presenting coordinates. Elegant stuff. I
couldn't follow it in form, but now it seems as simple as
Pythagoras.'

'Thanks to Pratt's sense of order,' Piers said. 'Thank God I
am innumerate . . .'

'Bugger off,' said Tom, affectionately.

Passing the Library, he caught his grandmother's eye
through the window pane, as she sat listening to Hubert reading some document. She smiled at him. But it was not
Grandma's 'sweet smile'. Perhaps it was just that, absorbed in
what Hubert was saying, she smiled absent-mindedly,
without that self-conscious 'love' that made her seem like a
pecking bird. Yet it could hardly have been a purely absent-
minded, automatic smile, for she said something to Hubert,
who turned, laughing in a manner that blew away in one gust
all the rolls of pomposity that normally protected him from

feeling, and he, too, waved to Piers. No, they were both giving him what they had to spare from their own delight, and what they had to spare that afternoon was considerable.

Oh, it was an enchanting afternoon and the house was the enchanter that brought them all together in pleasure. While, upstairs, the old man slept peacefully, his secret shaped and told.

Piers entered the Great Hall with more than usual elation, for, if the others were all content with their parts, what was to keep him from giving himself up to the giddy pleasure of staging his own play in his own theatre? He walked around for a while, simply delighting in the proportions of the vast room, the strength of the great Solomonic pillars (not Samson himself could pull down this temple) and the powerful majesty of the great keystones of each door. Looking to his left towards Pratt's East Wing, Vanbrugh's receding classical columns were like a Roman street in a *trompe l'œil* painting. To make the real seem contrivance and the painted solid, this was surely a triumph of art – baroque at its best that could easily survive Verrio's feeble hand.

He glided across the great marble Hall in a trance of what he would do of his own, of what he had it in him to do. The May weather was close, but the marble and stone were delicious refreshment to the eyes. And what seemed heavy in their force and pressure turned to airy grace in Tijou's delicate wrought-iron staircase balustrade. Placing his hand upon the ice-cool iron, Piers felt his cock stiffening with the first three steps that he trod in ascent to the Gallery above. It was only a momentary excitement, yet its surprise gave the strangest sense to him that in this Hall, this symbol of all he aspired to, every sense was united, even sex, which he had always thought of as so separate from his aesthetic appetites. And now, as he reached the Gallery above and started to descend, would begin that extraordinary experience which he had known from childhood, but had refined throughout his years of visits from school – the rapid, startling and always changing peep show of the Hall as it came in fragments to him through the wrought iron flowers and leaves of the staircase, the glimpses of the heavens seen through the enchanted forest. Now a twist of a great column, now a flash of the lantern, now a grey patch of Jove's beard, or the sudden wild eye of a bolting horse, now the flamelike disappearance of the twisted pillars through the rosy light of the lantern out into the sky, now the muscled calf of Phaethon's leg writhing in descent. Now he was Phaethon – now he would fly!

CHAPTER VIII
Rosemary's Confession

AFTERWARDS, TOM blamed himself for most of what happened. He, who was ever conscious of the ice cracking beneath us, who already at sixteen read all the newspaper
accounts of statesmen's top level meetings and knew how
often the 'exceptional cordiality' of one day presaged the
'grave diplomatic rupture' of the next, should have been on his
guard, should have found some way of lowering the emotional
temperature, or even, at cost to himself, of providing a sudden
distraction. Piers, for whom the death of Kings unsung by
poets was meaningless politics, was not to be expected to provide statesmanship. It was enough that he gave them all
sudden inspirations. But this had been the occasion for restor-
ing order and civility and he, Tom, had failed to do it. First he
had said nothing and then, at last, he had lost his temper and
joined in the tumult. Why? he asked himself for many years to
come. And all he could think of was that the pattern of order
and civility he had set for himself was not an easy one; it often
came near to contradiction. For, if it demanded from him
foresight and direction, it also insisted that, as the youngest
person present, not yet a man, he should not presume to intervene in his elders' intimate relationships. He could only hope
that it would be easier to practise a philosophy of maturity
when he was more mature.

Chef had done them proud for tea. And Tom could see that
Grandma was proud of it – all these sandwiches and cakes must

have been a part of her adaptation to English life, he thought, or what she supposed English life to be; now they were adaptation to youth's appetite, or what she supposed youth's appetite to be. After the heavy luncheon, even he couldn't fancy more than two éclairs and two tomato sandwiches.

'Now, this must all be eaten up,' she said. 'I rely on you boys. We mustn't hurt Chef's feelings. He takes so much trouble with his pâtisserie.'

Strangely, Tom thought, no one was made more genial by the licence to eat than Hubert. He found Eustace's schemes for the parterre 'very encouraging'.

'They'd fit in extremely well,' he said, 'with the ideas I'm putting to the old man for ridding the place of a certain amount of the accretions of the last two centuries. Of course, I have to go slowly. So many of the heavier, more inappropriate Victorian objects have some sort of sentimental value for him, dear old chap. And then I have one critic closer to me than Grandfather.' He cast a mock frightened look at his mother. She leaned over and put her hand over his.

'My dear boy, you must do just what you think to be right. As long as you do not forget that this is a beautiful *home* where happy people *live*, and that is what gives happiness to those who come to see it. I think your ideas sound "just grand", Eustace,' she laughed, Tom supposed, at her own little American vulgarism. 'There cannot be too many spring flowers for me. Spring time is life time – it is the waking out of a long dark dream. Not too many tulips though, please. Flowers should never be stiff, they should be graceful and friendly.'

Eustace assured her that the liveliness of the colours and shapes of the Bizarres and the Parrots would banish all tulip stiffness.

'Well, you are the expert,' she said, 'as long as there are plenty of blues. I shall have a little talk with Tucker. He is such an intelligent young man. And he likes new ideas. He was born a rector's son. There cannot have been many new ideas around in *his* boyhood. There is no need to be afraid of change. God made a changing world. He does not want us to turn our backs on the future.'

'I suggest you make us some detailed plans,' said Hubert, 'and, of course, we must pay you a retainer.'

Eustace said, 'Oh, well, of course, I suppose, mm.'

Tom hoped they would not take his uncle's demur for genuine.

After this friendly transaction, Ma's keenness to plant, as a present from herself, twelve Malmaisons by the South Wall seemed an act of largesse.

'We shall pay for them,' Grandma said, 'you are not running the Nursery as a charity.'

Ma insisted that only she should superintend their planting.

'That is very good of you, dear Rosemary. I am sure they will be very beautiful and a great pleasure to all who visit here. Like a waterfall, you said, tumbling down the wall. Well, if they give pleasure to a hundredth of Niagara's visitors. The name is a little sad though, isn't it? Malmaison. This is such a happy house.'

Piers stepped in to explain about the Empress Josephine's palace and her love for rose culture.

'Ah. You must be the historian of Tothill, Piers,' his grandmother told him. *The Royal Divorce* – such a moving play. Poor injured woman, Josephine. With that dreadful, warmongering Napoleon divorcing her after all those years. A sordid broken marriage. I hope the roses brought back some of the smile into her eyes.'

Something made Ma suddenly begin to talk very fast. 'I'll come and look at them when they flower in July. Although, of course, they won't be much of a show for a year or two. But it'll be a celebration. Jim and I begin our new life that month. I hope you'll be happy to let me bring him here with me . . . Jackie? Hubert?' As she looked in turn to them in appeal, Tom felt the floor tremble beneath him.

But there was no immediate earthquake, only an iciness as Grandma and Hubert tried to assess her words.

Grandma asked in her sweetest interrogative, 'Jim?'

Ma had taken out her lipstick and was re-doing her lips to control herself before speaking. But her hand was shaking as she fitted a cigarette into her long jade holder and as she flicked her lighter.

She said, 'I think you . . .' She stopped. 'Jim Terrington,' she said in a loving voice that alarmed Piers now also. 'You've met him a few times when you've come to the Nursery. And in the old war days with Jerry.'

Hubert said, 'Of course, Mother. He was one of Jerry's best friends. A very nice fellow. He must be a major by now, isn't he?'

Grandma said, 'I know Jim Terrington, yes, but not just as Jim. He talked to me so affectionately of Jerry one afternoon at the Nursery. He seemed a little limited for a friend of my son's. But mothers are rather silly about their children. I could see that he was a very good sort. He was so good with the boys. Wasn't it he who taught you to swim, Tom? That must have needed some patience. But I don't quite understand you, dear. A new life? If you are trying to say that you are to be married again, I am sure that we shall all be very happy. But what a way to tell us! Like a moonstruck girl of sixteen! You *are* a baby, Rosemary. You need a man to look after you. Let us hope he is as nice and simple as he appears to be.'

In turn Piers and Tom kissed their mother. 'We hope you will be very, very happy,' Piers spoke for them both.

'Oh, darling hearts.' She was crying a little. She answered her mother-in-law. 'He *is* a very nice man, if by nice you mean loving and thoughtful, Jackie. And he's very simple, too, if by simple you mean good.'

Grandma laughed. 'I mean whatever you want me to mean, Rosemary. He is lucky to have someone as hardworking as you are, so much in love with him. Well, I am very glad, Rosemary dear. We all are. I remember him quite well now: faithful brown eyes and a Scots accent, I think. Yes? Anyway a real honest body. Quite a boy himself, too, when he talked of the boys' games – their football and chess and so forth. And surely he had a son of his own who was good at diving or climbing or something. I had not realised that he was a widower. Well, I am sure these dear boys will not grudge another fellow a little portion of your love.'

Even Uncle Hubert seemed to feel disturbed by all these

manoeuvres. Perhaps he would come to Ma's assistance.

He said, 'Really, Mother darling, you speak as if Jim Terrington's private life was our concern. If he is *divorcing* his wife to marry Rosemary, it's nothing to do with us.'

'Love cannot be built on unhappiness, Hubert. But it's you who are attributing all sorts of unpleasant things to Rosemary's happy news. I was just thinking of the motherless boy and all Rosemary would be able to do for him. When are you to be married, dear? I hope so much that it will be a registry office ceremony. Those Church of England weddings are so theatrical. And, of course, we shall be happy to give the reception here. I really think that a good buffet luncheon is right for a second marriage . . .'

Tears made the mascara which Ma always put on for London glisten like black shoepolish. She said, 'There isn't going to be a wedding. Jim and I have been lovers for years, but his wife won't divorce him. She's a Roman Catholic.'

Piers noted Grandma's click of disapproval at this information. It seemed just possible that her hatred of Catholics might save the day.

Ma went on, 'Yes, it's a cruel religion, I think. At least in what it's done to Jim and me. But I don't think Esther would have been any different whatever her religion had been. She's just a bitter woman who grudges other people happiness.'

'She has some reason to be bitter, perhaps. And she has her son's happiness to fight for.'

'Oh, believe me, Jackie, please. I've always had Marius' happiness in mind. Just as Jim always thought of what was right for *my* boys. That's partly why we've lived this hole in a corner life all these years, until they grew up. But we can't go on forever. In any case, as far as Marius is concerned, his life is settled. He's going to be a priest. He started at the Seminary this year.'

Grandma was genuinely dismayed. 'Oh dear, what *have* you got yourself into? The Roman Catholics are always working against the Truth. Especially the priests. I heard a lecture at Third Church recently about these dreadful conversions they make. It's all animal magnetism. What an atmosphere for these boys to grow up in!'

Piers walked over and kissed his grandmother's cheek. 'Don't get in such a fuss,' he said. 'We've never met Marius Terrington. Or at least hardly. And as for Uncle Jim's wife, she's only been twice to the house that I can remember.'

'And then there were awful rows,' Tom mumbled.

'Not a very happy home for the boys, I am afraid,' said Hubert judicially.

'You're wrong, Uncle Hubert,' Piers said. 'It's been a *very* happy home. A bit of a muddle. But then Ma is a muddler. Well, you are, darling. But it's always been happy. Never any rows. Yes, well, twice, as Tom said. When that woman came over. But any other disturbances were me making scenes.'

'He's very good at it,' Tom mumbled – they must produce laughter.

'Look, if we must talk about this, Mother,' Hubert said, 'wouldn't it be better for the boys to go out into the garden? They obviously don't grasp the seriousness of the situation. And in a way it's better they shouldn't.'

'We want to hear *all* Mother's news,' Piers said. 'And we're both very happy with all we've heard so far. You see, we know Uncle Jim and how good he's been to us.'

It was true, he thought, look at the trouble he had taken about the *Phaethon* machines. Although, as they'd grown older, they'd both found his simplicity and his high spirited jollity a bit of a bore when he stayed at the Nursery. Feeling that this might be in his brother's mind, he stared at Tom to force him into confirmation.

Tom, too, was hesitant; but not because he found Uncle Jim a bore, that wasn't important. No, it was because he wondered if this news didn't spell the upheaval of everything. But Ma loved him. That was all that mattered. He said, 'Uncle Jim's a very respectable man. I mean I like – respect him.' His voice came out in unwanted falsetto.

'I'm afraid you haven't been brought up in a way that makes you a very good judge of respectability, Tom,' Hubert said.

Uncle Eustace rose. 'Mm,' he murmured, 'I think we could leave *them* out of all this, don't you?' He picked up a book from a side table.

'Hardly a moment for books, is it? Or are you? yes? looking

for something to quote to us?' Grandma asked.

'I was looking for something to take the taste of all this moralising out of my mouth.'

'You will not find that kind of book here, Mr Gordon. There is enough ugliness and error in life without writing it in books.'

Eustace said, quite sincerely, what he had said to his nephew earlier. 'Mm. Oh! I quite agree, Lady Mosson. That ghastly Lady Chatterley. If a man can't *do* it, then he should leave it alone.'

'I think we'd better keep to the point,' Hubert told them. 'We can understand that you may have fallen in love, Rosemary. And that you were lonely. Although, for many women, two loving, growing sons would have been enough . . . But not all women are made of the same stamp.' He looked at his mother with pride. 'We believe you, of course, when you say that you and Jim Terrington did all you could to keep it from the boys. But surely you must have known that it was bound to get through to them . . .'

Ma made a gesture of protest, but Piers took it upon himself. 'Yes, of course it did, Uncle, though Ma's too simple to realise it. I think I've known since I was fourteen that they were in love. Pratt and I haven't talked about it, but he's known, I'm sure. And it's made the house a wonderful place when Uncle Jim was there. Surely if two people are very much in love it's bound to make a house happy.'

'Love! My dear boy,' Grandma cried, 'you will know one day that that sort of thing isn't love. It's necessary, of course. It is part of nature. But thank the Lord there are so many beautiful things in life without making a horrible fuss about *that*.'

'*I've* found it very beautiful and enjoyable,' Piers said, to all their consternation. 'But I don't know that I should have done if it hadn't been for Ma and Uncle Jim. Sorry, Ma, I hadn't meant to let you know this but it's best now to out with it. I must have been about fourteen. I think all boys at boarding school are a bit squalid at that age – or, maybe, just curious. Anyway I heard Uncle Jim shut your door in the usual way one night. It had a special click about it for me. And I suppose it had for Tom, too.' Tom nodded, but he could have sunk through the floor with embarrassment.

'Because we weren't supposed to know,' Piers went on. 'Anyway I made up my mind to peep through the keyhole. Of course, it ought to have been the end of me. To be so furtive and inquisitive. But it wasn't! You both looked so happy. Oh, more than that! You looked as if for once you'd really experienced something. Sorry . . . I mean but Uncle Jim isn't exactly a very sensitive man. Anyway, it was beautiful. And I think it completely cured me of being dirty-minded about sex.'

Grandma had closed her eyes. She was murmuring some Christian Science truth. 'Now I understand exactly Mrs Eddy's interpretation of the seventh commandment. Adultery goes far beyond any pathetic, trivial thing like sex. It adulterates truth with error. Just look at the confusion in this poor boy's mind.'

Hubert gave her a loving smile, but he said, 'Let me deal with this, Mother, I think. Rosemary!' he began.

Tom shouted, 'She's not in the dock. She doesn't have to stand up to receive sentence.'

Grandma cried, 'Tom! After all the talks we have had. All your good sense. Are you going to encourage your silly mother in this squalid muddle?'

Tom tried to put love into his voice. 'I know you've suffered, Grandma. I know just how all that nasty Marina business . . .' He checked himself, but it was too late. She had drawn in her breath like a snake's hiss.

Uncle Hubert shook his head sadly. 'If I may go on. We can understand, Rosemary, that you were lonely. And perhaps it was natural that someone of your temperament and upbringing should have let herself be carried away. A theatrical boarding house isn't the best nursery for a child. And after all, he *had* been Jerry's best friend. It was natural that you should look up to him. And though I can't condone his treatment of his wife, let alone his young son, an unhappy home can drive a man to lose his head. But after all these years. We're middle aged, Rosemary. You and I. And so is he. What a moment to make it all public. To tie it round these boys' necks, just as they are starting out in life.'

'Do you imagine, Hubert, we wouldn't have been together all the time before, if we could conceivably have done so? What do you think my life has been like without him for days, for weeks, two years once when he was sent to Germany? But it's the army. Oh! they aren't so narrow minded as they were. But *she'd* have stopped at nothing. She'd have gone to the colonel. And with a wife making rows at H.Q. and me being a brother officer's widow, they would have requested Jim's resignation. And he just couldn't afford it. Not to keep her and Marius. But in the summer he comes up for retirement. The pension will go to her. *She* won't lose. And I think Jim means to read for accountancy. But he's been so worried lately. At your wonderful play, Piers darling! I behaved so badly. But that was it. She'd promised to release him. And then she went back on it. He was so upset. He rang me up at the school. I didn't mean to tell, because you'll think he's selfish. But he isn't. He's just been goaded and goaded by her.'

Grandma laughed bitterly. 'Accountancy! So this Terrington man has his practical side. This wretched love of yours isn't all house maid's daydreams. Well, let us hope he keeps you sober enough to deal with the money business. Oh, do not look so innocent. These things are bound to come out.'

Hubert resumed his chairmanship. 'You still haven't explained to me, Rosemary, why you want to wash all your dirty linen in public after all these years. Terrington can get himself a house near the Nursery. You can see each other whenever you want. But all this!'

'I'm sorry, Hubert. I'm afraid you just can't understand. And how should you? We want to be together *all* the time. To be the husband and wife to the world that we should be. And, all right, I'd better say it, I want more of his love, yes, his physical love. I want to be held by him, kept warm by his body. I need him to be able to take me whenever he wants. God knows, as you say, we haven't so much more time . . .'

Grandma gave a little moan. 'If that is all it is, there can be no question of bringing him here. This is a house where we *care*. In fact, I think, Rosemary, you must feel so out of it that you would be happier not to come here yourself again. Physical love! What a way to counter a false sense of loneliness when God is always with us.'

'I'm sorry. As you know, he's *not* with me. Oh, it's no good talking to you. But you'd better know. That's how it all began. It was when they sent Jerry to North Africa. He was in danger. I was so frightened for him. I couldn't bear the loneliness. Not that poor Jerry was much good in bed. Darling that he was. And he did give me these two boys. But sex wasn't his strong point. I didn't realise it then fully, of course. I couldn't believe it when Jim first made love to me. It was like Heaven opening.'

'My God!' said Hubert. 'My poor brother. So this was what he died for!' And he went over and put his arm about his mother's shoulder.

Piers said, 'Daddy died for the things he believed in. Can't we stop all this?'

But the accusing horror-struck look of mother and son was too much for Ma. She cried out, 'Oh, for God's sake! What in hell made me think you *could* understand? It's not your fault, Jackie, it's your upbringing. You've never known what real life means. They taught you as a young girl to cock-tease all the men who were after your millions. And then, of course, it was "Please! not now!" . . . and "Don't touch me in that way."' Her imitation made Eustace give a short barking laugh. 'How my poor father-in-law got you to open your legs long enough to get his two sons, I don't know. He must have been a magician.'

Piers said, 'Oh, Ma, for God's sake.' Tom sat tense and silent.

Hubert said, 'That's enough of that filth. Gordon, would you take your sister away, please?'

But Ma laughed. 'Oh poor Hubert! Mummy's boy. Even that Luzzi wasn't gutsy enough to break Jackie's hold on you. Jerry never believed you'd marry even. He laughed about it. He thought you weren't even man enough to be a queer. A doctored Tom!'

Eustace said, 'Look, old dear, you'd much better not start on things you don't understand. You haven't even got it right.'

Grandma said, 'She is drunk, of course, but she understands well enough to try to wound and hurt. She must go. I will not have the harmony of this house broken. Will you take her away, Mr Gordon? And I think I should say that as this unpleasant *ménage* appears likely to have to depend upon the profits of the Nursery, I must ask for the return of the money I have lent to her. At her convenience. Boys, you had better say goodbye to your mother.'

Piers said, 'What ever do you mean?'

'My dear boys, we love you very much. *I* love you very much. And I love you for loving Tothill so much. But Tothill House cannot be mixed up with all these squalors. You must choose.' Tom put out his hand towards her. 'Oh, yes, Tom, I know you love me. And I love you. But that is what you have to do – choose.'

Ma shouted at her, 'They're *my* sons. I have the legal right . . .'

'Of course you have,' Grandma intervened, 'if you want to cut the boys off from all Hubert and I have planned for them.'

Ma, crying, spoke to Hubert. 'Please say she's wrong . . .' And when he said nothing, she cried, 'Hubert!'

'I think they have to make the choice,' he said.

It was Tom who answered. He was hysterical in his anger. 'You're a filthy hypocrite. You pretend to admire the order that Pratt made here and all you and Grandma can do is to goad poor Ma on to destroy any order that remains.' He stared at them both for a moment. 'I suppose it's because you hate yourselves so much.'

Grandma looked at him pityingly. 'It would be quite wrong for you boys to make such a big decision in this atmosphere. Go back to school. And let us know your decision next week. If the boys choose that sort of world then they can have nothing to do with Tothill. It would not work. Of course, we shall continue to pay their Westminster fees until they finish there. But after that they must stand on their own two feet.'

'Four, surely,' Eustace murmured.

Piers heard himself giggle and, seeing Grandma's face, knew he had harmed his cause greatly.

But she said, as though she had not been interrupted, 'It is one or the other. We cannot mix this rubbish up with all that we have built here at Tothill.'

Eustace intervened. 'You can't surely want them to side against their mother, Lady Mosson.'

'Oh, you quite misunderstand me, Mr Gordon. I *always* want people to side with *me*.'

Piers stood up. 'I am afraid we can't, Grandma. I love Tothill more than anything I know, but of course I must go . . .' His voice faded away as he stared at the opposite wall of the East Parlour.

Tom, in surprise, took up the unfinished sentence, 'Of course, we must go with Ma.'

'I am sure Great Grandfather would want us to make that decision, wouldn't you?' Piers went forward to where the little old man had suddenly appeared through the concealed door of a dummy bookcase.

'I don't know anything about it,' he said. 'All I know is that you've woken me up with all your shouting. I can't have all this noise.'

'Grandfather, we have learned some terrible news,' Hubert spoke the address. 'Rosemary was not faithful to poor Jerry when he was fighting in the desert. And now she intends to live openly with the man she deceived Jerry with. We have told her, and I'm sure you'll agree, that Tothill House can't be open to someone so unconcerned for decency. Particularly in view of the very hurtful things she has said to Mother. Unfortunately, Piers and Tom have chosen to side with her. No doubt they'll change their position. They're very young. And the afternoon has, to say the least, been disgracefully hysterical. Meanwhile, we've told them that until they see the situation more clearly, *they* must stay away from here, too. I'm only glad that you were spared a very unpleasant occasion.'

Ma, Piers, Tom, in turn, all made their appeal to the old man.

'I was hoping after what you told us at luncheon that you'd understand, Grandpa, and I am sure you will. I've been deeply in love. And the boys are very fond of Jim. It's just his wife who stands in the way. I don't think she's sane. I've lost control of myself this afternoon and said all sorts of things I shouldn't have done, and I'm sorry. I am afraid I don't fit in here. Of course, if you don't want me here . . . But, please, don't visit it on the boys.'

'I'm sure after what you said this morning, sir, about love and horror being mixed together, that you'll see why Ma . . . she was so unhappy and frightened for my father . . . she needed love. It's just the kind of paradox that you showed us.' Piers sought for all his tongues.

Tom said, 'Of course, we're standing by our mother, sir. But we very much hope that you'll stand by us. We love Tothill and we are grateful for all you've done for us. And, and we're very sorry for all this unseemly disorder.'

The old man blinked.. 'I should hope so,' he said. 'I talked far too much at luncheon. I got indigestion. And I couldn't have my nap. That's bad at my age. And then when I *did* drop off, you all woke me up. It won't do.'

'You go back to rest, Father,' Grandma said, 'and leave us to settle all this vulgar emotionalism.'

'Yes, yes. I think that's best. I'm not getting younger, you know, and sleep's important to me. Anyway, Jackie's hostess here and she knows what's what. And Hubert, too. He'll be taking over soon. I shan't live a long time now.' And opening once more the shelves of dummy Hakluyt voyages, he went off to his own long voyage of sleep.

As he disappeared, Piers called after him desperately, 'Whatever happens, we can still do the opera, can't we? You'll be there on the first night?'

Tom saw Grandma look at his uncle with a pitying glance.

'They simply are not grown up,' she said. 'This is your whole life, Piers. And you talk about a school opera. I want you both to go away now and think, very, very hard indeed about what all this means.'

She rose from her chair with a regally dismissive gesture.

So there was nothing for it, but for Piers and Tom and Uncle Eustace to escort Ma to Victoria Station to get her train back to Haywards Heath.

By the platform barrier, with her ticket in her hand, Rosemary began to cry.

'I've let my boys down,' she said. 'I've cut them off from every chance in life. *They'll* never come round . . . I know their hardness. They've always hated me. And your scholarship, Piers?'

'Oh, we'll manage that somehow,' he told her, 'the school has a lot of influence at Oxford.'

'And Tom, my little Tom.'

'I shall be all right, I'm sure to get five full credits at least in A level – Physics, Maths, Chemistry, History and I should think Geography.' He detailed all the subjects not in pride but with some idea that such facts might banish his mother's hysteria. 'After all, you seem to forget that Piers and I are both Scholars. We're "up College".' He spoke the Westminster slang in inverted commas, hoping to make Ma laugh – for some reason she seemed to find all the school terms a sort of joke. But not this time. This time she looked wild and frightened. Almost, Tom thought anxiously, a bit mad.

'Dear God, I've let my boys down so desperately, Eustace.'

He bent his long, thin, spectacled body and kissed her cheek. 'You'll be all right, old dear. Things are never such hell as they seem. Or hardly ever.' He had to be accurate.

'Oh, Useless!' Piers couldn't believe his ears. It all sounded like something out of Wodehouse, but he supposed that that was how they talked when they were young.

Suddenly Tom felt that he, he and Van, *had* a right to protest. He said, 'For God's sake, Ma. Why didn't you give us some warning that you were going to burst out with all this? We could have thought up some better approach.'

She said, 'I did mean to, darling, I did. Jim was most particular about it. We've done nothing but discuss what the effects on you both might be. But we didn't see how we could keep it from them. They were bound to hear. Even if it had been honest, when one was getting money from them, which it wouldn't have been.'

'Oh, Pratt doesn't mean telling them, Ma. He understands that. Why didn't you tell *us* first so that we could help you?'

'Mm. I *must* say, Rosemary, you've made the most appalling balls up of it. I mean accusing Hubert of being queer. I'd told you all about his little ways. I sang, "Hold your hand out, naughty boy."'

'Eustace, it's none of it a joke. I meant to tell you all first. That's why I asked you all to come to Waterloo. But then when Piers wasn't there, I gave up the idea. Quite honestly, I wasn't sure of Eustace here and you *are* very young, Tom. I meant to postpone it. To say nothing today, and have a talk with you all first. But then Piers made everything so wonderful. And it was such a happy day. And Tothill seemed so much ours. Oh, I don't know, something came up about divorces and I thought there would never be a better opportunity. Well, you *had* prepared the ground so wonderfully, darling,' she said to Piers. 'Everyone was purring.'

Tom put his hand on his brother's arm. And Piers said, 'Oh, my God.'

Ma began to cry again. Eustace looked perplexed. 'Well, it's nothing to do with me,' he said. Tom made a strange choking noise, although Piers couldn't tell whether it was with exhaustion or with anger. Eustace looked at his younger nephew in surprise. 'Oh, God, is he often like this? Give him this from me, will you?' And he was gone. 'This' turned out to be a five pound note, which, considering that May was a bad month, seemed pretty generous, Piers thought.

They saw a tearful Rosemary off on her train. As she got into the carriage, she said, 'Darlings, at any rate you've saved me from being a drunken mum for the rest of my life.'

Each saw that the other had had this thought in his mind. Whatever the lost paradise, the broken dreams, the riches thrown away, the black nightmares of their childhood (never, never to be shared with anyone else) would not return. With Jim, she would be happy. They still had an hour before they had to be back up College. They walked, hardly seeing, into St James's Park and watched, in turn, a pelican and a cormorant dive from a rock. The pelican reappeared on the surface of the lake some distance away and sailed off like a small white ship, its bill an orange fishing net. But the cormorant surfaced with a small fish, which it swallowed, and then sat on the rocks, its wings spread out to dry – a strangely still dark sampan, its only movements the flashing in the dying sunlight of its iridescent feathers. Suddenly, its long neck stretched snake-like, it dived again. They could see its rapid shadow below the surface of the lake. Its grace, its swift hurled flight took Piers to the Great Hall. Furiously suppressing the memory, he found another subject on which to vent his anger.

'That fool, Virginia Woolf, writes of pelicans as "pouched birds". And she's a model of imaginative English held up to us. Pouched birds! They're sailing ships!'

Tom looked up in surprise, but also in agitation, for he could sense his brother's violent feelings. Piers could not suppress the image of Phaethon that the cormorant had produced.

'Promise me never to forgive those brutes,' he said. And Tom, alarmed by the sound of ice cracking, gave his faithful promise.

'It would have been all right if Great Grandfather had been himself again. Even Grandma said that he has authority because he sees Tothill and himself as one. Grandma and Uncle Hubert are so dreadfully unsure.'

Piers said, 'The canal is closed.'

Tom looked to see what canal he meant, then he realised. 'Yes, and the Russian tanks are in occupation.'

Piers turned on him angrily. 'Oh, don't always try to be clever. Don't you see that only one remark, my remark, was enough?'

In mutual despair they sat on a seat overlooking the lake. Suddenly someone had joined them.

A voice said, 'Mm. Look. I mean you're both very young, and I don't think I can quite leave you in the shit like this. I mean if Rosemary wants to marry this man, you don't have to let it bugger up all your lives. I mean they need each other, but you both need money. If people want to live their own way, they must, but they can't muck up everyone else. After all, you have got your own views of life or you seem to have . . . all that Pratt and Vanbrugh stuff isn't just talk, is it? After all, Piers, you can't fly like Phaethon and carry your family on your back. I mean it may be glorious, this life of risk that you want. I don't know. But it's got to be lonely, you know. You can't worry about mothers and all that.'

'Yes,' Piers said, 'I do know, Uncle Eustace. Thank you for saying it though. Of course what I want has much loneliness and sadness in it. *Phaethon's* a *tragédie en musique*. And I expect to have that loneliness in my life, however exciting and magnificent I can make it. And, of course, if I can get into the theatre, as I want, I shall be on my own. I shall have to leave family and childhood. But I can't do it at the dictation of frightened bullies like Grandma and Hubert. There wouldn't be any direction in it.'

'There'd be money, my dear boy.'

'Money with menaces. No, I couldn't accept that.'

'Well you, Tom,' his uncle said. 'This isn't much of a basis for your ordered Pratt existence – the sudden, ill-managed emotionalism of a silly woman, for Rosemary is awfully silly, my dear boy.'

'I see what you mean. And thank you for speaking to me. I shouldn't have expected you to bother with someone you don't like. And, of course, Ma's whole way of going on is quite against the sort of ordered world I want. But – oh, it's hard to explain without sounding soppy – there is an order of the heart, that's the only way I can explain it. I love Ma very much and, if I turned against her now, I'd be breaking up an order which lies deeper than any civilised orderly behaviour.'

Eustace looked at them a little sadly and a little crossly. 'I see, mm, well it's an enormous fortune lost. *I* can't afford to lose money. This is a very bad month for me. I think perhaps I need that money back that I gave to you, Tom. We've all been rather stupid and emotional.'

Tom gave him the five pounds and he went away.

'Oh, people!' Piers said. 'All their bloody little ways!'

'Yes,' Tom answered him. 'It's private emotion that makes

the whole thing so insecure, or so it seems to me.'

He sighed as they set off for school. Hawksmoor's West Towers of the Abbey came in sight. Piers, looking up, said, 'At the moment, as I see it, the spotlight is full on Phaethon in the bowl as the opera ends, with Climène and Théone in half light as they sing their last lines of horror at his fall. But I'm wondering whether we shouldn't end after the music has ceased, with lights on the two sculptured sisters mourning for his fall. The only thing is the material. It's called scagliola and I don't know how that will light up. I must try it out.' He added fiercely, 'There's no question of their stopping the opera, you know that, Pratt. That's just talk. It must be.'

Tom, looking at his brother, thought he seemed a little mad. He, too, looked up at the towers and, with the clouds moving behind them, they swayed, even rocked, ready to fall down upon the busy world below. A lorry thundered by and the pavement shook. He thrust his hands into his trouser pockets. He would not panic. He would not run away.

In the middle of the night, Nurse Harper woke Jackie and Hubert to say that old Mr Mosson was asking for them and seemed very agitated.

They found the old man sitting up in bed, the huge four poster that had been known as the Queen's Bed since the Queen Dowager Adelaide slept at Tothill one night in 1848 when she had supposed a thunderstorm to be the outbreak of revolution and had refused to return to Kensington Palace.

He said, 'All this is a lot of nonsense, you know. We *knew* Jerry had married a vulgar daughter of some twopenny-halfpenny tea planter's widow. She's turned out to be a trollop as we expected – we don't want her here again. But that's nothing to do with the boys. Of course, they'll want to see their mother, whoever she's living with. And quite right too. And they'll want to come here and we'll want to see them here. Just because you've both got cold, finicky feelings doesn't mean that my great grandsons are to be kept from this house. You'll write to them tomorrow, Jackie, and you, too, Hubert, telling them that whether they see their mother or not is their own affair, but that we want them here. Is that understood? Good. Well, now we'll all have a proper sleep. I.shan't need you again, Harper.'

Nor did he, for, in the morning, he was found to have died in his sleep. Nurse Harper, who was, after all, trained in geriatric care, was quite clear as to the cause of his death. It was all the fault of that boy working him up to talk like that at Sunday lunch. And this opinion of hers was retailed to Piers by Ralph Tucker when they met one afternoon by chance in Trafalgar Square.

'I know nothing about it, of course. But that's what that lot are saying.'

The old man's death could have reconciled, but instead it made the quarrel final, for each side affirmed that he had been killed by the other. And, once this had been said two or three times in public, it added heavily to the moral reasons against forgiveness or reconciliation.

PART III

1969

CHAPTER I
The First Night

OH, THE overture! He sat in the same agony of apprehension and of impatience that he had felt at each of the six full
rehearsals. Those slow pompous chords on the strings that
seemed to march in state to nowhere. Certainly not to *his* play,
to *his* production that would follow.

Nigel admitted that Lully's overtures, 'one of his greatest
innovations', never, in fact, gave hint by any melody or air – as
far as Piers could hear, never by any bar – of exactly what was
to come. 'They prepare the *mood*, Piers. A court, perhaps,
more than any other audience, because of its autocracy, its
strong-willed egotism, its chic frivolity, had to be charmed
into listening.'

Well, these solemn, 'stately' chords, no doubt, did 'prepare'
us for the solemnity with which the Prologue would present to
us the empty joys of the Golden Age returned, the solemn
decorums of Louis XIV's court; however little they led on to
the opera, they 'overtured'. And now this second movement
that banished the opening tedium, this hop skip hop of the
pleasing little minuet, gave notice of the many dances to come;
nothing so special in themselves, but, as he had come to learn
over the last weeks, conveying a happy sense of community, a
break into movement, an assertion of life, of some declared
emotion in the heroic, statuesque, recitative world of the gods
and heroes who acted out their basic human passions with
marbled restraint. And, of course, at the last, the overture's

239

third and final movement, the massed string drama of its close, in which, despite his musically untrained ear, he liked to think that after many hearings he could especially delight in the viola's playing, carried him away from all conscious criticism.

It had all come alive for him as the rehearsals progressed and, *Gott sei dank*, for the company. And now, as the last sustained chords of the overture died away in sober acceptance of tragedy, he hoped only that what he had done for the play's production might live up to what Nigel had done for its music. For it seemed that even after that intense study of the manuscript score in the Bibliothèque Nationale, Nigel had been forced to provide orchestration, even rhythm, again and again either from other Lully operas or to invent it from his great knowledge of that century's music.

Piers recalled suddenly, with relief, that this rare mood of humility before his collaborator's work had settled upon him during the first nights of his most famed and successful productions, all those he himself cherished most – the Edinburgh *Doctor's Dilemma*, the Chichester *Othello*, the Old Vic *Three Sisters*, above all the wonderful, unforgettable first night of *The Master Builder*. On all these he had humbly hoped that his hard work would be seen as good work; had moved from assertive certainty of genius to modest prayer for recognition.

That *Nigel* had succeeded could be felt at once from the evident continued applause and, more so, from the stillness of the bodies of this audience, as fastidious as it was distinguished, that filled the Great Hall, his Great Hall, he could now call it. He smiled to think that he was exercising his now intuitive sense of a real first night success not in a public theatre but in his own home. Oh, let it be, he murmured, let it be, here at Tothill, a wonderful flight, a repeat of the many joyous theatrical victories of the last ten years. Not, dear God, one of those few, but haunting, icy crashes that had here and there threatened his ever upward career. Don't, don't punish hubris just because it's the culmination of an adolescent's dream. Or, if it must be, let my fall, like Phaethon's, fill the world with astonished fear.

Automatically, he offered up his and Nigel's success with

Phaethon, if it came tonight, to the Olympus of the Arts –
mythical or existent only in some mystical transcendence,
what did it matter? – to Lully, standing there among the Great,
and to the paler shadow of the librettist Quinault (for one
could trust Lully to put his wordmaker into the shade even in
the World of Shades). He offered it this evening to Lully as, he
remembered with self-mockery, he had offered his past
triumphs to Shakespeare and to Chekhov and to Shaw and to
Ibsen. And, for a moment, he thought he saw one huge
merged cynical grin of all those great geniuses as his offering
reached them. For who could know more than they how little
an artist *could* offer anything up except to his Art, which was
precious hard to separate from himself?

But even Lully, he knew, that hard-boiled brutal climber,
would comprehend that the producer's work of art was also an
act of homage and love to the creator of what was produced.
No artist would wish to be realised by anyone – actor, singer,
conductor, producer – who did not burn with artistic ambition, or would feel honoured by any other kind of empathy.
Well, Lully's fierce will to succeed and his love of his art were
equalled this evening by those of Messrs Nigel Mordaunt and
Piers Mosson, not to forget the fierce artistic egos of that turb-
ulent, wonderfully impassioned soprano, Katherine White,
that maniacal, difficult, magical bass, little Ejnar Gösling, and
by our hero Phaethon, that insecure, sly, young, heavenly
counter-tenor, Marc Gorbeau. And, my God, yes, by twenty
or more others, by the whole fucking company. And so it
should be.

Nigel had one up on him; he enjoyed this early triumph of
the overture on his own, for his slightly amused cricket-
captain smile, as he called the orchestra to bow, showed how
he saw his team as part of himself. Damn him! No, bless him!
because that look of pretended assured disdain for applause
with which he now sat down at the harpsichord, after being
brought to his feet three times by continued applause, recalled
at once the incredible ease with which he, Piers, had found a
partnership with the Musical Director in this his first, and,
surely, last venture into opera.

Dear Nigel! There'd only been one *real* row – about the
siting of the orchestra. And look where Nigel was now sitting
– in the shade of the great stairway. Exactly where he, Piers,
had commanded, well, suggested, and he'd got his way. How
blessed are all those who give way to us. Anyway, he could
afford to bless them all, for no one else tonight but he, Piers
Mosson, was living out a dream that had been with him for
twelve years, perhaps even twenty, when he had stood, awed
but triumphant, beneath the great lantern at the age of eight.

And now light (thanks to Ralph's skilful management of the
professional electricians' team and the union rules) burst forth
to reveal the Golden Age, the gardens of the palace of the
goddess Astrée. And all was as he hoped; the four great black
twisted columns, reflecting the intense golden light that flood-
ed the forestage between them, somehow made the whole
scene more radiant. And, above, a golden haze hid the great
painted ceiling fall of Phaethon, as light poured down from the
lantern and suffused the whole scene. Truly the goddess
Astrée could, with her chorus, sing with reason, 'in this place
everything laughs without cease', and her followers could
dance their pastorals with true sedate gaiety.

It was a lovely scene. He knew at once that he had been right
about the back-cloth stretched between the great steel towers
reaching up to the Gallery. There, right across the South end
of the Hall, were not pale woody groves and temples of
Claude, as had been urged upon him, but the most formal,
sedate brilliance of tulip beds and the sharp symmetry of statuary and urns and oddly shaped myrtle bushes – this was the
glory of Louis' *real* Versailles gardens, not the figment of the
painter's imagination of classic pastoral Elysium. He felt that
he could almost hear old Eustace murmuring, 'Mm. Just as I
suggested. Perhaps my millionaire nephew will be a little more
forthcoming now.' Well, the old crook should have a large
cheque, even though the payments to him never ended.

Now the soprano voices raised in chorus were so enchanting
that he could take no more critical note – 'everything smiles,
everything is just as we wish.' Translating the words brought
back all the smugness that he had intended to satirise in that

aborted school production. He smiled at his youthful *naïveté* – he had been able to recognise smugness, had feared the Mosson blight ruining his visions of glory, but he had not then seen the full force of quiet joy, of assured happiness. He had not, of course, ever really known them *himself*, even now, but he had seen them too much in others to mock as he would have done ten years ago – in Pratt, for example, since they'd inherited Tothill, in Kate, in the early days of his own marriage, when even he had lived for months in a paradise of love and ease, in Ma and Jim, even in their absurd letters from Umtali ('Darling heart, if you could *see* how content and friendly the blacks are, quite a lesson to us over-sophisticated whites, as Jim says').

But he must not let the scene, the realised wonder of Tothill Transformed, distract him from the producer's eye. To wander down memory lane in this Tothill production, now that it was realised, was a danger that he had luckily foreseen.

He concentrated on Saturn's proud figure as he entered. The god of the Contented Golden Age. The full-bottomed black wig was altogether too high – a suggestion of Louis should be there, *that* he had rightly kept from his adolescent mockery, but it should not be a caricature. He made a note to have it lowered. All the same, this last splendid chorus of basses and sopranos – 'all the universe admires this hero, author of such sweet repose' – did reduce the Golden Age to the quietude of a well run old people's home, or would have done if it had not been for the splendid music and the magical stage.

Good for Marjorie, she allowed a little touch of a conventional Queen's complacency to accompany her divine singing of Astrée's aria. He was glad that he had given her, too, the high hair style of Queen Anne's Court, of Madame de Maintenon's. And Richard Dewey's first rate bass voice as Saturn came out from the face of Louis XIV at his most self-adoring. Enough to make the point, but not too much. The Golden Age was here, but it wasn't to everyone's taste.

Anyway politics – Kings, what did they matter? Though that was better than these bloody terrorists. He almost fancied that he heard a distant thud as he remembered how poor Tim's first night had been interrupted last year – and for all Tim's tiresomeness, he was a great artist, his first nights were world events. Damn the silly fools! What *did* they comprehend? To intrude their little political madness into such real things as the arts? But that was all over, that was 1968, and anyway it had been a very un-English spill-over of riot and terrorism from France. So much for Louis XIV de Gaulle.

The Golden Age and Prologue were over, Saturn and Astrée placed their divine forms on two satin upholstered thrones at the side of the forestage, where they prepared complacently (she with a special pleased adjustment of the shoulder of her dress recalling a hundred royal boxes – oh, darling Marjorie!) to watch the unfolding of this opera about Phaethon 'of which so much has been said'. Tiny happy laughs from among the audience told him that many had got his satirical point.

But not loud laughs. Nothing interfered with the first night's success of Libie and Théone, the rejected girls' wonderful soprano duet – '*Ah, qu'il est difficile que l'amour soit tranquille.*' Ah, how hard it is to love in peace. And again, he knew from others in his life how bitterly and sadly they'd felt. Kate telling him – 'We've talked for six nights this week, darling, about all the tension and conflicts of your production. Can I help you any more tonight? No. I'm going to ask you to help *me*, just by loving me a little with the peace and certainty our love ought to give to each other. Can't we just assume for this weekend that there isn't a crisis in rehearsal?' Of course he agreed. Being with Kate, not just her body, or even her sweetness, but the whole of her, had been, only a year before, all he wanted. But he'd failed, he was too het up about Cordelia's entry when she returned to England. It was absurd. But the play had to go on in his mind. That was how he was.

And now Théone was reproaching Phaethon in one of her most lovely airs – 'If you want to deceive, try to do so a little more convincingly,' she sang. And George's face suddenly appeared in front of him; George's unexpected sobbing as he turned away in that bed in the hotel at Norwich on tour – George, whose easy sensuality was such a solace after the sense of self-reproach following the divorce from Kate; George, who had set out to give him 'a good time in bed': 'If you can't kiss me with more pleasure than that, don't try. All right, I'm just a good fuck to you, go ahead and fuck me!' That had been the end of that! But George was an actor himself who should have understood that the disaster of the dress rehearsal didn't leave off nagging because a mouth was soft and searching. And now other faces – Maureen, Olivia White, the boy at Stratford – all asking him, reproaching him for not keeping a play going when the life had run out of it. He forced himself back to the stage, to now, to reality.

At last here was Climène to urge her son Phaethon on to glory. 'Your glory, my son, is my sole desire.' The recitative with strings and Nigel's harpsichord basso continuo made of this mother and son a wonderful symbol of united pride and ambition.

He *had* been right, absolutely right to maintain all the principal figures as statues – alive only in their facial gestures, their eyes, their music. Look how they stood, the superb mother and son, a stony force of ambition, as the rejected girl, Théone, in her sustained posture had been all marbled grief. He remembered with pleasure the battles he had fought with the singers – Katherine White, 'I thought a great producer would be here to give the opera the life of the theatre, not the death of the graveyard'; Marc Gorbeau, 'But 'ow do you mean? Stand? Phaethon is a young man, 'is 'ole character – do you say? – is to move. And you want 'im a statue! It is the dead opera of the past you are giving us.' But they *had* understood in the end, as the statue-like postures and the marvellously expressive facial changes this evening showed. No naturalistic fuss, no bringing gods and goddesses and heroes alive to modern psychology or social drama – just statues and expressions. Yet, from Martha Roddam's eyes as Climène, you could see – oh bless her blowzy old Yankee face! – love, ambition, fear, even cruelty glittering. Cruelty, certainly, as now when she told her son, whose future glory was her sole concern, to throw aside the girl who adored him – '*Il faut que l'amour soit prêt à s'immoler, sitôt que la GLOIRE l'ordonne.'* Love must be sacrificed, it's glory that matters. He couldn't love her French accent too much, but her voice was as much of a wonder as her eyes – she had been the first to catch on to what he wanted. 'She's a kind of statue with real eyes. Yeh! That's good, Mr Mosson. That's kind of scarey, but it's right.' If Ma had been able to flash such ambition from her eyes – where could he not have been now? But then for Ma there was always, first and foremost, Jim. Anyway, he *was* there – and, to give Ma her due, she and Jim had helped him, paying every Oxford penny after the horrible *débâcle*.

But it was movement time again. And testing hour for a new Piers Mosson – the master of machines. For, as the pastoral screens folded back to reveal the sea, in came the sea gods and all their strange marine followers. Yes, they had got it exactly right, Ralph and his team. To the expressive dance in triple time, to the sudden sound of oboes and bassoons holding up the glorious strings, the whole world was now again in motion – the clown's antic dance of the marine god's followers, and yet, beneath it, as he had urged them, a sinister sense of coming horror, for it was their leader, the god Proteus, who was soon to prophesy Phaethon's doom. But first the god must roll up and sleep in the grotto. Oh, hell, where *was* the grotto? Damn them, damn Ralph! But hardly was his damnation made, when, masked by all the dancers, the grotto was wheeled into place. Surely it was too near the great column on that side? None of the changing masks of the god, Proteus, as he tried to evade foretelling Phaethon's doom, could emerge from such a narrow space . . . no, Ralph had judged it to an inch – the lights went out on the sleeping Proteus and then shone again on the grotto's face to see in turn the huge lion's head (Winnie Bishop's triumph of design!), a great leafy branch of holm oak (apparently, according to Winnie, it had to be that, because it was Mediterranean – these travellers!), now a flame, and now the three-headed sea serpent waving in the air from the mouth of the grotto. But the sea serpent *didn't* work. He'd known it wouldn't. It looked coy and Disneyish. He'd scrap it tomorrow, whatever Winnie said.

But Proteus could avoid Climène's questioning about her

son's destiny no longer. His deep bass sounded and resounded over all the Hall – *'Dieux, je frémis* . . . Ambitious mother, fear for your son. Where are you going, young man? There you will find death.' How ominous were the strings now, and the basso continuo. And one searing, mortal thunder from the trumpets.

But nothing, no portentous, Great Grandfather Mosson warning, holds Phaethon back. First, he must win earthly glory, before he compels the gods themselves to do his will.

We are at Isis' Temple to offer thanks for the union of Phaethon with the King of Egypt's daughter, to offer thanks for his being heir to the world's throne. Suddenly, the irony of Phaethon's dreadful end compared to his own sudden unlooked for inheritance of Tothill's magnificence made Piers squirm with embarrassment, even fear. No! Nonsense! All the more reason why he should show the hero's tragedy as fated yet glorious. But he must not let Tothill's spell keep him from his producer's duties.

To loosen the spell he let himself go with Lully's celebratory music, only keeping an eye on the Temple gates – would the dancers react to their sinister abrupt closing with sufficiently sudden looks of fear? Yes, the reaction was perfect, and not only among the dancers, but in the change of expression in the eyes of the still statues of the King, the ambitious mother, the triumphant son. Even Louis XIV and his Maintenon-Saturn and his Queen – the royal spectators with nicely condescending look of interest in what went on upon the stage – trembled for a moment at what they saw. And then – music, dancers, statues, all broke up in fear and horror as the Temple doors opened again, revealing great flames and shadowy phantoms and furies – yes, the shadow projection was first rate.

And now Climène was allowed her one gesture as she raised her arm to check – even she, the ambitious mother – her son's fatal course. And beautifully the 'great Californian soprano', the 'Callas of Los Angeles' did it. But her son will have none of it. High the counter-tenor rang out. He will go up to his father, the Sun God – 'My glorious name will resound from pole to pole.' Marc Gorbeau's dignity, despite his small size, was everything Piers had asked for. It was Phaethon the heroic. The same Phaethon, apparently still statue-like – yes, Marc was far cleverer than he seemed – dexterous, almost unseen, made the movement on to the cloud-covered platform and in a second or so was carried up to and over the lovely Tijou wrought-iron balustrade of the South Gallery, where, in the glamour of full lighting, his father, the god Apollo, awaited him in the Sun's Kingdom.

Down below, Egypt, Isis, the world went dark. As the scene lit again, it was the dancing, singing Hours and Seasons of the Sun God's Court. 'Come, young hero, everything you want is yours, come enjoy your happy lot.' The sopranos, the counter-tenors, the basses all welcomed Phaethon to his proper regal home. How good the music was, Piers thought, whatever the experts said, suddenly so rhythmic, and it was so exactly right that no other instruments sounded above the strings. The two counter-tenors, divine father and half divine son, made their earth-shaking, fearful agreement in strange, high majesty, to let Phaethon drive the Sun's chariot on its daily course. It had worried him at first, this climactic moment with such unfamiliar pitch – surely a bass father, or a tenor son? But this evening's high strange sounds quelled all his doubts. 'In your chariot, Father, let me take your place . . . Ah, Son, what do you dare to ask? . . . How glorious, Father, if I succeed, and even if I fail, how splendid the design.' After that, no crash mattered.

Now came the short-lived glory – would it work? Yes . . . the hero stepped into his father's chariot suspended from the Gallery – and then was lost in darkness and the lights shone upon Verrio's painted triumphant Phaethon riding across the ceiling a hundred feet above the audience. And that strangely beautiful high voice was heard for the last time – in triumph: 'I fly. My glory shines from pole to pole.'

Below, to a degree that couldn't have been hoped for, his contrasts of hero – still statues – and crowd – ever moving dancers – worked, and worked well. For Climène allowed herself only the posture of a running triumphant woman, but all around her the crowds, Egyptians, Indians, Ethiopians,

whirled and spun around in amazement and adoration as the
lights followed the painted chariot across the ceiling. Every
instrument sounded as the voices, soprano, bass and counter-
tenor, pealed forth, 'A new sun gives us so lovely a day.' And
then – darkness. Jove's voice sounded way up in the lantern
where alone light shone. Jove's voice, a deep bass (the voice, in
fact, of Saturn, of Louis XIV). To Piers, knowing it was a
fake, it didn't appear quite to come from the sky. But he felt
the audience completely held. 'Fall in thy pride,' and, out of
the darkness, the Mother's voice shrieked out, 'O terrible fate!
O cruel fall!' And all the male voices – bass and tenor – answered her, 'O unhappy daring! O sad defiance!'

Then, suddenly, silence. Alone the light followed Verrio's
painted horses in their terror and confusion – the overturned
chariot, the driver, still proudly smiling, falling, falling
through the sky, fifty foot down to where, from the great
green malachite bowl, a hand (the singer's own), trailing life-
less over the edge, was caught in a spotlight.

And here he and Nigel had cheated, for Lully's score ended
abruptly in the air. But now trumpets and drums reverberated
through the Hall in a cruel parody of triumph, and Jove's great
voice sounded again from the lantern just once, '*Tombez!*' The
lights split apart to rest each upon a weeping sister turning into
a willow tree, guardians at either side of the great bowl in
which their brother lay dead. All animation had gone. Time
had stopped.

The applause was all and more than he had hoped for.

And the success was all heightened by the circumstances. By
Vanbrugh's exuberant, splendid fancy of the Great Hall, all
firmly based upon Pratt's order and sobriety. As his own
career owed so much to his dependable brother. Pray God that
brother Pratt's great feast tonight would be a triumph to equal
his own and Nigel's, would be something to relax the tension
of his brother's life, the endless hard slog of that law office, the
anxious life of keeping society on a straight path.

Tom, seated between the Countess of Chepstow and old
Lady Norah, had been conscious all the evening that he must
not allow himself wholly to relax, as he had at the dress rehear-

sal. There he had found himself weeping aloud at Théone's lament for Phaethon's desertion. Surely Van must have put into the singer's eyes her expression of lost misery, have taught her that tiny gesture of despair from some memory of poor Kate. Not that he could judge his brother, or wished to. Genius had its own laws and could not, probably should not respond to the needs of others too easily. And Van had tried to make the marriage work, he knew that. And Kate had never quite understood Van, that, when he was intent on a play, everything of him went into that. Perhaps he hated to think of it so much because of the divorce, because, since Hubert's death, all his endless work with the details of divorces at the office seemed only one reminder after another of man's sordid, pitiable nature, an endless repeat of the terrible chasm that Hubert's grim, squalid ending had revealed.

But that was all part of history now – the divorce, Hubert's death. Everything was so wonderful now – to be at Tothill, to share and feel the apotheosis of Van's triumphant career, had somehow lightened his own more trudging climb to success.

Yet, for a moment, when he had just heard Théone's piteous lament – how wonderful this Katherine White's singing was! – he had thought for Kate, how she would have loved being mistress of Tothill! How, indeed, she would have completed the order required of the place, the lady of the house who had been missing from the Mosson pattern for too long. And so he had wept – in public. He blushed to think of it – but not in much public, thank God. The dress rehearsal had had a very limited audience. And once bitten . . . Anyway, on this first night Lady Chepstow's formidable aristocratic charm and old Lady Norah's withering aristocratic zaniness had sufficed to forbid tears. And so he had sat back to watch Piers and Nigel – for really the music was so much more exciting than he had expected – plead the cause of a man who had bid too high. It was *his* job every month, pretty well, to make sure that some Phaethon or other met his just reward, in court. But it was wonderful to see his brother pleading so generously the cause of one who had tried to drive the Sun's chariot, as he had done, so magnificently, one who had failed as he had not.

Beside such artistic triumph, it didn't really seem to matter that Van had played down Earth's plea to Jove when the world was in danger of being set on fire. Probably all who walked on the ice field, as he himself did, exaggerated these dangers – look at all those riots that had spread last year from Paris like a plague, and the bombings that had followed. It had *indeed* been like a plague, and as soon gone as completely as a plague. It was almost six months now since that last explosion at Aldermaston.

How the audience were still! How the opera held them! Even the Countess had forgotten her gracious poise – her arm sprawled over in her intentness upon the stage action; Lady Norah seemed, in reverse, shaken into some apprehension of time and place, alert, held. He only hoped that the feast he had prepared for them – his own first public work of art – would be anywhere near as acceptable. Ah, if only Grandma could have been there for it all! Especially in her new open and easy mood which he must try to accept as everyone else did. He couldn't easily swallow change, however much it was for the good. But still she had seemed much better yesterday, far more on the ball than Lady Norah, except for her tottery walk.

But, as the lights came on and he joined in the wild applause, he gave Lady Chepstow a return of her look of delight, since no speech could be heard, and bobbed his head in acquiescence to whatever Lady Norah's extraordinary facial grimaces meant.

He felt immediately at his most alert and efficient. Lady Norah said, 'Dear Gobbi! He looked so youthful in his tunic. But his voice has a much higher timbre. Of course, he's getting on, you know.'

'That was Marc Gorbeau, the French Canadian counter-tenor, Lady Norah.'

She accepted it at once. Well, he supposed you had to be pretty adjustable to make every first night at the age of ninety.

'Ah! Now I understand. That's why I detected the French Canadian accent. I used to know Quebec so well. But of course! My friends were telling me of him. At the Met, I think they said. Tell me about him. Is he our coming singer?'

A counter-tenor at the Met didn't seem very likely, even to
his amateur knowledge. But he did his best to describe a career
he had picked up only from scraps of overheard conversation.
He feared that, by the time he had finished, Lady Norah could
have no clear idea whether he, she or Marc Gorbeau were
coming or going. But his effort clearly delighted Lady Chepstow. She smiled upon them indulgently and whispered:

'What a good and kind man you are, Mr Mosson. I judge
people a lot by their concern for Lady Norah. But we're all
inspired after that wonderful performance. I almost think,
you know, that an invitation to the Palace . . . But one can
never be quite sure. When you do another production here,
you must give me warning and I'll sound them out. And, of
course, Queen Mary so loved Tothill and spoke of it often. So
you're well known at the Palace. But perhaps the *next* performance you give? For you'll have to go on with these eve-
nings. We shan't let you off after this triumph.'

'It's Nigel Mordaunt's triumph and my brother's. But I
know Piers will be delighted at what you say. Of course, his
professional work doesn't give him much time for indulgences
of this sort, but I am hopeful that we'll be able to persuade
him. And what you say will help a lot. I suggest we lead the
way to the Saloon. There's champagne before the supper in the
Long Gallery. I think it the finest room in the house.'

'What? Better than this magnificent Hall of Vanburgh's?'

'I'm a bit of a heretic about this room. For me the original
house built by Roger Pratt is the more complete, the more
meaningful architecture. And the crown of Pratt's work is certainly the Long Gallery.'

'How you love it all,' Lady Chepstow commented. 'It does
one good to hear you, Mr Mosson, in these days when to reject
everything is considered so clever.'

He hadn't felt so approved since his early days at Clarke,
Bingley's when Sir Leonard had encouraged him for his précis
of the complicated Malcolm divorce case. Or even, perhaps,
since his law tutor at John's had approved his essays. If this
was the patronage of Court circles, it seemed most soothing –
but he'd always liked going up to get a prize. Only when it was

earned, surely. He realised almost with amused acceptance
that now, indeed in the last year since they'd lived at Tothill,
he'd begun shamelessly to enjoy things – whether he'd earned
them or not. I shall suffer justly, he thought, if the ortolans are
roast to a cinder or the *sauce suprême* of the *oeufs mollets* is
floury; but he knew the Chef wouldn't let him down. Getting
a really first class chef had been his chief contribution to the
household since Piers inherited.

Lady Chepstow said, 'If your food is as good as your brother's production, what an evening we're going to have. I'm
famous for my greed.'

'How did you know that I was in charge of the food and
drink?' he asked, not with anxiety, but with curiosity – could
it be that people connected with the Palace were given such information in advance? Perhaps some old tasting for poison
ceremony would be called for. He felt a longing to know
anything new tonight, to be open to everything that came
along. He'd chosen the champagne wisely, anyway, he
thought, as he drank with delight.

'Oh, I'm an avid reader of the gossip writers,' Lady Chepstow said, 'and, of course, they've talked about nothing but
the Mossons since . . .' recollection of the nature of Hubert's
death had clearly stopped her in her tracks, he realised, when
she paused. She went down a little in his estimation: people
oughtn't to be stumped by anything. However, he got her out
of it.

'Since my brother's romantic inheritance. Yes. He gets into
a terrible rage because little gossipy notes about his life keep
popping up among the press cuttings of his productions.'

'Well, it's you they're on to now. Cordon Bleu trained, up
and coming young lawyer. Bachelor dinners, a gourmet's
dream.'

Lady Chepstow was almost flirtatious in her teasing. 'However did you come to combine two such unlikely careers?'

'Oh, a solicitor's life is a very hard one. I realised early on
that I needed a hobby, something to relax me in the evening
when I got home, and I've always loved good food. I decided
to take a Cordon Bleu course immediately after I left Cam-

bridge before joining Clarke, Bingley's. It's meant that however much work I've had to take home, I've had something to
distract me first, something manual *and* cerebral – good cooking means using your head, you know – every evening before I
started on the work I'd brought back with me. And that way,
I've relaxed over something worth eating and a wine worth
drinking. It's a civilised régime, I think, and civilisation stops
panic and encourages work.' Except, he thought, when your
uncle's naked body is found in a suburban lodging house with
wounds still bleeding from whips. But the memory was
remote now.

'And you haven't put on weight?' she teased.

'No, you see, I play squash regularly every morning early
before I go to work.'

'You should have been royalty. It's regimen that keeps *them*
going, you know.'

'I think,' he told her, 'that it's the basis of all the institutions
that save us from chaos.'

But now Piers had joined them. 'I believe I have the pleasure
of taking you into supper,' he told the Countess. 'But I'm
afraid we have to wait for the singers to change. They objected
to appearing in their costumes. Actors and actresses are much
more obedient.'

Lady Chepstow laughed. And, Tom reflected, her laughter
sounded more at home with Piers than with him. 'But you
made them into actors and actresses, Sir Piers,' she said. 'It
was so wonderful to see opera *produced* instead of merely
presented. All that melodrama that singers usually give us.'
She pointed to Caracci's *Sacrifice of Isaac*, 'I know I shouldn't
say it about an old master – Caracci, isn't it? – but the average
opera singer's idea of acting is so much like a lot of painting we
are told to like. Gestures and attitudes. Whereas you put it all
into the eyes.'

'The great painters, I think, *could* do just that. Let me
show you Tintoretto's *Head of the Baptist*. Look at Salome's
excited eyes there!' And off he took her to see the masterpiece.

For a moment Tom felt that the Countess had been a little

less than courteous in letting him drop from her flattering hook. But, after all, Piers *was* the fish to fry! The play was the thing. Tothill's master the centre of the house. It was as it should be. And this evening he had his own role. He was to take in Katherine White, the first singer. Well, if the sincerity of her grief for lost love as Théone was even partly felt, he thought he could like her, even though to make contact with a great voice was awesome. He would get himself another glass of champagne to await her.

He felt no special demand for care, no tense scruple about extreme sobriety this evening, although his own show was just about to be judged. What a pretty girl over there! Simple looking without being unpleasantly boyish. So few young women could look intelligent without suggesting sophistication, but this girl did. He felt that he could talk a lot with her.

Then she said, 'I think you're taking me into supper, Mr Mosson. I hope it's good. I get so hungry after singing.'

Where her appearance without its Greek gown was unrecognisable, the speaking voice had, despite a touch of over-careful gentility, the wonderful, enslaving tone of the singer's.

The Countess had reminded him of the approachability, the affability that were the clichés of royalty and those connected with the Court. But, like clichés, it had been turned off as quickly. Somehow he felt that this goddess whose voice had moved him to tears was reliable, enduring.

He could not believe his own voice as he heard himself boasting.

'I hope you will like it,' he said. 'It's my contribution for the evening. I mean that I designed the food, not that I cooked it. Although I could have done.' His boyish rush of words embarrassed him; but, looking at her, he saw that she was pleased with him. 'Come and look at the menu,' he said, and took her to the placement table. 'That's what you're going to eat,' and she read the menu:

Oeufs Mollets La Vallière

***

Sole Colbert

***

Des Ortolans en petit chariot d'Olympe

Pommes de Terre à la Dauphine

Petits Pois Frais à la Française

***

Sorbet Soleil

***

Fromage Triple Aurore

***

Coupe Phénix

She said, looking at him, he thought, puzzledly but delightedly, 'It's all to do either with Louis Quatorze's court or Olympus. Your brother tells me they're the same thing. You're as clever as your brother, I can see. What's La Vallière? I don't mean the mistress who became a nun, I mean how are the eggs served?'

'They're in little tarts,' he said, 'on a bed of creamed sorrel and asparagus tips. With a *sauce suprême* over them.'

'I adore sorrel,' she said, 'but I hope the sauce is right. I've had it that shade too floury even at Picquier's before now. And, would you believe it? at that wonderful restaurant outside Rodez, I've had it when it was simply paste.'

'At the Cerf Volant – you shock me! Well, I can promise you it will be right tonight. The Chef is the man who taught me how to make it.'

'Ah! Our singing masters. We must never criticise *them*.'

They laughed. He said, 'I hope you never criticise yours.

You made me weep with your lament tonight.' As he drew to the end of his words, he feared her laughter or annoyance, but she took it delightedly and easily. Compliments had always been so impossible.

'That's nice of you,' she said. 'Actually, Nigel Mordaunt told me that I was in voice this evening. I have a suspicion myself that there were moments of strident singing above the stave. But self-criticism's never a safe guide. I am scared stiff about your brother's comments tomorrow on my acting. I can't help thinking, from what you say about my making you weep, that he'll give me hell for hamming. Coulsdon's Callas, he called me once. I come from Coulsdon, you see.'

'I'm sure Piers is never so rude.'

'What a snob you are!' she said, but she seemed to like him for it. 'In any case, of course he's rude. Really good producers must be.'

Tom could see that Katherine liked teaching him about his brother, but she said, 'Back to *your* production. What's Sorbet Soleil?'

'It's made with sunflower seeds.'

'It sounds very exotic. Not that ortolans are everyday birds. But they're delicious. All the same, I wish it were August and they were grouse. I can just see them sitting up high but not too high in their little chariots.'

Once again he found himself telling his thoughts. 'It's incredible,' he said, 'you sang so beautifully that I cried. And then you know about cooking. And you got the joke about the menu which I am sure almost nobody else here will. And now you say you would have preferred grouse and, of course, that is exactly what I designed when this occasion was first suggested because it was to be in the first week in September. And then it was brought forward to June. I can't understand it,' he said, 'I mean that you can be all those things at the same time.'

'You're a wonderful encourager for sopranos with self-doubts,' she said. 'As to food, well, when I began to make rather a lot of money, I thought I must have *some* indulgence. I don't really care about clothes all that much, or jewellery, and I have to travel anyway. So I decided never to eat any-

where except in gourmet restaurants. I mean ones *I* think are
gourmet. Not that the Michelin is always wrong, as silly snobs
pretend. It was a kind of insurance anyway. I think if you're a
real gourmet you're not a gourmand. At least, that's what I've
found. And putting on weight is the singer's menace. But why
do *you* know about cooking?'

He began to tell her, when a loud voice near them said, 'Ah,
Nigel, I see you cribbed a good deal of the orchestration from
Armide. Well, it's the Lully opera we all know. But shouldn't
you have consulted the manuscript of *Phaethon* in Paris?' The
sort of loud braying laughter that accompanied the words
made Tom shudder with memories of Hubert's life of fear.
'You *did*, but you didn't find what you were looking for.
That's what you're going to say, isn't it?' And the braying
laugh started again.

Katherine said in a quiet but not whispering voice, 'That's
Simon Harvester, the critic for the *Morning Advertiser*. He's a
very nasty man and he loves baiting Nigel. However he's what
he calls my greatest worshipper. So I can and must rescue
Nigel. You *do* understand, don't you?'

His disappointment must have shown, for she said, 'Please,
I must. But I'm looking forward to dinner enormously. And
to knowing about what you are and who you are more than I
can say. Anyway someone quite awful is advancing upon *you*.
That Marina monster, the Luzzi woman. She terrifies me and
you'll probably see me being rude from fright, which I don't
want.' She touched his hand and he pressed it against hers.

Then he heard the *Morning Advertiser* man saying, 'Ah! the
divine Katherine! My libation is at your feet as usual.'

And now, horror, Marina Luzzi was upon him, with,
horror of horrors, Uncle Eustace.

'Mm,' said Eustace, 'here's someone who wanted to know
whether the family had forgiven her. I took it upon myself to
say yes.'

'We sent an invitation to Signora Luzzi. It was an indication
of our pleasure in seeing her that hardly needed corroboration,
I should have thought.'

He felt a twinge of shame when Eustace's old purple face

twitched with embarrassment. He realised that he had used the voice he employed with clients whom he discovered had been holding back material facts in the evidence they put before him. But really the way old Eustace had sucked up to Piers, and even to him, since Piers inherited, sickened him.

He said to Marina, 'It was Grandma's special wish that we should ask you this evening . . .'

She interrupted him with all the old gush, 'Oh, but it's so fascinating. That she 'as changed, I mean. Everyone in London speaks of it. The fun lady, they call 'er. She wrote me a letter to Italy full of love. No Mother Gods and blue flowers! But all wonderful things that are 'appening 'ere. I'm worried she is still a victim of, 'ow do you say, mythomania? *Nothing* is 'appening 'ere in London. *Everything* is in Rome. But no, 'er letter made it all sound so funny. And not too much about 'Ubert. I was afraid for that.'

Tom wondered if strangling would stop her. And even Eustace was bending his flushed face forward and saying, 'Mm. Mm. Mm.'

Tom said, 'Unfortunately she has . . .' But the Luzzi torrent hurtled on.

'She told me she was to blame. It was true. 'Ubert would 'ave been 'appy married to me, she wrote. I don't know. But not to talk of it, I told 'er. 'Orrors are 'orrors. Now is the fun time, I wrote 'er. But why is she not 'ere?'

'She very much wished to be, but four days ago she had a stroke. Oh, don't worry. No horrors!' Tom heard his own malice with surprise, but he really couldn't take this woman, and, in any case, the whole subject of the changed 'fun' Grandma fussed and perplexed him. 'She's very much better. It's only affected her walking a little. And even that she seems to be coping with. They're wonderful at St Thomas's. She has a room looking right over the river.'

'Oh, good.' For once Marina's vowels were not elongated, but abrupt enough to leave the subject quickly behind. 'And Piers, where is 'e? What a triumph this evening! 'E's taught us all to love Lully! She is very good, that Katherine White! And Martha Roddam. I love 'er. She is so ugly. The Phaethon! I am not so sure. A French Canadian! That isn't very amusing. But anyway it is your brother 'oo is important. 'Oo else can make us listen to Lully? 'E is the only Englishman in Italy now. England is so boarring! Everything is in Rome. But of 'im they *are* talking. I was at Lily Farini's to dinner this week! She is rich American. She married Aldo. Everyone goes to 'er parties. My friend Feltrinelli was there. 'E's the cleverest man in Italy. 'E was talking to Pasolini – "The only one in London," 'e said, "is Piers Mosson." Pasolini agreed. "All the rest – finished," 'e said.' She snapped her fingers in imitation of the great film director's dismissive gesture.

Even praise of Katherine White and of Piers could not reconcile Tom to her. And, with her new flat chest and simple black dress like an orphanage girl, and her straight shoulder-length hair and scrawny old little boy's face, she looked worse than she had when she was all make-up and bosoms and jewellery and flounces ten years ago. But thank God, she had seen Piers nearby.

'Come 'ere, Piers,' she cried. 'You know very well I like to talk to the important people. Everyone in Rome is talkin' about Piers Mosson.'

Tom had never quite got used to Piers' assured party manner, which he had acquired in his swift rise to fame in the theatre, but he welcomed it now, for Marina was taken off his hands.

'And you, lovey,' Piers said, kissing her full on the mouth, 'you bring a breath of dolce vita to our stale city.' She clearly loved his undertone of sarcasm.

'Well, I suppose,' she said, 'we are living in Fellini's age. Not ten years ago.'

Now Tom felt free to look again for Katherine, but Eustace was upon him, speaking in a loud mumble that was intended apparently to be private.

'Oh God,' he drawled, 'I thought we were going to have a terrible thing about all that Hubert business, but she's such a snob, we were saved from it. Of course, I have my own view of the whole ghastly affair . . .'

Determinedly Tom interrupted him. 'Don't you like the

Luzzi whom you received back into the family on our behalf?'

Eustace ignored the sting. 'Like?' he drawled, 'I should hardly have thought anyone would *like* her. She's amusing enough, but a most dangerous woman, I should think. The main thing is she's frightfully rich.'

'Well, so is Piers. And for that matter I'm quite rich now with the generous income Grandma allows me.'

'My dear boy, I hope I've shown you both my appreciation of *that*.' With the openly malicious look in his dark eyes, and the new little upturned beard he wore, Eustace looked Mephistopheles himself. And he clearly felt a demonic power to say what he wished. 'Mm. About my Hubert theory. You see, I'm quite sure he was another victim of this beastly permissive society they all talk about so much. I mean everyone knew he liked being beaten. But of course it was never mentioned. Why should it be? And being a rich man, and a well known one, there were places where, if he paid well, he could get just what he wanted with the strictest privacy. Then they started all these saunas for people with his tastes to go to. Like Berlin in the 'twenties. And of course Miss Whipwell and Madame Birchezvous and all the rest of the professionals "came out", as the awful expression is now, as though they were going to be presented at Court. And they set up in Soho for the tourists with their names in lights. Naturally Hubert couldn't risk being seen at such places, so he was driven to amateurs – always a disaster! No wonder he was murdered or near to it in Surbiton or some other ghastly suburb.'

'Arnos Grove,' Tom said shortly, in his most law-office voice, 'and there was no question of murder, Uncle Eustace. The coroner's verdict was perfectly clear – death by misadventure. He had a heart attack and fell down the stairs.'

But Eustace was not to be put down by respect for the law. 'Oh! Coroners are notoriously corrupt or stupid or both. Everyone knows the old boy fell down the boarding house stairs and broke his neck. But he was obviously running away from some amateur bitch with a whip who liked her job too well. Too ghastly!'

But it was Tom's lucky night. Parties seemed to him then

such a wonderful thing, for now another familiar voice sounded in his ear, addressing Piers.

'My dear boy, quite superb! Far better than anything I had imagined.'

Of all the voices (save perhaps for one other now) that Tom knew, Sir Timothy Pleydell's famous tones had been his delight and marvel since Van had continuously lugged him to the theatre in their adolescence. He put his finger to his lips. 'Ssh!' he said to Eustace. 'That's Sir Timothy Pleydell's voice. The greatest actor of our time. I must hear what he has to say.'

This time it worked. Eustace said, 'Oh Lord! Mummers – I can't stand them,' and he went away. But as he went he sang in defiance, 'Teach us to live to Thee alway, Controlled and cleanly night and day. That we may bring if need arise, No maimed or worthless sacrifice.' Tom remembered the dreadful hymn all too well from his prep. school, where for some unexplained reason they used *The Public School Hymnal*.

'Ah! – Timothy, darling! 'Ow wonderful. You are right. Only this beautiful Piers of mine could 'ave made us all love Lully so.'

Sir Timothy directed his noble heraldic lion's gaze upon her.

'Marina Luzzi,' Piers said in explanation.

'Marina, my dear. I didn't recognise you. So "with it",' Sir Timothy said, and gave the cheek she offered him a manly buss. 'Oh, the opera, of course. "Superb." But that isn't what I'm so ecstatic about, I'm afraid. Naturally Piers makes a triumph of anything he sets his hand to. We expect that. But that wonderful room. The Great Hall. I've heard of it, of course. And I worship Blenheim and revere Castle Howard. But this is surely Vanbrugh's masterpiece. Why the man wished to write West End comedy when he could design such miracles, I shall never understand.'

'You could if you would agree to play in my production of *The Provok'd Wife* at the Haymarket next winter, Tim. It's quite wrong that the greatest high comedy actor of centuries should never have showed modern audiences that Vanbrugh was our greatest writer of comedies. Which *you* could do. And

only you, I think. He was writing *The Provok'd Wife* while he
was designing Tothill. That's perhaps why Sir John Brute is
the finest role he imagined. And it's cut out for you.'

Sir Timothy's old lion's mouth creased into as many pouts
and smiles combined as are usually only contrived by heraldic
stone masons. 'You're too flattering, my dear boy. But you
young fellows *will* type me for high comedy. You've got it all
wrong, you know. My forte is psychological mystery. The
man with doubts. The Hamlet soliloquies brought up to date.
However, if you'll do your beloved *Provok'd Wife* in the
Great Hall here, I might consider it. It would be a tribute to
the great architect.'

'Who did not, I am afraid, write his plays to be performed in
private houses, however magnificent. Even his own creations.
He wrote *The Provok'd Wife* for the West End, and that's
where it must be done.'

Tom could see that Van was shocked by what he evidently
considered the old actor's lack of sense of theatrical propriety
and order. It pleased him that, in professional matters, his brother had so Pratt-like a side to him. But he felt, also, unac-
countably miserable that an opportunity to repeat this
wonderful evening (and with this greatest of actors) seemed to
be fading.

He heard himself saying, 'Let me make it quite clear that *one*
Mosson, at any rate, would be overwhelmed if he could see
Timothy Pleydell acting anything he chose at Tothill House.'

Sir Timothy snuffled surprisedly. Piers said, with a glint of
malice in his eye, 'My brother Tom seldom offers public
praise, Tim. But we're eating a supper of his choice this evening and he probably wants to counter any complaints in
advance.'

'Oh, no,' Marina cried, 'you *must* do another play 'ere,
Piers. With Tim in it. It will make London interesting again.
And look what it is doing for your Tom who's usually so shy
and boaring. 'E is looking quite 'andsome and 'appy.' She
stroked Tom's arm.

His distaste must have been obvious, he feared, for Sir
Timothy rushed to his rescue.

The actor said, 'Well, if you can find a play, not too experimental, but not too conventional either, which has a thoughtful, self-analysing part for an old actor like me, Mr Mosson, we'll do it here at Tothill this summer when I'm supposed to be resting. And I'll do this Brute of Vanbrugh's for your brother at the Haymarket in the winter. Can you fix that? I'll tell you now what the snag will be. Piers will be under contract to three festivals here and two overseas.'

Van put on a special drawl. Tom could see that he did not want to lose hold of the old man's offer, but also wanted time to consider it. He said, 'I am, as a matter of fact, under contract to produce *The Master Builder* at Stratford, Ontario. And there was talk of taking it on to the Guthrie at Minneapolis.'

Marina cried, 'What barbarous names!' and Sir Timothy's frown was that of the King of the Beasts. But Piers took no notice, except, smiling, to draw a paper from his inside coat pocket.

'Far the most important offer I have is this from my mother. She sent this long cable, Pratt. I didn't have a chance to tell you before. "Every good wish for Tothill success from me and Jim. He says why not repeat out here at Umtali in peace away from all old England's terrorist bombs. What is happening to the old country, darling heart. Love. Ma." So there you are. Offers to play in Umtali! It's incredible, isn't it,' he went on in a voice Tom could tell was intended to leave the question of another performance at Tothill to one side, 'how people, when they go to places like Rhodesia, seem to lose all sense of what England's like. Terrorist bombs! They can't have seen an English paper for a year at least!'

Sir Tim's face grew solemn. 'I'm afraid,' he said, 'you may be speaking a little prematurely. I heard some rumour from Beale just now about another of these bloody incidents this evening. At Aldershot, I believe. Where did you say that bomb was, Beale?' he called in his loudest stage tone to that sergeant-major-like, opera-loving Lord across the room.

Lord Beale frowned and came over. 'Don't shout it around, Pleydell, there's a good lad. It's not released yet. But they seem to have landed one on Woolwich Arsenal. I don't know what damage the bastards have done.'

Piers' reaction troubled Tom a little. He said, 'Well, if anyone is going to know the damage, it'll be you, Beale. No doubt you'll get the commission to rebuild it.' His smile didn't prevent Lord Beale from walking away. He added, 'It does make me happy about my powers of hearing, though. I could have sworn I heard an explosive thud somewhere in the distance during the performance. And I was right. But one bomb doesn't mean a return to all that absurd rioting and nonsense of last year.'

'Oh, but no, your riots in London must 'ave been quite wonderful! The Paris riots were boaring. Everyone looks for 1848 there. But not in *London*! I wish I could 'ave seen those London riots. But not the bombs. They are ugly and boaring like all technology.' Marina gave a chic shudder.

Such frivolity in face of a possibility of renewed disorder made Tom feel that he should be in desperate alarm. And, mentally, he understood the need for alarm. But he didn't *feel* it.

And then a husky, deep American woman's voice said, very loudly and jarringly to the company at large, 'Oh, for God's sake, everybody, forgive me for being so late, but I got stuck in the bath tub.' It was easy to believe of the huge form before them.

And there Katherine White was by Tom's side. 'As you can hear, Martha Roddam's arrived, Mr Mosson. You can take me into supper now,' she said. 'Anyone who heard the Los Angeles Callas then can surely understand why the critics talk about her fine-spun mezzo.'

Tom looked at her for a moment, surprised. Then a deep happiness overcame him. She was being lightly malicious. He realised that he had been building up her virtues into perfection until he'd sowed doubts in his own mind. Now she had shown a failing – she was jealous – and she seemed, as he offered her his arm, all perfection.

CHAPTER II
A New Play

WHEN THE brothers arrived to see Jackie, the nurse told them that she already had two visitors – Mr and Mrs Tucker.

'They've only been here a few minutes, Sir Piers. I'll tell them they can stay another ten and then, if you and your brother are alone with Lady Mosson for a quarter of an hour, I think that will be quite enough. She's making such wonderful progress. Her speech is almost clear now and she walked the whole length of the corridor and back. She says the pulpit takes her back to her bicycling days. Has she always been so full of fun? Even when she wanders a bit, she says "what a lark!"'

It was clear that there was no undertone of sarcasm or irritation, as there used to be with Grandma's brightness and sweetness in her old Christian Science days, Piers thought. She's born again, he told himself, without our Father Mother God to guide her – and a jolly good rebirth it was proving. Tom smiled at the nurse, as he found himself regularly doing nowadays when people did justice to his grandmother; but then, again as always, he found himself shivering slightly – was this really any longer his grandmother?

But there was no doubt of Jackie's high spirits. 'Hullo, darling boys.' She accepted their kisses with a new touch of coquetry that amused Piers as much as it worried Tom. 'Now proper kisses. Not pecks. I *am* having fun. And so did you last night, from what the young people tell me. They don't seem to know which was better, the music or the food. More delphiniums for me?' But her glance at the many studies in blue was perfunctory. 'Put them in water, Nurse, please, and bring them all in later. We do not want to fuss with flowers when I have people to enjoy. So everyone was there that's fun to meet. And these two silly young people were too shy to talk to anyone so they can't tell me all the lovely gossip column names. But there is a piece about it in the Rodney Shannon column in the picture paper the nurses fuss over here. They read it to me this morning. "Everyone that is anyone" and all that sort of thing. And the brilliant young producer whose meteoric career and so forth. We are used to all that, of course. But "the rising young lawyer whose gourmet menu proved so much to everyone's taste." That *is* new. And there's something apparently in the *Telegraph* restaurant column thing about a wonderful dessert – ice cream and custard I believe it was. But then, people will enjoy anything if they are having fun.' She put the tip of her tongue out at Tom. 'We must not let him get too uppity.'

But she was much too anxious to hear all the guests' names to inquire further about the details of the opera or the supper. It seemed to Tom, as she clapped her hands with joy at every celebrity Piers named, that the whole evening was a fiction – three quarters of these smart first nighters must be unknown to her, she'd caught up a little with what she called the 'swing' in the year since Hubert's death, but not that much. He told himself to be happy with her happiness and, in fact, these days, his own happiness was too secure to be undermined, but if anything could do so, it was the sense of almost macabre pantomime her new, so much welcomed personality gave him. She who had been so rock-like, hard, egoistic if you like, but reliable, firm in her knowledge of the things she valued, appeared to be like a feather on top of a wave – pretty enough, because, for all that the stroke had pulled her mouth down slightly at the right side, her eyes had lost their old steely look and danced now, glinting yet gentle. But, to him, she seemed like a pretty but battered old doll. To feed her with what would have some meaning to her, he broke into Piers' recital to tell her of Lady Chepstow and Lady Norah.

It was a great success. Yet even here her reception worried him, for if she was delighted by Lady Chepstow's hint at Royalty's possible interest in another play at Tothill, she seemed transported by his account of old Lady Norah's confusion of Phaethon.

'Tito Gobbi! I am surprised she did not think it was Caruso. Well, that is rich. And fun, too. Fun cannot be all sweet smiles after all, can it? There simply has to be some malice to give it salt. And really the poor old thing's confusion is a bit of a lark. Why, she is only ten years older than me.' But she came back to Lady Chepstow's hints. 'So Royalty wants to see Tothill. Well, if they're anything like Queen Mary, Tothill will love them. Straight look, straight back, firm handshake. I worshipped Queen Mary. It is a royal command, Piers, you will have to put on another play.'

'So they all tell me, but I have a frantically busy programme.'

'Busy programme! Fiddlestick! And this time – no opera! Oh, I know you had your dreams about the Great Hall as a boy. And I am sure they were beautiful ones. I do wish that I had seen it, my dear boy. But you have got that out of your system. No, we must have a play to do with the history of Tothill. That is what I want. Hubert would have liked it too.'

Suddenly her voice trembled and her eyes filled with tears. Ralph and Magda moved to the window and looked out over the river. Tom was delighted with their tact. Piers patted Jackie's cheek.

'Cheer up, lovey,' he said. But Tom took her hand.

'You loved each other very much. That's what matters,' he told her.

But she wouldn't yet be comforted. 'Oh my dear, I don't know. He did not have any fun. I did not let him have any real fun. That is why he got involved in that silly childish nonsense.'

'He was a very clever man. He gave me my foundations in life.'

'Yes, he *was*, wasn't he?' Her tone had become lively, social. 'Well, no use a'dwelling on the past. It is this royal command we have got to think of.'

Once again she seemed to fly off at a tangent. 'You owe *him* a lot, don't you, Piers?' She waved her hand towards Ralph.

'Without Ralph's control of stage effects, *Phaethon* would have been nothing,' Piers said firmly. 'Nigel Mordaunt said that last night, Ralph.'

Ralph turned and winked at the company. 'You none of you knew what we were up to at the rehearsals until it all came together. We workmen had you in our hands to do what we liked – the lot of you, stars and all.'

'That's true. I only fully realised how brilliant your ideas were at the dress rehearsal. And we owe to Magda the whole *raison d'être* of the opera's presentation at Tothill. It makes me very angry with myself and with Tom that we didn't see that you met everybody interesting last night as you should have done.'

Magda's Dutch doll face had wrinkled a little with the years but it was still solemn, and pretty. 'Oh, I think English society does not permit such intrusions. At the performance, perhaps, but not in the intimate social gatherings.'

Tom saw that Piers was about to protest, but Ralph added his wooden agreement. 'Carpenter's hands. That would never do. On the other hand, you could have said, rectory bred. But a workman's hand. They might have refused to shake it. And then *I* might have spat in their eye.'

'Oh, Ralph!' Magda cried, reproving and worshipping at the same time.

But Jackie was delighted. 'Spit in their eye! What fun we are having.' She clapped her hands. 'Well – if he has been so useful to you, *you* can be useful to him. Put the boy's play on. He has written a play about Tothill history. Just what we want. Something to do with the Gunpowder Plot. I expect it has the old monks' passage from Tothill to St Stephen's Hall in it. It would be exciting to find *that*, wouldn't it?'

Suddenly the girl Dutch doll seemed to come to a kind of violent life. 'There is no monks' passage. There never was. I have proved it. I made it clear again and again. It is one of those old romantic legends. I am afraid families always want to preserve them. But history demands truth.'

It seemed, he thought, as though she, not her husband, was going to spit in people's faces. How touchy she is about her work, he thought.

Even her husband said, 'Steady, Magda!'

But Piers confirmed it. 'I remember Uncle Hubert telling me exactly what you say. That you had disproved the legend, I mean.'

But Jackie was intent on her own will, too. 'All I want is Ralph's play to be done at Tothill, Piers. You owe it to him, after all he has done for the opera.'

Tom noticed with approving amusement Piers' professional response.

'Ralph knows that I would never produce a play of his except on its own merits.'

'Which, given your response to my earlier plays, means no.'

'I'm sorry we've got on to the subject, for I realise it must be a sore one. I can only say that I've read all the plays you've sent to me over the last few years and I didn't think I was the man to produce them. I didn't feel that I could achieve what you were aiming for.'

'I don't know.' Ralph seemed as much puzzled as aggrieved. 'You're the producer who wants to do his own thing. You're famous for it. I should have thought my loose-knit happenings were made for you.'

'I do,' Piers said, 'the thing of the writer's words. *I* demonstrate what the words mean, but I must have the form to tell me what the mystery is. The foundation, the shape is the writer's.'

Ralph frowned. 'Well, perhaps *The Neutral Priest* will suit you then. It's my shot at the well-made play. After all it's cost me to write, I shall go over to happenings.'

Piers said at once, 'Send it to me. I'd like to look at it.'

Tom felt admiration for his brother's professional mixture of formality and friendliness; it was what he sought himself with long-established Clarke, Bingley clients who appeared to be embarking on unforeseeable courses. But to his surprise he felt a need, even a right, to intervene.

'There's only one point that worries me about this,' he said, 'if it's 1605, it means the old house. And apart from the fact that the old monastery buildings must by that time have been pretty unsightly with all the random Tothill additions, it seems absurd to lose all connection with the Pratt-Vanbrugh wonder – I mean it would have to be painted sets, wouldn't it?'

Magda's round cheeks flushed until Tom wondered whether her whole face would turn into an Edam cheese.

'I am sorry to say only some incidents in the history of the Tothills lend themselves to drama, Mr Mosson. I cannot alter that fact to suit fashionable tastes.'

Ralph once again seemed to pacify her. He said, 'I got the idea from Magda's researches. She's put a lot of work into it.'

'And you made a wonderful play from the dry facts, darling.' She drew her husband's arm under her own and hugged it to her firm little apple breasts.

Piers said, 'I'm sure Tom was simply thinking about possible practical difficulties. There was no criticism.'

'Certainly not,' Tom affirmed. The brothers exchanged a glance that said firmly to each other, oh dear, why do first rate people in their own fields have to stray beyond them?

There was a silence. No one seemed to have a solution. But it was a short silence. Once again Jackie clapped her hands.

'I have it,' she said, 'the Stables! There is a real foundation there of the old monks' original buildings. But they're really Vanbrugh's work, aren't they? Grandpa used to say he had tarted them up to give them class and make them Scots baronial. You know how he loved to joke.'

Piers couldn't remember such jocularity in his great grandfather, but he was struck by the idea. 'You are clever, lovey. They're one of Vanbrugh's finest fancies. They always remind me of his strange Gothic dreams at Seaton Delaval. It's his childhood – he grew up among the medieval ramparts at Chester. But then, childhood inspiration is the deepest. What do you think, Ralph? Could we set your play there?'

'I don't know. You read it and see what you think. But

now, our time's up, Lady Mosson. It's really good to see you
well on the road to recovery.'

'Yes, indeed,' his wife put in.

'We came because I thought you would like to know what's
happening in your garden,' he added.

'Thank you, thank you,' Jackie cried as they left the room.
Tom didn't think she was much concerned about the garden.

'Dear people!' she cried, when they had gone. 'I used to
make a rule never to know the people who worked for me in
the old days. One didn't, you know. But then they are not
quite that. And, in any case, it is such fun breaking down
boundaries.'

'Good for you, lovey,' Piers said. But Tom said nothing;
the concept did not seem to suit the grandmother he had once
so respected.

'Well,' she said, 'Mr Producer, what is all this fun going to
cost us?'

'It's not going to cost *you* anything, Grandma. It's my
dream realised, and I shall pay for it. I don't mind admitting it
will be costly enough. A star opera cast for three nights to a
very limited audience, even though we charged super Glyndebourne prices for the tickets with supper, means a large loss.
But it's been wonderful.'

'How much?' Jackie asked, and, when he didn't answer, she
added, 'Now you don't want to upset an old, hospitalised
woman, do you? But you will, if you don't tell me.'

At last he said, 'I think we shall be in the red to about fifteen
to twenty thousand pounds.'

'Oh, well,' she cried, 'you have to pay for fun. At least, you
do not. I am going to pay for it all. I haven't got Tothill to keep
up, you have.'

'But Uncle Hubert left such an immense fortune.'

'Oh! Do not remind me of the way I cheese-pared his life.'

Tom said, 'I think Grandma's is a marvellous offer, and you
should accept.' His eyes told Piers not to distress the old lady.

'Thank you very much, lovey,' Piers said, and kissed her on
the lips.

'Good boy,' she said. 'And you will think seriously of

Ralph's play or some others about Tothill, won't you? I
know, of course, that a lady's whims cannot guide an artist's
inspiration. But try.'

Tom could see that Piers was in danger of joining in
Grandma's tears, and he felt a little overwrought with happiness himself.

'We mustn't tire you,' he said, and bent down to the level of
her head. 'You can actually see the river flowing past. That's
wonderful. It's so blue today.'

'It is much more wonderful seeing you two boys. And all
my visitors. People are what I want. But I shall let you both
off today. I am to ride my bicycle this morning. That is my
name for the thing they call the pulpit, you know. It's so
bright and glittery. It reminds me of the cycle I rode as a girl to
visit friends on Rhode Island. They were all the thing then.
And it takes me out of this room. Among people. It is like
riding in the Row. Anyway, I shall be out of here soon, from
what they say.'

Her statement had an undertone of inquiry, so Piers said,
'That's what they tell us, too.'

'What fun we shall have,' she said. 'Not that they haven't
been very good to me here. Isn't it a lark to hear me saying that
about a hospital? Although in some ways they are just as silly
as the C.S. people were. *They* used to tell me pain was unreal.
Of course, that was nonsense. But these people here seem to
think they know exactly why pain happens, which is nearly as
silly. Goodbye,' she said. 'There will be a lot of clearing up to
supervise at Tothill and Tom needs his Sunday rest before he
goes back to that old office of his. Have fun.'

Piers kissed her again. 'You, too, lovey, on your bicycle!
Thank you for the money. But especially for that super idea
about the Stables.'

'Yes, indeed,' said Tom as he gave his farewell kiss.

'Oh, that was not *my* idea. It was Ralph said that.' She dismissed them.

They exchanged quizzical glances, half sad, half amused, at
the strange vagaries of her memory.

They had come by taxi, for they both hated the fuss of cars

for short journeys. And now they could find none to take them back to Tothill.

'Will you be all right walking over that bridge, Pratt?' Piers asked.

'I may have to take your arm.'

'Delighted, I'm sure,' Piers said. 'Anyway seeing Grandma so changed, so happy and real must make you feel more confident even about bridges.'

'I don't know about that. I don't really *like* the idea of people being changed. It seems to make nonsense of life. I mean, how can you build up order . . .?' He added quickly, 'But, of course, I'm delighted to see her happy. And I'm sure most of her is that. Did *you* like the supper?' he asked.

Piers roared with laughter. He felt able to, for they were on the bridge now and there had been no taking of his arm.

'It was fantastic and there must be many more of them. I *always* forget to congratulate people. I said nothing to Nigel last night. I can only think of my own work. In any case, you do so much all the time for Tothill that I took the supper as part of it. Without all you do for me, I couldn't live there. Not to carry on with the theatre which, of course, must come first. Uncle Hubert's lawyers and accountants have been first rate, but you've been the backbone, Pratt. The West Wing *is* what you want, for living, I mean?'

'I love it. Its order and symmetry. It's like a dream come true.'

'I think it has agreed with you. At any rate, that's what Leonard Bingley said last night. I haven't told you all the glowing report he gave of you. His successor at Clarke, Bingley's. That's what you are. And he seemed to feel that life at Tothill agreed with you greatly, gave that extra relaxation-stretching, he called it, that your work needed. Is he right?'

'I think he might be.' Tom was clearly very pleased. 'And I told you what the great Matthew Langton said of you. Do all famous critics boast as much as he did? So our school reports are satisfactory, darling heart. It's relaxing, isn't it?'

Indeed they crossed the road to St Margaret's in relaxed silence.

Piers said, 'You know, I'm sure, that if anyone came to share the West Wing with you, I should be immensely happy.'

'Anyone? A twelve-year-old girl? I'm sorry, Van, I've seen enough of that sort of thing, at third hand of course, in the odd case we get. I don't think I'm cut out for it.'

Piers guessed that this attempt to shock was a rebuttal of what his brother thought to be interference or patronage. But he determined not to apologise or withdraw or to be shocked; he would reply in kind.

He said, 'Well, of course, we could go to bed together, if you're determined to make a marriage of it.'

This time Tom bit. He said, 'Oh, Van, for God's sake.'

Piers apologised. 'I'm sorry. You know that I can't find any subject free from all mention, even funny mention. And then, I have been to bed with men.'

'I'm not as narrow as that. I liked that man George. He was a good man, I should have thought. Of course, I only met him half a dozen times. And the theatre talk was a bit hard going for me. And then perhaps I felt angry for Kate. I was so fond of her, Van. When Katherine White was singing that lament of Théone's last night, she came into my mind. She loved you so much. And I suppose, anyhow, marriage is the way I see things. It's more orderly.'

'It's strange you say that. I thought of her, too, just at that time. I suppose it's because Katherine White is so splendid, so nice, too, with it. But it didn't do, Pratt. Kate wanted more of my life than I could give her. My career – no, my art, however pretentious that sounds – must come first. And yet, you see there *was* a girl – my shy assistant in the provinces – Sally Leader, whose one wish was to sacrifice herself to me. A marvellous girl, too, beautiful, lovable and a very good assistant. But I didn't think it was fair.'

'If she *wanted* it? Aren't you being a bit managing, telling people what they should want?'

'Yes, perhaps you're right. I've regretted it many times since. There's a lot to be said for having a Hilde Wangel to urge you on, "Go up, master builder." You see. My mind is really on my next production. Anyway, why don't *you* marry? I'd like to see you looked after. And I think, too, if you married or lived with someone, I'd really know you felt a bit safe at last, or you wouldn't let anyone else in for what's coming to you.'

They had passed St Stephen's Hall and the gates of Tothill were in front of them before Tom answered. He said, 'It would be marriage, if anything. And it might be. At least I'm thinking of it now. I'm happy enough for the first time.'

Piers knew that he must ask no more. As they walked up the drive, he said, 'Well, one of us will produce an heir to all this. Let's hope old Grandma lives to see it. Meanwhile I must try and give her the play. I wish it wasn't Ralph, though, who'd written it.'

'Why ever?'

'His plays are so nasty.'

'Surely all modern plays are nasty.'

'Very few are as nasty as his – and they are sent to me in shoals. However, I must read this one and make some decision before I go to Canada. If it had a good fat part for old Tim that would lure him on to do *The Provok'd Wife*, that would be an extra reason. Look, Pratt, will you read the play as well as me? I may be prejudiced. I've seen too much of his work.'

'Certainly, if you want me to. But you know how much my judgment will be worth.'

'I do. That's why I want it. And then we could meet – you and me and Ralph and Tim – sometime in the next fortnight. And try to work things out. But it must be the last. Theatre is too serious for manoeuvres or sentiment or therapy or anything but itself. And Tothill was built as a wonderful house not a theatre. You agree?'

'Yes. For all my enjoyment of last night, I do. Everything in its place and order.'

They met in the Library to discuss Ralph's play. It seemed somehow the most suitable room in which to hold a meeting, for the office which Hubert had established for estate business was characteristically very small, very bare, very uncomfortable, very claustrophobic; *and*, Tom thought sadly, also characteristically almost certainly a privy. The Library, too, was appropriate, for it seemed that Ralph wished Magda to be present so that she could fill in the historical background of the play if needed, and she, in turn, wanted the documents from which she had gleaned her facts to be within reach.

It was certainly a most happy room in its effect on Sir Timothy. He was already in seventh heaven about the gentlemanly proportions of Pratt's rooms in general, but the globes, the books, the portfolios of drawings and designs, even Magda's index cabinets appeared to give him an extra satisfaction.

'Oh Lord,' he said regretfully, if a little self-mockingly, 'how wonderful it would have been to have spent one's life as a scholar and a gentleman. And I had many pretensions to scholarship. You wouldn't know that, Piers. I only just missed a First in History at Oxford. But my family, alas, had not the slightest pretensions to gentility.' He laughed and, save for Van, the others laughed dutifully with him.

Tom found this whimsical self-teasing of the distinguished old actor rather endearing, and Magda was clearly overjoyed at being invited to play opposite him. But the effect of his lengthy examination of the room's contents on Van was less happy. Tom thought, don't let him go on too long, or Van will curtail his cries of ecstasy with a nasty bite. Owing to some flight delay, Van had only just got back from Canada that midday, and Tom had returned from the office to find him in one of his rare states. Yes, he'd read Ralph's play flying over the Atlantic last night; indeed, he'd flipped through most of it before they'd boarded the plane, for they'd been kept for two hours' delay on the alert at the nightmarish airport. It wouldn't do, it was too dull – yet there *were* potentialities and it wasn't nasty. The central character of the priest was a fat part for Tim and with enough soliloquies and inner doubts and consciences, God help us, to equal Hamlet with Othello thrown in, only without enough sense of theatre – which God knows had *not* been the fault with Ralph's earlier horror comics. But it had potentialities, it could be done, he'd had some interesting ideas about it, but wasn't going to be forced into doing it, he'd tell Pratt that now. Anyway, he had to go back in two days to Stratford, Ontario, there were lots of problems, this Ibsen was important to him. Did Pratt think shaping a play in advance of its production was a simple thing like, well, reading through some evidence about who wrote exactly what libel, or was there sufficient evidence that the husband had bashed his wife? His head was naturally full of *The Master Builder* and would be for a month or more, he couldn't concentrate on this priest thing. Anyway, what did *Pratt* think of it? He was the one who'd promised to read it thoroughly.

Tom had had to say that he found it most interesting, not at all nasty, a valuable play for these times with its emphasis on the difficulties facing the individual conscience. Well worth doing, if Timothy Pleydell liked it. What he couldn't tell Van was that, not having read a play in detail before, he had found it very hard to concentrate – as he did with all fiction – and his impressions were therefore rather sketchy. Van had simply replied, 'Ah!'

But looking at his increasing scowl of impatience, as Sir Timothy delighted over every reference book Magda showed him and went down his University memory lane to recall his use of them all, Tom was really anxious lest Van would say 'Yah!' now, would snap. And then the whole wonderful project would be off. And indeed snap he did.

Sir Timothy had discovered that there was no copy of Stubbs' medieval charters and he could not leave off teasing Magda about the absence of 'this absolutely basic reference book . . . I relied on Bishop Stubbs to open the middle ages to me at Oriel. No Stubbs' Charters, no Firsts in History, my old tutor told me.'

Then Van bit. 'And, with Stubbs' Charters, you still only got a second class degree, Tim. And I'm not a bit surprised, if you wasted as much precious time as you have since we came into the Library. However, your picture of undergraduate reading in the late 'twenties should be of real interest to a distinguished archivist from abroad like Magda.' His tone left little room for passing his remarks off as playful. Yet, he wanted to please Tim Pleydell above everything, even if they decided against this play. He had told Tom so. Tom wondered at these self-destructive outbursts in his brother's successful life: how had he survived them?

Perhaps, as now. For it was evident that, however much Van wanted the old man to play in Vanbrugh at the Haymarket, the actor wanted quite as much to play in the Tothill surroundings that so roused his buried longings for gentility.

'My dear boy,' he cried, 'how unpardonable of me! And how unfeeling for this young man who very properly is bursting to hear what you think of his play. Or have you told him?' He sat down. 'To order now, everybody. This is a meeting. Don't look so alarmed,' he said to Tom. 'Your brother is used to my playfulness. It's a means of fighting off old age, you know.'

Tom found such descents into harsh reality in public much more difficult than the playfulness, but he smiled.

'I think the play actable, relevant, especially to Tothill history, and, my brother Tom thinks, to our times. It has a fat, moving part for you, Tim, as the priest and confessor of Lady Tothill, the Catholic wife of Sir Rayner Tothill in the reign of James I. But quite honestly it's a bit pedestrian as it stands. Which surprises me, Ralph, for as you know my complaint against your work generally has been that it mistakes sensational effects for theatrical shape. However, this touch of dullness is a less serious fault and, to a great extent, it's my job as a producer to give visual and formal novelty to what is basically a well-written, interesting psychological study with a good plot. I've got a few ideas. And, no doubt, when I've had an opportunity to think more about it, I'll have some more. If Tim likes it, I'll be inclined to do it. Meanwhile I'd like Ralph to outline the play. It'll be useful to Tim, and quite frankly also to me, because nothing helps one to see a play's potentialities more than the author's account of it. That's how one can tell what's the emotional force behind it.'

Tom felt a little disappointed at this somewhat rambling speech, the first he had ever heard Van give professionally. He wondered for a moment if perhaps his brother had got as

sketchy an impression of the play during his unhappy aero-
plane journey as he had trying to read it after a day's work.
Could that be why he wanted Ralph to outline it? But he
banished so unlikely a thought; after all, it wasn't just that Van
was his brother, he was a great producer. In any case, he was
very relieved that Van hadn't asked him to give *his* opinion
publicly. Perhaps, after hearing Ralph's synopsis, he could be
a bit more coherent.

Ralph said, 'Well. Where shall I start? The sources perhaps.
There are three things that got me going – three separate things
that coalesced. It's often like that in writing, I think.'

'Look,' said Piers, 'not the creative process, Ralph, just the
play.' Then he added, 'Sorry, go on.'

And Sir Timothy, a little flushed, commented, 'Fascinating!'

'Well, the second baronet, Sir Rayner Tothill, married a
recusant, a Roman Catholic, that is. She had to pay a fine for
not attending the Abbey, but there was nothing illegal about
being a Catholic at that date. What *was* illegal was her chap-
lain. He was a Jesuit. They were strictly forbidden. Father
Shoe.'

'I have found all this in Lady Tothill's coded diary,' Magda
said.

'Well, I hope you put it all in the next volume of the
Tothills,' Piers said, setting the research in its proper place.
'We're moving backwards in publication of the Tothill
history. God knows why. It was my uncle's idea. The next
volume goes back to the early Stuarts.'

Sir Timothy looked delighted. 'These family histories are
the central brick in the foundation of our knowledge of how
people lived in the past.'

Tom wasn't sure whether Van's stomach rumbled after his
long journey, or whether he groaned.

Ralph went on. 'Of course, she had to have an alibi. The
Jesuit was known as Seth Todd, a bit of a puritan, tutor to the
young heir, the future Sir Thomas. That was just what her
ladyship wanted, of course, a Jesuit to keep her son on the
right lines. And for a double alibi the supposed Todd taught

classes at Westminster School nearby, an usher they called
them then.'

'I have checked in the school records,' said Magda eagerly.

'Well,' Ralph continued, 'Sir Rayner was a member of the
House of Commons. And when I tell you the play opens in
October 1605, you can see where we're moving.'

'But Sir Rayner was not really a Member of Parliament.
That's Ralph's invention. It must be made clear somewhere.'

Piers looked so cross that Tom interfered quickly. 'A programme note about the sources, I should think.'

'Yes. Well. With Magda's permission, I'll go on,' Ralph
said.

She said, 'Oh, darling,' in penitence and remonstrance.

'The play opens with Father Shoe, alias Todd, taking his
usual morning exercise in the forecourt of the house. He is
reading his breviary, but he has to pretend it's a construe of
Ovid that he is preparing. This'll give a feel of the man's divided mind from the start. Suddenly there appears a Westminster boy from the Stable entrance – the Stables were much
nearer to the old house than they are to Pratt's pile. I want to
give the feeling of the uncertainty of this boy at the beginning –
is he a real boy? Shoe's never seen him at the school, but he
wears the school uniform.'

'I have found an exact description of this costume. The
archivist has been very helpful. It is of the 1570s, Queen Eliza-
beth's reign, but they tell me it will not have changed.'

'Magda love, please . . .'

'It is a very *pretty* uniform.'

Tom had never seen the Dutch doll so feminine as when she
tried to dispel her husband's impatience. She was more of an
actress, surely, than he'd realised.

'I wish,' said Sir Timothy, 'that I more often met ladies as
alive to beauty as they are to scholarship.' He gave a gracious
little bow, but Tom thought he looked a little impatient.

Ralph proceeded, 'Well, as I say, I want particularly to
make this boy a mystery. He gives a cryptic warning that Sir
Rayner should be prevented from attending the opening of
Parliament. And then he's gone. Is he real? Is he an angel sent

by God? Or the Devil's emissary of deception? Or is he a product of Shoe's mind, battered as he is by his life of hiding and
double identity? One thing is clear, the boy knows Shoe's true
identity, for he calls him "Father" and asks for absolution,
which makes his cryptic warning something like a confession.
And you probably know the contortions the Jesuits got into
over the sanctity of confession. Whatever, his warning puts
Shoe absolutely in the shit – should he go further in investi-
gation and perhaps sell his Catholic pals to King James's Star
Chamber and the torturers?'

'It was the dilemma of Lord Mounteagle and the other
Catholics at that time who were given such warnings,' Magda
said. Tom could not see that the word 'shit' in mixed company
had at all upset her apparent demureness. They were a funny
pair.

'I like the appearance of a Westminster boy on the scene,' he
said to encourage Ralph. It was effective.

'Oh, goodo. It was thinking of you two Mossons coming
here as boys when I first joined the staff that gave me the idea.'

'Yes,' said Piers. 'We don't want any more softening up. I
know what I want now. The divided conscience, the doubts,
the very nature of the apparition, all this seemed central to me
as I read your play. And I see you think it is, too. For the rest,
I shall tell you, Tim, that Shoe's plot to get the Tothills away
from London and play for time is in the form of a Restoration
comedy. Sir Rayner, encouraged by the priest, is anxious to
prevent her ladyship from getting into further debt by card
losses; her ladyship, egged on by Shoe, comes to think that her
man is having it off with the young and attractive housekeeper.
So both want to get the other down to the country house in
Gloucestershire. Which suits Shoe's tactics. You'll read it. It's
good fun. It's a rather pre-Restoration comedy, of course: I
am surprised, Magda, that you didn't see to it that Ralph kept
to his period – it should have been Ben Jonson not Congreve.'

Tom saw with relief from Van's smile that his ill-temper was
now dissipated; but Magda didn't respond to his teasing.

'I do not know English literature, Sir Piers. I think that
European scholarship is not so based on a general culture as in

England. We have a very high standard of specialised study.'

But Van was equal to her. 'I'm going to kiss your wife,' he said, 'she's a lovey.'

And Magda seemed as delighted as Ralph. It's all beyond me, Tom thought. He decided to start planning the supper for the first night as a relief from all these antics. He could see clearly now that Van intended to do the play.

'So you see, Tim, there's the fiercest possible inner struggle for you set against a heartless comedy, for Shoe's schemes end ironically and nastily. Trust Ralph for a touch of the nasty. The plot explodes, so he need never have worried, but his working upon the Tothill couple has set fires alight he couldn't have guessed. Her ladyship, of whose conscience he is keeper, frightened by her husband's violence about more card debts and wild with jealousy about his amours, pushes the young housekeeper down the stairs and kills her. And that's pinched from early eighteenth century Tothill history, as you can see from Magda's Volume I. Anyhow a wonderful curtain as the angel turns to devil above your head, Tim, and then seems to echo your own voice – is it all a product of your own diseased mind?'

'I can't wait to get at it,' said the actor. And Tom could see he meant it.

'What I really want to know,' said Piers, 'is whether we can adapt the Stables to represent the old Tothill House and whether Ralph can repeat some of his machine tricks he used in *Phaethon* to give eerie effects for the various appearances of this spirit-devil-angel-superconscious-subconscious boy. He ought to come at you, Tim, from all angles and at the least looked-for time. He'll be there when my Lord and my Lady are playing out their Millamant stuff. And only you will see him. Is that right, Ralph?'

'You're the boss.'

Tom found it hard to believe that an author could be so acceptant; perhaps he was wisely playing Van along at this stage.

Piers said, 'Oh, good God! It's *your* play. Anyway, let's go over and look at the Stables. I particularly want you to come,

Tim. It was our grandmother's idea that we should play it there. And naturally, after her death, both Tom and I are biased to want to do what she suggested. But sentiment can't rule the day or the play.'

'Lady Mosson's sudden death just as we are about to stage the play is *very* sad. I meant to write to you,' Tim said.

Neither Piers nor Tom answered, but Piers led the way.

'You needn't come, lovey,' he said to Magda, 'there's no research involved.'

And Tom saw that her smile of acceptance of dismissal seemed quite genuine. Then Piers added dramatically:

'I had a telephone call here today on my return, from Marina Luzzi. You'll be pleased to know that she's still longing for another play at Tothill. I told her we had a play we might do about a priest's conscience. I'm afraid it didn't meet with her approval, Magda. She said "priests' consciences are very boarring".'

Magda looked blank. 'Who is that?' she asked.

Ralph said crossly, 'You remember that rich Italian woman who had the row with old Primrose.'

'Oh, I had forgotten.'

'Didn't you see her at *Phaethon*?' Piers asked.

'Oh, no, she's too grand for us,' they said in chorus.

Tom said crossly, 'Really, this is too absurd. I'd have brought her up to you if I'd known. I could have sworn I saw you all three together.'

'No,' said Ralph quickly, 'we know our class and station.'

When they entered the courtyard of the strange long-converted Stables, their genuine Gothic pointed arches and their Vanbrugh confected 'medieval' towers and battlements thrusting forward and upward from the least expected places, they were all silent for a minute or two.

Then Ralph said, 'You see we could work something out for an apparition across that crenellated rampart and again high up in that tower, I should say . . .'

But Piers cut in, 'Marvellous, Ralph. Work it all out for me for my return from Canada. I shall be back in the third week of

July. I shall cancel the taking of the show on to Minneapolis.
Or they can go ahead without me. I suppose that we should
rehearse for four weeks and produce at the end of August. You
can serve us grouse this time, Pratt. We want good outdoor
weather if possible. Will the dates suit you, Tim?'

'Yes,' Sir Timothy spoke from far away. 'It's a magical
stage, isn't it?' he said. 'The real middle ages and the artificial.
And something else, I think, something almost twentieth century, almost functional and brutal in the force of some of those
towers.'

'You're right, Tim,' Piers said, 'Vanbrugh's medieval work
has often been compared with Rennie Mackintosh, the Scots
father of Functional. I suppose they were both influenced by
the castles and battlements of their childhood. Oh, I'm sure
it's going to work. You've seen exactly what I hoped – that to
interpret the priest's conscience, we need past, present and
future. We also need a good Sir Rayner Tothill and his lady.
Let me and you, Tim, go into the house and have a drink and
discuss casting.'

To Tom's amazement, Sir Timothy suddenly flounced and
patted his hair like some comic camp comedian. His voice
came out in high falsetto.

'Sirrah, I'm Boudicca, Queen of the Welshmen, with a leek
as long as my pedigree. I will destroy your Roman legions in
an instant.'

Ralph looked as astonished as Tom felt. Van's reaction was
immediate.

'You're going to do it for me then, Tim. Good! You'll be
better than you've ever been.' He turned to the other two.
'He's not come over queer,' he said, 'it's Sir John Brute in a
drunken revel, brought before the magistrates in his wife's
clothes. It means he'll do Vanbrugh's *The Provok'd Wife* at
the Haymarket. Doesn't it, Tim?' And they went off together
in mutual delight.

'Well! Fancy! I must say. Get him then!' Ralph's camp
imitation was bad. Tom didn't want to discourage him at the
moment of his play's acceptance, so he smiled a little but he
said firmly:

'I'm sure you are wrong. He's a famous womaniser.'

'Okay, I'll believe you,' Ralph said. 'Anyway, I haven't time for you lot now. I've got to concentrate on these scene effects. I'll get in some of the blokes I know to help me. But we'll need a big storage room for all the stuff. There's a cellar down here somewhere, I think. That'll do. Strictly private it'll have to be – we don't want a lot of Union snoopers asking who's doing what and all that crap.'

The weather became really warm towards the end of July. Tom said to Ralph as they walked once again from the East Terrace to the Stable block:

'Thank goodness, the forecast is good right through until September. The stars will be happy, for it will still be an outdoor production.'

Ralph said, 'I still don't quite understand what he's done.'

'Well, it seems that *The Master Builder* has been a huge success in Canada, and they're going to take it to Minneapolis – I believe it's called the Guthrie theatre there. Van did say he'd leave his assistant to produce it, but, with a smash hit, I suppose he feels he'd like to start it off himself. It's only natural. It'll only mean four days' postponement of rehearsals, but his tone on the telephone made me realise that he expects the cast to be a bit touchy about it. But he seemed to think that if I could tell him and them that the scene arrangements were well forward, that would oil the wheels. So if I could see a bit of what you're doing.'

'Certainly, mate. We're well on our way. What I won't do is to worry the blokes in the rear room who are constructing the rest of the stuff. Besides, the room is full to bloody bursting with props. I've marked it strictly private. Some of the gardeners and the carpenter had got in the habit of having their elevenses there, so I marked it off limits.'

'Quite right. If you've put up notices, you won't have any trouble, I suppose.'

But Tom supposed wrong, as he knew when they neared the great Stable courtyard that had once been the entry to the monks' refectory. Voices were raised, and how.

'I don't care who you fucking are,' said one. 'You can read, can't you? Strictly private. Keep out. That's what it says.'

'Mm. Oh God!' the other voice replied. 'I do happen to be Sir Piers Mosson's uncle.' And there before Tom was Eustace being led by the arm by a very tough looking young man, as though he were under arrest.

'That's all right, Len,' said Ralph immediately. 'The gentleman's a relation of Sir Piers.'

'Sorry. But I was doing what you said, Ralph.'

'Sure, you were quite right.'

'Hardly,' said Tom. 'There's surely no need for your men to be quite so violent.'

'We simply can't have any interruptions,' Ralph said. 'It's delicate and complicated in there, and intruders could muck up anything. The notices are perfectly clear.'

And indeed, Tom thought, they were.

'No one's to go through to the back, except my team. Signed Ralph Tucker.'

'Oh God,' Eustace cried, 'I can't imagine anyone *wanting* to go into that ghastly smelly hole. The people, the noise of those machines! Like those awful men that pull the very street up before one's window. London is hell now! The footman told me you were in there, Tom. Really, your servants!'

'Well, at any rate, I can tell my brother that you're working hard and will be ready any day, Ralph,' Tom said.

'That's right,' Ralph agreed, and he gave a sudden boyish grin, 'you tell him that.'

Tom walked the flustered and protesting Eustace back to the house and fed him whiskies to calm him down.

'I wanted to talk to Piers,' Eustace said.

'I'm sorry, he's in Minneapolis.'

'Really! Absurd! What *is* the point of your having so much money if you live such ghastly lives? Look, the point is I've arranged to live in Portugal. I can't stand all these bombs and terrorists.'

'I can only recall two bombs this year.'

'I don't know about that. It's two too many for me. It's the death of civilisation here, I think. And whatever else one says about Salazar, he's made Portugal a safe country for our lifetime. And then he's essentially a scholar. Have you ever seen the cloisters where he walked when he was studying at the University of Coimbra? There's such a lot of work to be done on the English in Portugal too. One's scholarship won't get rusty there. I don't mean Beckford and all those boys he buggered. That's been done. But Wellington, you know, had an affair with a Lisbon courtesan. It seems pretty certain he brought her to the mess at his H.Q. dressed as an officer. Well, I mean, that *would* be worth finding out about. And then there's the layout of the gardens at the Palace at Queluz. Oh! I shall be kept quite busy.'

Tom said, 'Good.' There didn't seem to be much else to say.

'Yes. Well. I didn't come here to waste your time. I'm going to settle at Estoril. And I wanted to make sure that Piers had the address of my bank there for the allowance. But perhaps you'd make certain of it?'

It was hard for Tom not to, since Eustace repeated it about six times.

'Rua da Lapa 2,' he said. 'Two is "dois" in Portuguese. It's pronounced "doish".'

He seemed very keen on this, although, as Tom pointed out, the pronunciation would not appear on the envelopes. At last, to stop the repetition of the tedious syllable, he persuaded his uncle to take a cheque for £500, because, as they both agreed, the first days in a foreign country were so difficult nowadays with all the exchange regulations. But a cheque could be cashed in London and Eustace apparently felt sure he could get the notes through the Customs. Even so, Eustace left the Saloon repeating, 'Doish. You won't forget that, will you, Tom? Doish!'

After he'd gone, Tom wondered whether he should go to the Stables once more to see the constructed scenery, but really, all things considered, and at the end of a tiring day's work, he thought he could do no better than to ring Piers and Sir Timothy and all the principal actors and tell them that the work was well in hand.

*   *   *

As he gazed up at the luminous twilit sky, in which wisps of the day's heat haze remained floating like so many tiny stage clouds, Tom thought, we shan't need the canvas top after all. It promised to be a perfect evening for a perfect performance. It was surely a splendid, though absurd, augury that he was flanked, as at *Phaethon*, by Lady Norah, a little somnolent after the 80 degree day, and Lady Chepstow, intent on Sir John Wallis' account of their visit to Mauritius and his expectations of the island's independence.

'It's certainly got everything for the tourist. Janey plans to go back for another visit.'

'Is there any more solid back-up to tourism?' Lady Chepstow asked. She hadn't been on so many royal tours for nothing, Tom thought. And he wondered how people could live in a world where interests and assumed interests had become one. He admired the discipline.

But on this wonderful warm evening of high expectation he found his attention more engaged by a moth circling in a beam of light. How pale it was, almost an amber white. How could he have lived all these years noticing so little of the creature world surrounding him? He would repair that in a new happiness that he felt awaited him. Travel, perhaps – to see humming birds, ruby and green, sipping from giant flower heads, to watch the slither of lizards on dead branches, or the sudden shutting of a chameleon's eyelids. And with someone who could tell him how to look, how to relax.

A breeze, a fine breeze, had arisen so that the audience were no longer fanning themselves with their programmes which he had feared would make an annoying distraction for the actors when the play started. Did Katherine know about wild creatures? He mocked himself gently as the question came into his head, but what mattered was that she had sent a telegram of good wishes for the performance from Milan, where she was singing, and she had sent it to him personally.

He had also forced himself to remember that he had been the recipient, in Piers' absence at rehearsal, of the telephone call

from that Scotland Yard Inspector. The exact words of it all
were etched in his mind – 'Ah, well, sir. Perhaps *you* can help
us. We want two tickets for your first night performance. One
fairly far forward to the left of the house, shall we say? And the
other, say, next to the back row on the right. We want to send
two of our men along. Just to keep an eye on one or two people
in the present state of affairs. Dinner jackets, I take it?' He
heard his own voice, absurdly snobbish surely, 'But this is an
invited audience.' 'Yes, sir, I know that. But people in high
places need protection these days. And there are other people
in high places whose motives we don't quite understand.
There's a lot of money behind these bomb maniacs. It's a
purely precautionary measure, of course.'

The police were quite right to be on the alert; but only asses
like Eustace panicked; and life was so sweet. He had wondered
a little in the days when Piers postponed his return whether
he'd taken on too much at Tothill; was it fair to Clarke,
Bingley? But Sir Leonard had especially commended his
detailing of the Hauptmann fraud case during those very days.
He'd been 'stretched' and he strongly suspected that supper's
delights would show everyone to what excellent conse-
quences.

A miraculously grass green moth was circling in a beam of
light – green moths? – they were probably a commonplace that
he'd never noticed. But he would now.

'Do you know Mauritius?' Lady Chepstow asked him suddenly. 'Sir John's so whetted my appetite to visit there.'

Damn her. But the strange opening wind music – half litur-
gical, half ancient Greek quarter-tone temple chant –
announced the entrance of Timothy from the main archway:
Father Shoe worshipping God in his breviary, disguised as
Seth Todd preserving humanities in his Ovid. The play had
begun.

Yes, thought Piers, watching from within the canvas constructed prompt entrance which Ralph's brilliant scene-
painter friend had so excellently disguised as the
Tudor-beamed West Wing of the old house . . . yes, it's going
to be good. A rather dull play in which the author seems to be

as null as he often is in life, and an oddly conventional play in
view of his other work. Why had he written it? But we've
tricked it out to give life and meaning, and with old Tim's
triumphant acting and, ironically, the author's machines and
contrivances, we shall bring off the evening. How good Lucy
Sainsbury was as Lady Tothill, too!

He knew he had been right to stage the Tothill plot outlines
in mime at the start. There was something wonderfully
mysterious and yet familiar about the fine lady selling her
necklace to the old Jew at one corner of the courtyard and the
fine gentleman dallying with the pretty maid servant at the
other, while the priest? tutor? intent upon his pagan loves? his
adoration of God? nevertheless saw every moment of these sad
allegories of human weakness – the gambler's ruin, the liber-
tine's folly. And now all this tripling would be swept aside as
the Westminster boy mysteriously (how cunningly Ralph had
contrived that trick entrance and how lucky to have found a
boy actor who hadn't a cockney accent) confronted the worldly scholar priest.

> 'Sir Rayner shall evade the fire
> Lest it prove his funeral pyre.
> Thus on the day they speak afresh,
> Let him be hence in mind and flesh.'

The boyish treble had the unearthly sound he had hoped for.
The very drabness of the costume contrived with its curious
(to modern eyes) shape to add to the sense of unearthly port-
ent. 'A sad new colour', the archivist had written, was the contemporary description of the Scholar's gown of that day, and
Miriam had beautifully caught it in grey and dun, a doublet of
sackcloth, pantaloons, kersey woollen upper hose, the dark
high hat. It was a kind of Guy Fawkes child-sprite. And, as
Father Shoe looked bewildered, the boy repeated his message,
adding, 'Father, I beg you, absolve me from my guilt.' And
hardly had the priest made the sign of the cross over him,
before the boy had vanished. Only apparently to reappear –
and this was his and Ralph's mechanical triumph – like Ariel or

Puck above on the ramparts in three places and three guises –
with angel's wings, with devil's horns and, in the very centre, a
null boy echoing, only deadly, the priest's bewildered cry,
'Who are you? Who are you?'

But before Piers could crane his head up to see how the dramatic effect held the eyes, a hand touched his shoulder, and a
voice whispered, 'If I could have a word with you, Sir Piers.'
And he turned impatiently to face a tall, long faced man, null,
pleasant in manner, yet somehow immediately serious and
authoritative.

'Inspector Bryant of Scotland Yard. We have a search war-
rant, sir. The matter is very urgent and I have sent my men to
search the back rooms of this building. Do you know anything
of Ralph Tucker? I believe he's one of your staff.'

'Ralph? Yes, he's worked here for ten years – head gardener,
head carpenter, head everything . . . I'm sure *he* wouldn't be
involved in anything criminal . . .'

'Do you know anything of a tunnel between here and Westminster Hall, sir?'

'Oh, there's some sort of legend about a secret passage – this
was part of the monastic buildings of the Abbey. Monks
always mean legends. This one has been shown to be false.
We'd liked to have used it in the play, but as our archivist,
Magda Tucker – she's Ralph's wife – pointed out, she's
exposed that myth.'

He heard his voice echo in the air. The words now made
sense to him, as the Inspector smiled dubiously. The man
would surely deliver a homily now on Mosson blindness, but,
if he so intended, events overtook him. A hatless, breathless
constable was at the Inspector's side.

'We've found the tunnel, sir,' he said. 'It looks as though it
goes a long way. They must have been at work there for weeks.
We've caught two villains coming out. The bomb boys were
down the tunnel like ferrets. We're trying to grab the others.'

The tunnel – Magda had denied its existence. Suddenly the
doll faces of Ralph and Magda made sense – dreadful sense – to
him; and Ralph's remarks about the system and the way
Grandma had patronised him. The Inspector was droning on,
but his words were drowned in a mixture of cries of surprise

and alarm, with clapping and shouts of 'bravo!', that came from the audience. Tim Pleydell burst into their canvas passage from the stage.

'What the hell is all this, Piers? Policemen and God knows what taking over the stage!'

'There's been an absurd terrorist fuck up going on here, Tim . . .'

The Inspector interrupted.

'Sir Piers, we don't want a panic. That would be a perfect cover for escapes – could you get on the stage and calm the audience down?'

'I suggest I tell them all to go into supper in the house.'

'A very good idea. Thank you.'

'Come and stand with me, Tim,' Piers said; he found it hard to credit what he saw. Police constables were bundling ten or more men out from the Stables and down the aisle that divided the audience in the courtyard. Some of the men were shouting obscenities. Ralph was among the prisoners, handcuffed; he was quite silent. Meanwhile many of the audience clearly saw it as part of an already over-clever surrealist play and were applauding vigorously or booing according to their theatrical tastes. Others were protesting loudly at what seemed to be a disorderly interruption all too typical of the way things were shaping these days. Others were preparing to leave, or demanding passage for their women to get through. One middle aged man was sobbing hysterically. Somewhere among those pushing their way through the side exit Piers glimpsed Magda.

'Ladies and gentlemen, do not be alarmed. It seems there's been a lot of childish, wicked, so-called political games going on here. The police, however, have it all in hand. For the moment, but let me assure you, it's only for the moment, these fanatical idiots have got in the way of art, but don't let them at least spoil your appetites. My brother Tom has prepared a splendid supper for you in the house. You can best help good sense and the police by enjoying it. Tom, will you lead the way to the house? I and Sir Timothy and the rest of the cast will be joining you all as soon as we can.'

Tom nodded to Piers. The ground of a whole wonderful

dream had sunk beneath his feet, but it was what he had expected for so long; his calm was automatic. He took the two ladies, each by an arm, and led them to the exit.

Lady Norah, now fully awake, said, 'Splendid, wasn't it? But I rather nodded off. So unlike me, but this heat. We'd hardly begun with that charming little boy when I opened my eyes and we were being sent to supper. Or was the play very short? So wise these days, when we're all so busy.'

Tom caught Lady Chepstow's eye, but neither of them had need to suppress laughter. The therapy of the absurd, Tom knew then, has limits. The occasion was too terrible to be helped by laughter.

Lady Chepstow said, 'I don't think it would quite have done for the Palace anyway. But your brother's splendid calm, the way he took charge, will give them great satisfaction. It's an absurd phrase, but he acted as to the manner born. I shall tell them at the Palace. Anything which challenges this beastly chaos they're after . . .'

Suddenly in Tom's ear sounded a voice – 'I adore chaos', and the Inspector on the telephone, 'people in high places whose motives we don't quite understand' – crazy ladies. He left the astonished, remonstrant Lady Chepstow and the bewildered Lady Norah in the covered passage to the house and pushed his way back through the incoming crowd. There were cries of 'Look here, watch out!' and 'Really, Mosson, this isn't a help.' Lord Beale shouted, 'I say, Mosson, keep your head.' And Lady Beale said, 'We must all be going the wrong way, darling. Is that right, Mr Mosson?' But he had no time to answer.

When he got back to the courtyard, Piers was still on the stage directing the audience to the house. He looked everywhere for Marina and there she was, still seated, but now collecting her bag and programme. Not a crazy lady, but a lady who'd kept her head. He ran up the steps on to the stage.

Sir John Wallis shouted up to Piers, 'What the hell were they after, Mosson? Not this house, surely?'

'Can you believe it, John,' Piers answered him, 'these crazy villains,' he heard himself use the policeman's word, 'wanted to blow up Parliament.'

The voice came in answer – guttural, shrill, rapid and clear, all in one storm-like mix-up of the elements.

'Nao! Not crazy! Not like you and your stupid boarring brother! You see! We *will* destroy all this . . .'

Piers only saw a Medusa face with arms gesticulating, hair streaming – but Tom saw the hand's movements. He rushed towards his brother and, saving himself from tripping, knocked him over. The noise came that he awaited, but upon the deadening of his eardrums followed a nightmarish pain of his stomach on fire.

He came to in agony. The movement of the world in which his pain lay and the abrasion of a blanket at his chin told him that he was in an ambulance. Van's voice came to him, connected with a hand that held his.

'I'm here with you, Pratt. Forgive me for bringing you to this.'

He forced back his pain to clear his mind, to answer what was true.

'Not you, Van. *We* led you into this. Me, Tim Pleydell, Grandma, all of us. Promise me you'll do your own thing from now.'

'I promise,' Piers said, 'but I'll promise you this too. I won't let these terrorist shits turn art and shape into any fucking happening.' He added, 'And you'll do your own thing, Pratt, and it will be good.' But Tom's speech didn't come, only a gush of blood that vomited on to Piers' arm.

As he waited in the little office room at the hospital to hear the result of his brother's operation, a sister came to tell him that he was wanted on the telephone.

'I'll put it through to you here,' she said.

'Inspector Bryant, Sir Piers. I just rang to know the news of your brother.'

'They're operating on him now.'

'Well, best of luck. That was a very brave thing he did. I thought you'd be glad to know that we've got the whole bunch of them now.'

'Yes. I am,' said Piers, and he realised that, though the

whole thing seemed a lot of political madness to him, through his desperate anxiety, he *was* glad. He said: 'I take it that Tothill was simply the means of getting at Parliament.'

'I'm afraid you exaggerate the importance of Parliament. No, the whole planned explosion was simply a diversion. Their real target was the Ministry of Defence. But we've got that lot, too.'

'Good,' said Piers, but it was all really outside his concern now. He knew nothing of defence. The agony of his anxiety for Pratt overwhelmed him.

'Well,' said the Inspector, 'we shall be meeting during the week, I expect. There are a few things to do with tonight that will need clearing up. I'll ring the hospital later for news of your brother. He's a very brave man.'

When Piers put the 'phone down, a man was standing by his side. 'I have bad news for you, Sir Piers. Your brother is dead. He never recovered consciousness.'

Piers nodded and walked out of the hospital.

It was only when he was walking across the bridge that panic seized him. Every step that he took, every step that those around him took, seemed to shake the bridge, seemed to shake the world. The water flowing below, the starred sky above him, seemed ready to meet, to burst upon the human insects, upon him, in one shapeless flow of eternity. Tothill in front, Pratt dead behind. How could he go on to deal with Tothill, to do all that Pratt would have wanted without Pratt – all the disorder to put right, all that talk with the Inspector, all that management and order to keep going. What good were his wonderful Vanbrugh inventions in a dead, chaotic universe? Then he thought of old Tim Pleydell, how would he have stood up to tonight's shock? He could not, must not let the theatre be without the old man's comic triumph, for it would be that, Brute in Vanbrugh's masterpiece. He must ring him up at his home, must go round there if need be. That play must be staged. It would be a wonder. He had promised Pratt. He *must* do his own thing. Go up, Master Builder, go up! Now. Lest delaying, you lose the power to ascend the towers of imagination.